ARLEE

Harold F. Hester

ARLEE
Collection of Harold F. Hester's Short Stories

ISBN 978-0-6151-9762-3

ARLee

DEDICATION:

Dixie Minor – SO, mother, grandmother, great-grandmother, quilter extraordinaire, and a lady that knows her mind and doesn't hold back when you deserve to hear it. So many times over the last years when something happened in mine and our lives she would say, "You need to write about it" and more often then not she would get a jaundice eye from me because I didn't have a clue how to write a short story or article. I can handle a novel, but telling a story succinctly while keeping all essential writing elements was not in me. That is until Dixie held my feet to the fire and with arguments for until I did not have an argument against.

Starting in 2003 till the end of 2007 Dixie talked me through and edited 31 short stories. All different but they all tell *A* story. Some give life saving information, others vent frustration while others are humorous. There is a sex in a couple and yes with some illustrated bare bodies but the story is the important thing here and not the sex. Trust me.

I owe the words under this cover to Dixie. Thank you… and …enjoy.

Hess

ARLEE
Collection of Harold F. Hester's Short Stories

ARLee

ARLEE - Title is an acronym. ALREE was a Blackfoot Indian chief and is the author's great grandfather descendant. **A R**eflected **L**ife, **E**tc, **E**tc are short stories by Harold F. Hester about everything from futuristic fantasies to first person accounting (as told too) of an air crises and from complete frustration of a government major agency to information that will save, or at least prolong your time on earth. This collection of short stories is one person's accounting of many things you have thought about, wondered about or just been afraid to think about. This book reflects parts of all living humans.

AUTHORS NOTE: There is a correlation between each of these 28 short stories but it is all in the author. The stories *themselves* do not flow from one to the other as chapters in a page-turner novel. The only orderly sequence of these stories is dates written and events in the author's life at that time. If I were to list these stories 1-2-3, etc I would have the story on page 199 first or maybe 253 or maybe 99, but that's just me. I feel sure you will have a different opinion – AND that's good.

A close friend told me this collection of short stories does not make for easy reading. Others have told me they read all the stories with either a smile on their face or a tear on their cheeks. This book is not a *page turner* but 28 stories with their own identity, personality and character. Of note, after the decision to write (pull together this book) and an outline formulated the decision to add pictures was made. Most of these stories were written in a matter of a few short hours but no longer then two days. The one exception is the lengthy *"We owe our Veterans"*. After I read the first draft it made me angry that our government could treat veterans so badly. I wrote more and the more I wrote the angry turned to total frustration. The end result after more then two months writing is worth your time. Congress has seen it as has a multitude of Veterans Administration workers so now it's back to the waiting game.

ARLEE
Collection of Harold F. Hester's Short Stories

index

Written between 2003 – 2007 – latest top to bottom

** - These are MUST reads if you are a veteran, a man, a woman, a warm body or human. All my stories are good to great reading BUT these two will get your blood boiling and your head shaking.

ARLEE
Collection of Harold F. Hester's Short Stories

Alphabetical Synopsis

airport. Her sexual orientation is a bit different then mine but I'm not real sure that does not make her a better person.

241...... *Predestination* - This is a true story from a Vietnam assault helicopter pilot. "If I had not flown it in myself, I would not have believed that a helicopter would fly in that condition." Parts of this story idea taken from my novel *Heaven's Luck*. The story is between the VC's automatic fire and a hover-hole just a bit too small for a medivac Huey helicopter in a night operation is 1969 Vietnam.

53........ *Seventy vs. Seven tenths of a Second* – Witnessed on the Washington DC beltway many mornings during early commute. Sex... some good...some not so good. Oral sex is normally very personal and when enjoyed in your own home or hotel room – nice. Where oral sex is NOT fun and becomes very public is in 70MPH morning rush hour.

141..... *Should I Turn Right or Left?* - Being retired military I was asked the other day what I thought about youth today going into the military - I gave a short, terse answer, then thought maybe I should expand that answer is the reason for this *story*. Before making any kind of life altering commitment I have always felt it best to know all I could about the subject and talk to all the *experts* as I could. Never make decisions alone in a closet.

179....... *Something I need to say* - I recently saw the 2004 Clint Eastwood movie, *Million Dollar Baby*. One of his last lines in the movie struck me as most profound. As Hillary Swank, in her rehab bed lay paralyzed and with absolutely NO hope of any kind of life other then life support he said, "I'm going to unplug your oxygen and you will go to sleep." He did and she did. He then took a full syringe of adrenaline and as he gave it to her in her IV he said, "…now you will stay asleep." I cried. I am crying now just remembering the scene and my feelings toward death and dying.

195....... *Steve Rogers* - Honesty, complete honesty is sometimes rare but always welcomed.

173....... *The DaVinci Code Commentaires de Roman* - The DaVinci Code novel raised many questions for me. I am sharing some as I sort others. What do you know about the Holy Grail? What do you know about Leonardo DaVinci? What do you know about the painting named the Last Supper? Why is the lady of the Mona Lisa smiling?

233...... *The Morning of the Contest* - Complete frustration on the subjectivity of a writer's completion. A fun 1000 word story you will enjoy - promise.

59........ *To Therapy or Not to Therapy* - As I select my characters and story-line it is sometimes difficult for me to differentiate, for them, between, love, hate, sex, hormonal drive, wanton desire, nomenclature of words and the professional person. Because of the frailties of the male human animal, changing times, attitudes and male-female relationships caused some consternation in the telling of this most professional and dedicated career field named *Therapy*. Remember - what was is not necessarily what is.

229....... *Two* - The Human mating season has neither boundaries nor time constraints and maybe because of this are much better at loving then other animals and things that fly, especially ducks. Nature tells me two is better then one and less strenuous then three. Enjoy each moment of each day and remember the next time you applaud someone or something.... It takes two hands.

93........ *We Owe Our Military Veterans...* If this is not THE Veteran Benefit Administration Solution, it is a good start...Objective of this rather long article outlines and justifies the new direction for rightful and earned military Compensation & Pension and a way out of VA/VBA stagnate bureaucracy waters. I lived and researched (interviews and Internet) the dickens out of the article. This should be a must read. A MUST READ

33.........*We Owe Our Veterans – Partie Deux* – I waited a year to see what congress would do after *We owe our Veterans* was published – this is that follow-up. A vision of the soul of the VA came to me one morning in what seemed to me was a blinding flash. WHAT?? You are always hearing of or seeing a light go on when a revelation finally hits you. Well, it happened to me just as the sun was coming up today. The Veterans Administration are all full fledged PATRIOTS! I am a decorated combat 20 year military veteran and some that I write was difficult BUT had to be said. A MUST READ

157..... *Why Sounds are Important* - Sounds, noises are wondrous and meaningful but they also do so much more. For example; listening to a child's heart beat during a sonogram or listening thought a stethoscope to your own organs as the body shuts down in death.

Our tribute to Peggy

A TSA Supervisor – Airport security are people too…

Which do you have the most extreme dislike?

A burglar
A rapist
A politician
An airport security screener
An overpaid professional athlete
An overpaid whiny celebrity
A person that gets away with Murder

Lois and Frank live in Woodbridge Virginia just outside the beltway. Both are educated, no children (yet), work for the U.S. Government in Washington DC so they have a comfortable income. Both travel in their work and for vacations.

They are world savvy and see many things around them as one. Where they differ is how they see people and their temperaments.

Lois is 28, Frank is 34.

This almost true story begins on a crisp morning in early February 2008 in a typical single-family home just outside the Washington DC beltway:

Frank and Lois were deep into raised conversation this morning and from Beth's vantage point next door their sometimes heated conversation sounded like a draw. Both had their points but neither knew all the facts. Frank was the hard head and would not listen to Lois's reasoning and Lois was too busy listening to her own voice to hear Frank's limited opinions.

As is typical, Lois seemed to have the upper hand as her words reverberated with strength and resolve; (Each topic noted above has been summarized and truncated here for brevity – In actuality this conversation covered an hour and eighteen minutes) Lois was clear and enunciating clearly as she said; "I feel comfortable in believing all people abhor burglars as they invade your homes and lives; rapist all deserve to be castrated; politicians need to tell the truth at least sometimes; athletes need to play their sports for the entertainment of others and be paid no more then $30.00 an hour; whiny and very young celebrities need to serve more then 85 minutes in the slammer if they have two DUIs and cocaine procession convictions while others should be made to keep their underwear on at all times; people with cameras should not be allowed to follow and record celebrities every moment and most of all the youth of our world should not make billionaires of these people that their only talents is singing (more often then not merely lip syncing) and acting. People that get away with murder… well what more can I say about O.J. and Blake?"

During Lois's soliloquy Beth reasoned Frank was trying to not get into any more trouble as she pictured him silently nodding at all the right times. She knew them so well.

Frank had finished his orange juice and just refreshed their coffee as Lois with somewhat are a wrinkled brow said, "Frank what did I forget from my litany? There was something else I wanted to cover but I guess I forgot it…any idea what it was?"

Frank squirmed in his chair, rubbed his stubbed chin while searching his memory bank for what they had been talking about. He found it! "Security Screeners… airport screeners" he beamed.

"RIGHT!" Lois's backbone suddenly became ramrod straight as she threw her shoulders back and took a few deep breaths for what looked to be some sort of sermon on a work group that she really dislikes.

In just her latest episode with airport screeners she had been on a United flight 917 from Washington Dulles to SeaTac in Seattle over the Christmas holidays. The flight had a passenger personnel problem and was diverted to Pittsburg that delayed their flight for over four hours. She was still very upset from having undress (her words) in the Dulles security screening while losing some of her liquid cosmetics and what she characterized as being wane raped.

When it rains Lois will blame the republicans. If she is late for work she blames the republicans and if her eggs are runny…yep… the republicans. Airport screeners she swears is a conspiracy of the republicans meant to keep the flying public subservant and brain washed. Public safety and terrorism? No, not really.

Lois travels a lot by air but she just hasn't yet gotten use to or accepted airport security and their procedure to try to keep her alive.

With her first deep breath she exploded with, "Those people are illiterate. For what they do they are grossly overpaid and besides they speak very poor English, if at all; they are fat, dumb and lazy. How in the world will a private security organization hire such complete imbeciles?" Frank knew *who* she was referring and because she was on a tear he just relaxed and sipped on his Baileys and coffee. He was taking mental notes so if she calmed a bit he could set her straight.

Frank is in luck this morning. The door bell rang and in steps a smiling and bouncy Beth, a neighbor and good friend from next door.

Normal morning pleasantries are exchanged before Beth asks Lois if there is anything she can help with or clarify on air port screeners.

You can see the light go on over Lois as she said, "That's right; you're a screener...Dulles – right? I had forgotten." The fact Beth had bluntly asked about the screeners had momentarily gone over Lois's head.

Beth smiled appropriately but didn't say anything, just yet.

"You could hear our conversation?" Lois asked.

Beth was quick to respond with, "Well kinda. The wind was against me a little but from what I could hear and what Betty Lou told me when she stopped by a few minutes ago" I got the impression it might not be a bad idea to stop by and bring you up to speed. There has been lots happening with us screeners since 911 and, you are right in some of your thinking, but ..." Beth's voice trailed off as Lois interrupted with, "We would LOVE to hear about the screeners... wouldn't we Frank?"

Frank knew when to be quiet so he merely nodded.

The propane fireplace was lit, Frank served Bailey's and fresh coffee and as the three of them sat on a comfortable sofa Beth began:

"Well, where to begin?" it was rhetorical. She took a short breath while saying, "There are 43,000 of us now. We work for Uncle Sam now but back in early 2002 we were all civilian contracted. There were 55,000 of us then. Those numbers are not that impressive because we service more then 5,010 major airports under the TSA around the States."

TSA?" Lois questioned.

"Transportation Security Administration. Since 2001, we have been mandated by law to appropriately screen air travelers to ensure that certain items and persons prohibited from flying don't board commercial airliners. We are most visibly present through our 43,000 trained and certified Transportation Security Officers stationed at over 450 airports across the country. Combined with over 1,000 credentialed security inspectors, these professionals screen over two million passengers daily and deliver both world-class security and customer service at your airport."

Beth appeared on a roll as she responded then continued with, "We work for the Government but we do not have the same rights and privileges as your normal white collar GS (general schedule) worker. Ok, there are benefits, but not like the other civilian government counterparts. A normal GS (general schedule) job has promotional steps and grades to make raises and advancement all but automatic. When we were created the administration made us specialized so there are no step advancements, so basically no raises. I can't see any of us being here long enough to enjoy the pension package....many of our employees are retired military so they might get something out of it. When we signed on we assumed that there would be grade increases and steps promotions. The best thing about it is the leave program. In the real world you don't earn useable leave right away, and we do. So I'm thankful for that. Otherwise, our starting salary is pretty much what we'll make forever, and for 12 bucks and hour..." Beth paused briefly before bristling with, "I will kiss no ones ass...but I will do my job." Beth lightened a bit saying with a knowing crooked grin, "But because I am such a nice person, on the job I am one of the friendliest even when we have problem passengers, I am the one who has to deal with them in a professional manner. It can be a quick painless procedure. Most people are pleasant and we know most of our frequent travelers, so they don't have to listen to the speech asking them for laptops etc. As for the shoe thing, I disagree with the procedure but I'm not a decision makers so am sure there's something, somewhere far above my pay grade that knows more than me.

Oh, while I'm thinking about it we are not called Screeners anymore. Since 2002 it's just the initials TSA"

Lois again questioned the letters as Beth said, "Transportation Security Administration".

Beth sipped her baileys and added something Becky had told her. "Not everyone that works for the TSA is suffering from low IQ. Most of us have college degrees, which unfortunately in this town do not guarantee a high paying job. Many are stuck in the $12-$13/hour positions. Some of us are military spouses, those with in-between jobs, students, and many just looking for experience. For me, I had a job I loved and enjoyed going to work, however this "opportunity" at the time seemed like a good chance to get a foot in the federal door. NONE of us knew how it would be when we signed on. It is certainly not a picnic for us dealing with holier than thou passengers who do God-knows-what for a living, but criticize what we do. We do not question how many people we piss off each day but expressions tells many stories. Ours just happens to be the public's most hated occupation of the moment. Everyone has someone that hates them because of their job. It just really is hard in ours. We don't want sympathy; we just want a little cooperation. We are not wand raping anyone or anal probing anyone. We are simply screening bags and passengers. I resent people saying they're naked, when they simply have to remove their shoes. Most of us try to do our jobs well. I agree a small percentage of the TSA folks are on power trips, but that's true in every profession – right?"

Frank finished his Baileys and substituted a VO and water. Lois was surprisingly very attentive as Beth seemed to have her undivided attention.

Beth began again saying, "When I started my screening position I had to learn a whole new language for TSA, ETD, IED, EDS, VAP, ETP and the occasional now famous synonyms: acclaimed, celebrated, distinguished, eminent, exalted, and of course; important." Adding with some importance – everyone is important!"

Lois changed Beth's train of thought quietly asking "Do you screen many each day?"

As matter-of-factly as Beth could muster she said, "2 million" She let that number sink in and followed with, "that is on average what we screen daily, nationwide"

The number appeared to astound Lois as it was repeated, "2 Million... each day" ... "Holy cow. I had no idea" The words were apologetic and sincere.

Beth saw this as a good time to tell some about what the TSA folks ran into each day. She said, "For me at Dulles I spend eight-plus hours a day standing watch at a security checkpoint, I have learned a few things about the traveling public. Among them:" Grinning from ear to ear said,

• "The condition of their socks is, for the most part, not bad.
• A surprising number are packing harmonicas.
• Passengers are much more malleable when they understand what's going on."

That last point can be a challenge for the screeners particularly in those weeks following a potential plot to blow up U.S.-bound airliners sparked a ban on carry-on liquids, gels and other seemingly innocuous substances.

Witness this exchange at *Dulles International Airport* where then screener Peggy Johns is fishing through a black carry-on finding a can of Edge shaving cream, a tube of Crest toothpaste and a bottle of Calvin Klein cologne.

The bag's owner silently watched knowing he could not affect what happened next.

"Is there anyone outside security you could give these to?" Peggy asks.

"Nope. No time," The owner said as he watched $40 or so in grooming aids unceremoniously tossed into a one-way gray plastic bin.

"I'm sorry but I think you understand." Peggy said with an apologetic crooked smile. He did.

It is just after 3:30 p.m., crunch time at the nation's 21st busiest airport, where Peggy and her colleagues are teetering on the front lines of TSA's balancing act between ensuring the safety of the 30,000 passengers who pass through here daily and delivering customer service.

The critics are vocal: The screening process is mere window dressing. The rules are inconsistent. (Why isn't lip gloss allowed on board, but KY Jelly is?) The enforcement is arbitrary, they say.

A quip among frequent fliers: TSA stands for Thousands Standing Around.

Seven years ago, the job that has put Peggy on a management track and brought meaning to her days didn't exist. But that was before terrorists crashed airliners into the World Trade Center, the Pentagon and a field in rural Pennsylvania. 911.

Peggy, now 28, became a screener with a private security company at Dulles in May 2002 and joined the first wave of government screeners when the TSA took over airport security later that year.

Beth continued speaking in a matter-of-factly voice saying "Dulles employs 671 full-time-equivalent TSAs at 21 security lanes at a single central checkpoint. By comparison, TSA's largest operation at Los Angeles International, which has eight terminals and eight separate checkpoints, employs three times that number.

Lois interrupted Beth saying, "I have seen some TSA people that didn't seem to meet the standards your describing Beth, There's...." Beth cut Lois short saying, "Screeners undergo criminal-background and medical checks. They have to be able to lift 70 pounds, be proficient in English and be U.S. citizens. New hires complete 40 to 60 hours of training, and everyone is subject to up to three hours of additional training weekly." That didn't satisfy Lois.

Beth added, "OK. Your right...in some cases." Then with wisdom far beyond her years she added, "We work for the government and like many of our government branches we have our dead-heads, our slackers and as little as we are paid, as much as I hate to admit it, even some of the TSA are overpaid. If I had to make personnel comparisons to other branches of the government I would say the Veterans Administration is far worse then us."

By this time Frank had offered and had been accepted fixing a VO and water for Beth. Two quick sips and she continued with, "Have I told you that Peggy is now a supervisor?"

Lois didn't answer one way or the other but shrugged her shoulders.

Good. Beth still had her undivided attention. Frank was happy with his VO. Beth sipped her drink then said, "This may not seem important to you now BUT as a TSA supervisor, Peggy's turf covers two to four security lanes, working with a team of six to 12 that rotates positions every 30 minutes to remain fresh in executing duties that could quickly become monotonous. Peggy and other like her must have people skills and be special in what they do."

From the look on Lois's face Beth felt she needed to explain further.

"Supervisors continually move from the walk-through metal detector to the X-ray monitor to the bag-search position to the secondary-screening spot to the explosive-trace detection machine and so on. They carry two-way radios but are always in ear-shot of their posts.

Peggy steps in when there's a questionable X-ray image, or a bag search that needs an assist, or the discovery of a weapon or, as she puts it, to deal with customer concerns that are escalating."

"Sometimes people are very attached to certain items," Frank tried.

"True... so very true Frank" Beth responded then added "Minor dramas play out throughout each shift. For example the woman who got separated from her son in the security line. The baby who threw up. (Peggy only has to call for cleanup; TSA does not deal with bodily fluids.) The forgotten boarding passes. The mother whose toddler is crying and fidgeting inside the *explosives trace portal – See on left -* (a walk-in device that shoots air from its walls and, in a child's eyes, might appear at best a funhouse amusement and at worst a torture device). Summoned by another screener, Peggy asks if the woman can make her daughter stand still but is told she has autism and could not stand perfectly still so Peggy enters the machine, wraps her arms around the girl and takes her through.

Amid this aural migraine, Peggy remains unflappable. After four years on the job, she has become weary of the strange (and strained) intimacies of the pat-down search, or the cluelessness of so many travelers after so long some still don't understand that box cutters are not permissible, she doesn't show it.

"When people are traveling, they have a lot on their minds. I have to believe that." Beth muttered between cold alcoholic sips.

She continued with, "Preoccupation would explain the man who departed his security lane wearing only one shoe. He later returned for the other one. Or the woman who walked away wearing the blue paper checkpoint-issued slippers. And speaking of shoes, the TSA screeners are repeatedly subjected to the ripe scent of feet unleashed from their stifling confines, August and is our worst month. The TSA thoughtfully provides air freshener at the checkpoints, to be used discreetly by personnel as necessary.

Beth relays that Peggy has unwittingly tipped off parents to their children's vices by withdrawing cigarette lighters, and in one instance, a bag of marijuana from their carry on. She and her colleagues have learned to watch for pet-toting passengers who absentmindedly send them through the X-ray machines. And she has caught travelers who are still bringing in banned sharp implements, which, when detected, are deposited in a metal cabinet with a one-way opening. Supervisors like Peggy help determine whether the offending carriers were simply absentminded or are artfully concealing, which can bring a civil fine of up to $10,000.

If Peggy was ever easily embarrassed, she isn't anymore. She sometimes tells the story that occurred once in Chicago, in which a young man packing a male enhancement device in his carry-on told the querying screener it was a bomb to avoid a humiliating admission in front of his mother. Peggy shrugs and says most personal devices are allowed and don't elicit so much as titters from screeners. "They come through so often, there's not much to talk about," she says.

In the days following the latest new restrictions, the TSA fielded questions that shed light on the remarkable stuff travelers feel compelled to tote along.

Was aerosol cheese allowed? (No.) Tanning towelettes? (Yes.) Goldfish? (Only without the water.) Peggy isn't one to question their motives. She has watched a chainsaw come down the conveyor belt (sans blade, but disallowed because it was loaded with gasoline). Then there was Thomas Jefferson's garden trowel being transported by a museum employee. (Not even a presidential trowel is allowed on board.) And a kitchen sink. (It got checked.)

And oddly, for reasons Peggy has yet to discern, lots of harmonicas.

Beth seemed proud of herself and the information she had given Lois and Frank. Actually she was a bit surprised with herself. Some of the information she gave had been the first time she had heard the words. She knew the facts to be true ; she knew she had been accurate and she knew, well pretty sure Lois had appreciated now knowing screeners are actually not all fat, dumb and lazy but hard working peoples that do the very best they can and under all adverse human conditions.

That should be the end of this story. Lois is happy now knowing her screeners are actually honest hard working people just like herself but as luck and fate have a tendency to not leave well enough alone the Cable TV History Channel that is featured in 52 countries ran a special on SCREENERS only two weeks after Lois returned from a weeks TDY in Paris.

October 19, 2008
The History Channel
SUBJECT THIS EVENING: Airport Passenger Screening

"It seems like every time someone tests airport security, airport security fails. In tests between November 2001 and February 2002, screeners missed 70 percent of knives, 30 percent of guns and 60 percent of (fake) bombs. And recently testers were able to smuggle bomb-making parts through airport security in 21 of 21 attempts. It makes you wonder why we're all putting our laptops in a separate bin and taking off our shoes. Although we should all be glad that Richard Reid wasn't the underwear bomber.

The failure to detect bomb-making parts is easier to understand. Break up something into small enough parts, and it's going to slip past the screeners pretty easily. The explosive material won't show up on the metal detector, and the associated electronics can look benign when disassembled. This isn't even a new problem. It's widely believed that the Chechen women who blew up the two Russian planes in August 2004 probably smuggled their bombs aboard the planes in pieces.

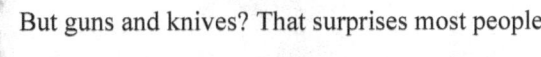

But guns and knives? That surprises most people.

Airport screeners have a difficult job, primarily because the human brain isn't naturally adapted to the task. We're wired for visual pattern matching, and are great at picking out something we know to look for -- for example, a lion in a sea of tall grass.

But we're much less adept at detecting random exceptions in uniform data. Faced with an endless stream of identical objects, the brain quickly concludes that everything is identical and there's no point in paying attention. By the time the exception comes around, the brain simply doesn't notice it. This psychological phenomenon isn't just a problem in airport screening: It's been identified in inspections of all kinds, and is why casinos move their dealers around so often. The tasks are simply mind-numbing.

To make matters worse, the smuggler can try to exploit the system. He can position the weapons in his baggage just so. He can try to disguise them by adding other metal items

to distract the screeners. He can disassemble bomb parts so they look nothing like bombs. Against a bored screener, he has the upper hand.

And, as has been pointed out again and again in essays on the ludicrousness of post-911 airport security, improvised weapons is a huge problem. A rock, a battery for a laptop, a belt, the extension handle off a wheeled suitcase, fishing line, the bare hands of someone who knows karate ... the list goes

on and on.

Technology can help. X-ray machines already randomly insert test bags into the stream, keeping screeners more alert. Computer-enhanced displays are making it easier for screeners to find contraband items in luggage, and eventually the computers will be able to do most of the work. It makes sense: Computers excel at boring repetitive tasks. They should do the quick sort, and let the screeners deal with the exceptions.

TSA doesn't just work indoors on people – There's also these cargo containers!!

Sure, there'll be a lot of false alarms, and some bad things will still get through. But it's better

than the alternative. And it's likely good enough. Remember the point of passenger screening. We're not trying to catch the clever, organized, well-funded terrorists. We're trying to catch the amateurs and the incompetent. We're trying to catch the unstable. We're trying to catch the copycats. These are all legitimate threats, and we're smart to defend against them. Against the professionals, we're just trying to add enough uncertainty into the system that they'll choose other targets instead.

The terrorists' goals have nothing to do with airplanes; their goals are to cause terror. Blowing up an airplane is just a particular attack designed to achieve that goal. Airplanes deserve some additional security because they have catastrophic failure properties: If there's even a small explosion, everyone on the plane dies. But there's a diminishing return on investments in airplane security. If the terrorists switch targets from airplanes to shopping malls, we haven't really solved the problem.

What that means is that a basic cursory screening is good enough. If I were investing in security, I would fund significant research into computer-assisted screening equipment for both checked and carry-on bags, but wouldn't spend a lot of money on invasive screening procedures and secondary screening. I would much rather have well-trained security personnel wandering around the airport, both in and out of uniform, looking for suspicious actions.

When I travel in Europe, I never have to take my laptop out of its case or my shoes off my feet. Those governments have had far more experience with terrorism than the U.S. government, and they know when passenger screening has reached the point of diminishing returns. They also implemented checked-baggage security measures decades before the United States did -- again recognizing the real threat.

And if I were investing in security, I would invest in intelligence and investigation. The best time to combat terrorism is before the terrorist tries to get on an airplane. The best countermeasures have value regardless of the nature of the terrorist plot or the particular terrorist target.

In some ways, if we're relying on airport screeners to prevent terrorism, it's already too late. After all, we can't keep weapons out of prisons. How can we ever hope to keep them out of Airports?

Several TSA screeners claim the agency has failed to adequately address a litany of problems they face at airports nationwide, including discrimination against minorities and veterans, selective hiring and firing practices, nepotism and management violations. They expressed frustration over the problems and said that in some cases security is being compromised. Some screeners want a congressional inquiry into the situation and an outside organization to provide oversight of TSA because they have lost faith in the agency's ability to resolve problems internally.

Remember also; Even though the government's 43,000 airport screeners do not have full civil service rights, they still can file claims under the Constitution a U.S. appeals court has ruled. RIF protection, yearly step pay increases, sick leave is not automatic. The TSA's starting salaries range between $23,600 and $35,400, and benefits include health care, life insurance, paid vacation and sick leave. The screeners receive 44 hours of classroom training, 60 hours of on-the-job training and a promise of advancement if they do well.

The next time you are standing in a screening line in your stocking feet try being patient and remember what Virginia Woolf, a British novelist once said;

"When I die, I want to go peacefully like my Grandfather did -- in his sleep. Not yelling and screaming like the passengers in his car."

and

As a last thought…. Don't let LITTLE things like this bother you. Relax, leave home a few minutes early and enjoy each minute of your life. *Remember the next time your feet hurt, think about the person that has no feet.*

At 30,000 Feet with a Crazy Person
As told by Sean Hester

A first person look at an in-flight *"Emergency"*

Perspective: Always remember, if a dozen people see the same thing happening, there will be twelve different versions and none of them may be 100% accurate. In the following story there were 182 passengers and a crew of eight on a non-stop cross-country flight from Washington DC to Seattle WA – This accounting is from one of those people using his senses, intellect, and a wee bit of literary licenses.

Remember the word **Predestination.**

I was born just three weeks before Neil Armstrong made his famous "One Small Step for Mankind…" statement as he stepped onto the face of the moon. I wanted to tell you this so you will know something about my time period growing up and mind-set of my schooling, my peers, the world and my parents.

My parent were not that religious but they believed in a Supreme Being, life after death, streets paved in gold and dead folks with wings and eternal happiness. As an adolescent they did their best by taking me to church and teaching me to sing off-key on Sundays. Mom taught me how to put Offerings in the plate and not take change out.

My dad fought in Vietnam so I have a feeling his thinking may have been a bit askew as he was always telling me about his thoughts, feelings and beliefs in life. He was raised in the Deep South and sometimes when he tried to explain Life I was never sure if it was a combat tale he knew first hand or a Southern Baptist belief.

When we would discuss life around us and life and death stuff he would most times throw his favorite at me; "If it's written in the book of life there is nothing you can do about it. It is predestination and if it's going to happen you can't affect the outcome. If it's not your time to die, you need not even think about it…"

My dad really believed those words… Me? Not real sure, but I always wondered.

As is my yearly custom I had gone home to Virginia for the Christmas Holidays. This year as I was sitting in the passenger lounge awaiting my flight back to Seattle when for no apparent reason I picked up a thin almost square well worn hard copy novel left in the seat next to me. The Soldier's Friend: A Life of Ernie Pyle.

I had no idea who or what Ernie Pyle was but soon came to realize he would be a most important part of my life.

911 made me a bit gun-shy while I was traveling by air. Each trip while sitting in the waiting area at pre-boarding I found myself eyeing the walkers in the concourse and all those waiting at my gate. Those of dark complexions with Middle Eastern origin I would try to judge how well their clothing fit; if there were bulges that could be C4 or box-openers or a Thompson sub-machine gun or bazookas. Plastic is fine for kids to play with and is fine as the main material in our autos; it's the C4 plastic explosives where I have the problem. I always check out the business suits to see if any had had a bad day, the middle-aged house wives that may look a bit distraught, and any GI combat soldiers that may be late for their PTSD meetings. As I looked over the old, the young the fashionable the nice-looking and the ugly my mind would always tell me to relax and think about my own problems and my own life. I tried, but I always found myself surveying the people that would be waiting to board the same aircraft wondering if their names had been written in their Book of Life. There always seemed to be the same mix of ladies carrying babies; adolescents; old men; old ladies; business suits, fashionable ladies, and of course the blue jeans and cowboy boots groupies.

I always hoped within these crowds there was no one that "Their time was up."

Today, my visit with Ernie Pyle and the wait to board was most enjoyable. There was this one guy that could have fallen into my "Weird" category but maybe because he was dressed comfortably and sitting with a rather pretty young lady, I dismissed the idea he could be a bad-guy or one short on time left here on earth.

It was the day before the last day of 2007; the wind was whistling outside the Dulles Airports windows and looked cold. The Ernie Pyle book cover was of a slight-built older man with hollow cheeks wearing a heavy military issue winters coat with its collar pulled up under his chin. Behind him were silhouetted soldiers wading waist deep ocean waters toward a shore. It was early into World-War II.

The books cover made me think of the movie "Saving Private Ryan".

Maybe that is the reason I picked it up. I don't know why I did but something told me to pick it up and read the pages.

By the time my United 197 flight was called I had scanned or read almost the entire novel. One sentence had caught my eye and I read it over and over. Ernie Pyle said "There are no Atheists in Foxholes".

The words burned their weight and power into my brain. I didn't know why I had re-read them so many times but something was telling me the words were important.

40 minutes into my flight, Ernie Pyle's and my dad's words rang in my head as United had an emergency.

"Relax Sean" I tried telling myself.

"Relax. Remember what dad always told me." My inner thoughts were trying to be logical but my adrenaline would not listen to reason.

Something was happening and at 30,000 feet I was seriously hoping United had a handle on the problem – whatever it was.

This whole trip to Virginia for Christmas was just enough different this year that for no apparent reason I decided to pamper myself to an upgraded seat assignment to relax and enjoy the almost six hour flight back to Seattle. Good idea but United computers took my

money but refused to change my assigned 32C seat. After I boarded the aircraft my apparent charm and a few empty seats up front next to the main access door got me moved.

After peanuts and soft drinks were distributed was when it all started. I was wearing my "noise cancellation" headphones which block most outside noise. But even so, I heard someone in the back of the plane yell **"Flight attendant!!! Flight attendant!!!"** The words were shrill and full of emotion. I also heard a baby cry. I figured someone had spilled something, or thrown up. A flight attendant bumped my elbow as she hustled toward the rear of the aircraft. At this point, I pretty much ignored it.

20 seconds later, the same flight attendant bumped my elbow again as she ran passed me again saying something to whomever would listen, but I didn't hear her problem because of my headphones. I decided I was missing something so I took off the headphones to see what was up. Glad I did as she was frantically talking to the purser telling her there was a major problem with a passenger back in economy. She bent over to talk to someone in first class I thought was a passenger, and he got up and hurried back to the back of the plane. He turned out to be one of the air marshals and by now I was getting use to having my elbow banged. The flight attendant followed him a few seconds later carrying some of those portable type nylon handcuffs. All doubt if there was trouble in the plane was erased the fourth time my elbow was hit.

Another flight attendant hurriedly moved toward the front and picked up the bulkhead phone, frantically dialed something, and said "We have a code three going on... right now!" The words were emphatic. At this point all the flight attendants are up and moving. Scuffling kind of sounds were coming from the back of the plane but I could not see exactly who was doing what to whom, so I relaxed – a little.

I figured this was bad, and knew something serious was going on. As soon as I finished that thought, the engines suddenly got quiet. I knew immediately that meant we were going down, hopefully for a landing and not a crash. As soon as I finished that thought, I felt the nose of the plane turn down. Now doubly sure we were going down, I started folding up my headphones thinking that; there's some serious stuff going on, and I might actually have to get up and tackle terrorists, or something like that. I'm no hero but the thought did actually cross my mind.

At this point, another first-class undercover air marshal got up and literally ran to the back. By this time I had my elbow out of harms way. Two flight attendants pulled beverage service carts into the aisles so people could not move around the plane and pretty much had, by this time, the emergency sealed off. The flight attendants were telling people to stay seated, that there's an urgent situation they now had under control, and we were not to move. Comforting words but they seemed a bit like they still weren't sure what to do. All the United crew standing and running in the aisle were all nervously looking around, looking at each other, shrugging, etc... There was actually a plain clothes flight attendant that got up to help them. She told us "I know I'm not dressed like it, but I'm a flight attendant so you have to follow my orders" I never figured out if she was just off duty and got up to help, or if she was another "under cover" type person. But she did seem to be the one that knew the most about what to do, and immediately became the boss.

After a while longer, a woman carrying the crying child that looked to be about 8 or 9 was escorted by one of the air marshals to the front, near me. They actually were told to sit in the backward facing flight attendant seats.

Several minutes later the captain gets on the intercom and tells us there's an emergency and that we will be landing in Pittsburg. We go through the landing instructions (seats and tray tables up, no electronic devices, etc, etc...) but it's very informal, not robotic like in a usual landing.

We are on the ground pretty quickly. Maybe 15-20 minutes? After we brake to a stop, we sit right there in the middle of the runway/airport surrounded by LOTS of emergency vehicles. Regular cop cars, black FBI looking SUVs and lots of fire trucks and such. The captain gets on the intercom again and tells us that since we made an overweight landing that our brakes were stressed more than normal, and the fire crews had to inspect them. I found it weird that he doesn't say we're overweight because we didn't use all the fuel we should have, even though I know that's why, and I wonder how many people figure that out or actually cared to know the reason. At this point my mind is a jumble of thoughts I can't control. There's that Book of Life also in my thoughts and I was wondering just who's name was in it with today's date.

It is amazing the thoughts that flash through your mind during a heavy adrenaline rush.

After a few more minutes, the captain tells up the brakes are ok and we taxi to a gate. We are told to stay seated, not turn on anything electronic like phones, and that police will be coming on the plane shortly.

At a time like this why are brakes more important then our emergency? Think about it, if you have a moving 65 ton airplane, you need brakes unless you want to stop 100 feet inside the terminal.

The door I'm sitting right across from is the one that opens to cold Pittsburg air and many official looking men and women.

Within a heart beat four white coated paramedics rush in with each carrying suitcase type bags and a folding stretcher. Lots of commotion behind me then what seemed only a few minutes the white coats carried a bloody stretcher toward my seat at the entranceway, bumping heads and backs of seats and more elbows in the narrow passageway. Everyone was now in the act and straining to see what was going on. I was the only one with elbows and head clear of the aisle. A blood stained blanket covering a very still person was the attraction as there was a plastic IV bottle being carried by one of the paramedics but I had the sense it was more for show then any real benefit to the person on the stretcher.

As the ambulance sped away is when the police got involved.

There was police (looked like local Pittsburg police to me) kneeling at the foot of the gangway on the tarmac. He looked ALL business. He didn't come on board at this point just seemed to a guard – but at the ready.

My neck was beginning to ach   from all the back and forth movement trying to see and understand what the hell was actually happening.

Emergency, crying kids, bloody stretcher, mass confusion, big burly air marshals with guns, pretty off-duty stewardess and lots of cold air. My mind had come up with so many different scenarios I could have been a soap opera producer.

Not sure what to call the guy taken off the plane next so for now I'll just call him "prisoner".

The two air marshal guys take the prisoner off the plane and out to the Pittsburg guard on the Tarmac. The prisoner is calm and doesn't say anything; he just walks off wearing his handcuffs. Not the nylon ones I saw before either, these are real metal ones. I guess the air marshals had them along with two steel blue 9mms.

They all stand right outside in the air/gate/tunnel area right where I can see them. Some more police and FBI guys come join the party, but they never move. Their conversations were hushed but I have seen enough Law and Order type movies the few words I could pick up told me they were discussing the injured guy taken out and his chances of survival. The "Prisoner" was talked about as if he was two week old lunch meat.

I'm right in the middle of everything with my seat. The door area is where the flight attendants and captain are standing, along with the two marshals and some witnesses that have been gathered to give statements. I can hear most of the conversations about giving statements and such. But when someone actually gives a statement, they are taken out to the jet way out of ear-shot of others.

After several minutes a flight attendant gets on the intercom and reminds us to not use phones or electronic devices.

Another 30 seconds pass as she gets back on the speaker and says it's ok to use phones, but no other electronic devices. As soon as she says that, 100 phones are turned on (including mine) as we all start calling people. My ride waiting for me in Seattle told me united had announced there was a medical emergency on the plane and it would be delayed.

I did hear the flight attendants talking about how everyone was confused about what went down in the early minutes. It didn't seem to go according to plan. People were in the wrong places, and not backing each other up right, and not covering their places right and such. I only caught bits and pieces, but they were all pretty shook up about it. A really pretty flight attendant sitting across from me talking to an older man and he appears to be trying to calm her down. She's also talking to us front row passengers a bit and saying that she needs a vacation. She also says she needs a backrub. I submit to give her one, but she doesn't take me up on the offer. Her home base is Seattle and she did slip me a phone number so may call her later.

By this time I and the other 181 passengers are wondering how long we'll have to be here, and how late we will be getting home. I figure it'll go pretty quick, but we actually spent around 3 hours on the ground. There was mass confusion about jurisdiction and lots of paperwork by United to be done before we can go. We all sit there with nothing to do for a while. Eventually they turn on the in-flight movie for us to watch. Not sure if they (airline) meant any symbolism but the movie was **The Ultimate Gift** which was a drama about *a life experience...* and a *wonderful journey.*

Every half hour or so the captain gets on the speaker and tells us they're trying to get us going but that there's no ETA. After the 3rd or 4th announcement he tells us we'll all get a free McDonalds chicken sandwich for out troubles.

Eventually all the witnesses are interviewed and the people outside wander off but we're still not going anywhere. The captain tells us something about how hard it is to work ourselves back into the air traffic rotation. We wait about 30 minutes after all the people

outside have left. Then the two carts of McDonald's sandwiches get rolled back onto the plane, and within 90 seconds the door is closed.

Pittsburg in winter is one cold place and our door has been open for hours.

After the door is shut the captain tells us we're cleared to go, and we start a pretty standard takeoff. The movie stops, we shut off the electronics, etc. The flight attendants make a joke about how we don't need to see the video about how the seatbelts and emergency doors work since we just saw it, but they play it again anyway.

The next to last day of 2007 on a cross-country flight to the West coast with 189 other souls, traveling at mock 0.8 MPH at 30,000 feet I was to learn that trouble is not always in the form of C4 bulges or bazookas or something mechanical malfunctioning but what can also be going on in a persons mind or just being very clumsy or horny.

Damn!

I was there. I know what happened. A television crew from KOMOTV was waiting for us as we de-planed at SeaTac to do their nightly news updates and a newspaper article the next morning gave their versions. Both were close in their details but not 100%. I feel they gave the public enough information to let them know something happened but the general public did not have a need to know ALL that happened.

The next morning I read in the Seattle Times that the unruly passenger taken off the aircraft in Pittsburg was Michael L. Hollander, 46. He made his initial appearance before a magistrate on a charge of abusive sexual contact, according to Ted Herskoski, special agent in charge of the Pittsburgh air marshals' office. Mr. Hollander was released on bond and the court was to appoint an attorney for him before he returned in one week for another court appearance, said Margaret Phillips, spokeswoman for the U.S. attorney's office in Pittsburgh. Hollander was held overnight in the Allegheny County Jail in Pittsburgh.

Abusive sexual contact is a federal misdemeanor punishable by up to a year in prison and $1,000 fine.

The one glaring fact left out of the Times was the details of just what really happened to all three passengers in row 32 seats A B C.

The lady that Hollander (in seat 32A) committed his "abusive sexual contact" was seated in 32B. She had been knitting and dosed off. Mr. Hollander used this time to stroke her hair and fondle her breast. As Hollander became more aroused in his groping he attempted to run his hands under her sweater, she awoke and in her sleep stupor, began frantically flailing her arms. She was still holding her knitting needles.

Mr. Louis Irby sitting in seat *32C* received a puncher wound in his upper left leg from one of the knitting needle and was treated by a flight attendant.

EPILOGUE:

The statement "There are no atheists in foxholes" is used to imply that atheists really do believe in God deep down, and that in times of extreme stress or fear, such as when participating in warfare or in an aircraft emergency, the belief will surface, overwhelming the less substantial affectation of atheism.

The precise origin of the phrase, coined some time during World War II, is uncertain. Various sources credit Lieutenant-Colonel William J. Clear, or Lieutenant-Colonel William Casey, but the phrase is most often attributed to journalist Ernie Pyle.

Ernie Pyle was killed from a machine gun burst on 18 April 1945 during the closing year of the WWII.

ARLEE
Collection of Harold F. Hester's Short Stories

Mr. Irby bled to death while sitting in his seat. The apparent slight puncher wound pierced his Femoral artery in the upper part of his left leg. He appeared asleep as he lost consciousness from loss of blood but no one noticed with all the other activities with the air marshals, harassed flight attendants and crying kids.

Curiously the 39 year old lady in 32B stayed in Pittsburg even though she was on her way home to Seattle. As of this time no criminal charges have been filed.

I did try to follow what happened to Mr. Hollander but assume he received some kind of

wrist slapping and told to leave his hormones at home the next time he flies. But, depending on his judge, this could be his home for a while.

Six week after being home I received a $50.00 credit from United for my "Being inconvenienced".

I lay awake many nights thinking…
What if?

    32C was my originally assigned seat.

ARLEE
Collection of Harold F. Hester's Short Stories

We Owe Our Veterans ~
Partie Deux

"We owe our Veterans" is on page 93

There are over one million old and new young veterans asking, begging for their rightful due that Washington, George and DC promised. Few remember the Bonus Army of veterans march on Washington in the spring of 1932. History has taught us that "...if you either do nor know or heed history you are bound to repeat it." I am hoping we do not repeat that march.

A vision of the soul of the VA came to me this morning in what seemed to me was a blinding flash.

WHAT?? You are always hearing of or seeing a light go on when a revelation finally hits you. Well, it happened to me just as the sun was coming up today.

The Veterans Administration is full fledged PATRIOTS! *(Tongue in cheek)*

It is now apparent to me they are in lock step with one of our founding fathers, Benjamin Franklin. He said in 1756 "A penny saved is a penny earned" and that is exactly what the VA has done and is now doing for the one million veterans pleading for their earned and rightful compensation.

By denying, protracting, and short-changing our veterans I estimate the VA has saved in just the last four years a bit shy of $49,323,746.12. Don't go getting all smiley-faced, that number also represents one million deserving veterans that must do without.

Are you asking, *without what?* That varies anywhere from a roof to sleep under to clothing for the kids.

If you know anyone that now works for the Veterans Administration, please ask them this one question. **How?**

How can you refuse so many deserving veterans?

How can you make deserving veterans wait years, or a lifetime for compensation?

How would you feel if you were the veteran and received your own VA narcissist responses?

(Read this "how" carefully – please) How would you feel if you asked for compensation - for example - for PTSD (post traumatic stress syndrome or being Shell shocked or battle fatigue) and the VA denies you because your PTSD (they say) was caused by being married and Title 38, U.S.C. does not recognize marriage as a cause for PTSD *(I realize this is a brainless and maybe unintelligent comparison/analogy but you should see a few of the actual (real) reasons I have received while denying me cancer compensation –* they are worse!). It makes no difference if you claimed three tours in Iraq and your nightly dreams are of your buddies body-parts crying to you from under your bunk as the cause and affect and you have twelve verifying civilian MDs official diagnoses, your family is broken and you now live on the street. The VA probable sent you a letter saying they are "Cognizant". So the beat goes on and they keep denying you …and your words and professional MDs words go unread or miss-understood or disregarded, or worse…!

That's not what Ben was referring when he said "…save…"

And the final "How" - How are you able to sleep nights then go to work and do the same day after day to still more veterans? Is that the reason there is an 18% annual "Action Officer" turnover rate and present to former Secretaries of the Veteran Administration (Mr. Anthony Principi and Mr. Jim Nicholson or Togo D. West Jr.) resigned prior to their full appointments? Does this "How" also include Mr. Harold F. Gracey Jr.? It should. You say "…that can't happen…" Yes it can and I have the VA letters as proof.

Benjamin Franklin would not approve of our present day VA.

There are so many things/happenings/events going on in our world I'm almost embarrassed in writing this article. In the big scheme of things these words don't mean a hill of beans to you. To me yes, but I am but one of over six billion folks alive on this blue marble we call Earth. Will you gain any insight or knowledge from this story if you read the whole thing? Yes. Will that knowledge do you or me any immediate good? No. Not today or tomorrow but someday down the road someone of you will have a light go on, take some seemingly insignificant action and that action will cause, if not the world, that action will change the well being and life of one or more persons. Promise. Scientist, deep thinkers, visionaries call it Evolution. The one major problem with evolution is I will not be here to see or benefit from it, me and one million like me.

That million number is growing exponentially so hang onto your scorecard to see the next thrilling chapter of our government's Veterans Administration (VA) in non-action.

ARLEE
Collection of Harold F. Hester's Short Stories

In our present politically correct world, why does our Veterans Administration aloofness continually surprise me? How can they do it? The VA attitude is NOT what Benjamin Franklin had in mind.

VCAA
Benefit of the doubt
6 Month approval time
Cognizant
BVA
Baloney (aka BS)
"On my watch"

The above words are for the most part the backbone of the Veterans Administration (VA) but in reality these words are merely words. They have no teeth. They merely are used to try to placate, are narcissist and generic form words.

"On my watch" is one phase I always deplored while I was a federal government employee. It means that the status quo will remain the same, no one makes any ripples and everyone is happy in their position and no one gets fired or called to answer for their actions or inactions. "Change" doesn't happen. Whatever the rules are at the time, those rules or interpolations of those rules/guidelines are static. "We don't want our retirement/pension damaged now do we?" or "...don't make waves." You know what happens when everyone around you is up to their chins in a cesspool and someone make a wave? Its call the Veterans Administration (VA) or more correctly, the Compensation and Pension (C&P) branch of the VA.

Hospitals and medical care are not the issues here. Veteran medical care can not be questioned. It is "First Class."

If you are not old enough to remember the TV show "Dragnet" Sergeant Joe Friday's penetrating monolog always contained his purpose in questioning people... "Just the facts mama, just the facts."

This article is just that – the facts. I would love to embellish, make more dramatic, stretch the truth, but my four year odyssey dealing with the VA trying for rightful C&P (Compensation & Pension or monthly government $$ in compensation for wartime or military caused medical problems – most times ending in death.), besides - the truth almost sounds stranger then fiction.

35

Let me start with my US Senator after I asked for help. The senator's response to my call for federal help was positive and reading the words told me, yes there is someone out there that will help and be on my side. I didn't ask my senator for anything not deserved or owed by law or regulations, I merely asked if they could build a fire under the VA and requested a fair evaluation… but preferable during my lifetime. The senator's official letter to the VA said I was a constituent and they were looking over the VA shoulder. The VA was then required to respond "…in writing… as to action taken on my behalf." The VA response back to the senator took less then a month and read as to merely placate, there was nothing positive in the typed two pages and was obviously generic – only my name had been substituted in an apparent standard "Senate" pacifying letter. The senator's office forwarded the VA letter to me saying, "…there you go… if there is anything else I can do for you, just let me know…"

Back at square one! Maybe... maybe not. As busy as the senator and her staff is, they called me at home to reassure me I had not been forgotten. That was seven months ago.

Growing up I had a younger cousin that was more then a bit slow that barely got him thought the ninth grade but his heart was golden and he always had a spring in his step and a ready smile. People, old and young always made fun of him to his face because he would always smile and never got mad. Anger was not in his personality. He never did anything positive, just never got angry. Our Veterans Administration is a lot like my cousin.

The really sad part of the VA is the people. For the most part they all fall under the category of "nice" or "normal". There are no axe murderers, malicious sub-humans

sitting in places of authority (action officers – mid and upper management) but there are many like my cousin. While these nice people don't know or understand the word rote, the lower echelon (the GS-5s, 7s and 9s are unfortunately those that first make line decisions on the veterans) practice *rote,* and that is sad. They just don't understand their position. In the civilian working community outside our federal government do you know anyone receiving more then $52,180 a year and doesn't have a clue what their job is all about? Our General Schedule Civil Servants has over 200,000 of them just in the VA alone.

I am not a tourist visiting a government office similar to a tour guide pointing out the first-class parts while visiting Europe's historic places in visiting seven countries in six days. I Lived in Paris for four years and in Germany for seven more years and a couple years in the Far East being shot at so I am not a Tourist. I lived the life and walked the walk. Similarly I worked on the rings and in the bowels of the pentagon for 24 years as an engineer action officer responsible for billions of USD ($$$) and in the War room responsible for military and civilian's lives and well being. I was not a tourist so I fully know and understand the inner working of the US Government and our VA system and it is not what Ben had in mind.

"If you know the system…why are you writing this article?" You are thinking. "Why complain if you know the treatment you will be subject too. Why beat your head against a stonewall while being stonewalled?"

Good questions. Actually they are damn good questions. Staring at the screen the only answer I can come up with is "Frustration". I have tried all the honest paths I can, talked to all those folks about what is happening, written letters – to everyone, done research till I am the resident expert on the VA, regulations, forms, querying the Internet but our VA system seems to me are a lot like the nursery rhyme:

For want of a shoe the horse was lost.
For want of a horse the rider was lost.
For want of a rider the battle was lost.
For want of a battle the kingdom was lost.
And all for the want of a horseshoe nail.

Bomb, bullets and shrapnel
are gender non-specific

 This Nursery Rhyme explaining consequences through its lyrics. A clever set of lyrics encouraging a child to apply logic to the consequences of their actions. Perhaps used to gently chastise a child and explain the possible events that might follow a thoughtless act. The references to horses, horseshoe, riders, kingdoms and battles indicate the origins of this nursery rhyme were probably set in English History but is as true today in our VA system as it was in 1754 when Benjamin Franklin wrote it.

Other then nursery rhymes, *Stonewalling* comes to mind.

The VA does not live up to their own rules and regulations. All you have to do is read Title 38 http://ecfr.gpoaccess.gov/cgi/t/text/text-idx?c=ecfr&sid=a3eb31fee1750ec515d3219f78412b17&rgn=div5&view=text&node=38:1.0.1.1.5&idno=38#38:1.0.1.1.5.1.98.3 - then talk to or be one of the one-million veterans awaiting rightful compensation to read what should be and receive from your government what they feel like granting.

The front-line VA GS-5s and 7s have the most impact on our veterans seems as if they are not allowed to act outside their own rules and regulations and their interpolations, or inside them for that matter.

Is there retribution in our government? Do civil servants always play by the rules, with smiles on their faces and a spring in their step? Are civil servants honest and give you an honest day's work for an honest days pay? Please read
http://www.mspb.gov/decisions/2001/ch00531d0644i1.html
before answering. This GS-9 was demoted to a GS-5 within the VA for inefficacy but then continued in their old job. I'm not sure about you but I am as honest as the day is long and love my fellow-man but IF I was demoted and left in my old position I'm not so sure I would be smiling all the time. You don't go to "efficient" from "inefficacy" over night. Ask anyone of the 3,000 plus veteran claims handled by this one disgruntled demoted GS. *(if* the above site is not working, ask your VA why they took it down.)

It seems to me the VA thinks nothing of protracting benefits for deserving veterans as they can not see the results of their inactions. Sad.... So sad... Ben would not approve.

I know Ben would have asked, "...how...?" or maybe "...why...?"

So... back to my article.

In December 2006 I wrote a lengthy and stinging article titled "We owe our veterans" www.haroldhester.com. Mailed it to 14 members of congress, six newspapers around the U.S.; was a guest speaker on a radio talk show in Phoenix. I had a phone call from my VFW representative telling me the Veterans Administration Regional Office in St. Louis had taken note and moved my 12" thick rubber banded C&P file to "...their congressional side of the house... for immediate action". Immediate is a relative term. To you or me the word mean "right now", "as quickly as possible", "ASAP", "rapidement", "bonne baise maintenant", or rápidamente or "schnell". To our VA friends those words only means "business as usual" and business as usual is extremely slow – even in the tourist season.

I had a VFW representative tell me two years ago "...you have to play the game. Pretend it is a game of tennis. You write the VA a letter that puts the ball in their court... they respond... the ball is then in your court... you hit the ball back with another letter, etc...etc...etc. – Love - 40 game." I tried that. In four years I have served 41 times, returned their high lazy lobs (generic VA letters) with stinging forehand (truths) smashes they never return – they simply ignore the bright yellow Wilson or Penn tennis balls bouncing at their feet and drop an old gray water-soaked Dunlop (generic) ball and lazily tap it under-handed over the net. In the past four years I have even received a few high floating badminton shuttlecocks (half-truth narcissistic answers to my senator). Two players, different balls, totally different rules BUT the same game. That can't be, you say.

There are USTA line judges, chair umpires, TV cameras, the senate, the news media all watching the "game" how can that be? Unfortunately for the American military veteran there is more emphasis and background qualification required to call a tennis ball in or out of bounds then what is required of professional Civil Servants that hold a combats veterans life and well-being at the point of their ball-point pen.

What qualifications do I have to write this story? In the big scheme of things, I'm actually a nobody. I am a college graduate, a professional architect for a brief time before being drafted, served with distention in the Army for 20 plus years until I was medically retired. A Bronze Star winner and combat soldier in sunny Vietnam was a.... well…you get the idea… just an all around good guy and even worked as a civil servant at the Pentagon until retiring in 2001 when they stopped shooting at me and started throwing airplanes at me. Medical-wise I'm not all that great; a couple heart attacks, a stroke, diabetic and kidney cancer to mention just a few ailments. I'm 73 now but don't go saying "…well he has had a good life…" – I have had these ailments since I was active duty military – since I was 43. The military – our government, the VA now have me on their hands to do with as they have promised in writing and in blood since 1776. Give me rightful compensation for those years I gave so much in defense of this country. *"Freedom is not free".*

I'm sure there is a question in your mind now. Let me try to phase it for you. Why should the government, the VA pay you monthly compensation? ANSWER: Without military service I may or may not have these same health problems but the fact is I do have them now and all my health problems are directly related to my military service as are the one-million other veterans in my same boat. If you are a civilian you may not be familiar with just how dangerous the military really is. In civilian life you do a job - to make money. In the military your job is to kill or help those that do the actually killing. When you are in a fight as a civilian you may get a bruise or a black eye – when you are in a fight in the military you are trying to kill the other person as they are doing the same toward you. Bullets and bombs kill as does disease and accidents.

A military veteran deserves all their government *has promised.*

In my December 2006 lengthy article I spelled out for the VA a way they can redeem themselves. I guess only time will tell if they (VA) ever read the article and if they will heed its words, advice and council. Unfortunately for

It takes five (5) equal stacks like this to make ONE Billion

the VA it is made up of humans and humans have built-in flaws but the folks in the VA don't even see or acknowledge their own flaws. "Why?"

Do you know how many parts go into making a Million?

Do you know how many parts go into making a Billion? How about **3 Billion USD** being spent PER WEEK in an Iraq war we should not even be in.

If you took all us veterans that have applied for and been waiting for years plus our new younger veterans in our current war(s) – if you added the USD that they/we are asking for in compensation of rightful service the total would be in the neighborhood of less then $48,000,000 for the remaining lifetime of the veterans – you can do the math comparing that number to 3 BILLION **PER WEEK.**

There are still a handful of WW1 veterans, and a few million WWII, Korea, Vietnam veterans and now Iraq and Afghanistan are producing young veterans that need medical care and compensation to live post military lives. Say that word again… Million. There are over one million old and new young veterans asking, begging for their rightful due that Washington, George and DC promised. Few remember the Bonus Army of veterans  march on Washington in the spring of 1932. History has taught us that "…if you either do nor know or heed history you are bound to repeat it." I would hope, at least, upper management in the VA knows enough history to get themselves out of their self-imposed quagmire called C&P.

There are lots I can not fathom about the VA but this is maybe the worst. How can a GS 5 nobody say no or only give a small percentage of what the VA's own rules and regulations specify to a new amputee, or brain damaged or PTSD veteran?? I am told a large percentage of VA action people are in fact, veterans themselves. If that is true then we have a LOT of hard-hearted veterans with attitudes. Could that be the reason there is more then an 18% yearly attrition rate within the VA?

There doesn't seem to be any way to build a fire under these VA people. Sure, sure they have a huge backlog of C&P claims. They do, and it is ALL their own doing – its called inefficiency. At the Bureau Veterans Affairs (BVA) the backlog of veterans awaiting rightful claim is in access of 493,000. When you have but 60 lawyers looking for errors and making sure eyes are dotted and tee's crossed in Regional Office (RO) submittals of deserving veterans it's no wonder the normal 4-6 year C&P claim is protracted another 4 - 7 MORE years. I wonder if anyone has noticed more then 56% of BVA veterans claims are "referred" back to ROs for further work. Backlog at the BVA (these are the lawyers and law judges sitting in Washington DC acting as the overlords for the VA) is >493,000 then you add the 57 RO's backlog of 638,408 you have that million number or 1,137,408. You know the really sad part of the million number? It's an INCREASE of over 44,000 just from one year ago. Four years ago when I started my rightful quest for earned C&P the total backlog was "only" 472,918. That's a hell of an avoidable increase. Remember that word – exponential? If you are a veteran all we can do is take tennis lessons and enjoy the days we have left on mother earth because the VA is going to fight you tooth and nail for your rightful due.

The VA has basically doubled their work force during the last couple years. They have doubled their budget and work force and their case load has more then doubled. Something is horribly wrong when you double the force and the money and your efficiency is cut in half. Shouldn't the case load go DOWN – not UP?

Remember the tennis game? *Follow this logic please;* Backlogged veterans claims are increasing exponentially over 4,000 per month; The 57 state Regional Officers (RO) are so over-loaded they forward most of their case-load to the BVA for adjudication (it's call passing the buck); the BVA, list, studies, catalogs then REFERRS over 56% of those cases BACK to the RO for further study; when a case is referred it DOES NOT go to the head of the line – it is a "first come first served" so the veterans case takes 4-6 years to work it's way to the BVA and then there is a strong probability that case will become a tennis ball adding another 5-7 years before it can be denied. Before the year 2000 the BVA had a favorite phase for denying rightful claim, "*...not well grounded...*" That phase kinda went away when *VCAA* (Veterans Claims Assistance Act of 2000), was made law now the VA and BVA play tennis with the veterans cases by referring them back and forth to each other – once referred it is a minimum 2 years before that claim sees the light of day again.

I'm not kidding.

Internet site http://www.index.va.gov/search/va/bva.html is searchable. Please feel free to verify these numbers – it's scary to see numbers the VA and BVA seem proud to display.

Here's another scary report: http://www.vba.va.gov/bln/201/reports/mmrindex.htm The VA calls it their *Monday Morning Work Load Report.* You can see weekly reports for the last EIGHT years. Scared the pants off me when I reviewed the numbers, but the VA just keeps plodding alone.

The VA will argue the veteran "…gets the benefit of the doubt… that the preponderance of the evidence must be against the veteran for his/her claim to be denied." That is just VA rhetoric. I personally had two professional medical MDs furnish proven medical facts from world renowned physicians and oncologists plus they included the American Cancer Society proven studies for me and was denied. Why? The VA's had their own IME say after a less the 3 minute physical examination "…there is no supporting literature".

HOW? How can a professional medical doctor turn a blind eye to facts and apparently NOT be held accountable?

The veteran needs outside help. Many can not afford lawyers nor IME (Independent Medical Evaluations – doctors that will review your records and render professional opinions to the VA – normal cost are in the $3,000 range and it's not guaranteed – that is just to get the VA opinion). The VA and BVA routinely turn to their on in-house MDs that parrot the party-line and turn a blind eye to the more honest civilian IMEs.

Remember that tennis game and the rules?

Remember that number – Million?

The military is funny. They will give you $20,000 to enlist but will fight you tooth and nail for $100 monthly compensation that you earned – all in contradiction to "their" rules. Some advice for the young soldier that one day will be a veteran and most likely be seeking Compensation from the VA just as – remember that number? – a million of us are doing today.
1.   Keep copies of your medical and service records
2.   Know that the smiling civil servant sitting across the table is NOT your friend and owes you nothing.
3.   If possible, tape (digital) record all your meetings and VA testing.
4.   Be VERY careful of your phraseology when speaking with the VA. "How are you?" if responded with "Fine,

thank you" translated into VA medical records means *"Veteran denies any physical problems – the veterans sits straight with no slouch – has an upbeat gait even with his Cain – is well tanned and centrally obese."*

I choose not to go on and on about the VA. I did that in my December 2006 article *(We Owe our Veterans)*. I choose also to say the

VA in understaffed – **They ARE NOT**!! They have plenty of work force – they just don't know how to use them. I covered the "how" in the December article. I choose also to not go on and on about the VA budget. *They have plenty of USD.* In fact, as soon as the VA stops saying how over-worked and underpaid they are maybe, just maybe these $128,757 a year middle managers will start doing something for the veterans they were hired to look after in the first place.

One final statement on the VA. They answer to whom they wish; they do not answer questions they do not want to but they answer questions you do not ask. A newspaper, the News-Record in Greensboro NC in early 2006 asked the VA 57 pointed questions many thousands of their veteran constituents needed to know. NC has about 800,000 veterans and many of them are seeking C&P. They asked the newspaper http://blog.news-record.com/staff/lexblog/archives/2006/09/index.html   if it could get answers because the VA was not responding to individual veterans. After a year, the VA finally gave the newspaper an answer: NO.

Do you know whose portrait is featured on our US $100 paper bill? *Benjamin Franklin.*

 I'm sure Ben would prefer his pictures were distributed more freely and openly to our present day veterans.

That stack of money you saw on page 39 - there are 200,000,000 of these.
One Billion = 1,000,000,000

ARLEE
Collection of Harold F. Hester's Short Stories

Life's Cycle and Walter Reed

Have you ever wondered about 'things' such as life, death, what your dog is thinking when you rub it's ear, is there pain for a fish as it is being filleted, do humming birds ever run into trees as they dart from red flower to sugar feeder?

This short story is dedicated to Walter Reed Army medical center and its military and civilian personnel with sincere appreciation for keeping me alive following a recent stroke and allowing me to attend my wife's funeral: Teresa Rader, Ms. Edith, Ms. Street, Dr. Hegde, Marie Mojica and a special young lady, Liz Tricozzi Loveless.

Before you make the wrong assumption as to my background and qualifications to write a short story on "Life's Cycle" I would like to assure you, upfront, I am no intellect, no genius, no deep-thinker, have never worked in a 'skunks work', was only a bit above the average student throughout college and actually in ever day life have always been just 'average.' There are a bit over six-billion people on our blue marble we call Earth and each and every one of them could have written this story, but until they do, this is my version. So, having said that, I would like to now say, "My mind is never silent and it is continually asking questions, making assumptions, observations and countless and ever changing events of daily living make me…wonder"

Does that qualify me to write this story?

Yep.

So… relax, sit back and enjoy the next few minutes. You just never know when you may glean something from my words that may have gone unnoticed in you everyday life.

The rain has finally stopped and there are patches of blue sky in this otherwise dreary morning. Sitting at my keyboard watching the squirrels, chipmunks and a buzzard overhead all looking for a meal, my mind is relating to them in the daily and constant quest for food and an existence and – I wonder.

Have you ever wondered about 'things' such as life, death, what is awaiting for us "On the other side"? Was religion invented to make dying easier? During conception when Mr. Sperm meets Ms. Egg how do all the dividing cells know where to go and what to develop? Do all ear cells always make an ear?

Picture this scene: you are walking a white sandy beach, or deep in a rain forest or dodging traffic on a busy street of a metropolitan city or in your own backyard and you find that mythical lamp that is the imprisoned home to a Genie. It gives you three wishes, what would you wish for?

1. Wealth
2. World peace
3. Long life

Sure this list of three will vary as there are many variables depending on who you are your background, education, age, etc. but generally those are the three frontrunners that immediately come to mind. If not then just go alone with me on this please – for now.

Wealth – Now this is debatable, but only amongst those that have it. "…having money is not that big of a deal…" I have heard this said many times, but always from someone that has it. Wealth is relative. When I graduated college back in the fifties a good living as a professional architect was considered to be $10k a year. Don't laugh. Frank Lloyd Wright was my idol and "building things" was my goal in life. There was no such thing as "credit" because if you didn't have the cash, you saved until you could pay for the item. Today my wallet only holds credit cards and enough green to buy a flower from the street merchant. The National armed forces draft was in-place; there was a cold war followed quickly by a couple shooting wars that changed the way we treat money and our thinking. To make a comfortable living, build things, contributing to man-kind were still visions dancing between my ears until people stated dying around me. $10k is now far below the official government poverty level and if I were still an architect my TurboTax return bottom line would have to be in the high six-figures to live as comfortably as I envisioned fresh out of college. But… I am no Microsoft genius so I settled – and I wondered.

World Peace – I know, I know that will never happen because of the pure nature of man and something Plato once said, "Only the dead have seen the end of war". Growing up in the south and listening to "World Peace" responses from honeyed red lips beauty contestants with their ever long-legs, high heeled, skimpy bikinis, and perfect figured young ladies, they were either baton-twirlers or short-sighted visionaries that young male adrenalin may have clouded my thinking a bit – but I wondered.

Long life – An elongated life span is relative. I have been in a war (Vietnam) and have seen death up close and personal. As you, I have or will have buried all my grand-parents, several cousins and nephews, a few neighbors, I buried my father, buried my mother, killed and buried a few bad-guys in sunny Vietnam, buried my sister, had loved ones die in my arms, and recently buried my wife. I have an expensive black suit that is starting to have shiny knees from constant use. A few years back I started losing body parts as they were wearing out but have always used my body the best I knew how. I smoked for a bit until I learned it was bad for me. I use to eat lots of white bacon grease gravy before I saw how it was made. It was hard to give up sausage and liver and onions but I did. Living on seven continents during my middle-years may have changed many of my bad southern eating habits as my fork is now used more in the European style rather then as a shovel from Arkansas. I was a pre-teen during WWII, have a son, not proud of the fact but I done everything once and many things twice. I have loved many, written twenty million words trying to tell stories…and I still don't have "life" figured out, BUT I have an idea I would like to pass alone. Even at that, some days, I wonder.

Have you ever wondered about why you are still alive? Look around and you will see folks younger then you dead and they were probable not murdered or died by accident, but something caused them to stop breathing. Something, somewhere is keeping book on you – I think – and I wonder.

As a youth I fell off a scaffold and a two-foot spike grazed my left side. Two inches to the right and I would have been impaled. Mortars destroyed my bunkers three times in Vietnam and friends died, but not me. I complained from pain from a hernia a few years ago but during some x-ray work-ups for that hernia, cancer was discovered in my kidney and was cured before it metastasized. I hate TV commercials but was suffering thought one a few months ago as they were talking about the three tests to recognize the first sights of a stroke; look in a mirror and make sure you have a symmetrical smile, raise both arms over your head and voice a complete sentence. That commercial saved my life last month as did an innocent x-ray as did just barely missing a deadly spike and not being in the wrong spot when hot molten shell fragments are killing all around me. Many days I sit looking at cloud formations and – I wonder.

Much of what I have learned came from listening and watching people and while occupying inpatient beds at Walter Reed Army military hospital in Washington D.C.

Trips to VA hospitals also played a role in my learning process but those experiences are well forgotten. For those of us that have spent any time in a hospital bed you remember there's lot of time for you to "think". I have many kudos for

47

Walter Reed and maybe the least important of all but personal important, to me anyway are the beds. During my last stay during April 2007 recovering from a stroke, the beds were actually comfortable. I am still alive so that, in itself speaks volumes for the Crown Jewel of the military hospitals and the dedicated military and civilian personal that run them. Don't get confused here. I'm only talking about the hospital personal and the care received NOT the VA and its broken compensation sorry program.

We are all going to die. Dying is a part of living. Because we are animals we will someday die. It is a rule of nature. We can change some rules of man, but Mother Nature rules were/are made by our Maker and they can not be brokered, challenged, debated or altered. We can be sent into an Earth orbit, we can sustain our breathing with the right combination of medications and tubing but there is no way out of Life – alive. We WILL die – someday. But I sometimes wonder.

What I have finally come to grips with is death. As I see it death is *"nothing"*. Maybe I need to qualify my southern use of that word. If you saw the Clint Eastwood movie, "Million dollar Baby" you may remember near the end when Hillary Swank was in her hospital bed begging to die Clint gave her a shot and said, "This will put you to sleep" and it did. He than gave her another shot saying, "…and this will keep you asleep." I cried and now I wonder. I have seen many die; most civilians die quietly and peacefully. No military person has ever died peacefully as they/we usually have either ugly holes torn from us or body parts scattered all over the country side. If there is pain involved the dying part is significant but death stops all your pain - promise.

I attended a funeral last year where a good friend had been fighting ALS and during the grave site ceremony the priest said, "…now Gary has won his fight with his cancer…" I frankly didn't understand how Gary had *"won"* but maybe the priest was referring to the fact Gary did not have to worry about controlling muscles, speech, and eating and toilet control anymore. I guess we all win or lose races in our own way and in our own mind, I wondered.

Frank Sinatra's last two spoken words were, "I'm losing."

My wife just closed her eyes and was gone, as did my dad, my sister and two VC I dispatched in Vietnam. A loved one smiled weakly, opened her mouth slightly to say something but couldn't. Her eyes dilated, her mouth drooped slightly, her arm around my neck fell lifeless to her side and she too, was gone.

ARLEE
Collection of Harold F. Hester's Short Stories

Gone where?

Do I believe in a God? Sure.

Do I believe there is a life or something after our earthly death? There are a few questions about this one but I figure I will just have to wait until I sit at the right hand of God - and I'll ask him/her. But having said that there is the question of reincarnation that I have always been interested in.

The Bible gives clear indications that reincarnation exists. In Matthew 3:3 a prophecy delivered by the prophet Isaiah was quoted, "A voice of one calling in the desert, `Prepare the way for the Lord, make straight paths for him.'" Later in chapter 17 verses 10-13, the disciples asked Jesus, "Why then do the teachers of the law say that Elijah must come first?" Jesus replied, "To be sure, Elijah comes and will restore all things. But I tell you, Elijah has already come, and they did not recognize him, but have done to him everything they wished. In the same way the Son of Man is going to suffer at their hands." Then the disciples understood that he was talking to them about John the Baptist."

Jesus clearly taught that Elijah had been reincarnated as John the Baptist. The disciples seemingly had no trouble understanding this.

I do but then again I was not a chosen one to be a disciple. If/when I am reincarnated I only hope I come back a lot smarter. Kinda makes me wonder.

THE LIFE CYCLE AND MAN (I found this on the Internet and it is a bit profound but I promise you will gather a bit of knowledge from the next short paragraphs. Trust me)

In the beginning planet Earth was only rock, water and air with a never ending supply of energy beamed down daily from the sun. But there was no life on earth.

There was no grass, trees or flowers on Earth because there was no soil. It takes soil to grow plants and sustain life. But, it takes decaying life to make and sustain soil.

At some point as our planet rotated in its planned orbit through space the Almighty saw fit to breathe life onto earth, very meager and primitive life, but life with a crucial mission.

As these micro-forms of life lived and reproduced, they fed on and etched away at the rocky mineral earth surface, and as they died, their remains formed humus and mild acids to etch away still more minerals. The process of their decaying bodies and decaying rock went on and on creating our first fertile soil.

Even though extremely small, the life, death and decay of each preceding life form has been creating better conditions for future life forms than were there before. The decay process builds with added interest to the soil's bank account, and after countless centuries of creating conditions for higher and more complex forms of life, Man, the most complex of all life, was able to exist and be sustained.

Walk into the woods and meadows and visit with Nature. You will be in the presence of much life. Especially in the spring, you will find many types of plants, grass, trees, animals and insects-large and small. There will be life in abundance.

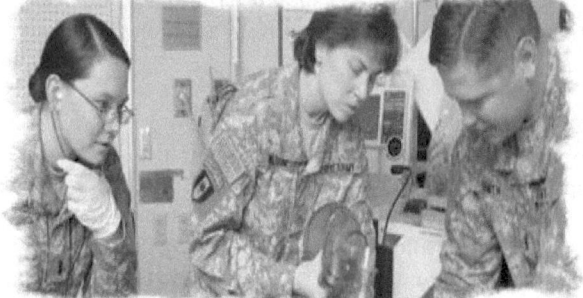

Now take a closer look. There is an equal amount of death, particularly in the winter. There will be dead grass and leaves, fallen limbs and trees, even dead animals and insects.

Every living thing will sooner or later die: no living creature, plant or animal, escapes death. In Nature, every dead thing is deposited in the very place it dies, and there it serves as a mulch protecting the soil until it finally decays and in due time is covered and replaced by still later deposits of expired life.

When a plant or animal dies, even though it may be consumed higher in the food chain, it will eventually be eaten by the decomposing microbes. They will decay or disassemble it and put it back into the soil. If they didn't, our planet would now be miles deep in dead things.

This life-death-decay-life cycle has built the thin layer of fertile soil that covers our land. It nourishes and grows our plants which are the bridge of life between the soil and man.

Man...Does he know? And can he trace his life support systems far enough back to understand the life cycles? Man has accumulated much knowledge, but in areas of his healthy existence he seems to be slow to learn. Man sees death as a loss, or something to be sorrowful of, and he considers decay as something ugly. He doesn't understand why Nature always returns the dead back to the soil from where it came.

If man understood the laws of recycle and return, he would without delay put back into the farmlands all the mineral and energy rich organic waste materials his life stile generates. He wouldn't be daily wasting the mountains of manure and thousands of tons of bio-solids and other organic materials that he buries in landfills that seal and lock them away from the life generating; natural Soil building processes that our food producing soils so urgently need.

In a natural environment, there is no waste. All is reused, and usually made into something of still greater value for sustenance of life.

If man continues to break this law of return, he will not only stop the life-generating processes of the soil. He will actually cause the soil to degenerate--a process that will sooner or later degrade all life ... including man himself.

ARLEE
Collection of Harold F. Hester's Short Stories

In all of us is a scholar, a statesman, a professional that is family and community orientated and admit it, there is a bit of ham and want-to-bee lurking in the shadows of our mind that craves the classics. For example the play *As You Like It* by *William Shakespeare (1564–1616)*, first performed in 1599 and first published in 1623. The famous soliloquy spoken by Jaques that begins "All the world's a stage" presents seven stages in the life of man, with the end marking a return to the beginning:

All the world's a stage, And all the men and women merely players: They have their exits and their entrances; And one man in his time plays many parts, His acts being seven ages. At first, the infant, Mewling and puking in the nurse's arms. And then the whining schoolboy, with his satchel and shining morning face, creeping like a snail unwillingly to school. And then the lover, Sighing like a furnace, with a woeful ballad Made to his mistress' eyebrow. Then a soldier, Full of strange oaths and bearded like the pard, Jealous in honour, sudden and quick in quarrel, Seeking the bubble reputation Even in the cannon's mouth. And then the justice, In fair round belly with good capon lined, With eyes severe and beard of formal cut, Full of wise saws and modern instances; And so he plays his part. The sixth age shifts Into the lean and slipper'd pantaloon, With spectacles on nose and pouch on side, His youthful hose, well saved, a world too wide For his shrunk shank; and his big manly voice, Turning again toward childish treble, pipes And whistles in his sound. Last scene of all, That ends this strange eventful history, Is second childishness and mere oblivion, Sans teeth, sans eyes, sans taste, sans everything. William had a way with words and they kinda makes you wonder.

So you see, it makes no difference if you are a scientist, a scholar, a romantic, or just your every-day average Joe or Jane citizen it all boils down to if you are a military veteran, don't trust your VA for benefits as they are budget driven but you can trust your military medical personal, the military hospital care and if you are a civilian you can basically trust all your medical dedicated people as they will keep you on earth for as long a time as you have been allotted – but some days I still wonder.

Thanks again Liz.

Seventy vs. Seven tentxs of a Second

A short lesson in physics, specifically, Newton's Third Law of Motion.

Four vehicle pileup on I-395 Snarled morning Commute

By Harold F. Hester
Washington Post Traffic Editor
Thursday, February 08, 2007; Page D04

All four southbound lanes of the beltway at the Bradlick exit were closed for two hours during this mornings commute because of a small sedan and three fully loaded tractor-trailer pile up apparently caused by the sedan. There were two fatalities in a crushed late model sedan. The accident happened shortly before 0800 hours this morning. Frank J. Neimrod, 36 and Becky Goodness, 24 died from apparent strange driving technique, as reported by eye-witnesses.

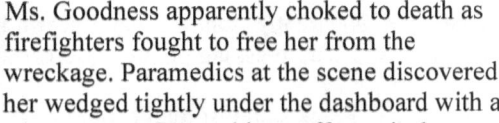

Ambulances and firefighting equipment from the Silver Springs ward 22 were first on the scene and took over an hour to get to the bodies. Mr. Neimrod apparently died from a crushed chest after rear-ending an eighteen-wheel tractor trailer that had slowed for traffic. A fully loaded tractor trailer that had been closely following the sedan 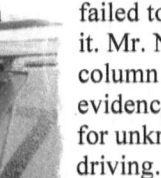 failed to slow in time and slammed into Mr. Neimrod's KIA - crushing wheel it. Mr. Neimrod was impaled on his steering column and died on the scene. There was evidence he had been wearing his seatbelt but for unknown reasons had taken it off while driving.

Ms. Goodness apparently choked to death as firefighters fought to free her from the wreckage. Paramedics at the scene discovered her wedged tightly under the dashboard with a male appendage (penis) lodged in her throat that apparently was bitten off near its base during the accident. Ms. Goodness was not wearing a seatbelt.

Drugs or alcohol were not a factor in the accident.

An investigation is on-going and no charges have been filed at this time.

Staff writer Dawn B. Daily contributed to this report.

***

Thirty-three minutes earlier at 0727 hours: *(The part that was not in the newspaper.)*

Frank picked Betty up from her home in Bethesda. They often shared rides with 'shag-line' commuters but this morning they were alone. Both were government employees at the Pentagon, he on the C Ring as a Systems Engineer, she on the A ring as a special assistant to the Chief of Logistics. They had attended many official social events together and over the course of a month and after many vodka martinis had developed a close bond as friends, lovers and companions-at-large.

Today was to be not that different then the normal hectic pentagon work-day. Directing the many arms of the military around the world is at best chaotic but today's calendars for Systems and Special Assistant employees and military personal on A and C ring was to attend a special "Sexual Awareness" seminar and workshop beginning at 1000 hours.

WMAL radio was softly playing 1960's music as Betty started the commute conversation by mentioning the class they had to attend. Betty said, "I talked with Mary-Beth yesterday after she went to this class and she said it was a real hoot. They had a slide show and Q&A and some of the Log Chief-of-Staff folks were actually embarrassed" she said.

Frank added to the conversation with, "Why the workshop, did someone get 'groped' in the cafeteria again? What started this mandatory sex class everyone has to attend?"

"No one was groped. This is just the annual thing we have to grace with your presence." Betty said. She hesitated a moment then added, "From the way I hear it, yesterday's class turned from ordinary sex and sexual practices, how to act and what can and can not be said or done in the work place to oral and that upset a few folks."

"Oral? Oral what? Upset...how?" Frank was curious and serious in his conundrum.

"Weeeeeell, apparently from the way I hear it is the older crowd couldn't follow the 'oral' part and started asking pointed questions," Betty said.

"Such as...." Frank said just loud enough to be heard over road and radio sounds.

"Well... such as Admiral Wise asked the meaning of fellatio and a young Log intern answered her saying, '...it's just a blow-job Admiral'".

Frank seemed to blush at the terminology Betty continued with what she knew from yesterday's classroom conversation saying, "The Admiral, as straight-laced as she is somehow came back at the intern with, 'I always thought the word for that was Cunnilingus'."

Betty was grinning from ear to ear as she remembered things she had been told about yesterdays. She said, "The whole class kinda lost it when the Admiral got into it and before the dust settled no matter what the rank or age group everyone left the class much smarter and introduced into today's language and terminology."

"Think any words learned at the class will show up in any White House briefing?" Frank said in jest but there was still the tone of seriousness.

"I'm sure it will Frank honey. You know how Washington works."

Other then road noises, WMAL and some now heavy breathing, inside the KIA was quiet as Betty leaned a bit toward Frank as she said, "Why haven't you ever allowed me to do that with you?"

"Do what - Fellatio?" Frank quietly said more toward the windshield then toward Betty. She was quiet for several more seconds before answering, "Yes".

Frank seemed to try concentrating more on traffic as it had picked up to a bit over 70mph and everyone now were bumper to bumper. There were huge trucks all around them and it made him feel as if he was in a rolling tunnel.

"Frank?" Betty's voice brought him back to their reality. "You have never asked me to give you a blow job – why?"

Frank let his tongue wet his lips a couple times, he blinked before answering, "You want the long answer or the short one?"

"Short will do for now. We are close to our exit and I need to know before class." She was grinning.

"OK. The short answer is – I feel – strongly feel fellatio, blow job, head, polishing the knob, etc... That it is very demeaning to the girls." He took a deep breath and continued, "I don't feel, honestly feel there is not a girl, female out there anywhere that services men with their mouths because they 'like' it. I have always felt they do it just to please the man and the ladies do not get any pleasure from it – at all." Before Betty could say anything, Frank said, "I once meet this young girl that had several 'piercing' on her eyebrows and lip and one she had was a 'knob' in the middle of her tongue. I asked her about it, 'why she did it, did it hurt, was it in her way' kind of questions and her answer surprised me. I had always thought when people had Tattoos or piercing they did it for themselves, that they were making a statement of sorts. She told me she did it 'for her boyfriend' that she did it '...because he liked the way it felt during her 'blow-jobs'. For him, for him, that was all

I was hearing. Everything was for him and nothing was for her. That's the short version... I'll give you the longer version some evening we have lots of time."

Traffic was steadily picking up as more feeder ramps opened and merging traffic speed seem to also increase.

The conversation seemed to arouse Betty a bit as she eased closer to the driver as she said, "Some of us get pleasure, Frank." She didn't sound convincing but she added, "Honest." She was in easy reach of Frank by now as she put her hand on his thigh and slowly eased her fingers closer toward his lap and his crotch.

The time was 0751 hours.

"Frank honey, have you ever had really good '*head*'?"

Her fingers were by this time in the crease of his leg and crotch. It was warm.

His eyes were darting from truck to truck to speedometer back to the trucks as Betty kissed his ear lobe.

The time was 0752 hours.

This was neither the time nor place but Frank said in his own defense, "I tried it once. Didn't like it – the girl wanted me to climax into her mouth and I tried not too but the way she was 'working me', I had no other choose but do what she wanted – I gagged and felt really bad for her all the while she was gagging, spitting and swallowing. She looked like she had white snot all over her lips and cheeks."

Frank shivered as he remembered that day so many years ago.

As Frank had been talking Betty had been busy unbuckling his seat beat and unzipping his trousers.

The warmth in her hands, her breath, her attitude, and his new attitude all changed in a heart beat as she reached inside his pants and pulled. "Frank honey, you have not had a blow-job until you have had one from me. I want you to relax and let me show you how it's done. I promise not to gag – OK?"

The time was 0757 hours.
She took as much of Frank into her mouth as she could under the circumstances... and he did relax, leaned his head back and momentarily closed his eyes as he felt a hot tsunami wave race from the tip and circumference of his penis, back through his anus, up his backbone, circle to his guts as he felt her tongue circle, suck and the warmth of her lips completely encompass him. His thoughts were not of *what* but **where** his penis was and what was happening. The feeling was euphoric for the split second he was in never-never

land then totally horrifying as he saw a blur of bright red truck tail-lights only inches from the hood of his KIA.

Betty's mouth was busy and Frank's was open but there was no time... no time...

The time was 0757 hours and 32 seconds as he felt the steering column enter his chest, the same time as he felt a searing pain in his groin.

The time was 0757 hours and 32.7 seconds as life left Frank J. Neimrod in a crumbled sedan in the middle of the beltway doing what he really didn't like or enjoy.

The time was 0812 hours and 12 seconds as life left Becky Goodness grotesquely and horribly broken under a crumbled Korean dashboard doing what she really didn't like or enjoy either but something that had become expected of her in her short life.

Not real sure about Monica, Traci or Linda at the time BUT for the present:

Monica now has a Masters degree in Science, (according to newspapers) has had an abortion, made purses and hosted a talk show for a bit. Her Master Thesis was impressive: *In Search of the Impartial Juror: An Exploration of the Third Person Effect and Pre-Trial Publicity."* She has spent the last decade making purses and hosting a reality dating show called "Mr. Personality." Jobs are now difficult to come by however.

Traci as a teenager, was an adult movie actress who has 107 films to her credit (all but one before her 18th birthday), done mostly while under the influence of drugs and management of some very unscrupulous people. It would have been easier for her to escape the spotlight and try to live a normal life. Instead she had the courage to pursue her dream of being an actress with dialogue, and withstood countless criticism and death threats. We should all be so brave.

Linda made a ground breaking "Deep Throat" movie in 1972. She said she was forced into performing some scenes at gunpoint by her former manager and husband, Chuck Traynor, and said that every time someone watched her on screen, "they are watching me being raped".

She later had two children and twice divorced and died in a car accident at the age of 53.

These vehicles took part in the telling of this story but do not have anything to do here other then just show you some of the things that can/will happen the next time you get pissed or feel amorous on the highways.

Looking at crumpled metal that use to be a fine 'set of wheels' is like looking at a piece of paper you just wadded up and threw away. Makes you sick.

to therapy or Not to therapy

As I select my characters and story-line it is sometimes difficult for me to differentiate, for them, between, love, hate, sex, hormonal drive, wanton desire, nomenclature of words and the professional person. Because of the frailties of the male human animal, changing times, attitudes and male-female relationships caused some consternation in the telling of this most professional and dedicated career field named *Therapy.*

Remember - what was is not necessarily what is.

After college Frank spent many years on the US East coast, lived in four countries of Europe, and two in the Asian Far East. Outside the confines of the boundaries of the United States there are roughly seven (7) billion other people and they all have their own way of looking at life, human and sexual laws, behavior, and the unique codes of idiosyncratic people…well for the lack of a better words let's use… differ.

If you ask any person that has a 9-5 job, or government worker that spends time at a work place, or day-laborer or anyone that is not officially retired from the work force what is their favorite day of the week they would give you most often, the week-end – Saturday or Sunday. For those workers that had to be on duty those two days serving the 9-5 crowd, they most likely would tell you Monday and Tuesday or any combination of a couple days 'off'.

Frank's was Thursday and it all had to do with Therapy, but at the time he didn't call it that.

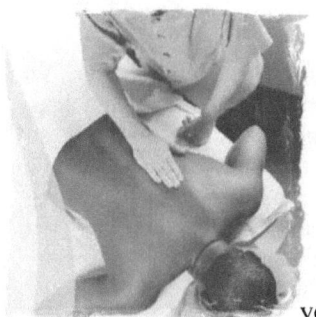

Just because during "therapy" there is normally much touching between men and women don't confuse physical therapy with anything sexual. Soldiers from all our many wars need these professional therapists to teach them to walk again or write with prosthesis but civilians also lose limbs, have surgical implants, and lose functional abilities in parts of their bodies. Wars use bullets and bombs to cause damage to flesh and bone while civilians, unlike their military counterpart will use a 3,000 pound automobile as a weapon of destruction. Have you even seen a 130 pound lady thrown from a tumbling or rolling car? Being thrown is not the problem; it's the hard landing that breaks bones and damages organs. The therapist is the one to help put a life back together after doctors and hospitals have done all they can. Don't forget also that disease can cause major limb problems and accidents can happen on your way to the beauty shop, hardware store or an evening partying. Therapists are the ones to put you back on your feet after you have done something dumb or a surgeon's scalpel has left you short handed or not in the need both shoes.

Bionic people also need the therapist to re-learn many functions of arms, elbows, knees, hips and the like.

A fact that may be difficult to understand that in the co-ed saunas of Berlin, Heidelberg, Chicago, Houston, Bangor, Whistle Stop SC, Piney Grove Arkansas or Frankfurt Germany, their thinking and treatments do not differ a great deal from their friends of the Far-East. No matter what you call it, massaggio, Θεραπεία, терапия, therapy is still therapy meant to help make your life and body healthier.

Therapy is not sexual and a therapeutic massage is not sex.

Frank recently had a major problem with a knee and the idea of having a therapist help in what was to become a long period of recovery NEVER crossed his male-Far-Eastern-European-sex-oriented-brain. That was until he reported for his first post-operation appointment with the doctor that gave him the metal knee.

"X-rays look good Frank. How does the knee feel?" Dr. L said.

"Feel? You mean other then the pain?" Frank said as he rubbed and fingered the swollen and painful knee. "I can't bend it without screaming and if I'm late taking my pain-killers the pain radiates throughout my body till new pills kick-in." It was an honest response to a doctor's standard question.

There was some bantering about pain before Dr. L said, "Who did you get as a therapist? What are they doing for you?"

"Therapist?" Frank tried. "What do I need a therapist for? You told me in the hospital I needed to be on the knee as much as possible, using and exercising it and if I didn't it would be stiff for the rest of my life. You pretty much put the fear-of-God in me so I have been moving as much as I can – pain permitting."

Frank tried to justify his words by saying, "I bought a stationary bicycle but I can't get the knee all the way around, but I'm working on that." Frank showed serious signs of frustration trying to explain his non-ability to bend the new metal knee.

"…and…?" Dr. L said with wrinkled brow, hands in pocket and raised left eye-brow.

Frank hates confrontations and by this time he was wishing for a hole he could crawl in or just wish this appointment away. Frank had always believed in his own body and his ability to heal himself and that he didn't need outside help.

"…and…and…" Frank sputtered. He knew he needed to say something but didn't know what. As seconds passed you could see manliness building as he sucked his waist in a bit puffed his chest before saying, "I don't need an outsider to massage my knee, I can do that."

Dr. L had been here before so as discretely as possible he sat Frank down and educated him on the differences between Massage, Therapy, sex and what a Therapist can do for you is always longer lasting then a sexual rub-down. Dr. L enjoyed the next few minutes as Frank squirmed but nodded at all the proper moments.

Dr. L began, "Physical Therapy is a dynamic and ever changing field…Frank. Physical therapists are health professionals who evaluate and treat people with a variety of dysfunctions. They assess joint motion, muscle strength and endurance, cardiac and pulmonary function, development, functional ability, sensation and perception, integrity of the skin, muscle tone and reflexes, and performance of functional activities. They evaluate patients' needs, diagnose physical therapy problems, establish plans of care, and evaluate their effectiveness. There is normally never anything sexual about true therapy."

Frank's eyes were a bit cloudy as Dr. L gave him a cup of water then continued with, "Physical therapy is a people-oriented profession - Frank. Physical therapists have many opportunities to improve the quality of their clients' lives as individuals or in small groups. Physical therapists educate patients in health promotion and conduct research to improve patient care. Physical therapists must have excellent observational and psychomotor skills.

Physical therapists are involved with restoring function and independence at all levels. I'm give you a couple examples: Helping someone to walk again following a stroke, helping a child to develop head control, or helping an athlete return to their sport. You may not even need to go to them because therapists practice in a variety of settings, including hospitals, nursing homes, private physical therapy offices, community health centers, sports facilities, rehabilitation centers, clients' homes, schools and pediatric centers. Physical therapists also conduct research and teach in colleges and universities and practice as researchers in private industry."

Dr. L was apparently enjoying his captive audience as he continued with, "…Physical therapists are valuable members of the health care team, who work with physicians, dentists, podiatrists, occupational therapists, nurses, speech and hearing professionals, psychologists, and social workers. Physical therapists may practice by referral from physicians, podiatrists, or dentists or have direct access to patients depending upon the jurisdiction."

Frank's face went blank but it looked to Dr. L as if he was trying to ask a question so he added:

"Frank, the term therapy covers a wide range of health professions and activities. In general, it refers to the treatment of an illness, disease or disorder. This can include training or rehabilitation of such basic motor skills as speech or movement; healing or rehabilitation of physical or intellectual skills lost or impaired due to organic disorders, accidents or medical conditions; or even social and behavioral adjustment.

The goal of all therapy is to enable an individual to live a more effective, satisfying and comfortable life. Look at the lady over there n the treadmill and you will see just one example. Last year she had all but given up. See what I mean Frank?"

By this time the water was gone, the paper cup crumbled and Frank was sitting on the edge of his chair wanting to say something. "Yes Frank, you want to add something?" Dr. L said as he poured a cup for himself.

"I'm pretty good giving massages." Dr. L sipped his cup of water waiting for the other shoe but that was all Frank apparently had to say.

Dr. L was the true professional as he crushed his cup, leaned forward a bit and said, "Where did you learn your techniques – Frank?"

"Korea mostly." His eyes seemed to glaze a bit – remembering then he added, "I use to go to a massage parlor in Seoul and the girls would let me 'practice' on them." There was an abnormally long pause as his eyes narrowed remembering. Frank opened his mouth again to continue but Dr. L interrupted with, "Any formal schooling or training Frank?"

"Formal school?" Frank said the words as if he had just been called a nasty name, but he finally did manage a quiet, "No."

Dr. L saw the expression of disbelief on Frank that someone would need to be formally schooled to rub sore muscles around or be a voyeur in the parlor.

"Frank, you have a degree from a college right?" Dr L asked.

"Yea. A University actually. Have an AS in engineering and BS in architecture." Frank said.

"Could you have been an architect without the schooling or paper?" Dr. L was taking this conversation somewhere and Frank was going along because he didn't have a clue what was required to be a Therapist. Dr. L handed Frank another paper cup of icy water and asked him to get comfortable as he was about to be educated – on Therapy.

"Frank most professional therapeutic positions require at least a master's degree as an entry-level requirement. Most assistant and aide positions, however, can often be obtained with a bachelor's or even an associate's degree. The higher the degree obtained, the more qualified you will be to compete for a position and the higher the salary range you can command."

That had Frank's attention.

"Physical Therapist and Physical Therapist Assistant/Aide: Physical therapists are health care professionals whose goal is to improve the overall physical functionality of their patients. This can include enhancing their muscle strength, functional ability, flexibility, endurance, or mobility. Physical therapists also work to relieve pain, prevent or reverse muscular degeneration and atrophy, and to restore independence in their patients."

Frank seemed to be searching for words for Dr. L and even stuttered a bit as he asked about other kinds – of therapist.

Dr. L recognized the wrinkled brow, tight lips, quenched eyes, nervous fingers and feet pointed inward to be the classic look of this southern man searching his brain for a question, an answer or in this case just searching the gray-matter to see what was up there that could be of any use, right now. Frank didn't find anything so after a few moments that seemed an eternity Dr. L tried to bring other kinds of therapy into the conversation that would not be offensive or making fun of Frank's stuttering.

Dr. L gently offered, "Speech Therapy?"

Frank beamed as if he had come up with the new word but stuttered as he said, "Yea."

Dr. L continued with, "Speech therapists are also highly trained health care professionals who work with people who have speech or language disorders. Speech therapists assess, diagnose and treat these language, voice, and fluency problems. They also work with people who have swallowing difficulties."

"Like me?" Frank offered.

Dr. L let the question slide as he continued with, "We also have in the field, Occupational Therapist and Occupational Therapist/Aide: Occupational therapists treat individuals with conditions that are disabling, whether mentally, physically, emotionally, or developmentally. They assist patients in developing or recovering the skills necessary for independent day-to-day living. The mission of occupational therapists is to teach their clients the skills they need to enjoy independent, productive, and fulfilling lives.

All States require physical therapists to pass a licensure exam before they can practice, after graduating from an accredited physical therapist educational program."

Dr. L paused only briefly then said, "According to the American Physical Therapy Association, there were over 200 accredited physical therapist programs in just this last year. Of the accredited programs close to a hundred offered master's degrees and offered doctoral degrees." Just to show off a bit Dr. L continued with just how well up-to-date his reading was by saying, "All physical therapist programs seeking accreditation are required to offer degrees at the master's degree level and above, in accordance with the Commission on Accreditation in Physical Therapy Education."

By this time Frank's eye had glazed, his mouth opened a bit as Dr. L said, "Physical therapist programs start with basic science courses such as biology, chemistry, and physics and then introduce specialized courses, including biomechanics, neuroanatomy,

 human growth and development, manifestations of disease, examination techniques, and therapeutic procedures. Besides getting classroom and laboratory instruction, students receive supervised clinical experience. Among the courses that are useful when one applies to a physical therapist educational program are anatomy, biology, chemistry, social science, mathematics, and physics. Before granting admission, many professional education programs require experience as a volunteer in a physical therapy department of a hospital or clinic. For high school students, volunteering with the school athletic trainer is a good way to gain experience."

Dr. L was on a roll and Frank was seemingly glued to his every word (actually Frank was marveling at how eloquently 4 and 5 syllable words were rolling off Dr. L's tongue – Frank didn't know many of their meanings but they sounded like important doctor words) as he continued with, "Physical therapists should have strong interpersonal skills in order to be able to educate patients about their physical therapy treatments. Physical therapists also should be compassionate and possess a desire to help patients. Similar traits are needed to interact with the patient's family.

Physical therapists are expected to continue their professional development by participating in continuing education courses and workshops. In fact, a number of States require continuing education as a condition of maintaining licensure.

Physical therapists held about 155,000 jobs in 2006. The number of jobs is greater than the number of practicing physical therapists, because some physical therapists hold two or more jobs. For example, some may work in a private practice, but also work part time in another health care facility.

Nearly 6 out of 10 physical therapists worked in hospitals or in offices of physical therapists. Other jobs were in home health care services, nursing care facilities, outpatient care centers, and offices of physicians.

Some physical therapists were self-employed in private practices, seeing individual patients and contracting to provide services in hospitals, rehabilitation centers, nursing care facilities, home health care agencies, adult day care programs, and schools. Physical therapists also teach in academic institutions and conduct research."

Frank was clearly impressed. As Dr. L refilled his water cup Frank walked slowly toward the front of the clinic and pointing and nodding at the same time said, "You have a really nice looking luxury sports car out there Doctor L, Mercedes 450 SE?"

Dr. L almost chocked on his water but while clearing his throat said with a huge grin, "No Frank. Don't I wish? "Mine is the one parked next to the butcher's wheels. Mine is the Ford, Fairlane'96. I would love to owe a Mercedes but they are a bit out of my price range. The Ford is all I can afford."

"Really? I would think your income would be in the six-figures." Frank was fishing but he got no bites.

"OK my friend; it's time for you to do ten-minutes on the treadmill." Dr. L said in a serious voice.

"But I…."

"No Butts Frank, now hobble over to the machine and get busy. Your knee is never going to get better just talking about it."

Eight minutes later Dr. L was standing next to the treadmill talking to Frank about what actually was going on with his knee, what would be required to get him back to normal when he said, "Remember the difference between a massage in the Far East to a real therapeutic massage you need be schooled, tested and certified. There are excellent therapists here and I want you to start going."

Frank didn't look thrilled with Dr. L but was curious as the good doctor had noticed then said, "Frank, those tattoos you have, where did you get them?"

"Basic training when I was in the army, just out the main gate of Fort Carson Colorado, and a couple in NJ, why?"

"Do you remember the person that did the tattoos?" it seemed an honest question to Frank.

Frank assumed that wrinkled brow, tight-lipped, toes inward position as he searched his memory of oh-so-many-years ago before finally saying, "Yea. A ... actually a tough but youngish looking woman with colorful dragon-like tattoos all over her back, shoulders and arms... and even legs." Frank looked to be reliving the moment. He continued describing her as he remembered, "If memory serves, she had spiked hair; tobacco stains on a sleeveless tee-shirt, no bra and was wearing combat boots."

After many years there are some things that will always remain in a male's memory. No bra and combat boots did it for Frank.

With concern in his voice and manner Dr. L said, "Frank, because you didn't get hepatitis, AIDS, blood poisoning, your arm didn't rot and drop off, plus you have a decent looking artistic skunk, and many other designs, you can thank our licensing system and that lady with spiked hair." Dr. L paused for an exceptionally long time before saying, "Frank... that tattoo artist...do you remember her name by chance?"

Her name was Joan or JoAnn. Why?"

Dr. L had a slightly crooked grin and it was now his turn to 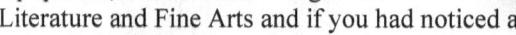 remember and reminisce. His voice was almost silent as he said, "Frank we are so regulated that that Tattoo artist had to be board tested, state licensed and monitored on a regular basis. If you had looked beyond her skin-art and spiked hair you would have seen she used all sterile equipment, had a master's degree in Literature and Fine Arts and if you had noticed a

few family pictures taped to the wall over her table next to her licenses and credentials you would have seen a picture of what I looked like as a youngster – when I too had spiked hair."

Ice, to Have or Have Not

Have you ever wondered…about "things"?

Of course you have! We humans have the most advanced and highly developed brain outside chimps and dolphins, so of course we wonder and think – about "stuff". That's the good news. The bad news is we only use less then 10% of this marvelous brain doing such things as - wondering and thinking while as far as science has been able to determine the other 90% in still undeveloped virgin waste-land.

An example of how one particular males' brain works is below:

Last evening the part of Frank's brain devoted to women was wildly thinking and wondering about Irene and how to 'pop-the-question' on marriage and if she would be his wife. They were having dinner in an up-scale restaurant and he was all nerves as she was miss-kool sipped her lemon-flavored ice-water and was the perfect vision of beauty in motion. Dimmed lighting, soft muffled conversational voices in the background, waiters scurrying between tables, soft romantic string music coming from a lone antique harp sitting in the corner with a gowned young lady playing it as if she had butterflies playing with her fingers. Irene had slowly raised her glass with graceful fingers, eyes flashing with anticipation, lips slowing parting, her pink tipped tongue unhurriedly moistening her lower lip to accept the cold ice filled glass, he felt a twinge of future anticipation for an lovely evening. Anticipation and adrenalin peaked as she held a small amount of cold liquid in her mouth letting it warm briefly before it slips down a scented throat, her eyes glistening as she held the glass only inches from her handsome face. Looking over the glass' now frosty rim toward Frank her eyes narrowed with passion and want, said in that sultry female voice now so familiar to him…

"Do you have any idea why these ice cubes are clear?"

He sputtered a quiet "…no."

She then engrossed herself in studying her newspaper sized menu. Maybe she dropped the 'ice' subject because she saw that blank look on his face that spelled 'I have NO idea'.

Frank felt as though he had just dodged a bullet, but the question still nagged him. He had never thought about it before, why should he, what difference does it make to him if ice is clear?

Orders taken, and small talk continued during cocktails and salad then she had to powder her nose just before the main entrée.

This was Frank's chance.

As soon as she left the table he dug out his new do-everything Blackberry and with nervous fingers quickly typed in Google.com. No response so he typed Ask.com still no response, then tried AskJeeves, then Dogpile.com before a search engine window to the world opened. His finger were beginning to sweat and was touching wrong keys in quiet anticipation Irene would be returning before the little machine could answer... but he typed on and finally there was an answer, or part of it. He had to put on his glasses to read the screen and scroll and scroll and scroll but finished a first scan only moments before she returned. He wished for a printer or at least for another fifteen minutes.

"What are you doing honey?" An honest question because she apparently saw his cupped hand in his lap just as he closed white-tipped fingers over the screen.

 "Nothing." He lied. Thinking back on it now he should have said he was checking e-mail but, maybe it was that guilty feeling because he didn't have a clue what "clear ice" was supposed to be as apposed "non-clear or dirty or foggy or hazy or gray or cloudy" ice.

"Ice is ice is ice" his male pre-occupied brain was telling him. Relax and think about it later.

Frank's brain was having fun with it 10% as it continues silently saying to him; "I wish Irene didn't smell so good, it's hard to concentrate... I love 'cleavage'". Never once did his brain wander off to subjects such as baseball, football playoffs, hall-of-fame inductees, republicans, democrats, war, car repair or new car models. It was centered on the lady across the table which was the love of my life, but sometimes also his tormentor.

Between her asparagus and filet mignon, Frank was able to steal quick glances at the little screen now being held between nervous knees. The answers were all there, but as he scanned again and again he could not find anything on "clear ice". Maybe 'clear-ice' is a synonym or antonym or even an acronym for something. He was perspiring, nervous and now lost as how to handle that seemingly casual question – "...do you now what clear-ice is...?" Maybe now what he should try doing is just deciphering all what was between his knees to make meanings and put the words into some kind of intelligent conversation. His brain yelled "BS" but he paid it no attention.

He had scrolled to portions of text that said, "CLEAR ICE – Clear ice does not have any impurities. That didn't say a heck-of-a-lot but that was all the little machine could apparently tell him – so far. Maybe it didn't know either but there was lots of data there saying such things as:

"1000 BC The Chinese cut and stored ice.

500 BC Egyptians and Indians made ice on cold nights by setting water out in earthenware pots.

Then around 1700 In England, servants collected ice in the winter and put it into icehouses for use in the summer and in 1720 Dr. William Cullen, a Scotsman, studied the evaporation of liquids in a vacuum.

1805 Oliver Evans of Pennsylvania, compressed ether machine, the machine is never built..."

Everything in the world about ice except what he really needed to know.

He was dead if he could not come up with something about 'clear ice'. There had to be a reason Irene mentioned it earlier. Was she testing him? Was it a simple observation? Maybe she was checking my intellect, my observation to details, my worldliness, jeeze-maybe even my man-hood. Frank's 10% brain usage right now needed expanding but all the questions, facts running around in his head were not running into any answers. Now there were only other problems and questions. He was dead meat.

Dishes were cleared and coffee ordered, "Yes. Black thank you AND another glass of lemon water with ice, please." She asked.

As in a funeral procession his brain was silently saying in a sad tone, "Now you're really dead. She's getting fresh ice and I bet it's as 'clear' as the other."

The restaurant's table and booth conversations were not especially loud but there was a constant buzz as all seemed to be intermingled and not 'words' per-sa just sounds. As luck would have it the gentleman sitting back-too in a chair almost touching his chair, Frank's ears and good luck picked up what could have been an appliance salesperson talking about refrigerators compared to the old style ice-boxes. The salesperson was saying something along the lines such as, "...when my mother got her first Electrolux refrigerator in 1925 she was so happy to get rid of her old leaking ice-box she..." when Frank could again pick up on the words he heard "... it had a freeze compartment that would actually freeze ice in small metal trays but it always vibrate so badly the water in the tray would sometimes splash out ... but the ice was always clear and had a cleaner taste, not at all like other cloudy ice." All conversations seemed to stop, the heavens open and an Angel came down to sit on his shoulder as he then heard, *"... seems all impurities would be vibrated to the bottom and left clean ice cubes..."*

BINGO.

There IT was. He had his 'clear-ice' ace-in-the-hole and as he smiled from ear to ear conversations picked up again but he stopped listening to the neighbor and leaning on one elbows looking Irene straight into her beautiful blue eyes behind her water glass. While thinking, "...yes there is a God."

As Frank relaxed so did his knees and the light-blue Blackberry slide off his lap onto the floor but no one noticed. Its small plasma screen glowed bright with data but there was no hurry now. He didn't need what the Internet had taken all of .002 seconds to look in all documents that talked to water and ice and refrigeration and Freon and freezing and who-did-what-to-whom over the years discovering, testing, perfecting the production of ice. He had his answer.

Even having the answer to satisfy his future Significant Other just the simple question raised questions in his own mind now:

> Where does ice come from?
> How was ice made during the hot summer months?
> If chemicals are used to make ice, what are they, are they harmful?
> Are/is there any substitute for ice?
> What about 'dry-ice', why is it hot and how does it keep 'stuff' cold?

The Blackberry screen was blinking with the answer but no one cared to look or read "...Dry Ice is frozen carbon dioxide, a normal part of our earth's atmosphere. It is the gas that we exhale during breathing and the gas that plants use in photosynthesis. It is also the same gas commonly added to water to make soda water. Dry Ice is particularly useful for freezing, and keeping things frozen because of its very cold temperature: -109.3°F or -78.5°C. Dry Ice is widely used because it is simple to freeze and easy to handle using insulated gloves. Dry Ice changes directly from a solid to a gas -sublimation- in normal atmospheric conditions without going through a wet liquid stage. Therefore it gets the name "dry ice."

No one was interested in dry-ice or clear ice, or cloudy ice or any kind of ice right now.

"Sweetheart" He said as he picked up his fresh glass of lemon ice water with 'clear ice'.

"Yes Frank" Irene said as she chewed a small sliver of *'clear ice'*

Before he could say another word there was a chiming from the floor. His do-everything-Blackberry, its bright plasma screen flashing with words of wisdom said:

"Make sure you tell her you know that clear ice requires running water is the main reason it is commercially made". Frank's brain whispered to whom ever might be listening, *"...damn thing is smarter then me..."*

Frank cleared his throat, hit the Blackberry's OFF bottom and turned ever so slowly toward his beautiful soon to be partner – he hoped.

"Irene, sweetheart - I have a very serious question to ask but before I do, have I ever told you about my grandmother's 1925 Electrolux absorption refrigerator and her running water?"

ARLEE
Collection of Harold F. Hester's Short Stories

Muscle, Blood and Electricity

Just some information I learned the hard way and would like to share...to maybe save your life.

Lightning is one of the most prominent effects of electricity. The leader of a bolt of lightning can travel at speeds of 60,000 m/s, and can reach temperatures approaching 30,000 °C (54,000 °F), hot enough to fuse soil or sand into glass

I am deathly afraid of Fire and Electricity.
I am also very cautious of and when handling electricity – and rightful so. Electricity is in our everyday life and ALL around us, all the time. Not only does your flashlight, your car, home, lights, Blackberry and cell-phone need electricity, did you know your body is also electrical and *your heart actually creates electricity?* Your heart requires about 80 microAmps (μA) or about 60 Hz to maintain it's job of pushing your six quarts of blood about 12,000 miles, daily through your veins. Did you know your  Aorta (main blood vein) is just a bit smaller then a normal garden hose whereas capillaries supplying blood and oxygen to certain parts of your body and heart are up to six times smaller then a human hair?

OK – So much for your schooling. I just wanted you to kinda understand what we are dealing with.

Do you know what exactly is happening to your body when;

     a. **You have a Stroke** = your brain is attacking you but how do you "know" it is a stroke? Do these three things;

          1. Raise both hands over your head
          2. Smile
          3. Say a complete sentence

IF you *can not* do those three things you are having a stroke. **Go IMMEDIATELY** to a hospital.

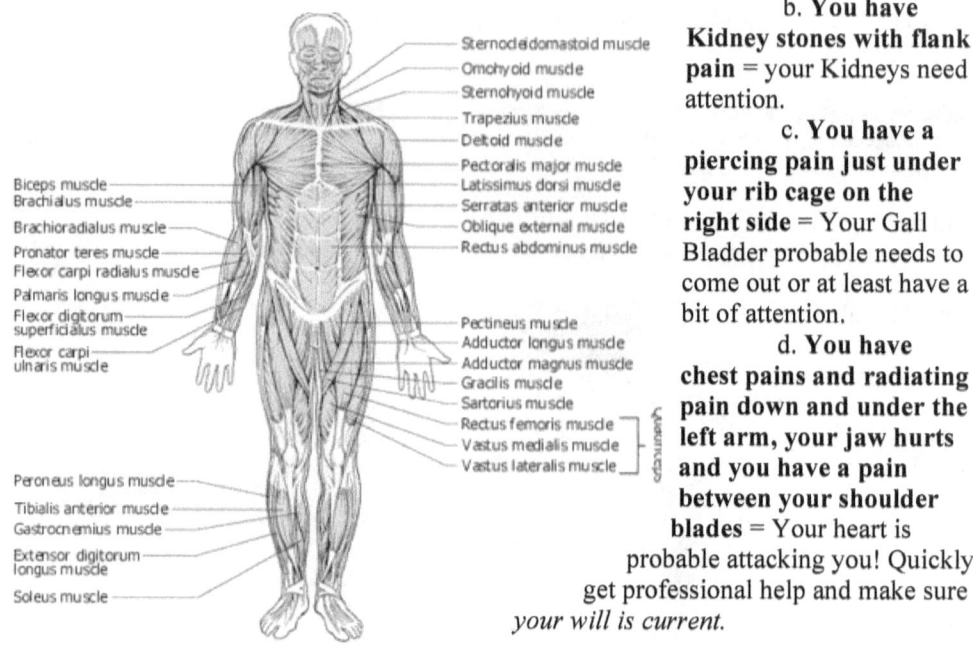

Sternocleidomastoid muscle
Omohyoid muscle
Sternohyoid muscle
Trapezius muscle
Deltoid muscle
Pectoralis major muscle
Latissimus dorsi muscle
Serratas anterior muscle
Oblique external muscle
Rectus abdominus muscle

Biceps muscle
Brachialus muscle
Brachioradialus muscle
Pronator teres muscle
Flexor carpi radialus muscle
Palmaris longus muscle
Flexor digitorum superficialus muscle
Flexor carpi ulnaris muscle

Pectineus muscle
Adductor longus muscle
Adductor magnus muscle
Gracilis muscle
Sartorius muscle
Rectus femoris muscle
Vastus medialis muscle
Vastus lateralis muscle

Peroneus longus muscle
Tibialis anterior muscle
Gastrocnemius muscle
Extensor digitorum longus muscle
Soleus muscle

b. **You have Kidney stones with flank pain** = your Kidneys need attention.

c. **You have a piercing pain just under your rib cage on the right side** = Your Gall Bladder probable needs to come out or at least have a bit of attention.

d. **You have chest pains and radiating pain down and under the left arm, your jaw hurts and you have a pain between your shoulder blades** = Your heart is probable attacking you! Quickly get professional help and make sure *your will is current.*

If you are female your chances for survival during a heart attack are pretty good because you will seek help as you know "something is wrong".

If you are male your chances of survival are greatly reduced because you will *gut it out* and be *manly.*

God made at least one mistake when he made Adam because he gave him vanity, muscles and external plumbing but not enough blood to run all three at the same time.

Let's pretend for a few minutes you are male and you suddenly can not smile, you can not raise both hands over your head and you can not say a complete sentence. That is your first clue something is wrong with that body? Yesterday you could bench 300 pounds while laughing and telling *blond* jokes. Today you can't remember that joke and one arm is even too heavy to wave. Do you have a problem?

Yes is the short answer and that problem is called a Stroke. The longer answer is if you can get professional medical help within a short few hours your chances of telling more 'blond' jokes are pretty good. But If or when you gut-it-out because, "…it will be better as soon as I stretch or in just a second…" you become the joke as friends will then be saying such things as "…poor Bill, or Fred, or Jim, etc. did you hear he had a stroke and is now paralyzed on the "right/left side. If he had only gotten to the doctor a few hours earlier he would be better - Poor dear."

When your brain is having a blood supply problem, no amount of vanity *manly* boloney will save your muscle bound sorry self, but a doctor can.

If you are female and you can't smile or snap your bra you know you need to get to a hospital and quickly.

You do not need to be doing "heavy" or "strenuous" things or being overly emotional for your heart to yell at you either. I was 40 years old sitting quietly at a friend's house in a wonderfully soft recliner sipping on morning coffee when I suddenly knew I had a problem. I felt "funny" unlike all other feeling. The pain in my chest and jaw went away but then would come and go as a wave washing the shore. It never dawned on me anything other then I was just maybe "hung over" because of several drinks last evening, but in the back of my male vanity brain I kept hearing "…something is wrong… something is wrong.."
"Bill… I need to go to a hospital" I said, or words to that affect.

"What's wrong Frank?"

"Not sure. My jaw is killing me and my damn shoulder blades hurt…" Frank stuttered as he headed for the front door saying more to himself then Bill, "I need to get to a hospital, I need help, I need…"
"I'll drive you." Bill interrupted his thoughts but Frank knew he had druther finish his Sunday paper then nursemaid a grown man at a hospital.

"Where's the hospital" Frank tried. "I promise to be right back?"

The directions were turn for turn to the hospital front door but when you're in pain directions are not your priority. Frank had to stop twice to ask further directions in the three miles to the hospital while his heart was busy attacking him.
Because Frank is writing this story tells you he did several stupid things but survival has not been pleasant or a short recovery.

Why am I writing this story? I have something I would like to share.

Why are you reading it? I have something you need to know and this information is always something you have though about but just never asked.

ARLEE

Do you know your body is made up of muscles, blood, water, lots of other 'stuff' AND Electricity?

Now pay attention!

Frank is an army decorated combat Vietnam veteran that has done more then most and when ask will answer "…I have done everything once and some really bad things twice…" he often says and in truth had always felt, for the lack of a better word, "indestructible"… until he met Marine Master Gunny-Sergeant Victor (Vic) Gonzales. Vic kept the traditional white side-wall haircut, had a round clean shaven face, was barrel-chested that had to have all his uniforms tailored and could not wear anything before having being altered for his 67" chest, 32" waist, 230 pounds and 4% body fat on a 5'11' frame. You did not have to see him in uniform to know Vic was a Marine and a damn good friend. Semper Fi (Always Faithful) my friend.

Vic died at the age of 44.

His heart killed him. An organ no larger then the size of your closed fist did what droves of Vietcong had failed to do. A tiny blood vessel did what bullets and mortars and a steamy Vietnamese jungle could not.

War had spared his life yet the lack of a liter of oxygen supplied through microscopic veins to vital heart areas did not function properly one day and Vic died. His heart muscle basically exploded as it needed oxygen and blood and there was none. His body had given him warning sighs over the years but they all went unnoticed. A twinge here, a brief stabbing pain there, shortness of breath, slight things, diminutive insignificant signs easily overlooked by not only people like Vic, but down to the smallest, frailest, most insignificant person, male or female.

There are 60 organs in our living body and they all must function the way they are designed or you get sick and some die. All living matter will eventually die so it is just a matter of time until one or more of your organs wear out. Until that time your body "…is your temple…" and no matter what you may think, what you put into your temple…. matters. Even if you are Lon Chaney starring in the 1956 movie "indestructible man" or as Will Leitch said once "I'm young and indestructible. I'll worry about such matters when I'm older and living in the suburbs and car pooling and having my special Friday night dinner at the Outback."

Some have said over martinis that a heart attack is Gods revenge for eating his animals. I don't know.

But, what I do know is…

Heart Attack Warning Signs.

A heart attack is a frightening event, and you probably don't want to think about it. But, if you learn the signs of a heart attack and what steps to take, you can save a life— maybe your own.

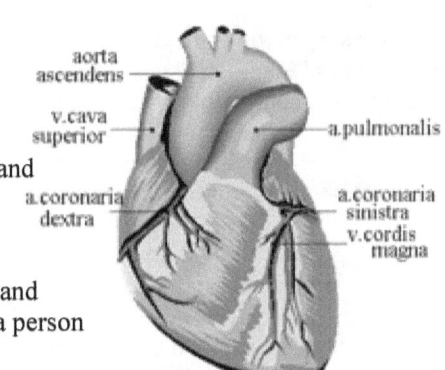

Many people think a heart attack is sudden and intense, like a "movie" heart attack, where a person clutches his or her chest and falls over.

The truth is that many heart attacks start slowly, as a mild pain or discomfort. If you feel such a symptom, you may not be sure what's wrong. Your symptoms may even come and go. Even those who have had a heart attack may not recognize their symptoms, because the next attack can have entirely different ones.

Women may not think they're at risk of having a heart attack–but they are. If you have a heart, you fall into the category of those eligible.

It's vital that everyone learn the warning signs of a heart attack.
      a. **Chest discomfort**. Most heart attacks involve discomfort in the center of the chest that lasts for more than a few minutes, or goes away and comes back. The discomfort can feel like uncomfortable **pressure, squeezing, fullness, or pain**.
      b. **Discomfort in other areas of the upper body that can include pain or discomfort in one or both arms, the back, neck, jaw, or stomach.**
      c. **Shortness of breath**. Often comes along with chest discomfort. But it also can occur before chest discomfort.
      d. Other symptoms may include breaking out in a **cold sweat, nausea, or light-headedness**.

Each year, about 460,000 people die because of heart attacks. The next time you need to go into a hospital and they tell you, you are their 459,999 patient – don't go in!!

What Is Angina? No, Angina was not in your senior class in High school. Angina (an-JI-nuh or AN-juh-nuh) is chest pain or discomfort that occurs when your heart muscle does not get enough blood. Angina may feel like pressure or a squeezing pain in your chest. The pain may also occur in your shoulders, arms, neck, jaw, or back. It may also feel like indigestion.

We talked about electricity earlier.

What is electricity in the context of this story? This question is impossible to answer because the word "Electricity" has several contradictory meanings. These different meanings are incompatible, and the contradictions confuse everyone. If you don't understand electricity, you're not alone. Even teachers, engineers, and scientists have a hard time grasping the concept. Just for your edification knowing what is happening inside your chest is IMPORTANT – Do you have any idea how much that 80 microAmps (µA) that is needed to run your pump actually is? Well, in terms we all can relate too are primary (non-rechargeable) zinc-carbon AA batteries are 400-900 milli-Amp-hours capacity are common and a microAmp is 1000 times *smaller*. Just know to enjoy each day to it fullest before you are short-circuited.

Remember life is not the length of the journey but the journey itself.

Remember also, years are merely a way to keep score and longevity is not meant to be the only meaning to your life.

Why did I mention I was afraid of fire? Fire had nothing to do with this story but I just wanted you to know – Amongst many things, I am deadly afraid of fire and what it can do.

I wrote this story so you might be a bit more informed about what your body is doing when it "does" different things. I hope you have a long and healthy life, because you now know what certain pains are and what they can do.

One final word for the guys: You can "gut out" most arm or leg muscle pains, cramps, back spasms, etc, BUT the one MUSCLE you can NOT mess with is your heart.

If you don't believe me, ask Vic.

Concrete Ribbons of Frustrations

Two or more vehicles seldom come together on purpose. That's why its call *accident*.

Jake, Frank and Eileen lives come together - by accident

PROLOG: This story has been difficult to write and only using words with some any kind of civility. Since I have had driver's licenses I have experienced "Road Rage", as I am sure much of the reading public has so I am sure, as mine was, your immediate reaction was one of animal instinct. Mine use to be but now... It has taken much blood pressure medication to finally turn the other cheek – but I have learned. Some say I learned the hard way before it sank in that there are lots of people out there that have worse problem then me.

So.... Once upon a time....

If your name is Jake... you are in trouble. Look over your shoulder, there is a lady diving in the car next to you that is "out to get" everyone on the highways named Jake. Actually

that isn't 'exactly' true as she is not out to get ALL just one particular 'Jake" that took "her space" at 70mph while traveling south on I95 just south of Washington DC. A "Jake" abruptly cut her off a couple years ago and his actions caused a major traffic accident that he didn't even bother to stop and investigate. The driver she dubbed 'Jake' showed disturbing and discourteous driving habits and she now wants to teach him better driving manners. He put her in a hospital, destroyed her car and three others, caused her to loss two months salary while putting her further in debt and she now "owes" him retribution.

How will she do this? By doing the same to "others" every chance she gets at the off-chance "Jake" will be one of them and by being discourteous each time she is behind the steering wheel, by always being in a hurry behind the wheel, by having a deep-rooted belief she is right and the world is wrong and by simply parroting your actions – Jake. "Jake" you may be the sweetest and nicest guy to other but in a moment of carelessness or stupid ness I fear you have created a monster.

Why the name "Jake?" She feels it is a nicer name she gave you while in the hospital and just in case there should be others in the car with her then her normal emphatic "&%^&%$". Jake – she has you in her cross-hairs.

She is looking for you - Jake. So, Jake be forewarned the next time you get "flipped off", run off the road or tailgated by a very pretty little lady it is because you were acting and behaving rudely (the posting of this story on the Internet does not allow the kind of words needed to fully describe your character while driving so I must just say…) and not following the "rules of the road" – Jake!

Chances are, Jake you are not the only person in the world that has been minding his own business while on an expressway, highway, autobahn, back-road, Interstate that may not have been the aggressor but the "victim". Being the kind gentle person your mother raised you could have smiled and moved to an outside lane all the while smiling and thinking "nice". BUT… you didn't. You had a bad day at work, your girl/boy friend is mad at you, you just came from the doctor's office with bad news that you have herpes and you have a big date this evening… or pick a reason, any reason. No one has any problems in their day-to-day lives other then you so the world needs to "…stays the hell out of your way".

Jake, your thinking is flawed and you need to relax.

It is a known fact someday we will die so there is no need to rush that fact while on a road in your shiny whizmobile. Another shiny whizmobile or bucket-of-rusty-bolts or 18-wheeler or just plain dumb-SOB cut you off so it is your duty to retaliate. It's human nature. It is the only positive response to reacting to stupidity. It is nature's way. It is….

Dumb!

While on the subject of dying, you may not "die" or be seriously injured during or shortly following any "road rage" incident but your attitude and reactions while driving or as a passenger has been medically proven to raise hell with your body parts. Just to give you some numbers, there are sixty (60) major organs in your body that must work (function) in unison for you to survive. The pressure you put on these organ during periods of temporary aggravation raises hell with your BP, heart, kidneys, bowels, muscle grouping in the arms and inner thighs and vocal cords, just to name a few.

Relax.

I had the opportunity to live in Paris France for four years when I was young and fresh out of college. I knew everything about everything and to some was known as a lead foot under a steering wheel. I and eleven million Frenchmen soon were in for a rude awakening. I should have been in youth heaven living in Paris, the city of Lights and free love as I soon learned that vous vous inquiéteriez pour dormir avec moi aujourd'hui would put a smile on my face and a spring in my step where vous fils sourd-muet d'une chienne would and did get me into all kind of trouble. When I finally tried Je suis désolé my life got and stayed much better.

Item of NOTE: Paris was built circa the 11th century. Like Washington DC it was designed by a Frenchman and those guys are crazy about wheels. The Arc De Triomphe

is Paris's hub connecting Thirteen (13) Major streets. Look to your left...Around the arc are six (6) lanes of meshing traffic and all moving as if everyone is late for lunch. When I was feeling indestructible I use to have a few beers, then join the madhouse by moving as quickly as possible from the outside lane to the inside and back again. I always made sure my Will was current. In four years I saw many accidents, shooting, folks having all kinds of sex in and out of cars and that is where I learned all my French swear words.

Comment: I'm using the French in this story as "samples" only as I actually lived there and they make really good cannon-fodder for this kind of story. If France is offensive to you are you preferred another nationality or local, please substitute your favorite. Some suggestions might be; Arkansas, Tennessee, Mississippi, Louisiana, Texas or California.

What took me a long time to understand about the French people at that time was the automobile was a toy to them– was new to the masses and they didn't realize it was not only transportation but also a weapon. Following World War II the few Citrons they did have, they had used in fighting the Germans and they quickly discovered a thin skinned Citron was NO match for a 40 ton Panzer tank. Actually the Citron was no match was anything larger then a B-B gun. During WWII the French did not manufacture war goods but opened dozen of White-flag factories. After the war the automobile and "driving" was so very new they didn't know the rules of the road. If asked when the best time to be on the roads in France is, the answer is between 12 noon and 2 PM. Their lunch break.

In France most of the cars on the roads are; Citrons, Peugeot 404 and 405s, Renaults, two cylinder Citrons (shade-roller) the occasional Mercedes. I had a French Simca. My Simca was brand new as I special ordered it from the factory, and personally drove it off the end of the assembly plant in Paris. New but its four cylinders were not a lot better then the 50cc Honda scooter I used for transportation before I could afford four wheels. Gutless translate to "staying out of the way and don't piss off anyone". A lesson I learned the hard way. If there is any doubt in your mind what is meant by "hard way" picture this: Have a perfect stranger pull a handgun on you, point it toward your groin and you say, "…your yellow, you don't have the nerve to pull the trigger…" Kinda like the same thing when you retaliate on the highway.

European autobahns are and were very different then the highway system in the States. Three lanes each direction with no speed limits – the far left lane (hammer lane) is reserved for Porsches, Mercedes BMWs and anything else with flashing headlights. One fact our European friends have yet to fully understand is that a blow-out at 220 kph is far more dangerous then at 120 kph (70 mph), or should I use the word "survivable"? Blow-outs are not the only problem you may encounter on the road. Have you ever "over-reacted" with a steering wheel and does "losing-control" ring any bells?

Consider this – Three lanes of rush hour traffic moving at 120kph or 70mph or even slower bumper-to-bumper and a car cuts you off barely missing your front end and you JERK the steering wheel in a "reflex action", you barely miss neighboring cars and trucks but your adrenaline kicks in and you are "…going to get that SOB" for taking *your space*. No need for this story to describe the scene all you need do is picture in your own mind, what you did and the consequences. Wasn't pretty, was it?

Do you know or understand Kinetic energy? Kinetic energy is the energy by virtue of the motion of an object.

Do you know or understand what a weapon is?

Do you or have you ever realized the many times you have been evolved in Road Rage you have a 3,000 pound weapon you are controlling and it's kinetic energy can cause serious physical damage to others?

In traveling the world I have found it makes NO difference your skin color, the shape of your eyes it you roll your "Rs" or speak in the language of love or guttery slang or if you drive on the left or right side of a highway, human nature toward Road Rage is universal.

In the USA on the highway you need to know certain rules of the road. For example, a new shiny Cadillac, a BMW, Mercedes, and most everything else that is new and shiny will never 'intentionally' cut you off or try running you off the road – when they do, it is always unintended – so cut them some slack.

That rule changes a bit for folks driving beat-up pickups, anything with rust, or has a bumper sticker that reads: "go ahead and hit me, I need a new car". These people you really have to stay away from so if one of them cut you off, bump you from behind or is simply annoying DO NOT try to retaliate because you will lose. These are the times to wave politely and smile and if anyone wants "you space on the highway", let them have it.

A road *rage* can become upset because you accidentally cut in front of him or her, or other reasons that were not intentional. A key factor in reversing the process is an apology. Over 85 percent of road rage said that they would drop the matter if the other "careless" driver simply apologized. Instead, road rage claim, the "careless" driver seems to be unconcerned about what they just did and, therefore, needs to be taught a lesson.... And you're just the right person to do IT.

Dumb...

One small step for you and mankind is to make a sign. No, not a middle finger sign but a real cardboard sign that can be read from thirty feet. Make a "SORRY" Sign and keep it handy as road rage can and does happen in less then a heart beat.

So you may live to fight another day try: staying in the car; do not respond with an angry gesture or action; keep your "SORRY" sign handy in the car and use it when needed.

I'm a military combat veteran with accredited kills so I know and understand rage but I keep a **"SORRY"** sign in the map holder on the driver's door and the passenger's door. I have used it many times and found it much easier then killing the other guy.

Life is too important and valuable then to lose it in some stupid manner on a highway loaded with "strangers" that have their own agendas and their own problems. Don't make their problems yours!

Relax; don't take traffic problems personally; avoid eye contact with an aggressive driver; don't make obscene gestures; don't tailgate; use your horn sparingly (the polite honk can be misinterpreted); don't block the passing lane (some drivers think you're doing something to them when you do this); don't block the right hand turn lane; use common sense.

Road rage need not always happen on the open highways at 80 mph. It can and does happen to little old ladies at 5 mph in parking lots. I never really considered this act as Road Rage before until it happened to me – in Monte Carlo. I was in my Simca looking for a parking space. I spotted an empty place that was just open enough that I figured I could parallel park but there is a woman standing in the middle of the space obviously

saving the space for her husband or someone who is nowhere to be seen. At the time my French wasn't that good so I tried in animated English telling her to "move her fat butt" but that didn't work. Several minutes passed as my BP topped out when a van full of kids and an obviously distraught man driving pulled into the "my" space.

As I yelled at him all the kids leaned out of windows in the van and waved and smiled as did the man and now lady I have been berating. Their van had Spanish plates and they were simply tourist trying to see-the-sights and enjoy-the-day, as I was. Being in France at the time I felt like the universal owed me- Stupid American!! This was not an isolated incident happening to me but one that takes place every minutes of everyday, somewhere. When it happens to you, relax, and enjoy the moment as it just might be a defining

moment for you as my experience was to me in that small kingdom in the south of France on a bright and warm sunny day oh so many years ago.

EPILOG:
When Jake was released from his last hospital visit following still another car accident he was divorced from a beautiful lady that must now work two jobs to support her three small children.

Frank is now happy in his average life-style driving for Pizza Hut but his family of five love him for who he is and his high moral and principles.

On our highways you need not even have "Road Rage" to hurt or kill. 16 February 2008 this car pictured above was having fun "drag racing" on highway 210 in Maryland when it ran thought spectators killing eight and putting 6 more in the hospital for a very long time. *"Body parts, shoes and clothing was scattered more then 300 yards."* The *stains* seen on top of the car is BLOOD, lots of blood from several different people.

Never say Oops

This is a must-read if you have teeth, vote Democratic, Republican, Green or Independent, have a few patriotic bones and a couple minutes to reflect, grin, wonder and grimace all the while your mind is telling you about decisions made and not-made. You really need to read and reflect on this short story and what it says.

"What do you want to be when you grow up little boy?" It was a standard adult type question while speaking to a youngish southern born wide-eyed youth. Art Linkletter once had a TV show titled something along the lines as '...out of the mouths of babies...' so asking an innocent question of little Frankie could have interesting responses. Today, young Frankie said in all honesty, "...anything but a dentist..."

Young Frank is your typical grammar-school aged boy but has been asked the same thoughtless question so many times he now has pat responses - mostly. Depending on what holiday it is or who was asking and the time of day, he told me he could remember thinking when he was four going on nine that when he grew up he wanted to be a fireman, or a policeman, an engineer, fly navy jets, be an astronaut, a soldier, THE President, a pimp, most anything but never a dentist ... "What did I know, I was just a kid" he would say if asked. He didn't have a clue about the world other then what the TV, Google, his blackberry and game-boy told him.

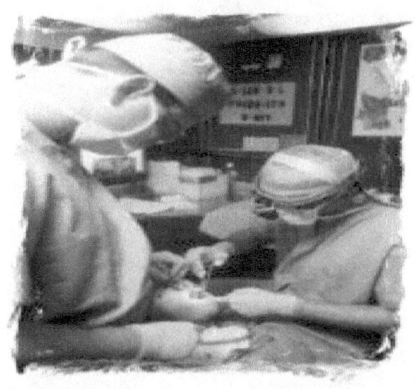

Frankie's father was a dentist as was his father before him. Dentistry in his family actually goes back to where anesthetic was half a bottle of Jim Beam (rot-gut) and forceps that doubled for shoeing horses or ice skates (did you see the movie "Cast Away"?) Dentists in the immediate family were well respected community figures, God-fearing and church-going Protestants and very good dentists. Their patients loved them and they made a good living. His dad loved his work, "...his passion..." he would say and always with a glean in his eye with the right side of his lips slightly curled. The sedimentary, home, uneventful, routine life was good for him, but he worried about little Frank. Father and son had the normal 'birds-n-bees' conversations but he never pushed young Frank into following his business and he never tried to talk him out of dropping out of school or joining the military. The few times he did try talking about dentistry young Frankie's standard response was a screwed up face, top teeth bared, both hands extended palms pointed outward and a very wet and emphatic "Yuk".

Frank told me just yesterday, he wished his dad would have tried harder.

Frank is now in the military fighting in an unpopular war and at ten minutes past high noon today he is having serious second-thoughts about not becoming a dentist.

Have you even been in 120 degree heat? Have you even been in a desert or any desolate area of earth that God forgot? If no to these questions, picture yourself in a country named Iraq then picture yourself as a non-commissioned officer (a sergeant) sitting on the side of a folding cot, flies the size of small sparrows sitting on your mess gear, sand everywhere, a family of scorpions living in you spare boots, the wind directions has shifted and is coming from the latrines and the drums have not been burned today. If this is difficult to imagine, the next time you are visiting great-grandparents in any southern hilly state, when you use the "out-house" stick your head in hole number one and take a deep sniff – that is the same for Frank right now. The air in the tent is heavy also with sulfur and there is a knot in your gut.

You are now inside Frank's twenty-year old head;

"Getting ready for our daily patrol of the northern sector of Baghdad I sometimes reminisce about my dad and move along through my favorite list of 'what-ifs". What if I had listened to him, what-if mom had not died giving me life, what-if I had not been so stubborn and thinking I wanted more out of life then working in peoples mouths. I remember having to go to dad's office after school hours to wait until he finished the last patient of the day so we could have dinner together or just quality time. We never did have 'quality-time' but different patients in the waiting room would always offer lots of free advice and help on home-work assignments. It wasn't until I was in the fourth grade then my homework got too difficult for the grown-ups that I had to do my own work.

Always go over your check-list: Rucksack with extra water and MREs, grenades, MM40 with extras rounds, CBR protective mask (just in case) and the most comfortable combat boots ever designed. I was almost ready. I had to field-strip my M-16 and clean it before this patrol because yesterday evening I was too bone-tired from an all day fire-fight with insurgents so I just had an MRE (meals ready to eat) and passed-out on my cot till almost 0400 hrs. I remember my dad telling me he could clean and polish a full set of teeth in ten minutes. I use to take that long to get all the sand and carbon from the working parts of my old SAW (Squad Assault Weapon - fancy military acronyms for a rifle with lots of fire-power) but during this combat tour I can now field-strip the weapon, clean it and have a fresh round chambered in less then two minutes. For my back-up 40MM I can do the same. Did I mention that two-minutes is blindfolded or in a black-out condition. The first two months of this tour I have lost three good friends from my infantry squad... and I personally have more then a dozen accredited kills, but that's another story.

Many days I lay awake too tried and exhausted to sleep so I normally reflect what it would have been like to have grown up and spend all my working days in others peoples mouths? Right now at high-noon in this blistering heat, that prospect sounds inviting.

"Frank, saddle-up, we leave in two minutes." The voice coming thought the tent flap belonged to Becky. Combat units do not allow 'girls' to actually carry offensive weapons and do any actual 'fighting' but they are allowed into combat areas. Becky was our Hummer driver. Guys go for weeks between individual washings and your nose can tell you 'ripe' from 'riper' but Becky is different. She is in the same living conditions as the guys but she always smells 'good' like a lady, even through dust, dirt, IEDs, suicide bombers and bullets she looked like the all-American-girl-next-door with a blond pony-tail neatly tucked under a Kevlar helmet, BDU uniform buttoned at the neck, sleeves rolled up just a bit above the elbows, flak-jacket snugly tied over ample breast and a smile minted by the Gods. Just last week Becky was awarded the Silver Star for bravery "...above and beyond the call of duty". Enough about her, this story is about Frank and dentistry.

"What is Dentistry? Wonder why I stayed away from it? I wish.... I wish... damn."

As Frank packed and cleaned his gear his brain was on full alert, thinking, remembering and wishing.

As a youth Frank remembered many talks with his dad about 'the after life', 'heaven', 'hell', 'purgatory', 'fire & brimstone' and 'Predestination". That was the one that always seem to stay in the back of his mind and sometimes he felt he only had a measured number of days here on Earth. Every time Frank would see or hear of an extraordinary event and the person survived Frank just figured "...it was not their time..." and on the other side of that predestination coin a person could step on a crack in a sidewalk and be killed in a drive-by shooting "...it was their time..."

To most people dentistry means teeth, which, of course, it is – but don't forget that teeth are attached to people's mouths, which in turn are parts of actual living bodies. Although teeth may not seem a priority in the great scheme of things, their health and appearance can greatly influence people's lives. Apart from helping us to eat our food, our teeth and our smile can greatly influence other people's judgment of us, whilst extreme toothache can be extremely debilitating for the sufferer. Being a dentist nowadays involves an awful lot more than just doing fillings and scaling teeth. Dentistry is really a major branch of medicine.

"While I'm thinking about teeth I need to pass along the essence of a History Channel TV program I saw just before deploying to the Near East. Today we take life around us as routine, commonplace and natural like for example, tooth paste & mouth wash. The producers of this History Channel show knew how to hold my attention because I had seen their shows on the building of the Hoover Dam, the Harley motorcycle, where money came from and how it is made, how "things" work, etc... so when they started talking about teeth, I figured they had something I needed to know.

Ever wonder where toothpaste and mouthwash came from? Have you ever thought about what people used for toothpaste before the invention of Crest, Colgate or Aquafresh?

If you are squeamish please skip the following three paragraphs:

Presented in HDTV and in full color a narrator was saying, "Our mouth contains one or more of 500 types of microorganisms. Some of these, mainly streptococcus mutans, create sticky plaque from food residue in your mouth. Microorganisms in our mouth feed on left over food to create acid and particles called volatile sulfur molecules. The acid eats into tooth enamel to produce cavities while volatile sulfur molecules give breath its foul odor. Toothpaste works with toothbrush to clean teeth and fight plaque bacteria. Toothpaste contains abrasives which physically scrub away plaque. In addition, toothpaste abrasives help remove food stains from teeth and polish tooth surfaces. Some toothpaste contains ingredients which chemically hinder the growth of plaque bacteria. These include ingredients like natural Xylitol and artificial triclosan. Phew..."

I can't believe I said that all in one breathe.

Maybe I'm just getting warmed up. Remembering the show, the narration continued with "...the activity of keeping the mouth clean dates all the way back to the religious figure Buddha. It has been recorded that he would use "tooth stick" from the God Sakka as part of his personal hygiene regimen. In 23 - 79 AD the practice of oral hygiene included: Drinking goats' milk for sweet breath, ashes from burnt mice heads, rabbit's heads, wolves' heads, ox heels and goats feet were thought to benefit the gums. Picking the bones out of wolves' excrement and wearing them (maybe in the form of a necklace?) was considered to be a form of protection against toothaches. Washing your teeth with the blood from a tortoise three times a year was a sure bet against toothaches as well. Mouthwashes were known to consist of pure white wine, or (get ready for this one) old urine kept especially for this purpose. Urine is basically ammonia and ammonia is a cleaning agent. I can hear it now, '…Alice have you peed this morning, I need to gargle…?'"

My eyes are dimming and I'm cold, why in the world am I letting my mind wonder… I need to concentrate but I can't seem to hang onto any one subject for more then a second.

Four letter words are used in our world to convey orders/direction, expression of hate, love frustration and attitude. Most civilianized countries can and do use their full compliment of words and expressions, and that's good. However - there in ONE four-letter word that is FORBIDDEN to the dentist. Dentist must NEVER utter the word 'Oops' when in a patients mouth.

Career wise, dentists have many options open to them. They can work in general practice, both for the government or privately, in the community or in the forces, at home or overseas. As well as becoming a general dental practitioner, all sorts of other openings are on offer, from oral and maxillofacial surgery to orthodontics; from children's dentistry to prosthodontics (that's implants, false teeth, etc). You could specialize in periodontology (gum disease), restorative dentistry (fillings, crowns and bridges) – or become a lecturer and researcher in any of these. (Those that can – do… and those that can't – teach) Oral pathology is another possibility: analyzing lumps bumps and so on for cancers and other diseases. Dentistry can also be a flexible career for those wishing to take time out, to work irregular days or hours, or for those who wish to work in more than one location.

Pay is not that bad. You might not become another Bill Gates but $140k plus isn't that bad for 50-60 hours a week. Sure beats the hell out of $24k a year a GI receives for shooting bad-guys.

Would I have enjoyed Dentistry? Maybe, maybe not. My dad once told me if I became a dentist and if I ever tired of bad breath and smoking teeth I could run for president. It's Just a thought anyway as I'm pretty sure it's too late for me now.

My mind keeps going back to better times, civilian times, times when I didn't have to kill. I remember thinking once as I sat in a dentist chair admiring a pictures on the facing wall of a cat hanging by its nails captioned *"Hang in there baby"* that civilian dentists

Hang In There, Baby

are different then their military counterpart. I once had a civilian root channel and crown in the States and other then being a bit sore for three days afterward the experience wasn't that bad. Kay, Dr O (real name is difficult to pronounce) and I had an interesting two hours; I was in a horizontal position, Kay was handing Dr. O "stuff" as he asked for them and she kept busy with a vacuum the size of a hollow pencil as she kept my mouth clear of debris. Dr. O and Kay worked well together. Not once did I hear him mutter the unmentionable word. My military experiences with dentist for the same procedure went something like: "This may sting a bit" as he put a liter of nova cane into the roof of my mouth with a two-inch needle as big around as a soda straw, then filled my mouth with a rubber blanket "thing" and told me to breathe thought my nose. Not sure about other people but I gag at the slightest thought of anything other then food in my mouth. The rubber blanket was kinda attached to teeth not being used. I tried taking my mind off the burning smells of tooth enamel and flesh and flying chips from a tooth "being repaired" by playing with the rubber with my tongue. In dozens of dentist visits I have never learned where and what to do with my tongue as they drilled, poked and surveyed my mouth with that tiny bent mirror on a stick.

Dr. O was different. He deadened the area where he was to give me a few (4) shots of Lidocaine. He wore a "D" powered head lamp to better see the dark crevices of my mouth as he went fishing for a nerve. I have always marveled at the finger dexterity dentists and the young ladies that clean my teeth. They have all mastered the art of these curved and pointy "picks" all moving in conjunction with that tiny crooked mirror on a stick.

Two main differences between a military and civilian dentist for a "crown" are:
Cost - Military = 0$, Civilian = $1,500 (before insurance) I use to think the reason they wear masks was the same reason as a highway robber but it is just to protect them from our bad breath. Actually for what they do, the equipment used and the experienced needed they are mostly underpaid.
Pain - Military = Plenty vs. Civilian = None

Did you even see the movie, "Joe and the volcano" with Tom Hanks? He had a "Brain Cloud". Right now I feel the same but the sunny side of the brain is still thinking "What-ifs".

For example, oral and dental health is a very important part of general health. The ability to smile, eat and talk without pain, discomfort or embarrassment contributes greatly to a

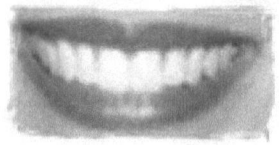

sense of well being. Dentists are health care professionals who are experts in the diagnosis and treatment of a range of problems that affect the mouth and teeth. This demands diagnostic, clinical and social skills. Some dentists will become teachers or lecturers in dental schools, others will be employed in hospitals, or community clinics but most will become general dental practitioners. Often, they will be managing a team of people encompassing dental nurses, hygienists, receptionists and others so good administrative and managerial abilities are needed. It's not being a philanthropist but it isn't a bad living either.

Significant Points; not all dentist play golf on Wednesdays; drive expensive foreign cars and retire with golden umbrellas. Dentists are fellow normal humans like you or I that have paid their dues by completing at least 8 years of education beyond high school (I was lucky to make just 4).

I found this tidbit of information on the Internet that bears repeating; "Dentists use a variety of equipment, including x-ray machines; drills; and instruments such as mouth mirrors, probes, forceps, brushes, and scalpels. They wear masks, gloves, and safety glasses to protect themselves and their patients from infectious diseases." And "Most dentists are general practitioners, handling a variety of dental needs. Other dentists practice in any of nine specialty areas. Orthodontists, the largest group of specialists, straighten teeth by applying pressure to the teeth with braces or retainers. The next largest group, oral and maxillofacial surgeons, operates on the mouth and jaws. The remainder may specialize as pediatric dentists (focusing on dentistry for children); periodontists (treating gums and bone supporting the teeth); prosthodontists (replacing missing teeth with permanent fixtures, such as crowns and bridges, or with removable fixtures such as dentures); endodontists (performing root canal therapy); public health dentists (promoting good dental health and preventing dental diseases within the community); oral pathologists (studying oral diseases); or oral and maxillofacial radiologists (diagnosing diseases in the head and neck through the use of imaging technologies)."

No pun intended but even thinking that was a mouth-full.

I'm getting colder and the mid-day sun seems to be dimming. I'm hearing strange sounds from deep inside me now. I'm cold but not afraid. If I could have my "druthers", right now I wish I had followed my Dad in being a dentist. I should have stayed in school…now as the sun is just past 12 O'clock high I could be working in an air-conditioned building in a mouth full of rotten teeth rather then laying in a pool of my own blood dying in 120 degree blistering heat on a dusty road in Baghdad Iraq."

The roadside explosion (IED) left most of Becky laying next to me in her own pool as her dying body pumps her life's blood onto the sand from a gapping hole in her face where her jaw and teeth use to be.

I should have been a dentist but maybe it was not to be and this was my time.

ARLEE

We Owe Our Military Veterans...

If this is not THE Veteran Benefit Administration Solution, it is a good start...
Please do not just scan but read. Lots of good information/data here!!
FACT: *The VA has enough money and way too many work force –* **They just don't use either correctly!!!**

NOTE: This article is rather long and detailed. If you are not a veteran it will read like a fictional piece of literature but is, in fact all true. If you are curious civilian or work in congress this article can be used to *change the rules –*

Secretary of State Rice in 2004 said so.

Author of this short story/article is *Frank* but could have been written by anyone of over 24,387,000 living veterans. I am two fingers he enlisted to tell you a story of "what was; what is and what should be.

Objective: Outlining and justifying the new direction for rightful and earned military Compensation & Pension and a way out of VA/VBA stagnate bureaucracy waters.
A CHALLENGE near the end of this paper (page 133) will re-enforce my words and the words of ALL veterans.

Timeliness processing rightful C&P claims is only one of many problems confronting the veterans. We don't have much time left and we need earned and rightful compensation yesterday. Too many of use arrive here before the VA gives us our earned compensation.

Numbers quoted in this paper: Depending on which report, who is quoted and on any given day, numbers change. Please view numbers quoted here as "Yardsticks" and not "verbatim – locked in concrete". No numbers quoted here are "made-up" but came from official documentations.

Assumptions:
There are no inherently bad people in our VA or VBA system. There are no veterans applying for C&P that have not earned it.

Meet "Dumb Horse"- a warrior. He is believed to have initiated the VA circa 348,000 BC and is also believed his Neanderthal ancestry now controls our present day Veterans Administration.

The Reality of the game: Rules and regulations for the VA and its VBA arm are quality documents, well written for the most part and offer criterion for existing and growing areas of compensation. The *interpretation* and action (or non-action in many cases) of those regulations, the *action officers* that make decisions for the veterans and the pure bureaucracy of approval are the focal points of this paper.

1. It is time to change the way our VBA does business. Everyone from congress to everyone who has worn the uniform says it's time for change and this paper shows how we can actually "change" and gain from it. This paper shows a "win-win" situation.

2. The many problems within the VBA are exponentially compounded by its action officers and antiquated government thinking on how to fix a problem. Studying the problem for 50 years, adjusting procedures, adding/deleting report procedures, adding people and throwing money at phantom problems does not work. VBA action officers are also discusses a bit later.

3. The Board of Veterans Appeal (BVA) is a major bottleneck but much of their problems percolate back and forth between the Regional Offices (RO) and procedures designed to protract claims as much as possible. More on the BVA later.

4. Congress, the VA, the VBA and Joe Public all realize there are major problems so this article will cover much of the same plowed grounds then offers virgin land for developing (Recommendations). 5. Most recently www.va.gov/budget/report/2005/MMC-Summary.pdf The Office of the Inspector General (OIG) surgically reviewed the VA and its VBA arm reported several reasons for slow responses and inconsistency of the organization; See GAO items # 4, 4A, 4B, 4C, 4D and 5D. As thorough and comprehensive of this OIG report was it still did not address what the VBA must do to accomplish their charter as envisioned 50 years ago. Their charter = the veteran. Nowhere in this report does the IG address the VBA *action officers*. They address:

a. "…complexity of 'inferred medical issues…' that refers to issues Not claimed by the veteran but which are reasonably raised by medical evidence of record (See item #4A Inferred issues).

b. Systematic Technical Accuracy Review (STAR) process reported the VBA at a low 59% efficiency.

c. VCAA process passed in 2000 'to help' the veteran has added more steps to the overall approval process lengthening time it takes to develop claims.

d. Major inconsistency between all its ROs.

e. "March 2005 a working group of subject-matter experts identified rating elements needed for medical conditions." This references Title 38, U.S.C. and the heart of rating disability claims.

f. Sharing of electronic health information.

g. The word "inconsistency" was paramount throughout the OIG report. See item #4B

See page 127 "Craig Kabatchnick" – Authoritative words from a person that has been "in the trenches"

Preface comments: I am humbled in relaying facts lived and the responsibility of

required detailed research and this story/article. This paper that reads like a story will give you facts, reasoning, history, drama and final recommendations that should cause you to sit back and rationalize the real dilemma for your veterans and an other promised benefits we should not have to fight for - again!

*You are to participate is a **CHALLENGE** at the end of this paper – please pay attention.*

We live in a world of instant communication with computers that control our groceries, gasoline, banking, medicine, phones, our every technique, practice and mode of life but we still rely on nineteenth century philosophy, paper and pencils, chalkboards, the sequential steps in making decisions and the USPS when it comes to our veterans. WHY? *The root problems of the VBA are the VA thinking, its structure and workers **apathy** toward their job.* The three visible benchmarks are; guaranteed bi-weekly paychecks, a comfortable retirement at the end of the working days for the VBA workers and vastly protracted C&P for the veterans. These are hard words, harder to write and still hardest to admit.

How can I make such a challenging statement about government workers Apathy? I worked in the Pentagon for too many years not to recognize *apathy* when I see it in my VA correspondence!

Along these same lines is the story of the dead horse (VBA) and the governments (VA & Congress) attempt to revive it by beating the carcass with long handled sticks (OIG studies, congressional meetings and reports and Monday morning reports, etc.) while having visions of a Phoenix arising from the souls of disabled forgotten veterans. It ain't gonna happen! Change means change, not camouflage.

The VA and our government are both fast moving trains. What is true at 0800 is not necessarily true at 0806 hrs or 0807 hrs. There is no one answer for ALL people/veterans but there is a solution for our veterans and *'light-at-the-end-of-the-tunnel'*. We veterans acknowledge our government, the VA and its one arm named VBA are trying to do the best they can for the veteran, but *their thinking* is flawed. Handicapped as they are because of much wasted efforts and resources there is clearly a new direction needed. We no longer can afford to take three steps forward and slide two back while trying to nail Jell-O to the wall. More is not better. Having action officers running in circles looking for and trying to justify "inferred" claims is trying to catch smoke in a bottle.

We MUST stop thinking and saying, *"...we have always done it that way..."*

You will soon realize which finger to use in what dike.

Mini PROLOGUE: If your business is Service and your clientele is say 1,000 people and 993 of them are dissatisfied – would they be an indicator you maybe needed to change something? It is a know fact portions of the Veterans Administration (VA) are broken / dissatisfied. *This article/story addresses the Veterans Benefit Administration (VBA) organizational arm and to offer a way to make your business a more pleasant place to work.* If you have read any of the VBA Annual Benefits Reports for the last five years "broken" is maybe not the word you would select to describe a train wreck, but the meaning would be the same. The misguided (wrong direction) reports words are superbly written by intelligent people, but they are just well used words and numbers with no teeth.

Veterans have bitterly complained for years, congress has ordered studies and held meetings, the VA has looked inward and they know there are major problems awarding just Compensation and Pension (C&P), but no one has figured out (or admitted too) yet where to put what finger in what hole in what dike. The government and the VA have thrashed around in the bureaucratic waters since it's inception in July 1930 and even as late as 2000 gave itself an over all grade of only a bit above average with a B-. *"...The Veterans Benefits Administration, long notorious for slow performance, ran into a whole new buzz saw in 1998 when the Veterans Affairs Department's inspector general found errors in VBA reports of how long it took to process veterans' applications for disability and pension benefits. The mistakes made claims processing look faster than it really was - and the incorrect figures were none too swift. For example, VBA reported that it processed disability claims in an average of 128 days - more than four months - but the actual average was nearly a month longer, 151 days, the IG said. Today, VBA says, it's about 168 days."* In civilian terms that works out to be 5. 6 months... months. Those 5.6 months is not a bottom line, just one small decision step in a LONG decision making journey, as you know and is reiterated in this paper.

PROCESSING FACTS and CONCERNS: when you look at the real ramifications to the  Veteran and the Veterans family, processing becomes cumulative damaging in nature when compared to how the Social Security Administration handles a much similar process. The main difference being of course that Social Security is looking for a 100% disability medical conclusion justification; where as the VA is administrating disabilities that range from a 0 (zero) percent to 100% or a combination of disabilities that renders the Veteran Unemployable status. The difference between the two federal agencies is the process of additional information as the medical condition develops or additional evidence is submitted.

The VA states a 5.6-month processing time-line on average. On the surface that sounds reasonable but this is a series of 5.6 months, which could be a multiplying factor of any X number of 5.6 months culminating in years waiting for a final decision. Please read the next paragraph a couple times for it's reality to sink in.

This is a fact totally misrepresented by the VA as they clearly indicate that any changes to a claim, the claim goes back into the X number cycle of 5.6 months. Of which the 5.6-month is a conservative plus side performance to promote the agency in a good light to congress. At the local VA shops, this time line is even worse as every change or new evidence is *estimated to be a **cumulative** additional 12 to 18 months.*

A conflict of interest is clearly indicated when automatically associated Service Connected claims in some medical areas that require no (zero) complex medical decisions still take 12 to 18 months. This lack of performance is not only unacceptable by VA, it is indefensible. When a veteran dies, his/her claim dies - is there bias somewhere when compared to the government's other disability agency - Social Security?

Recently the Veterans Affairs Committee in the House of Representatives tried to explain why veteran's claims were not handled in a timely matter at the VBA levels. After much spin on the why of this over a many years concern, no conclusions were reached. What was brought forward that most Veterans were not aware of was the doubling of the VBA staff and costs that resulted in a net gain of a 50% reduction of claims processed. Something is horribly wrong here. To double the staff and reduce the output by ½ is unacceptable and again indefensible.

More on VBA a bit later – please read on … and carefully.

FACTS that turned up the last time the VA looked at it self:

In today's systems our GS 5s and 7s "Examiners" (action officers) corps is **a quantifiable failure**: It is not the fault of the individual workers but of the system.

    a. The first stop for a veterans C&P claim is a VBA Examiner (and there-in may be the problem.)

    b. Attrition of over 15% is twice the number of new hires then all of the VA.

    c. **Examiners are hired as GS 5 ($29k) and GS 7($36k) and can go no higher then GS 10 ($61k).

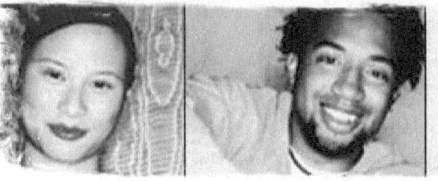

    d. Examiners are "trained" by OJT (On the Job Training)

    e. There are **NO** special educational *OR* special experience lever requirements to be an Examiner or Action Officer. *These three pictured are just typical post High School students that our government hires to made first decisions for combat military veterans.*

    f. New action officer performance is in direct relationship to the supervision and their attitude.

    g. http://www.va.gov/budget/summary/1514Chapter1.pdf - Please review your own Strategic Goals and Tables beginning on your page 1-23 – Especially Goal #1 Objective 1.2

    ** http://www.opm.gov/strategiccomp/whtpaper.txt dated April 2002 says such things as the federal government GS (General Schedule) system, "… Its structure suits the workforce of 1950, not today's knowledge workers." See also page 10 that begins, "…this point is…." and page 17 that begins, "The System Is Performance Insensitive"

REASONS FOR CONCERN:

    1. VBA Examiners (Action Officers) are the first people that review and make decisions on veteran claims. They set the tone and direction for the life of a claim. Once a mistake or misstep is made it never goes away and is carried from mistake to fact for the life of the claim. You will see true life examples as this paper unfold.

    2. *These action officers are all very young and inexperienced in a position that represents our government's policies. Being young and at a low position in the "food chain" of government workers tend to follow orders, verbatim or how you 'perceive' the orders making any interpretation weak and recommendation and actions disastrous for the veteran. They are the wrong people sitting in the wrong pew in the wrong church.* New hires, especially at the GS 5 and 7 lever are always young (mid to late 20s) with NO life experiences and usually not much formal education past High School. Even a college education is NOT helpful for this position – Kinda like putting a confectionary maker in a slaughter house with a dull knife. Having little to NO background for a VBA position is not good when a military combat veteran asks for compensation and your new office worker doesn't have a clue who or what is on the other end of the claim. Claims then

become just numbers. This low-level government position must be more then just a "job", a "paper-pusher" but must have a person that sees their position as omni important – A quick and honest E-mail to these action officers will tell you ramifications of their actions are not their main consideration. *Quantity not quality* is all important and most likely their only goal.

3. "First line examiners are trained and supervised." You will see these words in every official supervisors report but is not entirely accurate; Trained = OJT, supervised = "…read these rules and regulations, check with me on anything you don't understand, all claims must meets our highest standards before approval, turn in your 'progress sheet' to me by noon each Friday…" Everyone will make mistakes, but the VBA has built into its systems guaranteed pitfalls just from the sheer numbers of hands a claim has to go through.

4. First-line supervision of examiners is critical; Supervisors, for the most part take the word of their examiners because it is not their job or position to do the leg work and filter information. Supervisors are not expected to make the recommendations of a claim but to trust, to a certain extent, their underlings have questioned a claim and would not pass it to the next lever without being correct. That said all supervisors will change something within an action if for no other reason then to justify their position.

5. It is common practice for a government first-line action officer to do "bare bones" work on any action because they learn at an early age in the organization what they do *will* be changed. Makes no difference who you are (rookie, supervisor, manager, CEO, Senator, President) the one above you will change something in whatever you recommend – guaranteed. That's not bad. What is bad is after a short time the rookie seeing this progression will stop doing 100% of their fact-finding and do just enough to "pass an action". Supervisors will catch some problems but then numerous un-noticed errors will "fall in the crack."

6. First-line supervisors have supervisors that have supervisors that have supervisors and as information, data and recommendations are passed up and down this chain the veteran's words are lost in translation. In the present organizational structure there are too many eyes trying to make the right decisions.

7. In too many cases, what a veteran's claim says and what the third or fourth lever supervisor sees are two entirely different sets of facts.

8. The Department of Veterans Affairs regional office in Wichita shares some of the same problems that plague offices around the country, including a large caseload and a shortage of fully trained workers. They added that as bad as their RO is, St. Louis and SF is worse. Their article needs reading:
http://www.mercurynews.com/mld/mercurynews/news/special_packages/veterans/11066

795.htm the disturbing, to me anyway, part of this article said, *"Claims are handled by 10 service officers representing nonprofit service organizations such as the American Legion and VFW."* Does this Kansas article then mean each state has it own "system" and untrained civilian Joe Average is processing C&P claims? This point was addressed by the last OIG study mentioned above.

9. Does the VA have a handle on their TDA organization? Is the structure too layered? Are all these layers necessary or are they merely the way business has always been done? Go ahead and answer these questions – I dare you to be honest during the CHALLENGE part of this paper.

10. In an IME system these problems go away.

Two kudos for the VA: 1.The passage of Veterans Claims Assistance Act of 2000
                          2. The veteran is FINALLY seeing Title 38: Pensions, Bonuses, and Veterans' Relief *§3.102 (reasonable doubt)* taken into account, sporadically but at least now - *sometimes.*

-the Good, the Bad and the Ugly-

Mind-set. The many very bright people trying to do the right thing by making the VA better are stuck in a well-worn government rut ('we have always done it that way') and the only difference between this rut and a grave is the depth. The present mind-set needs to stop trying to make a flawed arm of the VA manageable and concentrate and listen to both the spoken and unspoken words of your valued veteran. The many whispered voices all cry out, "Change the VBA / C&P arm. Stop bandaging a festering wound and look outside the envelope." Just because "is what is" doesn't make it right. There is a way out of this RUT and I cover that direction later in this paper.

There are many good people in the VBA but sometimes they can't see the forest for the trees. To say that another way; there's many good people working the problems but they all have their own agendas, their own problems, and most importantly they have their own priorities, their own supervisor to answer too and their own marching band. What the VA leadership (at the GS-14 and 15 level) doesn't have is the free reign of their positions as such people as say, the first Emperor of China, Qin Shi Huang when he started building the Great Wall of China in 220 BC. Few people do and it will take the fortitude of a thousand brass monkeys to do the right thing, here now, for the Veterans. The Great Wall of China is known as the world's longest cemetery. If we *"stay-the-course"* with our current VBA rules and direction we are destined to repeat the sins of our fathers, not learn from history and fill another long cemetery with bodies of our veterans that will die waiting for fair government promised compensation and pension.

Can the VBA be fixed? In its present organizational configuration, probable not because the current bureaucracy will need to die-off or retire before fresh ideas will be tried – current work force will immediately throw up their hands in rejection saying, *"...we have always done it that way..."* **We need to cut off the existing VBA arm.** I'll explain this amputation later. The VA as a whole is not all that bad. Most huge organizations have both good and bad elements and the VA has its share of warts. The worst wart has been developing since 1953 and is named *VBA* with its generic name *C&Pitus*.

txe Good – The VA provides care at a fraction of the cost of civilian due to big government discounts in medication, prosthetics and surgery. Medicare and Medicaid are going to adopt the VA way of purchasing so we are talking here about osmosis, growth and savings of major dollars. In 1938 President Franklin D. Roosevelt leaned on congress to approve the building of major "arrow straight" concrete highway systems; he advocated portions of interstates would have one to three miles of "straight" stretches that could be used for emergency landing strips. Today, the VA hospitals are designated as a back-up medical system in case of large scale war or disasters like Katrina, Rita or when another Texas City or Galveston blows up leveling whole towns and the killing of thousand of citizens.

txe Bad: Four are listed but are only the tip of this iceberg.

1. Approval ratings for veterans C&P claims are embarrassingly low? According to VBAs own Monday Morning Workload Reports http://www.vba.va.gov/bln/201/reports/mmrindex.htm is only actively *working* less then 8% to 13% of its claims (depending on which column is read – "pending" or "total") per year. Because this report has over eighteen (18) categories it is difficult to say just how many active claims are actually approved/denied/remanded for any given reporting period. *Frank has personally been waiting five (5) years with no end in sight.*

2. There are too many and unnecessary wickets a valid veteran's claim must go through. Too many eyes must see words that are meaningless to them and they must approve (chop on) subjects they don't have a cue about other then it being a number on a rating chart. IMEs change this.

3. Many whispered voices have said and a few have yelled; "I have noticed that treating physician statements are not given the weight and authority they should be given; instead, the VA will rely on VA physicians and doctors under contract with the VA (claiming that they are 'Independent medical advisors'). These VA physicians and doctors under contract oftentimes examine the veteran in a cursory manner, sometimes within a matter of minutes, and thereafter render an allegedly 'independent medical opinion' stating that the veteran's current disabilities are not related to injuries sustained in service. Sometimes

the VA physicians who are under contract are not certified by the American Board of Medical Specialists in the areas for which the veteran claims disability. (See op-ed, Craig M. Kabatchnick, Greensboro News & Record, October 29, 2006)

When a VA examination is cursory, lasts only minutes and is done by a physician not ABMS board certified in the area for which the veteran claims disability, it is virtually impossible for that examination to fairly serve as a basis to deny the veteran his claim. Such 'Independent VA examinations' represent both factual and legal error and are an injustice to the veteran. In many instances, the VA rating board will offer no explanation for why it ignored the veteran's physician's opinion supporting the grant of the veteran's claim and only considered the negative 'independent medical opinion' of the VA physician." (See op-ed, Craig M. Kabatchnick, Greensboro News & Record, October 29, 2006). I have a tape of my last VA interview. It's scary to *listen* to narcissism in action.

4. Systematic Technical Accuracy Review (STAR) process reported the VBA at a low 59% efficiency. National average for all businesses using STAR is something close to 90%.

Bad – bad – bad - http://www.gao.gov/new.items/d03452t.pdf - **OJT** (on the job training) is a way of life and is used successes fully in many fields of endeavor. Two fields that OJT fail miserably are as a rifleman in combat and as an examiner in the VBA.

txe Ugly – Hundreds of thousands of deserving veterans still are begging for their rightful due.

Is there a magic bullet out there to help? *No* – Yes - W*ell, maybe* … you decide after reading Franks story.

Take a deep breath and let's chat a bit.

Who or what is this guy named Frank writing this article? For starters I am one of your disabled veterans that is a statistic here. Having said that, I, like so many in our all-volunteer military am a college graduate, married family man, honorable person that lives by my word. I am a Bronze Star winner from Vietnam, a Masters bowling champion (the year before being sent to Vietnam), a military precision drill team member and leader for nine years, cartographic and architectural teacher and a 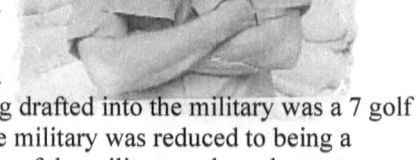 leader of men. I practiced architecture before being drafted into the military was a 7 golf handicap but then being medically retired from the military was reduced to being a draftsmen and computer operator when the ravages of the military and combat put me into a sedimentary life style. The master life plan of being a career military person was cut short, but not to worry, *"The Military takes care of its own"*.

We military people and fingers know and understand discipline, honor, know how to give and follow orders and deeply respect our government. To some, that mind-set is backward and antiquated but this is our lives shaped by discipline, fighting in wars, killing, burying our friends and believing in others.

As a nation we have basically lived in isolation and until lately never perpetrated a war. The world has always seen the United States as the "good guy", the "land of milk and honey" and where our allies could call on us when in trouble by a neighborhood bully (Hitler comes to mind).

Our war history is long and heavily stained with blood of our youth. The numbers of veterans, living, dead or disabled is in direct ratio to our civilian politicians.

Following our *Revolutionary War 1775-1783*, President George Washington said, *"we owe these veterans a debt of gratitude, indeed a debt of honor."*

In the year 344 BC Plato wrote *"Only the dead has seen the end to war"*. History is proving him right.

Our wars continued with; The Indian Wars 1775-1890; Shay's Rebellion 1786-1787;The Whiskey Rebellion 1794;War With France 1798-1800; The Barbary Wars1800-1815; The War of 1812 - 1812-1815; Mexican-American War 1846-1848; United States Civil War 1861-1865; The Spanish-American War 1898; U.S.-Philippine War 1899-1902; Boxer Rebellion 1900; The Moro Wars1901-1913; The Banana Wars 1909-1933; U.S. Occupation of Vera Cruz 1914; World War I 1917-1918; Allied Intervention in Russian Civil War 1919-1921; World War II 1941-1945; The Cold War 1945-1991; The Korean War 1950-1953; The Second Indochina War "Vietnam War" 1956-1975; U.S. Intervention in Lebanon; 1958; Dominican Intervention 1965; The Mayaguez Rescue Operation 1975; U.S. Libya Conflict 1981, 1986; U.S. Intervention in Lebanon 1982-1984; U.S. Invasion of Grenada 1983; "Operation Earnest Will" 1987-1988 ; Invasion of Panama 1989; Inter-State War Panama; Second Persian Gulf War "Operation Desert Storm" 1991;Inter-State War Iraq; "No-Fly Zone" War 1991-2003 war Iraq; U.S. Intervention in Somalia 1992-1994;Civil War & Foreign Intervention Various Somali Militias; U.S. Occupation of Haiti1994; U.S. Embassy bombings and strikes on Afghanistan and Sudan (The bin Laden War)August, 1998; Kosovo War 1999 Civil War; Attack on the USS Cole October 12, 2000; Attack on the World Trade Center and the Pentagon September 11, 2001; Afghanistan War (Operation Enduring Freedom) October 7, 2001-Present; Third Persian Gulf War "Operation Iraqi Freedom" March 19, 2003-Present.

In our war history, hundreds of millions have served and 37,296,663 became casualties of which over 35 million now have no voice.

-ℳℍɪꜱᴘᴇʀɪɴɢ ᴠᴏɪᴄᴇꜱ~

Outward appearances; a veteran surprisingly looks just like anyone else. The veteran may have a limp or sitting in a wheelchair, but so do non-veterans. How a veteran differs is in their eyes and nightmares and bank account. A veteran's physical needs are no different then non-veterans, but what the veteran does not need is our government treating us as common numbers and faceless individuals in a sea of humanity. Sure there are many of us, so our government needs to tend to us one at a time. It is their job, their obligation and purpose in life. What the veteran does not need is to have to beg for what George Washington and our government promised. We volunteered to serve and protect, not to become casualties.

So… you volunteered for a few years, carried a rifle, killed some bad guy, drove a tank or flew a jet then after you hung up the BDUs, desert boots and dress blues and have prosthesis and a medicine cabinet crammed with pain killers, where do you the veteran go for help - the VA of course?

There are several government organizations set up for help such as; The VFW; The American legion; AMVETS; DAV to name but a few of the 46 other Veteran Service Organizations ranging from the War Mothers to Submarine Vets from WWII. No need to get all smiley-faced on me because that was the short answer. All of these organizations are *the few* – while you are *the many*.

Then there is the Independent Medical Examiner (IME) --- What is this?

What our government says and what they do to and for our veterans are two entirely different directions or so it seems. That is a broad statement and is not entirely true for ALL government and ALL veterans but when we talk about the Veterans Administration's VBA, it seems to be.

Frank is telling this story because he is your every day, run-of-the-mill *typical person/veteran.* He worked in government for 23 years following a twenty (20) year, three-month and thirteen day military career so much of what you read here will *not* be biased but what Frank and his friends saw and experienced. If we didn't see the world from our own eyes and using our own intellect to intrepid then we would be just robots plodding along doing what we are told. Human nature is designed to question and that is what he is doing here, questioning and expressing views and making recommendations. Some folks would say: his *two-cents* may well be THE solution for this major government sore.

However, if there are clear defined conflicts of interests by government with no (zero) separation of powers involved, then bias becomes more than a different view or opinion; and rewards are now the goal, not the human flaw.

For those of us with children remember when your young were learning to talk and questioned the world around them? Remember the incessant questioning of WHY? For years Frank tried to answer his son with correct answers as he knew them but with "why", "why", "why" never stopping he finally reverted to the standard parent answer; *"Because I said so!"*

That answer never worked but it made him feel good to assert a bit of parental power.

When Frank set out on his quest for what the government calls C&P (compensation and pension) the government or more correctly the VBA arm of the Veterans Administration (VA) took the Parent role and Frank assumed the child role. It is so because they say it's so. I'll cover the make-up of *"they"* shortly.

Of the over 24 million veterans currently alive, nearly three of every four served during a war or an official period of hostility. About a quarter of the nation's population -- approximately 70 million people -- are potentially eligible for VA benefits and services because they are veterans, family members or survivors of veterans. The task for our VA is not an easy one but consider their benefits, their take-home pay, they are well paid for doing their job. A mid-level VA General Schedule (GS) when finally retired from the work force their *average* government pay is just under $87,000. When you consider the normal Government workers pay ranges from something around $35K entry level to $105K mid-management, those are not bad numbers for an honest days pay. Where there may be a few exceptions it is an oxymoron to use "honest days pay" and "government worker" in the same sentence. The VBA numbers are a bit different that we talked to earlier in this paper.

Frank worked on the Pentagons A, E rings, in the Army War Room as a player and in the bowels of the building on a computer wired into 'the world' for many years, says he can not entirely fault the VA for their short-falls. They may be short-handed (I'll give you how many people they employ in just a minute); they may be over-worked (much because of their own organizational fault) with a workload rivaling the 1920's and 30's sweat-shops of the NY and SF garment industry but they still have obligations. It is not uncommon for a veteran's claim to drag on for 4 to 7 years or until the veteran gives up or dies.

I call it a "bottleneck" others just call it a "wicket" but just an example for protracted claims is the **Board of Veterans Appeal** (BVA) in Washington D.C. Their current and standing case load is in access of 475,009 active claims. The Board of Veterans Appeals is divided into four decision teams divided up by geography. Each team is comprised of at least two veterans' law judges, staff attorneys and clerical staff. The BVA consists of 14 veterans' law judges (including two chief veterans' law judges) and at least 55-60 staff attorneys, some of whom have 20-25 years of legal experience. Each veteran's law judge is assigned four or five staff attorneys who have varying degrees of experience. The duty of a staff attorney is to review the claim and draft a decision for a veteran's law judge to proof and sign.

Is this overkill? The Board of Veterans Appeals reviews the rating decision rendered at the regional office level looking for errors in fact or law. Because the BVA is not a finder of fact, the board must rely on the record established at the rating board level. Thus, frequently the rights of veterans are lost because no legal assistance was available initially. The Board of Veterans Appeals allowance rate between FY 1982 and FY 1991 ranged between 12.8 and 14.4 percent. That rate rose with judicial review to 20.8 percent in 2005. The remand rate back to the VA regional office is much higher. It was as high as 48.8 percent after passage of the Veterans Claims Assistance act of 2000, which broadened the VA's affirmative duty to assist the veteran in the development of his claim. But remanding back to the VA regional office causes even more delay. In most instances the whole process will be delayed for months, if not years, if such an event occurs. (See op-ed, Craig M. Kabatchnick, Greensboro News & Record, October 29, 2006)

Each RO has smart and ranked professionals so; the real purpose of the BVA is beyond this veteran's comprehension – maybe it's just another "Checks and Balance" barometer. If yes, then its usefulness needs to be re-evaluated because don't we have smart finance people that watch the government's purse strings? While we are chatting about money let me throw this tidbit at you. It's all perfectly legal but have you ever wondered why government checks are all 'rounded' dollars? I have never been paid, say, $536.49 cents. It was $536 – Did you ever wonder what happened to that .49 cents? You know if you take a few million 'rounded' government checks (1,000,000 x .49) would pay a LOT of veterans miseries, just a thought.

One final word on the BVA and I will leave them alone, for now. They have nine (9) 800 numbers but the main one is 1-800-827-1000 but don't waste your time calling. Their Internet site is accessible at http://www.index.va.gov/search/va/bva.html and anyone with more then two fingers and knowledge how to query (ask a question) can read their cases and decisions. The BVA receives their cases from Regional State offices (ROs) (as of 22

November 2006 the ROs open claims load is in-access of 399,502) to make final decisions as to who shall benefit from their budget dollars. The way the system seems to work is a claim starts with the veteran that sends his paperwork to their state Regional Office who does the leg work looking up medical records, verifying the claims as factual and worthy to receive monthly C&P. If they can make that final C&P decision, they do. Someone called a DRO at the RO is the "decider". If you are a GS 13, 14 or 15 you have had lots of experience and being in the $100,000 plus salary range "deciding" should be easy. But…sometimes decisions are difficult so the claim is forward to the BVA so they can be the "decider". The BVA looks at all the records and verifies the veteran may or may not be eligible for Compensation or Pension. This is done by law people using law terminology, lawyer logic and the law - verbatim. This process is so far protracted it doesn't seem to bother the BVA when 56% of their 475,009 cases are remanded back to the RO for further study and/or review. Each remand averages more then 400 days till the next time the claim see the light of day. The process is likening to rides at an amusement Theme Park. Wait in one very long line for a short ride then wait in another very long line for still another short ride, etc.etc.etc. Do I understand this picture correctly?

A veteran's claims action folder that lives in the RO or BVA must be complete for rightful decisions. This folder should have ALL correspondence from the veteran, all hospital and doctor files/records, rebuttals, recommendations, back-up literature, etc. (An average folder has over 400 pages of data – Frank has more in three folders with heavy rubber-bands holding them closed) so the VBA action person can make an intelligent and rightful decision. *When a veteran is to be denied…* make it for the right reasons and not just because an eye is not dotted, a tee crossed or a "certain" paper has not been requested or worse, not read correctly, *or miss-filed.* Under the present VA/VBA structure, a workable idea would be a way for the veteran to access their files electronically to check their accuracy. Make sure all "players" are on the same sheet of music. See OIG report mentioned above.

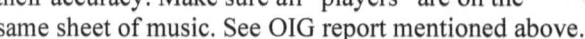

But right now the system says until that happens you can now view your claims folder or request hard copy of the complete folder. See: http://www.hadit.com/library/freqrequests/reqcfile.htm that says you can view your claims folder at the regional office by calling 1-800-827-1000 and/or request an appointment to view your c-file. It took seven months for Frank to get a roster of his Vietnam unit from the government so not sure how long it would take to get more then 400 pages copied and mailed from his claims files.

Frank has sent (three times) a list of his chronological correspondence to his RO to make sure the RO and he was on the same sheet of music – He has yet to hear back from them that yes they are or no something is missing. There has to be a way other then the sited web site above to assure the RO or BVA has all submitted records! *Action Officer Apathy or a file clerk error should not be factors in a claims denial.*

American Legion quality audit:
http://www.house.gov/va/hearings/schedule107/jun02/6-6-02/jfischl.html Statement of James r. Fischl, Director Veterans affairs and rehabilitation commission The American Legion Before the Subcommittee on Benefits Committee on Veterans' Affairs U.S. House of Representatives On implementation of the VA Claims processing task force's recommendations June 6, 2002 "…The American Legion's Quality Review Team visited the St. Petersburg VA Regional Office. While there, they were confronted with graphic evidence of premature and erroneous denials of claims, a general lack of compliance with the Veterans' Claims Assistance Act (VCAA) rules, and other types of inappropriate action. It almost appeared as part of an orchestrated policy of manipulation of the station's production figures as a means of meeting its mandated production quotas. Management, rating board members, decision review officers, and front-line claims processors are under tremendous pressure from VA Central Office to produce the expected monthly quotas. There were cases in which veterans received letters stating that their claims were being denied, because their military records may have been destroyed in the 1972 fire at the National Personnel Records Center. The problem was that these veterans got out of the service years after the fire took place. As disturbing as these tactics are, what was even more shocking was the intentional neglect of the backlog of pending appeals and remanded cases from the Board of Veterans Appeals. Remands are not being worked, because the station receives no work credit toward their mandated monthly production quota. (See Charles Kelly - Sources November 2006)

This is not just a local issue.

"At St. Petersburg, there were over 1,300 remands in which The American Legion holds power of attorney. Some of these cases had been remanded by the Board more than 'five years ago' and were still waiting final regional office action." (See Charles Kelly - Sources November 2006)

IN ADDITION to inefficacy, auditors' uncovered 136 cases of potential fraud or mishandling in the distribution of veterans benefit checks from offices in St. Petersburg and St. Louis, including the approval of $475,000 for a veteran who may have died 21 years ago. The whole story can be seen at http://www.sptimes.com/News/080100/TampaBay/VA_office_targeted_fo.shtml

Not all claims for C&P are as dramatic as the above St. Petersburg syndrome, amputation and PTSD or as profound as cancers and not all claims require the same amount of time to sort-out, gather medical background, etc. so not real sure why *Trauma to tooth #9* takes as long (4 -7 years) as PTSD. I suspect the GS 5 VBA action office is not given *any* approval authority and must have his section chief sign off on each claim then have a branch chief sign off, then a departmental chief before the claim ever gets to the C&P Associate Deputy under Secretary for Policy and Program Management desk who asked their DSO their thoughts on any particular claim. (I'm a little weak on this pecking order but the idea is a lot of folks have their hands in every decision) There are better and faster ways to get an official yes or no but the present organizational structure guarantees a need for more people that guarantee more jobs that guarantees higher positional rating that guarantees nicer retirement. Having worked on the Rings, in the Army War Room during some major decision times plus in the bowels of the pentagon for 23 years there has been too many organizational diagrams, coffee breaks, life and death decisions, Christmas parties and good-old-boy smokers that personnel, retirement and titles were discussed to not fully understand government hierarchy.

Growing up, did your mother ever say to you, "Always know which side of the bread your butter is on?"

If you follow this paper **RECOMMENDATIONS** (page 130) all this lost time and wasted effort goes away. You will see your own graphic results when you conclude **THE CHALLENGE** (page 133).

To clarify some numbers it is important to know that each of our fifty states plus the Philippines, Puerto Rico, and Guam has at least one RO (California has 3, Pennsylvania 2 and Texas 2) and they all have their own case load. To see the numbers reported in the Internet, see http://www.vba.va.gov/bln/201/reports/mmrindex.htm - what some of these numbers show is of 11 November 2006 there are 398,519 outstanding cases in just the ROs then add the BVA cases you are looking at 873,528 disabled veterans waiting for their just compensations & pension. Still more disturbing numbers in the same report show in January 2006 369,081 active cases – This case load should be *decreasing not increasing* by over 29,000 cases for a time period covering just eleven months. Rabbits don't multiply this fast but the word exponential comes to mind.

COMMENT: If you know about a problem and over the course of seven (7) years that problem exponentially manifests itself, you may need to re-look your procedures and direction. http://www.vba.va.gov/reports.htm

172 - Remember this number.

Then there is the Independent Medical Examination (IME). Is this important?

President Lincoln in his Second Inaugural Address indicated the importance of caring for the Nation's veterans said: *"To care for him who shall have borne the battle and for his widow and his orphan."* These words spoken by President Lincoln reflect the philosophy and principles that guide, or should guide the Department of Veteran Affairs and the Vocational Rehabilitation and Employment Service as their endeavors are focused on serving our Nation's veterans and their families. So says the VA doctrine.

Mark Twain wrote "Get the facts first. You can distort them later." Albert Einstein wrote "The important thing is not to stop questioning."

Not sure, but I think Mark Twain may have worked for the VA while our veterans reflect Albert's theory.

The stated Goal of the VA is: *"...to provide excellence in patient care, veterans' benefits and customer satisfaction. We have reformed our department internally and are striving for high quality, prompt and seamless service to veterans. Our department's employees continue to offer their dedication and commitment to help veterans get the services they have earned. Our nation's veterans deserve no less."*

These are stellar and honest words when written but extremely difficult to live up to when dealing with a Government Organization as large and diverse as the VA. The VA is manned by GS Government workers that are told the day they begin work, *"...begin planning for your retirement..."* and *"...an action passed is an action completed..."* Ouch! Frank said that his dealings with the VA it seemed the Action Officers (AO) were given a set of rules for handling and answering veteran's claims and to not deviate from them. Deviation converts to budget dollars so no matter what the veteran's claims says, what medical documentation are submitted it seems AOs believe a veteran claim must match a number in their rules to "win". What that boils down to is the AO looks for a number and awards or denies the claim based exclusively on that number. Most military people will tell you they consider themselves "second class citizens" and the actions of the VA amplify that feeling through their actions and deeds. In England the soldiers consider themselves "sixth class".

More on these Action Officers later.

Claims, Cause and Effect~

The government and/or the VA does not automatically give you anything. You have to ask for it, justify it, over and over, prove you deserve it, dot all the Eyes and cross all the Tees, jump through prescribed hoops and forms before any meager budget dollars show up in your name. A recent conversation between a veteran and the VA went something like this:

Vet – "My medical records show I have had Hypertension for seven year."

VA – "That's correct."

Vet – "Hypertension is 'ratable', why aren't you paying me compensation?"

VA – "You haven't asked for it."

Vet – "I have to ask for it?"

VA – "Of course – we don't know anything unless you tell us."

Vet – "OK. Can I have it and make it retroactive?

VA – "No."

Vet – "You told me to ask for it."

VA – "That's right, but you have to ask for it nice like. You have to say please and you have to fill out all the forms, get in line then wait."

Vet – "How long will that take?"

VA – "Did you ever read Violet Fane (1843-1905) in her poem - Tout vient ß qui sait attendre when she said, *'Ah, all things come to those who wait,'*

Vet – "Yes, yes I did, but didn't she also say, *'but something answers soft and sad, 'They come, but often come too late.'*

After much strained heavy puffing mixed with white-eyed-rolling embarrassing moments from the VA side of the house, she stomped out of the room muttering something that sounded like… "I just work here… that's not my problem."

Where do these "claims" for compensation for military physical problem come from? From the veteran, and remember the veteran, just as their civilian counterpart does not initially know ALL the rules and ramifications of his request. Mass communication or the lack thereof comes to mind. Also, the veteran is just a guy or gal that has done their duty for God and Country, put their lives on the line for politicians and now is only asking for what Washington, George and DC promised.

Depending on the Governments needs is a direct ratio to Government speed. Frank's medical retirement was swift and non-compassionate – Laying in a Walter Reed Hospital bed recovering from a major heart attack (MI) the following conversation took place:

MB – "We are retiring you and you must vacate your government quarters and return your TA-50 and any monies you are now not eligible."

Frank – "I don't want to be retired. I don't have anywhere to move my family and I don't have a civilian job, besides I feel fine now. "

Medical Board (MB) member – "You are not *'fine.'* Your heart has two major tears we call an MI and even if you survive the next two years you will not be able to function as in the past. Not having a place to go or a job is not *our* problem. *You* were the one wounded because you didn't duck so now we can't use you anymore. You are now *Permanently Unfit for Military Service*."

    Frank – "But… I don't have a job. Can I have more time?"
    MB – "No. We awarded you 30% disability – that should help"
    Frank – "How much is that?"
    MB – "30%"
    Frank – "No, I mean what will my retirement money be after you retire me?"
    MB – "30%"

The June medical board really didn't know that the 30% translated to just twelve ($12.32 rounded to $12) a month. It seemed to make no difference to them anyway as they gave Frank two chooses in his forced medical retirement – July or August. He chooses August then he was gone.

As many of Frank's fellow veterans, he is dying and the VA has yet to open their doors to him to help pay bills and live out his days in some kind of comfort rather then to just exist from day to day. What the VA is doing is denying any rightful service-related health problems and is saying for low-cost medical help all he needs to do is drive 300 miles to the nearest VA hospital any time he can get an appointment for his cancer and heart problems and *"…they will treat you…"* Have you even visited a VA hospital? How about an automobile assembly plant? Or Krispy Krème donuts shop? They are all similar in their assembly-line approach to health care.

When Frank was medically retired his base military pay was $800 per

month. He had a wife and young son as Frank was only 43, in the prime of life, military fit and trim… but his heart attacked him – twice - so the military gave him 30% retirement disability and deemed him *"permanently unfit for military service"*. Not to worry, the 30% disability was "tax-free". That number does not fall into the WOW category as it only relates to about ½ tank of gas per month for his sixteen year old Nissan. Over the years Frank has provided for his family as best a disabled man can but when a service-connected cancer struck, he asked for help.

Percentages of disability are established by regulations. Government regulations are black and white with NO grays when it comes to, well - regulations. For example, METs (Metabolic Equivalent) is the benchmark for establishing C&P percentage you can be awarded if your heart is involved. If you have a MET of 3 or less, you are rated 100% disabled, a MET of 4 but <5 you are 60%, >5 but <7 you are 30%, 7 to 10 is 10% and more then 10 = 0%. A MET is the energy cost of standing quietly at rest and represents your oxygen intake… In other words METs are nothing more then normal breathing. METs can be measured BUT more likely then not for VA rating purposes your METs are *ESTIMATED* using your BP and heart-rate during a Bruce protocol treadmill exercise or climbing stairs. What happens if you can't walk a treadmill? Well then the VA Cardiologist takes your pulse and *ESTIMATES.* You know the difference between a 100% to a 0% disability in dollar terms? Round numbers is $2,400 monthly compensation. That is a *huge monetary difference* for a 3-4-5-6-7-8-9 *ESTIMATE,* especially if your "estimator" is having a bad day - - or even a good day!! There are more criterion in Title 38 that should be considered and not JUST METs.

*Another unit of measuring one MET is how long it takes to climb stairs. There NOTHING scientific about these – as it too is ALL subjective… There is a formula that can be used which is the same as automobile mechanics use in monitoring a dynamometer. "**Can be = but isn't".** It says: 15.1 + (21.8 x speed of treadmill = - (0.327 x HR) = - (0.263 x speed of treadmill x age =+ (5.98 x genders) 0 = female and 1= male. This give Vo2 - now take that value divide by 3.5 for your MET.*

Take a deep breath….I am sure all these numbers are explainable BUT, if you are diabetic and depending on what RO is servicing your claim, awarding criterion is different: For example, the benchmark in the H.S. Truman VA hospital for one RNC is, if your Hemoglobin A1C is 7 you are ratable diabetic. Another RNC at the same hospital, the same day the yardstick used is Glucose, BP, Urine sample numbers. These RNCs essentially are your "deciders". The way the system works is, remember this when I tell you about the all important *VA interview.* That interview report when read by the RO action officer and whatever numbers and words are read is parroted to the veteran in a form of approval or denial to their claim for diabetes. Also, remember that BVA site I told you about http://www.index.va.gov/search/va/bva.html ? Some real head shaker numbers you see there are approved A1Cs below 5 and some A1C above 13 denied. Sounds like your deciders, decide each day what they will decide on any giver decision. See the OIG report Item #4D mentioned earlier about inconsistencies in the ROs.

To add insult to injury on this heart compensation drill, the regulations (Title 38: Pensions, Bonuses, and Veterans' Relief) says the first three months following a heart attack (MI) you shall receive 100% then revert to whatever rating your estimated METs say. This portion of the regulation is seldom made available to the veteran. The veteran is usually busy just trying to survive and the VA doesn't give the extra 100% because the veteran doesn't know to ask for this rule that has been on the books since 1964.

There has got to be a better way.

Before you start thinking the veteran is maybe getting something for nothing, consider this. When a civilian retires they receive a retirement (usually monthly half salary), stock options, pay for occurred leave, any disability (bad back or bunion on their butts, trick knees, etc.), IRAs, etc... In other words retirement may not be a golden umbrella as some CEOs but its not peddling apples on a street-corner either. The military retirement is a bit different, especially if the veteran has a low (under 50%) ratable disability. As the civilian counterpart the veteran, at 20 years, goes out with 50% of their base pay but any percentage disability is deduced from the retirement total and given then as "tax-free". Statement by Daniel L. Cooper, Under Secretary for Benefits, Veterans Benefits Administration, Department of Veterans Affairs, Before the Military Personnel Subcommittee, Senate Armed Services Committee, March 27, 2003 maybe said it best when he described what his VA was doing for the veteran, he said, *"...instead of **merely** a percentage of military retirement pay tax free"*. **Merely!**

Social Security (SS) is also very different for the military and civilian. SS is based on your first forty working months and we all know military pay is just above the poverty level so to just give you the numbers: SS for a retired enlisted military person is under $700 a month while the *average* civilian is over $1,700.

Military and also civilian people seldom know if anything is physically wrong with their bodies. When we do have a pain we most often take an aspirin and forget about it. That works for most but not for example - cancers. By the time you see a doctor for a nagging pain caused by a cancer you are stage IV (you usually have a few months left) on a very downhill slippery slope. More on cancers just below.

Military life can be hazardous to your health. Walter-Reed and Civilian doctors have discovered not only does Frank have a bad heart and Kidney cancer he is diabetic, has out-of-control hypertension and Chloracne. During the last three years Frank has written twenty-seven (27) letters to the VA sending official medical documentation, lay statements and has justified over and over and over how he qualifies for just compensation – all according to their rules.

To offer just one example of VA action officer apathy and narcissism toward Frank's cancer, he gathered necessary medical documentation, forwarded to the VA RO in St. Louis citing the military connection to the *cause and affect* was from the diuretic and BP medication he was put on during active service. Medicine, The American Cancer Society agrees as did his civilian doctors ALL agree with Frank but the VA has denied compensation three times. Why? Because, read this next part carefully and try not to laugh, or shake your head in wonderment, but they said Frank's cancer claim was denied because it was not caused or secondary to Agent Orange (not presumptive). Frank was in Vietnam during the massive defoliation of the country in the late 1960's early 1970 so according to the VBA, Agent Orange (AO) can not cause his cancer so because he was in Vietnam and exposed to AO he can not be granted compensation for his cancer as AO couldn't have caused it thus not making his cancer "service related" and compensate able. Remember Bud Abbott and Lou Costello's routine about who's on first? In three year now *the VBA has yet to even address the original cited cause and affect.*

Not sure *where* VCAA is during this VBA thinking process.

NOTE on Cancers: There is not a MD, oncologist, DO, etc anywhere on the face of the earth that will or can say for any certainty ***where*** cancer starts. They can only tell you what kind you have and when it will kill you.

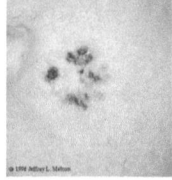
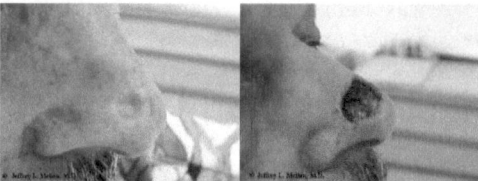
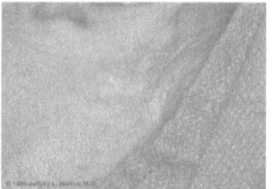

Just some sampling of compensatable skin cancer I wanted to share: L to R: Cheek, Nose, Nose, Cheek

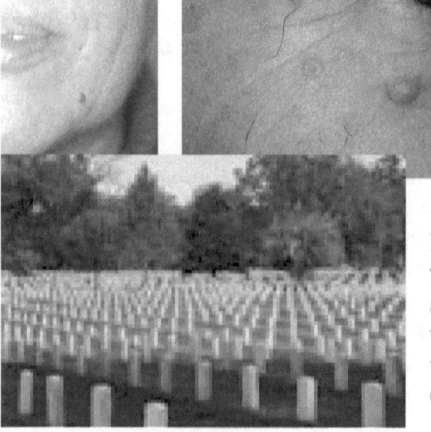

BASEL CELL CARCINMOMAS: Pigmented, Nodular and Neglected.

I hate showing these but these are the reality of what many of our veterans and I are dying from while awaiting C&P from our Veterans Administration.

On a cellular level, any type of cancer is caused by abnormalities in a cell's DNA. These may be inherited from parents, or they may be caused by outside exposures to the body such as chemicals, radiation, or even infectious agents. All cancers involve the malfunction of genes that control the growth of cells in the body. Genes can be damaged (mutated) throughout a person's life by many different things such as hormones, certain viruses, tobacco, chemicals, sunlight, and substances in food. Most of the time, it takes many years for the damage to produce cancer. And, as people get older, they are more likely to have damaged genes. There are over 200 different types of cancer. You can develop cancer in any body organ and there are over 60 different organs in the human body. (see the renowned Dr. James A. Goodyear North Penn Hernia Institute) Knowing this and knowing there are very young VBA GS action officers that can definitively deny a veteran because their rating charts may not specifically note the veteran's cancer is beyond human comprehension or mine anyway. Maybe a criterion for the action officer should talk with and hold the hand of a cancer patient in a VA hospital so they could fully see and appreciate the *power* of their government position. I know… I know… the action officer doesn't have that medical decision power as he/she must send the claim to a medical doctor BUT depending on what that doctor says the action officer should not have to *interpolate* stated findings and should NEVER have to send a denial letter to a veteran with cancer, any cancer. We have to *assume* the action officer handling your folder is doing all they can to get the right/correct answers so they can make the right/correct decisions and also remember - that action officer does have **§3.102 (reasonable doubt)** power. Please don't take our word for this cancer criterion – Please ask, check with any and all Oncologist and they will ALL tell you the same.

Agent Orange (AO) is, to say the least, *controversial.* In AO issues Vietnam Veterans are not the arguable points of this paper they certainly have been a major concern to those

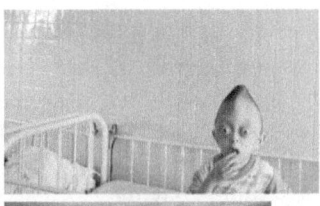
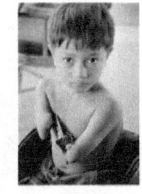

Veterans now dead, those Veterans that are going to die, like Frank, and those that are disabled from government causation directly due to herbicides (plural) exposures. Alternatively, the more recent developments of what is being called Gulf War Syndrome.

We have all heard horror-stories out of Vietnam babies and also about hospitals where you go in with a minor problem and a leg is amputated or a civilian buying a tainted leaf of spinach with e-coli and dying at the local pharmacy. If understanding the after-affect of what Government sponsored Agent Orange in the Vietnam War zone can do, has done and is doing, consider also the patient with hypertension (high blood pressure) in-service documented in several military doctor visits. This one particular patient, an atypical female major eventually exited service with a normal physical and nobody bothered to check her blood pressure in exit physical or during his VA exam for benefits. She went home with 10% disability and no medication for or diagnosis for hypertension and 5 years later had leg swelling went to an MD and found out that she had lost most of the function of her kidneys due to hypertension and now needed dialysis to live, Before she could revisit the hospital for treatment she had dizziness and a stroke from a hypertensive brain hemorrhage and she ended up spending 2 weeks in the ICU and lost function of the right side of her body, all of which would likely have been avoided with good treatment earlier from the military and VA. Coincidently the major's military partner developed headaches and was discharged only to get a civilian MRI one year later that shows inoperable tumors.

IT IS DIFFICULT TO IGNORE FACTS AND TRUTH BUT on this AO issue OUR GOVERNMENT SEEMS TO HAVE TURNED A BLIND EYE and A DEAF EAR TO THE VETERANS OF KOREA and VIETMAN:

Admiral E.R. Zumwalt, Jr. in his 5 May 1990 **CONFIDENTIAL** Report to congress on Agent Orange (see http://www.gulfwarvets.com/ao.html) and its affect

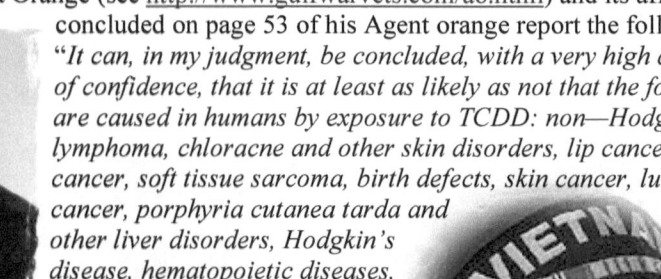

concluded on page 53 of his Agent orange report the following:
"It can, in my judgment, be concluded, with a very high degree of confidence, that it is at least as likely as not that the following are caused in humans by exposure to TCDD: non—Hodgkin' s lymphoma, chloracne and other skin disorders, lip cancer, bone cancer, soft tissue sarcoma, birth defects, skin cancer, lung cancer, porphyria cutanea tarda and other liver disorders, Hodgkin's disease, hematopoietic diseases, multiple myeloma, neurological defects and auto—immune diseases and disorders. In addition, I am most comfortable in concluding that it is at least as likely as not that liver cancer, nasal/pharyngeal/esophageal cancers, leukemia, malignant melanoma, kidney cancer, testicular cancer, pancreatic cancer, stomach cancer, prostate cancer, colon cancer, brain cancer, psychosocial effects, and gastrointestinal disease are service connected."

HOWEVER: The U.S. Government and the Veterans Administration has disregarded those disease its *fighting forces incurred in Korea and Vietnam that would be overly* *costly and allowing **ONLY** the following: prostate cancer, respiratory cancers, (lung, trachea ,bronchus, larynx), soft-tissue sarcoma, non-Hodgkin lymphoma, Hodgkin disease, chronic lymphocytic leukemia (CLL), and multiple myeloma.*

I could go on and on with thousands of real examples - but you get the idea.

If we can have, *no child left behind* can't we also have *NO Veteran left behind?*

In our present system, veterans are not always the target, sometimes it can be the physician. A physician at a well known military hospital in the Mid West wrote favorable opinions for veterans and lost his job as specialist but being in the right, continues to support veterans and was assigned to the research floor. The doctor continues his support and was put in a room with no phone or computer while the physician continues to help as he could – honest help. He finally resigns and files suit and wins for an undisclosed amount. He won a few dollars but it cost him dearly. (see source – Dr. Bash)

Every coin has two sides emphasizing the VBA has major problem.
Another physician is told to not put anything supportive of a benefit claim into patent's records. He doesn't and is alive, prosperous and now chief of his division. (see sources - Dr. Bash)

The VA may have a duty to assist but the system seems to prevent the rank and file from supporting any veteran....for example, only certain MD's at certain hospitals are allowed to write IME's. The IME process should be randomly assigned to prevent bias. Drunken roulette player in Las Vegas have better odds.

Then there is the Independent Medical Examination (IME) --- Why wasn't I told of this?

Benefit of the Doubt within the "VA Journey"

When Frank first applied for compensation he had to be added to the VA *"roles"*, get in-line for testing then start down the VA gantlet. First was an Agent Orange examination. This hurts to even tell you what that examination is because it is nothing but an interview with a VA nurse (an RNP), a standard blood test and chest x-ray. That maybe doesn't sound that bad but consider in medicine there are only two laboratories in the world that even test for Agent Orange (AO) and they are expensive (over $1,600) and they only work on cadavers, *BUT the VA **requires** its veterans have this worthless "test" that seems to be public relations oriented more so than fact finding .*

IMPORTANT!!! VA interviews! Interviews with VA RNP (Registered Nurse Practitioner) personnel the veteran has to be very careful of his/her words. For example, how many times does someone say to you, "how are you?" and your response is "...fine, thank you" when you may be suffering from heart palpitation, have diarrhea, headache, just finished a gut busting lunch and feeling like what the cat hauled home. However "…fine thank you…" when spoken in the presents of a VA person your words are then locked into concrete and translated into, *"…the veteran denied symptoms of…", " centrally obese…", "…there are no thumps, thrills and rubs…", "…the patient plays golf 5 days a week… has regular sex 3-5 times weekly… walks the dog two miles a day… well tanned…"*

To be a veteran during a VA interview you need be two people. Dorin Gray comes to mind, however; **One** – You need to possess the same type personality as the beloved Labrador retriever. As their canine friends, the veterans need love, affectionate and patients with civilians. Don't lie; just be careful of your *phraseology*. **Two** - veterans are also vain and use to telling war-stories so if truth be know, they watch golf on TV, reminisce about a fantasy sex-life from their twenties and the dog died fifteen years ago, shouldn't have had that extra slice of Pizza and his heart will not allow any activity more strenuous then sitting behind a computer so why not sit in the sun and tan as much as possible. All sounds quite innocent BUT when the action officer at your VA Regional Office reads that interview report they do not see any of the numbers on their Rating Charts and immediately send you a denial form letter.

Dorin Gray led two lives – In person (his physical appearance) never changed BUT his portrait grew more grotesque with each of his sins and transgressions. Our VA does the same, only their transgressions are reflected in the >1,000,000 deserving veterans.

Why is so much importance place with the VA interview(s)? Having been down this path as an over-worked AO in the pentagon it is my impression is because it is easier for a VBA action officer to parrot simple and abbreviated words of a VA RNP then by doing their job deciphering 20 years of medical official documentation.

What's a Rating Chart? I'm sure it has many names but what we are talking about is what tells the Action Officer the parameters of claimed compensation outlined in *Title 38: Pensions, Bonuses, and Veterans' Relief.* It is a government regulation like all others that govern our lives. Where do "regulations" come from is not relative in this format but the simple answer is they evolve. The long answer would take all day trying to explain "…is what is…" Similar to the Bible and all written words, government regulations need to be not only read but to be *interrupted* as to their meaning and intent.

To get back to being denied.... After receiving a few, a denial form letter from the VA is fun to read because you know it took NO time for a clerk to print the form letter and just add your name to the envelop. You know what the letter says before opening as they are usually heavy, thick and smells of sulfur. They are always long and wordy but never say anything of substance. When Frank received his first four letters denying additional heart and new cancer claims they all gave long generic explanations of what the VA regulations say but never tied their words to his specific medical problems. Generic letters designed to appease and placate rather then give the exact cause of denial. Remember the parent role "…because I said so…" is the common thread running throughout VA letters.

VA letters never talk TO the veteran. They talk generically and usually condescending and more likely then not will leave the veteran muttering, "…what the hell are they talking about, that is not what I said…"

As many of our disabled Vietnam veterans out there Frank has Chloracne. (see examples this paragraph) Chloracne is a skin disorder akin to adolescent acne. Chloracne is a by-product of Agent Orange and is listed as one of the VA's eleven *presumptive* diseases. Frank furnished the VA *thirteen* 1970s thru 1980s medical care official document three years ago asking for compensation but the VA has *denied the request four times.* Why? Because they said so. By the way - the official military documentation Frank submitted, four times, stated in clean and plain language *"…condition is a result of the Vietnam war".* The decision

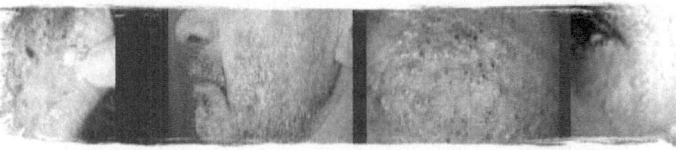

makers get a bit fuzzy here because Frank's four denial letters all said, "…did not manifest within 12 months of exposure to AO…" It did, but there is no way to prove it 36 years later other then by carbon-testing and for that they would have to kill the patient. Everyone knows what precedent means and all you have to do to see where precedence lives and is at work is check out the BVA online files. There are 1,270 approved Chloracne claims in the BVA case files all dated within the last five years and in all cases the approved veteran was exposed 30-35 years ago. *Maybe Frank's medical records were not understood when they said, "…caused by the Vietnam war…"??*

CONSISTANCY: In some cases the BVA is trying to do right for the veteran by giving them the benefit of the doubt. Don't get all bubbly because they only just started. Before 2000 they routinely denied claims because *"the claim is not well-grounded".* In today's BVA files you can find 4,726 claim that have been approved in their 1992-2006 case files all citing, *"… under the benefit-of-the-doubt rule, for the veteran to prevail, there need not be a preponderance of the evidence in his favor, but only an approximate balance of the positive and negative evidence. In other words, the preponderance of the evidence* *must be against the claim for the benefit to be denied."* Not sure if this has filtered down to the VBA or if it has, IF it is understood and honored.

EDITORAL: In any legal system, the order of legal precedence is the backbone of the legal system. Yet for our BVA this order of precedence does not seem to exist. Many bad things can be the fall-out but for the veteran the processing and ambiguity of individual issues leads to years and even decades of (pick a bad sounding word describing frustration and wasted effort).

Take a few minutes and rummage through the case files of BVA decisions, you will get a mixed bag of outcomes for almost the exact same numbers in different claims.

For example the Benefit of the Doubt rules. One claim will deny because even though the evidentiary facts are clearly stated as 50/50 the medical issue or issues are associated to exposures to the herbicides, diseases, military problems while others will even approved. Nevertheless, an identical case will also say disapproved. On the other hand, the ruling may be remanded back to the lower level. Who's on first?

The Benefit of the Doubt rules say, *"....the preponderance of the evidence must be against the claim for the benefit to be denied."*

Now you would think the courts would have some concern on why their directions are not being followed. It seems no one, including our congress, has any concern over this totally government biased mandated budget process which seems to track only budget; not justice for the Veterans or their widows. (see Kelly, Sources, November 2006)

These decisions are all searchable on BVA computer database.

~txe Solution~

Then there is the Independent Medical Examination (IME). --- Finally! What is this IME?

The IME is a way for the VBA to step out of their rut/grave and do right for their charges – the veteran.

The MES **IME** Network has over 17,000 credentialed physicians and allied health professionals across the country that are expertly trained and prepared to deliver evidence-based opinions. Now... 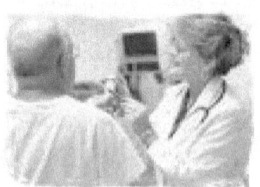 these guys/gals are there, in place ready to go. Our government doesn't have to develop any, they are already there. All Uncle has to do is now hire them and sic them on our veterans population.

MES Solutions, (MES) was founded in 1978 and was the first organization ever established to provide the claims community with access to physicians with expertise in conducting Independent Medical Examinations and Peer Reviews.

IMEs are current NOT affiliated or aligned with the federal government. When (if) hired, the IME will take your records, review them and come to their own conclusions. It would be nice if the veteran could *suggest* the IME find in their favor for "xyz" problems but that doesn't happen and is a quick way to the exit door. The civilian medical profession is one of the most ethical on earth and  because of what the IMEs do, they lead the pack in morals, principle for just and honest evaluations.

IMEs charge a fee for what they do and any report they submit to the VA for you. There are no free lunches out there.

Not sure what the different IMEs charge for their services but an educated guess for the bottom line would be a percentage of one month compensation you would receive for whatever compensation your VA claim asked for or how complicated your case might be. For example; if you can't hear it thunder and asked the VA to approve a Tinnitus 20% claim you might be looking at a IME bill for around $485.00 or if you had higher claim expectations of say 100% for a really bad heart and reams of legal documents your IME bill might be around $2,393.00.

As in life, the same holds true for the IMEs, there are no guarantees. The IME will give you an honest evaluation, submit to the VA in all the proper formats and in language to support the claim, then it is up to the VA to accept or deny yours and the IMEs words.

HONESTY – Now that would be a breath of fresh air.

To lessen the pain in the pocketbook just a bit consider this: Remember the story of the retired engineer that was called by the Turkey Point nuclear plant in Florida to solve a major problem that had everyone baffled for a solution? He inspected the machinery what was sick, walked around it several times, poked this, turned that and after fifteen minutes turned to the plant manager said, "Turn this handle ¼ counter clock-wise every hour on the hour for four hour and that will fix your problem." He did and the problem went away and the plant is happy and humming. The following week the plant received a bill for $50,000 for "service rendered". A quick phone call to the retired engineer complaining of the high charge when the engineer worked only fifteen minutes and actually didn't do anything other then tell them to turn a handle. "Your right, but I knew where to look for the solution and you didn't." The bill was paid in full that afternoon.

Now… go take this pill and call me in the morning.

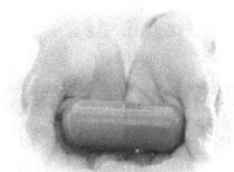

~Prelude to a Decision~

A stated goal in 2001 from the BVA said, *"…the Annual Benefits Report (ABR) has become a meaningful tool for VA, VBA and a variety of interested program stakeholders. Similar to the first three years of publication, this edition of the ABR does not attempt to analyze work processes associated with the day-to-day administration of these benefit programs. However, one of our goals is to broaden the analysis and use of the data contained in the ABR. Towards that objective, we are exploring the feasibility of including in future editions information about our performance against established measures."*

Do you hear that dead horse syndrome drum beat in the background?

Government workers are not overly compassionate and to them, a letter, a claim is just words on paper and not a living human being on the other end. To them the veteran is a number (C12 345 678). The VA doctrine says differently but those are just words written yesterday. The mere fact they work for the U.S. Government tells you that. Decisions made on you are a numbers game. If your claim numbers and medical history numbers match their action manuals you have an even chance to being awarded just compensation. Few government people *"answer the mail"*. In civilian board meetings ever utterance is addressed, ever note is finalized, ever phone call is answered and every letter, e-mail, fax is answered. Government workers and the VA seem to answer what they please - see parent rules.

*If you are warm, have a heart beat, know someone that knows someone and have decent credentials, you can work for the government. Where you work is a crap-shoot unless you know somebody. Not to worry because what cubical your desk is, they will train you. You will be trained to look for a number, a phase, certain wording and that's OK. What isn't OK is the action officers within the VA must or should process the ability to **ANALYSE** words in a veterans claim. Analytical ability can not be trained but it can be learned and one way is through dedication to the veteran. VBA action officers need to be special because they service special people, the veteran.*

VBA action officers are the key to the system we now have.

IF the system is to remain status-quo criterion to be a VBA action officer MUST change.

The most disturbing facts toward the VBA action people they are all basically nice and decent people but they are not overly smart in ALL fields of medicine and anatomy and they are required to made medical decisions because that is what medical disability

124

compensation is. Our body is made up of hundreds or trillions of cells that each one has a mind of its own. They have their own names, terminology and language. The VBA action person deciding your claim is probably not a PhD, MD, or even have a masters degree is Liberal Arts or even an engineering BS, BA or even a AS but when a claims folder is setting on his/her desk with words like, "This is a Positive study with an inferior fraction, scar and periinfarct ischemia" not even a PDR or Webster's can help... *BUT the IME can.*

Before closing... I know there are at least a couple questions still in your mind.

1. Are we bound by any set of rules that REQUIRE us to continue down this same slippery slope? Not really. Rules can be amended, changed or broken as long as it is for the good of the people. Rules that applied to yesterday's world do not necessarily apply today. ***For example:*** *On 18 Jan 2005 during her Senate Confirmation hearing Condoleezza Rice said to a Senator Dick Lugar question as to how the United States should now and in the future deal with the Soviets for world peace. She responded, "...work to do the right thing... if there are laws or rules in the way, **then we must break them**..." A follow-up question from Senator Joe Biden about her chooses of words about "breaking" the rules, she clarified her response from Senator Lugar to mean, "...change the rules..."*

...and the one I like best, maybe because I was sitting in the briefing and heard the words;

*For me, an unforgettable moment when....*In a 1984 pentagon staff meeting Vice Chief of Staff General Maxwell R. Thurman was being briefed by a LOGCENT Major General and he said to a Thurman question, "... those are the rules...", General Thurman replying in a tone and words that left no one in doubt as to his feeling, "...G_d-damnit general, we make the rules... change them...!!" Few enjoy having that kind of influence but Secretary of State Rice, congress and the VA does.

2. Are IMEs our magic bullet? *I'm sure there are folks out there that will argue the point, but from this ex-military, ex-government servant and current disabled veteran the answer is YES.*

Prelude to Recommendations

The VA is the second largest department run by the U.S. Government that employs just over 235,000 people. Just the benefits portion of the VA's 2006 budget alone is $38,525,965 of which over 35.8 Million is labeled *"discretionary"*. The 2007 budget calls out 80.6 Billion for veteran's benefits and services and 38.5 Billion for discretionary spending and 42.1 Billion for entitlements. What these billions represent is just an arm of one government department. What I do know if you take the 235,000 workers and multiply that number with their average salaries you get a very large number and there is a very real way to make that number smaller – a lot smaller. *Franks suggestion to Outsource and IMEs will, over time, saves more federal dollars then spent on Katrina and the whole Iraq and Afghanistan war.*

IMEs are the key to better run a more efficient care-taker sized C&P VA organization and Veterans receiving rightful compensations.

Think - IME and change.

VFW just completed a 7 year review and found that for each 1 dollar spent on IME claims the return to the veteran was 55 dollars in retro benefits!

If I were a VBA action officer would I approach my supervisor with this IME suggestion? I might as would Frank and 20 million other veterans BUT if I were that supervisor and knowing the more people I had under my supervision the higher my pay would be, I would file your suggestion where it would never see the light of day.

A couple really scary claims today would go away if change within the present system took place: Some physicians are told to not put anything supportive of a benefit claim into the patent's record; the VA may have a duty to assist but the system prevents the rank and file from supporting any veteran; only certain MD's at certain hospitals are allowed to write IME's. The IME process should be randomly assigned to as to prevent bias.

Remember that number I told you to remember? There are **172** VA hospitals where any one of thousands of remanded claims can be sent. Not sure if this is good or bad for the veteran, but continuity and time constraints comes to mind and must be considered.

Did I just hear you say, "That could take a long time?" Your right, it can and does but that is *the system we now have.* Does *"...is what is..."* and *"because I said so..." ring* any bells?

The way the BVA is now structured it can send opinions to local RO or any RO in country. Maybe VA headquarters is already thinking IMEs because recently they just approved 2000 opinions a year to be paid at $500 an opinion from anybody outside the VA... (?)

The VA has favorite medical school staffs but nothing has been made public as to what the thinking is within the VA. Sometimes when the opinion is not supportive they will send it back for a second look. A bit unusual but it has happened that opinions have been sent back three times to have the doctor write against the VA and in favor of the veteran and it is not uncommon to see the VA form Physician committees to over rule one of their lower level staff Doctor or have Congressmen put pressure on the VA to have a doctor change his opinion. If a manipulation can be made, it has and is done.

Being raised in Texas it shouldn't have surprised me when a few years ago my mother was telling me she had to send her federal income tax paperwork to the Three-Rivers Correctional Facility as her CPA was doing two years hard time. What did surprise me was when I heard one VA lawyer in BVA who is in prison because he removed positive evidence from a veterans file so as to make the veteran lose benefits.

During the last 7 years the VA has undergone a profound transformation. They are trying to redesign the Top heavy, top down organizations network.
http://www.va.gov/ofcadmin/ViewPDF.asp?fType=1 page 7.
Note: VA is in the process of rewriting whole medical evaluation process; in fact Institute of Medicine met 8-9 November 2006 in Washington to write recommendation for March publications. If they are NOT on the right track for the veteran, then everyone needs to seriously consider the below recommendations.

- Craig M. Kabatchnick-

The below article was written 29 October 2006 by Craig M. Kabatchnick an attorney who lives in Greensboro NC. He is now a full-time law professor of the North Carolina Central School of Law Veterans law Clinic, one of the first and largest law school law clinic's in the country. His office number is 919-530 -6605. Tell people to try the law school number and the cell phone number 336-456-3751.

His law school address is:
North Carolina Central University School of Law Veterans Law Clinic
1512 South Alston Avenue
Durham, North Carolina 27707

He is the Director and Supervising attorney of the Veterans Law Clinic.
Mr. Kabatchnick is and has been a long-time player in this theater we call C&P.
He writes.....*"The $10 limit*

Because of a $10 limitation on attorneys' fees for helping with veterans' initial claims — a limitation that dates back to the Civil War! — Veterans usually can't obtain legal counsel initially. For example, for nearly two years I was the only attorney registered with the N.C. Bar Association's Lawyer Referral Service to handle initial veteran's claims. I did so primarily as a public service and because I had acquired *unique experience with veterans claims while I served in Washington in the VA's general counsel office.*

Veterans need the support of permanent legal representation at the initial claims adjudication level. That attorneys can only receive compensation after the VA has rendered a final Board of Veterans Appeals decision creates a vast void. There is great need for immediate long-term assistance for veterans through a permanent veteran's law clinic, such as the one that will open at the N.C. Central School of Law in January 2007.

Veterans' problems are further increased because oftentimes denials by the Board of Veterans Appeals are based on a defect made because the claim was not initially processed by an attorney. Thus, frequently the rights of veterans are lost because no legal assistance was available at the beginning of the claims adjudication process.

The average time for an initial claim for compensation and pension to be processed and a final Board of Veterans Appeals decision rendered is four to seven years. Oftentimes an elderly veteran will die before his/her claim has been fully adjudicated. VA rating boards are slow and lackadaisical in processing claims for benefits because of heavy caseloads caused by inadequate staffing, poor supervision and inexperience among rating board members. Oftentimes rating board employees are hired right of high school. Many have little or no college and little or no medico-legal, military or pertinent work experience.

Adversarial climate

Normally claims are handled by rating boards made up of one or two VA employees, and a great number of these claims are handled by junior level employees who are evaluated with an emphasis on productivity and quantity of decisions produced, rather than quality. Often, haste causes crucial items in the veteran's claims folder — items that would favor granting a claim — to be overlooked. Furthermore, the VA's statutorily mandated affirmative duty to assist the veteran in developing his claim is often overlooked.

All of this makes for a veterans claims adjudication process that is bogged down and adversarial.

Regional rating boards are to review the evidence contained in the veteran's file, assist the veteran in developing his/her claim and to render a decision. Under law, rating boards must give veterans the benefit of the doubt when deciding whether current disabilities are connected to injuries and incidents that occurred during military service.

But many decisions do not apply the benefit of the doubt standard or, if it is applied, it is done in an inappropriate fashion. The VA will fail to fully develop the medical evidence and will instead base its decision on medical evidence in the record favorable toward a denial. Sometimes the VA rating board will fail to assist the veteran in obtaining appropriate medical records and military records (many of which are stored in Greenbelt, Md.), buddy statements, unit reports and any other information that might assist the veteran in developing his/her claim.

The VA rating boards also often fail to examine the veteran's claims folder for claims not raised by the veteran but which exist and must be evaluated by the VA rating boards in light of evidence already of record. The VA also must inform the veteran of what information is necessary to make his claim for benefits sufficient.

I have noticed that treating physician statements are not given the weight and authority they should be given; instead, the VA will rely on VA physicians and doctors under contract with the VA (claiming that they are "independent medical advisors"). These VA physicians and doctors under contract oftentimes examine the veteran in a cursory manner, sometimes within a matter of minutes, and thereafter render an allegedly "independent medical opinion" stating that the veteran's current disabilities are not related to injuries sustained in service. Sometimes the VA physicians who are under contract are not certified by the American Board of Medical Specialists in the areas for which the veteran claims disability.

When a VA examination is cursory, lasts only minutes and is done by a physician not ABMS board certified in the area for which the veteran claims disability, it is virtually impossible for that examination to fairly serve as a basis to deny the veteran his claim. Such "independent VA examinations" represent both factual and legal error and are an injustice to the veteran. In many instances, the VA rating board will offer no explanation for why it ignored the veteran's physician's opinion supporting the grant of the veteran's claim and only considered the negative "independent medical opinion" of the VA physician.

Appeal process
Veterans dissatisfied with the regional VA rating decision can file a substantive appeal with the Board of Veterans Appeals in Washington. Veterans who appeal must file a Notice of Disagreement with their regional office within one year of the VA rating decision along with a VA Form 9.

The Board of Veterans Appeals is divided into four decision teams divided up by geography. Each team is comprised of at least two veterans' law judges, staff attorneys and clerical staff. The BVA consists of 14 veteran's law judges (including two chief veterans' law judges) and at least 55-60 staff attorneys, some of whom have 20-25 years of legal experience. Each veteran's law judge is assigned four or five staff attorneys who have varying degrees of experience. The duty of a staff attorney is to review the claim and draft a decision for a veteran's law judge to proof and sign.

The Board of Veterans Appeals reviews the rating decision rendered at the regional office level looking for errors in fact or law. Because it is not a finder of fact, the board must rely on the record established at the rating board level. Thus, frequently the rights of veterans are lost because no legal assistance was available initially.

The Board of Veterans Appeals allowance rate between FY 1982 and FY 1991 ranged between 12.8 and 14.4 percent. That rate rose with judicial review to 20.8 percent in 2005. The remand rate back to the VA regional office is much higher. It was as high as 48.8 percent after passage of the Veterans Claims Assistance act of 2000, which broadened the VA's affirmative duty to assist the veteran in the development of his claim. But remanding back to the VA regional office causes even more delay. In most instances the whole process will be delayed for months, if not years, if such an event occurs.

If after filing an appeal with the Board of Veterans Appeals, the veteran or his lay advocate submits a newly discovered material piece of evidence, the veteran will lose any back benefits he might have received had the claim been adjudicated in his favor *solely on the basis of evidence presented when the initial claim was filed. Of course, had the $10 limitation fee not essentially barred the veteran from obtaining legal assistance in preparing the initial claim, key material that weighed in the veteran's favor probably would have been presented initially?*

Indeed, veterans are at a distinct disadvantage until after a final decision is rendered by the Board of Veterans Appeals. It is only after that time that they can hire an attorney for a reasonable fee.

It is my hope that the student involvement in a permanent veteran's law clinic will help veterans seeking legal assistance with their claims." See op-ed, Craig M. Kabatchnick, Greensboro News & Record, October 29, 2006

Recommendation(s):

1. Reduce the C&P (VBA) arm of the VA to caretaker strength.
    a. 57 Regional Offices
    b. BVA
2. Award C&P requested by veterans with valid DD 214s and supported IME and two or more certified lay statements.
3. IMEs will become the Standard Bearer for the veterans C&P
4. IMEs will be paid their going rate – Procedure to be work by smart finance people.
    a. Hire 10,000 IME doctors
    b. Because of the tens of thousands of case files awaiting decisions transfer those files to an IME for finalization.
5. Exercise a one-year BETA test.
6. 2003 GAO report on VBA personal needs to be seriously re-read and analyzed for another direction to do business for the veterans.
http://www.gao.gov/new.items/d03452t.pdf
7. All ROs and scaled down BVA will have access to all IME on the pay roles. All ROs, BVA and IMEs will be electronically connected with 24/7 capabilities for anyone - anywhere.
8. A veteran with an open claim must have access to their, ROs and BVA files and interaction capability.
9. At the outside, a valid claim should be in the new VBA channels no more then six months.

How to implement these recommendations… DO NOT FORM A STUDY GROUP OR TASK FORCE OR HOLD TRADITIONAL Government style MEETINGS!!(Remember the dead horse). Send this paper to all ROs, VA headquarters, VBA, OIG, Budget Office, and any "Deciders" I can't remember, and make sure there are some financial (budgetary) smart people involved. Have this paper staffed amongst the "deciders", hold a video-conference of 1-3 deciders from each office that are authorized to make decisions and talk to each of these items of concern in this paper, i.e. RO Action Officers, apathy, low grade deciders, inexperience, IMEs, staffing procedures, etc.. Send final decisions to the Director of the VA, Congress and Cabinet members. Set realistic due-dates and expect final decision(s) within three months. Have all "Deciders" chop (approve) the charts produced by the **CHALLENGE** in the following pages.

Who will be the "Deciders" under the new IME program?

1. RO buildings and staff will be no more then one floor of now leased multi storied building and a total staff of no more then 21(plus administrative staff) will be required (1-GS 15, 4-GS 14s, 8-GS 13s and 8 GS 12s) – This personnel configuration will be different for each RO because of demographics.

2. The one GS 15 in each RO will be its "Decider"

3. The BVA will be no more then 9. Supervision and "Decider" of 1 SES V with 8-GS 15 (one per time zones within the lower 48 and 1 each GS13 for Alaska, Hawaii, Guam, Philippines and Puerto Rico)

REASONING:

1. The VBA numbers just do not lie. They tell a sad story of many good people thrashing around trying to make do and make a sick system workable but in 50 years it just isn't happening. It is time to bite the bullet and go in another direction (see brass monkey theory). If the VBA was rated against its own criterion it would be 130% disabled.

2. Statement of James P. Terry, Chairman, Board of Veterans' Appeals before the Committee on Veterans' Affairs, United States Senate July 13, 2006 where he testified saying: *"...Other factors that may affect the increase in appeals to the Veterans Court are not so readily quantifiable. There is a heightened awareness among veterans of their access to the judicial process. It appears that veterans have become increasingly knowledgeable about their right to appeal to the Veterans Court and are increasingly willing to avail themselves of that right."* He continued by saying; *"These changes would affect cases that have already been filed. As noted earlier, however, the sheer number of potentially appealable decisions from the Board of Veterans' Appeals is staggering. The problem of backlogs will be a theme that continues into the future, unless steps are taken to meaningfully reduce the actual number of appeals or to employ an expeditious means to dispose of them."*

3. Our government has been thrashing around with this problem since 1953 with no solid solutions in sight. Wasted cost: Unknown but has to be in the hundreds of billions.

4. Veterans do not deserve having to beg for their rightful due.

5. C&P staffs or another name is VBA range from a bit over 600 for California to the Philippines's 78 so total numbers of GS employees look to be in the 8,250 range. These numbers need not be RIFed (fired) but absorbed into the 1.9 million (or 15.4 million – depending on which chart you reference) federal full-time civilian work force. This alone saves over $200,000,000 annual VA budget dollars.

131

6. Our VBA system is broken, there are honest people trying to do the honest and honorable things for the veterans but visible actions are similar to nailing jell-O to the wall.

7. C&P awards will initially increase but only proportional to the current back-logged claims.

8. New claims will not increase as the veteran has never accepted anything they did not earn.

9. Some pain now will save major pain down the road.

10. The present system simply does not work. Yes the system keeps lots of people employed and yes it works "sometime" but not all the time as it was designed over fifty years ago. The VA and VBA have enough band ads already so it is time to try something else. LET'S TRY IMEs. What do we have to lose?

11. The VBA said in 2001, *"...Through the assembly, assessment and interpretation of historical participation and performance data, VBA can reasonably construct decision-making models that utilize knowledge gained from the past."* The 2001 BVA structure has exponentially decomposed itself. NOTHING has changed for the better! It is time to change!

12. The new VBA system will sure make long-range-budget (5 year) planning a lot easier, smarter and reliable.

POSSIBLE SHORTFALLS:

1. Initially, a shortage of IME qualified doctors.

2. Bricking at the highest levels within government as to who finally came up with THE solution that works by saving budget dollars and making 20 million veterans content in the knowledge their country finally acknowledged their sacrifices. George and Abe would be proud.

IF YOU HAD YOUR *"WHAT IFs..."* as a veteran which would you choose?

1. ...being awarded just compensation would be no worst then what is promised.

2. ...your widow did not have to apply for your C&P.

3. ..."Request" to "Approval" would be only three months and not 10 years.

4. ...there actually is a "genie" that granted wishes, and it gave you two?

5. ...keep what we have. What If Congress changed the VBA and it got WORSE?

EPILOGUE:

The Constitution of the United States, Amendment 1, and The Bill of Rights has given you a voice and a genie has given you two wishes. Now.... Use them.

EXPECTATIONS:

FACTS: *Abraham Lincoln in 1862 proposed to his congress and the people of the Union (North and South) that to stop the looming civil war the federal government would pay each state $400 per head for each slave and then the state would have 20 or more years to come up with legislation to abolish slavery (The reason for our 1861-1865 civil war), the estimated cost was $173,048,000 (1862 dollars). The actual cost of the civil war was 5,233,000 dead and wounded and >3,000,000,000 (2 million per day) 1862 dollars. Afghanistan and Iraq is costing >3Billion per week and just under 4,000 young American military lives as of the fist of March 2008. There is no way to determine civilian causalities. Only history will determine what happens to our veterans and our wars.* ***I am NOT optimistic. See page 130 for the modern day Lincoln thinking!!***

txe CXALLeNGe: for the VA and VBA – Give your VBA an honest test! Not the congressional White Paper "numbers", finger pointing report, "we know the problems and working it", meeting after meeting till the numbers seem 'manageable' - but a HONEST look at the NUMBERS and people.

RECOMMENDED PROCEDURE:
a. Select 4 people (two will be ladies, two will be male. Age needs to be greater then 50 except for the GS5 or 7 – A civilian, A veteran, A GS5 or 7 RO Action Officer, A GS14 VBA manager
b. Make four charts:
1. Dollars v. time spent on existing VBA procedures – use 100 to 300 random claims.
2. Using the same sampled claims – grant (approve) the claims as submitted. This is the one of interest as I feel the numbers will show the process will be cheaper and more efficient in the long run by automatically granting of claims rather then beating the claim to death until it matches the arbitrary numbers of a regulation. ***By the time you save all the middle processing dollars caused by "people- handles", re-handling, massaging, the claim pays for itself.***
* Read through the claim, if it sounds honest, logical, either within your present guidelines or close and your gut tells you compensation is needed / warranted, and then grant. If claims have accompanying LAY

statements read them to get a feel (another gut reaction) if the words are honest. Put yourself in their shoes as if you were asking for C&P then ask yourself, "Do I deserve what I am asking my government for?" A real veteran with 'needs' will never lie about that.

    3. IME – using an average of $2,000 per IME times the sampled claims will be a line on the dollars chart.

    4. Compute for how long? Assuming the average life spans for a veteran as:

    aa. Female = 73 years

    bb. Male = 66 years

Five years has been taken off the National averages simply because of wear and tear of the military on the human body.

c. Challenge to be completed within one month.

d. Publish honest findings on the Internet.

e. This same procedure can be repeated for 1,000 and 10,000 claims as time permits, but the bottom line will show proportionally huge savings in manpower and budget dollars as we move away from multi-layered bureaucracy to serving our veterans.

I strongly suspect your numbers will show the VBA is too large, inefficient and not a lot different then most any government organization.

If I am wrong and the numbers show you (VBA) are doing the absolute best you can under the circumstances and I have wasted your time with this paper then name your prize you require of me and I will do it.

I was further disappointed this week after I asked the VA if they would like to comment on this paper: *They said NO*. On 27 November 2006 M. Marsh, Veterans Service Center Manager said "No, we do not want to make a comment on your article."

Thank you for staying with me throughout this hard-to-read story…. But there just was no easy way to say… "We need to help our veterans"

This is ALL the Veterans are asking for…

Daddy, I want to...

Many of us owe much to nurses...

Dedication of nurses (RNs).... reg•is•tered nurse (rĕj'ĭ-stərd) n.
(Abbr. RN, R.N.) A nurse who has graduated from an accredited school of nursing and
has been registered and licensed to practice by a state authority.

Korea is known as "The Land of the Morning Calm."

This morning as I stood in my back yard, coffee in hand, watching the Eastern sky turn

from black to gray to misty grays to streaks of
burnt orange to red back to orange to finally
streaks of grays to blues I pictured myself
back in the Far East. The cool morning was
void of all sounds and as my coffee cooled the
far shore tree line began to take shape against
a clearing horizon. A huge Blue Heron flew
past me at eye level; neck extended looking
more pre-historic then modern day hungry and
looking for breakfast.

For no apparent reason, I was thinking about Linda.

When your body needs mending or a part repaired, an SNU sometimes comes to mind.
Survivability is mostly 100% but it all depends on your attitude and your nurse.

Recently an article on the Internet said of a newly opened medical unit, "The new 14-bed
Skilled Nursing-Care Unit (SNU) provides post-hospital care and a full range of
rehabilitative services for patients who are not yet able to care for themselves at home.
The focus is to help patients regain their strength so that they can return to their own
homes quickly and be self-sufficient." Those are seemingly cold words that convey a
message of need and where to find it and what is available. The message may be chilly
but the nursing you receive is warm-hearted and professional.

If you have ever had the opportunity or necessity to be an SNU patient I am sure you are
silently nodding your head remembering the experiences.

If not and you are still very young, healthy and have all your parts in working order, sit
back with your older friends that have been there, and enjoy this ride.

Three short years ago I experienced chemotherapy, radiations, an array of experimental
drugs, several surgeries and some fairly rough emotional times when I was looking at my

own mortality. "You have cancer." The words still rattle around in my subconscious during the wee hours of cold mornings as lights flash in heavy REM or lying awake looking at a dark ceiling trying to make sense of what my body was doing. This mortality-thing is not the kind of demise you have any control over like when facing an enemy in a World War, a Vietnam, Panama, Bosnia, Afghanistan, and Iraq, Watt's district in LA or politicians in Washington DC but "Natures Mortality". In a war zone there are certain things you can do to stay alive. Duck, cover, shoot first, have more ammo then the bad guys comes to mind. Nature is not that exact, pristine or predictable. Nature, like science has its own set of rules. 'All living things will die' comes to mind as does 'you can't fool mother nature', but when you are young and indestructible bullets and shrapnel can be avoided but with each passing birthday Nature and military caused physical problems gets a better foot-hold on your body parts.

'What, me worry?' That kind of thing always happens 'to the other guy' so I never gave it serious thought until folks started calling me "Sir" but when my doctor used the word "hospice", my blood turned icy cold.

But, death and dying is not what my mind is telling me this morning. It is telling me about life and the many people that help us keep the life we have, and even make it better; a wife/husband/friend to share a smile; your worries; and how best to enjoy broccoli; a baby(s) to love and rear and spends your life's saving. Some children make our life a bit better, some not, but the fact is for better or worse and whether the car is running smoothly, the bank account is anemic or the garden needs weeding, we keep breathing and it's all because of medicine and…:

Nurses.

"God bless um…"

Nurses come in all ages, sizes, shapes, sex, age groups, ethic backgrounds and personalities. I once had one tell me she was 'in shape'… "Pear is a shape."

When you have to spend time as an in-patient of any hospital you see nursing is not just waking you at 0400 to give you a sleeping pill or someone putting a few gallons of your blood in those little-bitty glass tubes or scheduling an appointment after decrypting a doctor's scroll or garbled verbal instructions. Nursing is hard work and hustling from one blinking call-light to others and normally in a fast gait.

Laying in your uncomfortable rubber protected hospital bed, your drugs wearing off and your back-side exposed, you see; nursing is not a 9 to 5 job; is not a profession where you can function by rote; or nursing is many times not a safe in-door, air-conditioned profession.

My sister was a mother, homemaker and a nurse (RN) that specialized working the psychiatric patients and drug dependent. She died from an overdose of drugs at the age of 48 alone in a one bed-room Houston apartment and wasn't missed for two weeks.

A cousin had just graduated nursing school and was into her second week carrying bed pans when she was strangled to death by a patient recovering from a simple gall-bladder procedure one early morning. It was learned later Mr. Gall bladder had been hallucinating from excess pain contributed by a two-week on-set of hic-cups.

My mother's sister was a mother, homemaker and a surgical nurse. She was approaching retirement age when she tripped on artificial grass breaking her neck falling into a six-foot deep hole while attending her husband's funeral.

Then there was my dad's sister who was a mother, homemaker and nurse that specialized in Skilled Nursing Units. As of yesterday morning she is 93, spry and from what we hear from the household handyman, "....active".

Of the 2,909,467 active nurses we have in just these Unites States, I'm sure there are close to 3 Million stories of love, hate, violence, compassion and sacrifice. This is but one of those *sharp* stories.

If the above image is fuzzy... that's a needle...!!

One thing I do know about nurses is they do not go into the profession for the money or job security. If those were the only goals all you have to do is work for the U.S. Government, show up for work, sometimes, and that would put you into the $85k to $100k pay bracket and... it takes an act of congress to be fired.

As a race we Americans are self-centered, we can not see passed our incomes, our family, and our own mortality. I often thought I was one of those storied ugly-Americans, until I met Nurse Linda.

Linda is your average American woman. B's and C's in high school, mostly 2.3 to 2.6 in college before switching to the School of Nursing and a 3.8 GPA.

During her third semester in college a reading assignment about nurse and fore-bearer Florence Nightingale was profound. Linda described Ms. Nightingale as

137

her 'calling' of hearing the voice of God calling her to do his work. For Linda, she must have heard the same words as they became the lynch-pin that rattled around in her head ever time she saw posters or ads calling for or describing "Nursing".

Linda may have inherited come of her nursing genes. Marie, Linda's mother had a World War II recruiting poster in her attic that she would unroll sometimes and tell stories about her military service in France in field hospitals during the last years of the war in 1944-45 and occupied German two years after V-E Day. Marie had been a beautiful young lady, married a young medical captain shortly after the war when she was stationed at occupied Landstuhl. Marie had been one of only six WWII nurses to have been awarded the Bronze Star for Valor. Marie never talked about it to Linda but the blue military awards box that is home to the bright red, white and blue striped ribbon with attached golden star is nestled in the attic trunk under now yellowed and brittle rolled paper wall posters.

Sometimes after a few cocktails Marie would talk about nursing and 'back then' when RNs worn pristine white uniforms, white starched caps bobby-pined on the back of freshly combed and managed hair and always smiling. In the military a 'rank' or 'pay-grade' is shown as sleeve chevrons for the enlisted and bars, leafs, eagles or stars for officials. Nurse's caps use to have black bands of ribbon on their caps with differently widths to show 'rank' or seniority. Multicolored and multi pin-ed smocks have taken the

place of all-whites and the starched caps are next to WWII posters. Now the all visible stethoscope hangs on necks designating medical person.

Times have changed a bit as we now have PCs that can fit into your pocket, automobiles without fins and cell phones stuck in every ear incurring instant and constant communication. I can't remember the last public pay phone I saw, but I will always remember Linda.

June 1985 Linda's parent's home in Houston was the reunion site for the WWII 352nd Field Hospital staff, and what a reunion it was! The 40th reunion's rank and file showed signs of thinning as only 33 original war staff members show up but 214 "past patients" were front-N-center. The partying patients had lost limbs, sight, had suffered severe mental problems but the 352nd and it medical staff had kept them alive. Many are now productive politicians (now that is an oxymoron if there ever was one), professional people, family members and a few writers. Young Linda would be 16 come that October and this reunion would be remembered in her early college days. At sweet and innocent 16 Theories and Concepts of Nursing, Pharmacology, mental health, Pediatric, Clinical decision making and Pathophysiologic Process's were the furthest thing from her mind.

ARLEE

Boys and pajama parties were the order of the day, but that was yesterday.

Today Linda and all the 'Linda's' that care are professionals that have dedicated their lives to others and their well being. Linda is now sick and looking at her own mortality, but still works 12-14 days in a SNU. Less then 100 yards from her SNU duty-station is her treatment station were ever 21 days she reports for chemotherapy. On her way home after exhausting days she stops at a wig store before stopping at Wal-Mart and her favorite butcher shop for a deserved filet.

Tomorrow is another day, the same but different.

I have been Linda's patient for the last few days and it is because of Linda, her constant smile and positive attitude I was released to go home - early.

You see, Linda is special. She is close to middle-aged, nice looking, a nurse and she is bald.

Chemotherapy kills white blood cells, 'all' hair follicles and hopefully the bad cancerous rogue cancer cells.

Linda has stomach cancer.

As I was walking out of the SNU last evening my five-year old grand-daughter looking at the stars and full moon said in the hospital parking lot, "Daddy... when I grow up I want to be a nurse just like Ms. Linda."

There was a tear in my eye as my emotions squeezed my heart.

EPILOG:
1. The highest level of preparation for an estimated 17.5 percent of RNs (510,209) is a diploma; for an estimated 33.7 percent (981,238) the highest preparation is an associate degree; for 34.2 percent (994,240) it is a baccalaureate degree; and for 13.0 percent (377,046) it is a master's or doctoral degree.
2. 5.7% are male.
3. 81.8 percent of the RN are white or non-Hispanic
4. The actual average annual earnings of RNs employed full-time in 2006 were $57,784 which appears to be an increase from average earnings in 2000 ($46,782).
5. Nursing has high burnout and dropout rates. Nearly 20 percent of all licensed registered nurses have left active nursing. For nurses trying to combine working and raising a family, the widespread hospital practice of mandatory overtime imposes a particular burden.

6. America's hospitals are hurting for nurses—a fact of life, new studies warn, that may have deadly consequences for some of their patients. Nationwide, more than 126,000 hospital nursing positions are unfilled (one of every eight), placing patients at a higher risk

For further information on these wonderful people log into:
http://bhpr.hrsa.gov/healthworkforce/reports/rnpopulation/preliminaryfindings.htm

Should I turn Right or Left?

Being retired military I was asked the other day what I thought about youth today going into the military - I gave a short, terse NO answer, then thought maybe I should expand that no is the reason for this *story*. Before making any kind of life altering commitment I have always felt it best to know all I could about the subject and talk to all the *experts* as I could. Never make decisions alone in a closet.

President Bush once said and I feel it worth repeating "We're in a fight for our principles and our first responsibility is to live by them", I agree.

2,346 years before Bush a Greek philosopher named Aristotle said, "Young people are in a condition like permanent intoxication, because youth is sweet and they are growing." Again, I agree.

Because I agree with both men, I had to write this short story.

People long ago stopped asking my advice or even how I feel toward different subjects because they learned I usually told them the truth or how I truly feel about a subject. Why? Because I have found it is much easier telling the truth then trying to remember a lie. Within limits, I speak my mind, especially when someone I know is about to make a life altering decision. I have always believed that those kinds of decisions should be made after knowing ALL the facts and from as many perspectives as possible.

DISCLAMER: This story and comments are from my experiences and as seen through my eyes from a lifetime of living in or around military communities. One of my hero's is Mark Twain and he once said "I have a higher and grander standard of principle than George Washington. He could not lie; I can, but I won't." Neither do I.

I need to start at a point we are all comfortable, so why not define Career vs. a Job: Prior to the mid 1970's when our government did away with the Military Draft and turned entirely to an all-volunteer military force *career* meant *lifer*. In those days the lifer's intent was to stay in the military as long as possible doing as little as possible while others did the heavy lifting but he still receives a monthly pay check. That concept changed as the lifers died off and the military ranks began filling with youth looking for adventure and some *life experiences* and of course, at government expense and '...all-paid world-travel' would be nice.

A job is flipping burgers or any position where your name is embroidered on your shirt.

For the purpose of this story a *career* is not meant to be ...*a life-time commitment* but we are merely talking about the next couple three or maybe four years, a change of pace, or a place to *find yourself.* Some would even say "...taking time off from school to see what the world is really all about." For the sake of this story we will be talking about 18 year olds that do not know their butt from third base about the world and how it works. This story will try to be gender-neutral as at 18 there is not a lot of difference between boys and girls. OK – right there I'm wrong. One has breast and the other has raging hormones. OK – wrong again. Girls and boys have the same raging hormones but in today's world you only hear about the boys.

Following WWII president H.S. Truman pushed the military to integrate itself and by the time the draft ended so did 'only white males' in its ranks. If you have ever been in the Pentagon in Washington DC you probable noticed there were twice as many restrooms as needed. The reason is because the building was put up during WWII (1943) when blacks and whites were still very much segregated.

Before enlisting in the military please take a few minutes and completely read this story AND especially Rule Eleven.

Rule one: Girls are just as sexually oriented as her counterpart. Am I being sexist making this kind of statement in the context of the military? I hope not - but with the military ranks now filling with females and it is known facts their sexual drives are equal to all humans so it might not be a bad idea to address it here. The bastions of the Citadel, West Point, Annapolis, etc. have fallen and we are now all equal so this story is not about the girls but about the military and the military rules seldom differentiates genders, as does shrapnel.

Rule Two: For the sake of argument the age 18 as used here can mean anywhere from 17 to 30.

Girls and boys at 18 generally know only what they see on television, what they hear/see at home from parents and maybe a few high school classes where all experiences were from a text book. Those few things they may learn from each other is simply the swapping of bodily fluids. Depending on the programming they watch on television will tend to bend a viewpoint. For example, Fox news Bill O'Reilly's segment is advertised as "The No-Spin Zone". Traveling the world I have yet seen that to be true as there is no such thing as "no-spin", everyone puts their own spin on any subject.

Rule Three: Everyone is bias. That's not all bad, it just says everyone has their own view of the world and what they see.

Before reading further you should know where I am coming from; Born in the USA in a southern state; graduated college in the late 1950s and because the draft was in place enlisted in the military at 22; in my 20 year military career I lived in France, Germany, Korea and sunny Vietnam; I vacationed in Italy, Spain, Holland & Thailand; I skied the slopes of Austria; swan the warm waters of the Mediterranean; smelled the tulips in Holland; tried to prop the leaning tower of Pisa to the vertical, several times; witnessed glass-blowing and held my nose in Venezia; rooted for the bulls in Spain and camped out in the Louvre and on Rue Pigalle in Paris for 48 straight week-ends. During this same time frame I would see visitors from around the world trying to see all of Paris in one week and there I was 23 and living there; I truly enjoyed the co-ed saunas in Berlin; lost all bashfulness in the unisex restrooms of Europe; feed elephants in Bangkok; froze my buns in Korea; hated civilian contractor working for the military; and killed the enemy in Vietnam. I have been terrified for my life many times and truly hated to kill but that was in my military job description. See the small print on page two of your enlistment agreement "...follow orders..." That means some days you may have to either throw yourself on that grenade or kill the guy before he throws it. In my mind it was an easy choose.

My intent when I enlisted was to serve my three years mandated by my government for universal military training (the draft) and return home to Texas. My problem came when at the end of my third year I was stationed and living in Paris and the military gave me the preference of staying in the City of Lights and Free Love or going home to Texas. To stay I would have to re-enlist (give the military another three years). I was in my mid-twenties, what would you have done?

The military is not ALL bad..... Where else can you be guaranteed a job and monthly income, have only olive-drab or camouflage clothing in your closet along with spit-shined black low-quarter shoes and three sets of boots; three meals a day, a place to live, a company of others to keep you company, and not really know what tomorrow would bring? If you make it to a 20 year retirement, you receive half your base pay for life, have hospital and medical privileges for life and can have the military fit your prosthesis at most any Veterans Administration (VA) hospitals. Because of your job description "your natural life" may be foreshortened by many years but when you enlist you agree to this possibility. Pay depends on your rank. First year enlistees receive $1273.00 monthly and at a 20 year retirement that number is roughly $3516. As an officer (with your college degree) first year monthly pay is $2416 and at 20 is roughly $7003.00. There are monies tacked on to that monthly pay for 'quarters allowance', 'separate rations', clothing allowance', 'proficiency pay', combat pay, etc. that can add another $800 or so but retirement is based solely on base pay. See http://www.us-army-info.com/pages/ranks.html

Rule Four: As in civilian life you can be most anything in the military that ambitions, drive, motivation and education will take you. The military is made up of three classes; Enlisted (E1-9), Warrant Officers (W1-5) and Officers (O1-10). Enlisted are the "doers" and backbone of the military; Warrants are the Technicians and Officers are your administrators/supervisors/managers. Everyone has a "boss" and as many of my military friends will point out.... "Shit always rolls down hill" so always try to be *'up'* the hill.

Rule Five: No matter what you are promised before being sworn into any branch of the military you CAN NOT be an officer without a college degree.

Rule Six: Promotions are more time-oriented then demonstrated proficiently. "Time-in-grade" is paramount. While on the subject of promotions there are several sets of rules the military uses; enlisted grades pretty much will guarantee you an E-7 rating in 20 years if you keep your nose clean; officers are a bit different – for example if you are "passed-over" for promotion twice you will not be allowed to remain on active duty. Being passed over can be easier then you would think. All you need is having a bad or even a mediocre (a tad less then perfect) efficiency report. Unlike enlisted personnel you can be an average to good officer looking at normal retirement and be told you must leave the service. Weight and physical conditioning carries the same conditions – all military personnel must pass a yearly physical examination and if body fat gets out of control and your test scores do not meet the minimum, you are discharged. That is the bad news, the good news is "minimum" scores are normally well within reach if you have a "normal" body.

Rule Seven: Before enlisting, if promised a military producing MOS (Military Occupational Specialty) school following basic and advanced basic training, you will attend whatever school you selected: mechanic; armor, artillery, infantry, aircraft weaponry, medical, computers, signal, etc...etc...The last I looked there were around 620 MOS's in over 20 disciplines in the Army. As best I can figure, the Air Force has around 174 "Air Force Specialty Codes" while the Navy has something over 200 "Navy Enlisted Classifications". BUT now hear this...the military contract you enlisted for ends at graduation of that school. Further assignments for all services depend on the military's need for your MOS or Specialty codes or Classification skills. You asked for an assignment in Hawaii but they need you in Alaska. Pack your long underwear. Close your mouth. I have seen this happen to not only myself but every warm body in the military. Why do you think I went to Korea?

A brief word on Basic Training. Depending on your MOS, basic training is from six to twelve weeks of hell. The old saying about the more you sweat in training the less you bleed in combat is true. If you saw the movie GI Jane with Demi Moore will give you some insight. Her training was for the elite Navy Seals but normal basic is close.

A recruiter friend told me this a few years back and it stayed with me. "Regardless of what your recruiter told you, being a member of the United States Armed Forces is not just like having a civilian job. You need to understand this right down to your toes before you sign that contract and take that oath. In the military, there will ALWAYS be someone telling you what to do, when to do it and how to do it -- and you've got to do it. Sometimes they'll tell you to do something that you don't want to do, or tell you in a way that makes you angry. Failing to do it is not an option. The willful disobeying of a lawful order won't just get you "fired," as it would in a civilian occupation, it can get you sent to jail."

Rule Eight: You can serve your enlisted time and return to the civilian world or re-enlist each 3, 4 or 6 years until the minimum required for retirement of 20 active years. Under special considerations you may be allowed to be released earlier, say at 15 years but that is not your full-fledged all-benefits retirement. You pay a price for the early out. Some that do find a home in the military will stay active long passed their 20 but 30 years is mandatory retirement. Retired pay passed 20 is calculated in two year increment but once at 26 years retirement pay of 75% of your retired base pay tops out.

Once you "sign-up" can you get out before serving the number of years you agreed to? Tough but you need to know the consequences; There are three discharges that can be given administratively - honorable, general under honorable conditions, and other-than-honorable. There are two that can be given at a court-martial (trial) - bad conduct and dishonorable. An honorable discharge is exactly that "You served with distinction and honorable – you are a good person". Generally, the other-than-honorable, bad conduct, and dishonorable will all preclude reenlisting, and most will prevent or inhibit future civilian employment. Every job application form asked if you had military experiences and they ALL ask type discharge received. If you are in the position to hire someone, would you take a dishonorable or bad-conduct person?

Rule Nine: Soldiers are second class citizens. There will be lots of disagreement to this statement but that is what I have seen. An example is coming home after a full combat tour in Vietnam and having to take off the uniform before being allowed out of an air terminal or the guard units returning from Iraq and not having their jobs waiting.

Rule Ten: Sometime during your enlistment if you are female chances are you will be sexually harassed either by deed, word or innuendo. If you are pretty or nice-looking and/or have heavy breasts you can count on it – learn to live with it. Confucius said in 473 B.C. and is true today, "Respect yourself and others will respect you."

The military is not a garden party but a life and death career where in the history of wars fought by the United States people die. Dating from the revolutionary war of 1775 .02% of our soldiers have died and over 30% were casualties of one sort or other. If the .02 number doesn't get your attention then said another way 575,185 died of 37,772,566 that served or said another way, four complete generations in only two centuries of warfare. Very few of us who have served or serving now will or have escape with a whole body. The bulk of these causality numbers are male but bullets, shrapnel and disease are always gender non-specific. Both male and female in the military are considered "soldiers". That is OK as the military now furnishes maternity clothing to pregnant soldiers. There is that old joke in the navy where 1000 men would put out to sea for a few months and 500 couples would come back. Women are now allowed to serve on all naval shipping so unless men or so inclined there are females around while out to sea - to chat with. The land forces do not allow women in combat units or to hold a combat MOS (i.e. 11B) but women are allowed in combat areas where remember, shrapnel is gender non-specific.

Just to made sure we are on the same sheet of music when talking about war and "fighting"....Fighting is not arm-wrestling, fisticuffs, shouting nasty words... but killing; killing the other guy before he kills you and killing anyway you can using bullets, artillery, IEDs (try not sitting next to a suicide bomber while having tea or your "body parts" will be sponged up by your buddies). War, killing is not pretty and does not smell like a rose garden. Fighting is also sitting at your post with a buddy and his head suddenly explodes because of a sniper round fired from 1000 yards away – and you never hear it. Do you know how far 1000 yards is? Over ten (10) football field lengths or imagine a parking lot 1000 yard wide and your car is parked on one side and you are on the other side. The car would look like a dark burry fuzz ball, if you could see it at all. The next time you listen to news and they are talking about "fighting" you will know the troops are out there killing and trying hard to make it home with all their parts in working order.

Every nation must maintain a ready military as someone out there is always looking to take away those things that belong to you. Following World War II the United States has maintained a strong ready fighting force ready to fight many brush-fire conflicts anywhere in the world. Today the US has 67,742,879 available forces. Of those 471,500 is active duty serving overseas and here at home plus of those 220,000 are frontline forces. Not bad considering we have only a total population of 281 million. One point here is, read the small print of your enlistment contract. If you enlist for two or three years that is not the end of your commitment as after active duty you are committed to reserve time and/or call-back for up to eight or more years.

I hate war. Wars are usually good for the economy but bad for your health. Wars are normally political or politically motivated. Mao Tse-Tung said, *"Politics is war without bloodshed while war is politics with bloodshed."* The United States has always defended itself against aggression and Iraq is the only war we have initiated. Some will argue without 911 we would not be at war "against Terrorizes" while others will say, and rightfully so, Americans are notorious for being patriotic and fighting for a cause. Senator Barbara Boxer said "Iraq was a war of choice, not necessity." Having said that, Sun Tzu said in 450 B.C "All warfare is based on deception."

Unlike wars of yesteryear when opposing forces would form battle line facing each other only a few dozen yards apart and begin shooting until the last man was standing or someone with a lick of intelligence retreated. Musket ball ammunition was notoriously inaccurate over 50 yards whereas today .30mm ball ammo from an M-16 will accurately knock the eyes out of a knat at 500 yards; aircraft will kill a target over the horizon and never see it; there is no hiding from the M1A2 Abrams 70 ton main battle tank with it's 120 mm smooth bore computer guided cannon that can move at speeds rivaling NASCAR all the while the navy can pound an area 30 miles inland with large guns and rockets no one can hide from. The US are the good guys but remember your enemy has the same or better capabilities and you too can be on the receiving end of rounds fired that you never hear. Large 120mm mortar rounds however do give you about 3 seconds of warning before impact. Remember shrapnel is not gender or nationality specific.

I often reflect some of the great quotations of history and many have to do with choice.

In the words of *General George S. Patton:* "No bastard ever won a war by dying for his country. He won it by making the other poor dumb bastard die for his country."

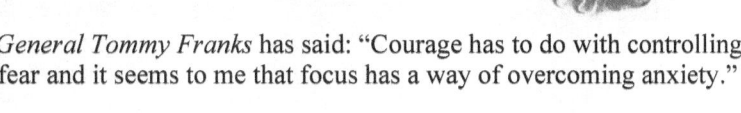

General Tommy Franks has said: "Courage has to do with controlling fear and it seems to me that focus has a way of overcoming anxiety."

147

General Norman Schwarzkopf has said: "Fear will keep you alive in a war. Fear will keep you alive in business. There's nothing wrong with being afraid at all." "Fear tends to cause you to focus, it tends to cause your adrenaline to run, and it tends to cause you to perhaps see things in much, much sharper perspective at that instant." "There's more than one way to look at a problem, and they all may be right." "Somebody's got to do it. And if you don't, who will?"

Secretary of Defense Robert McNamara said in 1995 in his book *In Retrospect:* "We of the Kennedy and Johnson administrations who participated in the decisions on Vietnam acted according to what we thought were the principles and traditions of this nation. We made our decisions in light of those values. Yet we were wrong, terribly wrong. We owe it to future generations to explain why. I truly believe that we made an error not of values and intentions, but of judgment and capabilities." Some believe we are in the same place now with Iraq.

Rule Eleven: What you have just read has been one person's viewpoint and perspective… for others and very definitive viewpoints from what some refer to as "The Horses Mouth" log onto http://www.objector.org/before-you-enlist/myths.html

If you are thinking about a career in the military your time in uniform will be exciting to monotonous to an adrenaline rush experienced by a very few, kinda like flying, ….hours of shear boredom and moments of pure terror…. What you will NOT get out of the military is wealth or even a good living but if you survive, your closet will be stuffed with memories no one will ever believe and you will sleep well knowing you gave it your all.

Rule Twelve: Following service and for the rest of your life; your eyes will pop open each morning before 0500; you will accomplish more before 0900 then most civilians do all day; you will learn to love SOS; you will

use the phonetic alphabet and the military 24 hour method of telling time and be puzzled why the civilian world doesn't already use them; Your pallet for gourmet foods will become severely restricted and you will tend to eat to 'fill the hole' rather then for 'taste'; sitting at the family dinner table you will always finish your plate first and wonder who will not finish the five-mile run you have planned for everyone...

Rule Thirteen - I saved this rule to be near the last because of all things civilians can not understand about their military, the language used is the hardest to fathom - The military uses all known and many yet un-coined four-letter words and one twelve letter words beginning with 'mother****er'. They exclusively use f*ck in its many forms as a means of expression and feelings in communicating with ALL. The reasoning is not for lack of education (you will see more college graduates in service then you will at most businesses) but is used pretty much the same as writers do when they write at the eighth grade reading level. The military's language is meant to communicate orders and feeling in as a direct method as possible that will be understood by all. For example, if mortar rounds are 'walking' toward your bunker you don't say, "…ok guy, looks like it may be time to relocate as I have a feeling they seem to have our range…" You say with explicit tone and volume, "…shit... move your asses! Let's get the fuck out of here!!!" These expressions are not easily turned on and off so these terminologies tend to stay in place – the words are not meant to be offense to anyone - just communication to the many. The next time you hit your thumb with a hammer listen to what comes out of your mouth. Will it be "Ooooh shucks" or ".#%$^&(*()*&%^." ??

Rule fourteen: SEX. I have tried to stay away from this rule as there is no clear cut yes or no answer or advice. Sex in the military is no more prevalent then on any college campus or civilian work place. Some folks might argue with male and females thrown together in a combat area, sex would be rampant. Not true. The boys and girls have sex yes, but it by no means 'rampant' where the ladies need fear for their virtue at all hours of

DON'T BE IMPATIENT, MABEL, I'LL LET YA SEE THE FINISH!

the day and night. Why isn't there lots of sex between soldiers in a combat situation? Simple answer and easily understood for those of us that have been in combat. You are usually too tired and too dirty and you have other priorities then having an orgasm. Combat and combat areas your main concern is staying alive and keeping your buddies alive. You can have all the sex you can handle on R&R or when you get back to CONUS (Continental US – the States). The military awards all kind of medals (awards and decorations) for many things (heroism, valor, campaigns, good conduct, unit citations, service in specific theaters, etc.) but they give no awards for sexual activity – not even an 'At-A-Boy'. If you have a daughter going into the military don't worry about her. Just because there may be 500 males for each female doesn't make your daughter any more vulnerable then an office with 50 males per female or any campus where both males and females 'keep score'.

"Where so ever you go, go with all your heart" said Confucius in 551B.C. And don't forget my friend Mark Twain that said, "Don't go around saying the world owes you a living. The world owes you nothing. It was here first.

Rule Fifteen: "Only the dead have seen the end of war" - Plato – 334 BCE

Now…do you turn right or turn left? Choose.

Brenda, Snuffy and the Computer Store

What do you do and where do you go when your computer hic-cups?

The year is 1941 and you have a need to feel power. Most likely you went roaring down Route 66 better then 100 mph in your dad's 1936 Mercury coupe or enlisted in the military to fight against the evil Axis powers.

In 1950 with that same need for power you most likely borrowed your dad's 1949 Ford big-block V8 and tried out route 66 again.

In 1960 – 1970s you taught your kids about love, honor, money, power and God and Country and they enlisted in the military to fight communism in sunny Vietnam.

1980s you traded stocks and bonds but the exhilaration of losing your money was not the feel of power you expected.

1990s you hired illegal field hands and the feel of power partially returned.

At the turn of the 21st century you master your computer by learning the word "boot" meant something other then footwear and "crash" and "freeze" meant a feeling of helpfulness, but you can now use MS Word and Excel programs as power was again in your grasp.

Have you again reached your pinnacle of gratification for power? Not yet.

The year is now 2008 and the adrenaline rush in your soul is bursting from your finger tips as you again feel the need for power - but where is it?

If you could have your druthers, would you druther have; your groceries manually checked with guaranteed errors; air traffic controllers looking out a window to control your landing; weather people wetting a finger and holding it outside to predict the weather or having to re-learn your math tables or having a calculator handy?

Smart computer people have given us our druthers... and much more.

It is difficult to imagine counting without numbers, but there was a time when written numbers did not exist. The earliest counting device was the human hand and its fingers. Then, as larger quantities (larger than ten human-fingers could represent) were counted, various natural items like pebbles and twigs were used to help count.

Merchants who traded goods not only needed a way to count goods they bought and sold, but also to calculate the cost of those goods. Until numbers were invented, counting devices were used to make everyday calculations. *Just above is a Motherboard – I have been known to call it by its other name...*

In today's world of milk-and-honey we have large numbers and a real need to monitor. Smart people have given us the means to do just that. They started us slowly with paper and pencils then calculators and now - computers. It use to take several minutes to add a long column of numbers then divide that total by another number then check those totals up and down then sideways and more times then not those numbers would not accurately total. When adding the same column three times and getting three different answers you kinda knew the brain was not listening to your pleas. A truism of math is that the same column of numbers will add the same top-down as it does from bottom-up. During the early hours of a work day that is correct but later in the afternoon that truism doesn't always work. Calculators and computers do not have that fallacy. When calculators were conceived their main function was to handle numbers and especially 1s and 0s and now they do that very nicely as they calculate, compute and advise in a blink of an eye and do it accurately, mornings, noon and night.

Computers are not smart. It's the bright people that make the hardware and software of computers that put them on a like plane with humans.

Computer people are naturally smart and I listen to them – up to a point.

Modern mechanical computers have been around since before WWII when it took a whole floor to house those ten-ton monsters with more wires and connectors then you see in mega-store electrical and hardware departments. Computers as we know them started small then outgrew technology evolving from gargantuan to back sitting in the palm of your hand.

If you look in history you will see computers in use in ancient times in 500 B.C. China when they were called Abacus. Whatever we call them today from PCs to ^%*&# damn things; computers now rule our world and are misunderstood by the masses and only loved and cared for by a hand-full of people, or geeks as we lovingly refer to these very sharp numbers folks.

Geek is not a bad word. Computer folks are mostly nerdy and there are lots of brainy and rich geeks such as Bill Gates. Give me a few billion dollars and you can call me anything you like.

Geeks understand numbers but between their ears they are wired differently then normal folks. They think, play and work in another world. They even have their own language: motherboard, byte, folders, sub-folders, partitions, windows, hard-drives, monitors, wired or remote mouse, notebook, laptops, dialup, wireless, DSL, etc... Now these words are the same as normal folks use but to the geek, the words mean different things. Yesterday if you had told me you had a wired-mouse the picture in my mind would be a four-legged rodent high on moldy cheese and if you had said you had a hard-drive would have pictured to me a difficult journey with vehicle problems along the way. If you had told me your hard-drive crashed I would have pictured your wired mouse wrecking your car.

Education and travel are broadening experiences as is a secondary language. Traveling the world I discovered my second language had to be Computereez. The language is as complex as Chinese, as guttery as German, as romantic as French and is as misunderstood as English, but I am trying.

As a human race we use communication as a way to live, love and survive. Sometimes our communication skills fail and people are left at odds with others. For example when someone says to you, "How are you?" they are not asking a question but is meant mealy as a greeting. Granted, the question is a question but not meant as a question but in the language of greeting it is understood as not asking a question but mealy a way to start a conversation. Remember Bud and Lou? Computer folks are a lot like that. They understand the meanings of many unspoken words.

I told you computer men and women are clever.

This story could easily had been written as a He said – She said or a verbatim discussion between a customer and store owner, but you see that in everyday life and reading about it here would be similar to the last time you did not get your way – or even close to your way. Now if you think having-your-way is the only way, you may consider moving to another planet. That is not the way this world works. We all have our own specialties and things we understand. Our world today has made many of us into Jack-of-all-trades and masters-of-none or as some are referred to as Smart-Asses that given a grain of knowledge think we deserve the Nobel Prize for sophistication. It's called; Give-and-take; Finding the middle ground; or Compromising.

A person's age has everything to do with compromising and it is all because of perspective.

Your typical high-school graduate today doesn't have any clues the combatants in our Revolutionary war, Civil war or WWI of II or even where Korea and Vietnam is located on this blue-marble we call Earth or reason for those wars. We are still struggling with the reasons for Iraq. A world without television or a radio with vacuum tubes is also difficult to believe those things have not always been there. Few of this teen generation know history but they all know their way around a keyboard and fully understand Rap, Bon Jovi and the Boss. They also fully understand computers while anyone older then fifty probable still spell computer with a "K" and are afraid of them.

The spelling "K" comment is tongue-in-cheek and if you have not had a fiftieth birthday you probable do not understand that "afraid" attitude. Under 50 age groups know computers can not bite your finger if you make a mistake or can not advertise to the world their master is an idiot if a wrong key is pressed nor can they do permanent damage to your bank account if you erase your hard-drive, but remember, of the 281 million humans in just North America, 104 million are over 50.

Hard-drive is a geek word that if you think about it, is truly an amazing piece of machinery. First think speed, then vinyl record players or tape player then bytes, then light-speed, then reading. Ready?

I fully understand if I take a hammer and hit a nail as hard as I can I will cause something to happen. I see it, I hear it and sometimes I feel it. What is many times difficult for me to understand is how a small disk revolving up to 7200 RMP (my vinyl record player's speed was 33 and read by a needle) and not having anything in contact with its surface other then a beam of light that "reads". What does that beam of light read? Bytes.

If you are old enough to remember Bud Abbott and Lou Costello you may be trying to see who is playing second base right now rather then understand "Bytes"

I choose not to beat the byte subject to death but just for edification: A byte is the unit most computers use to represent a character such as a letter, number, or typographic symbol (for example, "g", "5", or "?"). A gigabyte (GB) is a measure of computer data storage capacity and is roughly a billion bytes. A gigabyte is two to the 30th power, or 1,073,741,824 in decimal notation. I am not going to even mention Terabytes or Petabytes because in that rarified air even I get a nosebleed.

*Your keyboard is funny sometimes. You know what to do when a message appears on your screen to tell you to "Press any key"? **This is what it means....***
My first computer was equal to the IBM 650 that could hold up to 2000 words. My current computer has a hard-drive capacity of 60GB or said in another way, enough space to hold that first set of encyclopedias which I paid over a $1000, all the 40,000 pictures I

took traveling the world and probably the whole library of congress (I may be stretching that a byte or two but the point is - Huge in a Miniature frame.)

Computer folks understand this.

Circumference 24,902 miles

Have you ever taken a corner in your car going just a bit too fast? Remember what happened? Have you ever chased one of your kids around a corner in your house and didn't slow down before banging into the far wall? Have you…well, you get the idea. Now picture a beam of light traveling at the speed of light (186,272 miles *per second*) moving around inside your hard-drive looking in folders, moving around partitions in many different programs and doing it at light-speed is beyond my comprehension. That beam of light not only finds your data but it displays it onto a screen in a way you can understand. Computer folk understand this and how the whole show works. If the speed-of-light is difficult to understand, picture this; you know a bullet is fast; you know many times your reflexes are quicker then an eye-twitch so just for a frame of reference consider this; If you could get a bullet you fired from a rifle held at shoulder lever to travel at the speed of light and once fired it would not run into mountains or tall building, that bullet would travel the circumference of the world and hit you in the back eight times before you could jump out of its path.

Stop shaking your head, I told you *light speed* was fast.

All computers have built in electric fans to dispense heat - for obvious reasons.

Computer folks understand programs, partitions, folders, upload and download, drivers, HTML, USB, .exe, .dll, .INI, .xls, .doc, .jpg and many, many more.

Hopefully I am bright enough to listen to computer people and sharp enough to understand and learn from them. Everyone has bad days and even on good days I have been known to not listen and not learn. This world is a beautiful place to live and I thank God for the breath in my body, the spring in my step and the taste of honey after a tablespoon of caster-oil.

Now, today when you have a need to feel power, go create new files on your computer. Create new or just move a few hundred thousand of your files from one hard-drive to another. Send them over the Internet to the other side of the world. Move your money, shop for a new automobile, buy a tube of lipstick or rent your forehead on the Internet.

You have the power of the computer at your fingertips.

You can accurately do it and do it in a heart beat, thanks to many smart computer folks.

Computer people are different from most but intelligent in their own way. Listen to your computer people. If Brenda is not always 100% right, she knows what is required and what happens inside Snuffy's computer much better then you or me.

A Typical Motherboard

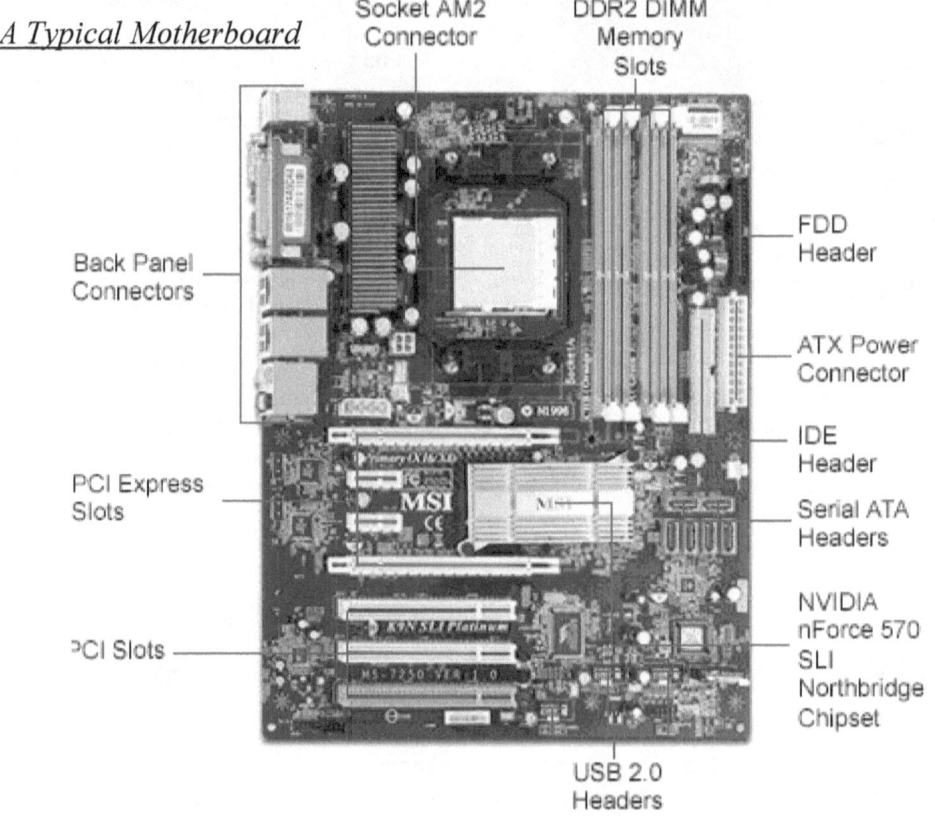

Socket AM2 Connector

DDR2 DIMM Memory Slots

Back Panel Connectors

FDD Header

ATX Power Connector

PCI Express Slots

IDE Header

Serial ATA Headers

PCI Slots

NVIDIA nForce 570 SLI Northbridge Chipset

USB 2.0 Headers

Why Sounds are Important

Sounds, noises are wondrous and meaningful but they also do so much more.

What is sound? Why do I need to know?
What are some of the Laws of Physics?
Why do things wear out?
Why do we have to die? Does sound have anything to do with our dying?

As a youth I did what most boys did growing up in the south; I had summertime jobs, killed time standing on street corners, chased girls (didn't catch many), hung out, thought about college (but not that much), chased girls, hung out at the ice cream parlor during the day and pool hall and the movie theater in the evenings. At this time in my life there were no shopping malls or credit cards and drugs were not on every street corner and alcohol was covered in plain brown bags. It was a time when full-service service stations checked your tires, cleaned your windshield, checked your oil, filled your gas tank

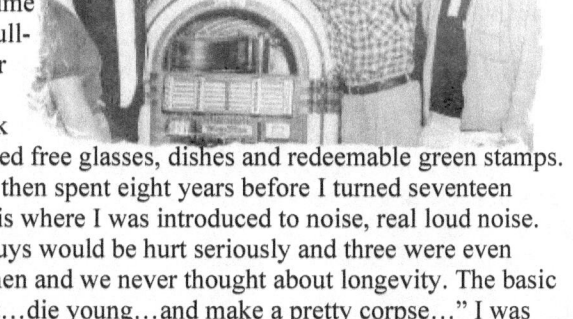

for .29 cents a gallon and you received free glasses, dishes and redeemable green stamps. I worked a bit in oil as a roughneck, then spent eight years before I turned seventeen working in a shotgun sawmill. That is where I was introduced to noise, real loud noise. There were times at the mill when guys would be hurt seriously and three were even killed but that was our way-of-life then and we never thought about longevity. The basic motto of my crowd was, "…live fast…die young…and make a pretty corpse…" I was just a kid during WWII and in college during Korea so I was still naïve when it came to the likes of death and dying as I was still chasing girls and still not catching many. It wasn't until I served in Vietnam that I fully understood how a youth grows up very quickly and just how loud exploding shells can be.

One of my summer jobs between college semesters was in Flint Michigan working on an assembly line building Buicks automobiles. The summer was 1955 and Buicks were built like tanks and the girls like gazelles. Maybe that was one of the reason I could never catch any. My dad was some kind of supervisor that allowed him access to all divisions of the GM plant which I guess was good. "You wanna see the boiler-plate division?" Dad asked one evening as he was downing draft beers and I was ogling the ladies prying their $5.00 trade for a quickie.

"Sure" I said with naiveté written all over my teen face.

The boiler division turned out to be where GM receives old engine blocks, cleans and recycles them into new V-8 throaty 452 cubic inch monsters that were the power-plant for those two-ton Grand Sports with mag wheels. Did I mention they got around 8 MPG when finely turned but in those days I didn't care as the only real decision I had to make were to give one of the ladies my $5.00 for a quickie or fill up my Buicks gas tank.

The first process of recycling old engine blocks was to clean them in a huge steel vat-like cylinder. If you have never heard metal engine blocks being tumbled inside a huge steel cylinder the noise is similar to standing behind a 747 as it approaching take-off speed. Dbs exceed 16,000Hz on the -8.5 on the C dB scale. What does that say? The 747 is in the neighborhood of 140dBA so that says, Noise with a capital N.

I never paid much attention to noise until that day and then only because as I left the plant with heavy ringing in both ears I found myself saying "huh" for a week and missing out on all conversations around and about me.

"If a tree falls in a forest and no one hears it fall, was there sound?"

Physics rule our lives. You don't necessarily need to know all the "rules of physics" but sometimes it helps explaining life.

Do you have any idea why people die?

Did you know at the turn of the nineteenth century life expectancy was 47 years and now in 2009 men can expect 77 years and the ladies another eight? Men can stretch their 77 years to a few more if they still have a "quickie" now and then and do it quietly. Works for the ladies also, but if they want to be noisy, it is allowed. As a man I did not learn that lesson till late in life that women have the same or stronger sex drives as men.

Many things can kill a person. Actually *anything* can kill a person; car accidents, bullets, knives to name a couple obvious threats. Paperclips, ballpoint pens, banana skins, water, bare hands, etc..etc. are some of the not so obvious threats but when you get right down to the facts, anything can be used to kill, even your mind.

The human body does not have to be killed to stop living. Most of us will live out our programmed life and die a "natural" death. I never fully understood "natural" but then I found that "sounds/noises" can push us toward that "natural" death.

Do you know the human body is delicate and tough at the same time?

Delicate is the touch of a rose, a tender kiss from a lover, a kind word when the world is going to hell or being told you are beautiful during your third trimester or being bald and fat is OK.

Tough is the intangible of life. Tough is something that has a job and does it without fanfare or reward. Tough is the body that carries your soul until your tissue, cells and blood and most of your tubing wears out or clogs to be replaced with hog guts or something synthetic that is not bio-degradable. The body does not have to be killed… given time it simply wears out from day to day usage.

Wears out? Now that is a profound statement.

Automobile have built-in obsoleteness, as do highways, building, toys, and everything man-made. If we made it… it will eventually break or wear out just from doing what it was designed to do – promise.

I learned tough and delicate from two young, very pretty, talented and obviously educated ladies named **Peggy Newell** and **Amanda Holliday** a couple days ago.

Peggy was the operator of an Ultrasound machine at the Lake Regional Hospital in Osage Beach Missouri. Osage Beach is a place people go to vacation, to play, to be free and loose and not wear your bikini top if you so choose and to stay up evenings partying till the sun comes up, if you so choose.

What does all this have to do with Noise?

Did you know your body is a very noisy place? I didn't, but   then Peggy showed me REAL noise and it was all *inside* me. Many times   in the quiet of an evening I can hear and feel my heart beating and constant ringing in both ears. Several times during fire fights in Vietnam I was so close to mother earth I could hear my blood rushing through all my veins. When your adrenaline is topped off, the things you hear see and feel are maximized.

Peggy showed me another way.

The other day during a kidney ultrasound exam she had me laying on my side, shirt up, warm grease smeared over my hairy stomach and side. She began by placing a hand-held gadget in all that grease, clicking a few keys, turned a knob then turned the volume up a bit on her machine. The sounds I heard were

159

coming from my body, from my organs; from me…I thought I was back in Flint in the middle of that boiler plant.

I didn't say anything at first then as Peggy and Amanda explained what was happening and what I was hearing, my first thought was, "…I now understand why body parts, organs, veins, tissue parts, and stuff wears out after a few years. All my working parts were in constant motion! The sounds were indescribable to me but to Peggy each mummer, rub, thrill meant something. To amplify just what that means to average-Joe, me, she was not only just listening to my body working, she was recording, interpolating and measuring it. Measuring!!

The human body, like other man-made things also come with built in obsoleteness. Some Biblical folks had over 600 birthdays but as Bill Clinton said on his fiftieth, "…I have had more birthdays then I will have…" Sobering… but all so true .

Both my hands had long ago gone to sleep because of the cramped position I had them under my head, but other then all fingers tingling, I was comfortable. The exam room was a 10' x 12' non-descript normal hospital room with a sink, a couple cabinets, some shelving with clean towels and a good sized Ultrasound machine/recorder/player unit that would have made Star Trek's C3PO proud.

As Peggy listened she would occasionally pause, reflect, and tap a button on her small menu selection pad or twist a dial, then look seriously at the monitor while drawing a dimension line from point A to B on the screen and measure.

"Measuring something important?" as I tried to be flip and relaxed.

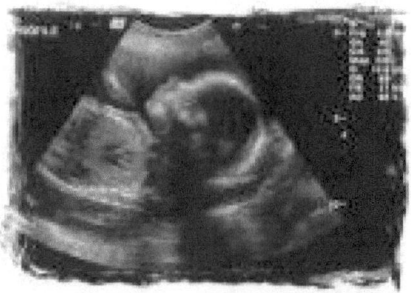

"No…" then a slight crooked grin, "…just some blood vessels." Peggy was cute in her seriousness.

She was actually measuring not only the working size of the blood supply to my kidney but speed and amounts of liquid being moved. She was measuring my kidney, its tubing, its construction, its functionality.

When I lose my right kidney to cancer a few years ago I was told the left would most likely "grow a bit" to help compensate for doing all the work rather then sharing with another kidney. Peggy was measuring the organ to see if it was doing what it was suppose to be doing.

In a matter of only a few minutes Peggy and Amanda knew more about what made me tick, rub and mummer then a long-term wife and more then a few lady friends from all corners of the world.

Talented people that play the piano or surgeons working inside you have great hand, eye coordination. It's the same kind of coordination with people that can type on a keyboard. Really good typists can listen to music, carry on an intelligent conversation, look around the room and drink a beer all at the same time. Coordinated is not a strong enough word to describe these people. Peggy and Amanda are in this elite group.

Type? No not me. I use the religious method when faced with putting words to paper.

I use to think of ultrasound technicians as people pregnant ladies went to be told if their unborn child had a willy or not.

These ladies that operate an ultrasound machine are highly intelligent and dedicated. They can look for willies, but these technician ladies can do so much more those babies born today would be entering school before I could finish outlining their qualification and abilities.

Ultrasound machines, some are also refer to as Dopplers but whatever you call it, is much more then just looking at a fetus to see if there is a willy or long curly blond hair to be welcomed into this world. Today's technology allows non-invasive techniques to see, and hear what our body is actually doing.

Doctors still "practice" but with more and more sophisticated machine being built they are burying fewer mistakes.

Just a couple more facts and specification and I will let you go and say thank you for taking a few minutes to read about – Sound.

1. Your ears are designed to receive sounds and pass those vibrations to your central nerve system for interpolation, and they do that efficiently, but sounds are the most damaging elements the ears will ever have to endure.

2. Sounds are generally audible to the human ear if their frequency (number of vibrations per second) lies between 20 and 20,000 vibrations per second, but the range varies considerably with the individual. Sound waves with frequencies less than those of audible waves are called subsonic; those with frequencies above the audible range are called ultrasonic.

3. A sound wave is usually represented graphically by a wavy, horizontal line; the upper part of the wave (the crest) indicates a condensation and the lower part (the trough)

indicates a rarefaction. This graph, however, is merely a representation and is not an actual picture of a wave. The length of a sound wave, or the wavelength, is measured as the distance from one point of greatest condensation to the next following it or from any point on one wave to the corresponding point on the next in a train of waves.

4. Sound travels more slowly in gases than in liquids, and more slowly in liquids than in solids. Since the ability to conduct sound is dependent on the density of the medium, solids are better conductors than liquids; liquids are better conductors than gases.

5. Sound waves can be reflected, refracted (or bent), and absorbed as light waves can be. The reflection of sound waves can result in an echo—an important factor in the acoustics of theaters and auditoriums. A sound wave can be reinforced with waves from a body having the same frequency of vibration, but the combination of waves of different frequencies of vibration may produce "beats" or pulsations or may result in other forms of interference.

6. A typical ultrasound machine ranges in cost from $30,000 to $180,000.

7. A basic ultrasound machine has the following parts: a. Transducer probe b. Central processing unit (CPU) c. Transducer pulse controls d. Display e. Keyboard / cursor f. Disk storage device g. Printer.

Don't go away…. Just a few more minutes...

What is Ultrasound? Ultrasound or ultrasonography is a medical imaging technique that uses high frequency sound waves and their echoes. The technique is similar to the echolocation used by bats, whales and dolphins, as well as SONAR used by submarines. In ultrasound, the following events happen: The ultrasound machine transmits high-frequency (1 to 5 megahertz) sound pulses into your body using a probe.

The sound waves travel into your body and hit a boundary between tissues (e.g. between fluid and soft tissue, soft tissue and bone). Some of the sound waves get reflected back to the probe, while some travel on further until they reach another boundary and get reflected. The reflected waves are picked up by the probe and relayed to the machine.

The machine calculates the distance from the probe to the tissue or organ (boundaries) using the speed of sound in tissue (5,005 ft/s or1,540 m/s) and the time of the each echo's return (usually on the order of millionths of a second). The machine displays the distances and intensities of the echoes on the screen, forming a two dimensional image like the one shown below.

What sound does *one* hand clapping make?
What is sound? What are some of the Laws of Physics?

ARLEE

Why do things wear out?
Why do we have to die?

You now have those
answers and a lot more
you never thought you
needed.

*Look closely to see me
smiling while hanging
by a finger nail --* →

ARLEE

𝕸𝕽𝕴 or 𝕮𝕬𝕿

Acronyms can be confusing... especially in the medical community.

Last week as I was leaving my doctors office I was going over in my head what he had said and what he wanted me to do to help him solve a new problem my body recently came up with. I use to think the white coated men and women that had; MD, DO, PhD, etc. behind their names could look at me, feel around a bit then listen to my bodily sounds with that thing they all hang around their necks, give me an aspirin and I would be fine.

That's not quite true. Actually not even close.

Last week I saw a neurologist for the first time. I figured anyone that could stick me with that many needles and say, "Uh-huh" and "Hummmm" so many times certainly had me figured out. Maybe not. He wanted a test first so he had me report to the hospital for an MRI.

Everyone knows what an MRI is, right?

In our world of acronyms we smile at the right times and nod our heads when we should be thinking as we just plod along in our own little world. "You need an MRI. I will schedule it for you." OK. Three months ago another doctor said, "You should have that checked by a CAT scan. My secretary will schedule it for you". OK. Many of us have heard those words from our doctors. Some of you even know what they meant and what was involved while the rest of us just figure the MDs know their business and we will report to whatever appointment is made.

I discovered this morning there is a big difference between MRI (pictured on the right) and CAT (left). NOTE: The MRI is very deep much like a torpedo tube!

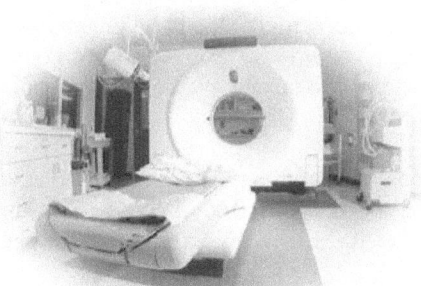 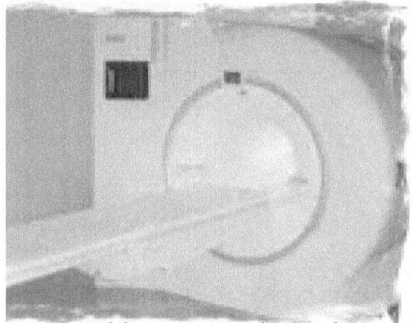

A pretty young lady named Kelly called me from the waiting room and my adventure began. "Good morning Mr. Hester, have you had an MRI here before?"

"Yes." I said. "In the last three years I have had several." That was a mistake but I didn't realize it until I had to take my pants off.

"I have just a few questions and we can get started." Kelly was saying as she handing me neatly folded off-color faded orange cotton something. "Please strip and put on these one-size-fits-all cotton hospital utility pants. If they are a bit loose the draw-string rope should hold them up. You may keep your socks on if you wish." Kelly was being the true professional. She was a petit young lady, short chopped blondish hair, dancing dark eyes, all smiles with a bubble personality that put me immediately at ease. She was good. I was to find out later she had a behind-the scene partner named Daphnia that was equally as professional (she punched the keys and monitored the screens). They made an excellent team.

Kelly bounced to my side with clipboard in hand as she chatted and positioned my half naked body with that wrap-around all-purpose tent onto what looked to be a steel-like gurney. A first impression was the same as seeing the table convicted criminals are strapped just before they receive that lethal injection. My mind was wandering and conjuring all kinds of visions and scenarios as I took in my new surroundings. The room was not 'star-wars' but in the dim lighting, could have been. One door that had my attention had yellow and black diagonal 2" tape indicating – 'special'. My gurney looked to be targeted into a long metal-like mechanical contraption. The forward torpedo department in the movie "Das Boat" flashed behind my eyes.

"This isn't a CAT scan machine" my brain whispered as my eyes watered and my tongue dried.

"Are you claustrophobic?" Kelly began. No. Looking at the hole where my gurney was aimed the question made sense and was not comforting. A picture from my youth flashed between my ears as I looked at that hole and remembered two of my favorite uncles tying a rope around my ankles and lowering me into abandoned water well. They were my "favorite" kin and I just knew they would hot hurt me – intentionally. I had the same feeling about Kelly. Why would she try to hurt me? I was her patient. Besides a pretty sweet young thing like her was not old enough to have formed that many bad habits, so I trusted her. I convinced myself I could handle being a little "close" for awhile. The one problem I didn't know just how long "awhile" was going to be and my tongue was too dry to ask.

"Are you wearing a pace-maker?" No. I know I look ancient to a twenty-something year-old but other then being bald, overweight, paunchy and knobby-keeled I could still walk upright and could still chew my food with my own teeth. Heart is still active just the body around it was losing steam.

"Have you ever had eye-surgery?" No.

Kelly must have sensed my winkled brow was silently querying her questions as she said, "I just have a few questions I have to ask for your own safety. They are all metal related and will not take but a few more seconds." I blinked, she smiled and I nodded thought the other questions.

Then she was ready. I was becoming more apprehensive but with the clipboard finished and my pants in a locker, the procedure was at the-point-of-no-return so I just hoped she would not drop me into any wells.

"Good." Kelly said basically to herself. She had done this many times in her young life but she apparently didn't recognize a chicken-heart in a grown man. Kelly was still grinning and happy. "Would you like a blanket? You will be in there for awhile?" No. I have a hairy chest but that macho response would shortly prove to be a very wrong answer. There was that "awhile" again. I should ask but I couldn't.

"Eye plugs. Did I give you your ear protection?" Kelly asked. No. I had told her I had other MRIs so she knew that I knew the procedure was going to be a bit noisy and didn't explain further. I accepted the small sponges and buried one in each ear. Kelly said something to me but all I could do was nod and grin as I was now in my own muted little world.

Kelly helped position my head into a padded vise after placing a rolled cushion under the knees. Even on the cold metal gurney Kelly was making me comfortable. The vice was secure but to make it really secure she placed a couple wedges next to my temples to make sure my head didn't wander. It's not called a vice for nothing. Just as I was thinking the only direction my head could move was up Kelly placed a clamp over my forehead and secured it. I now knew how the eighteen century colonials felt in those punishment chocks and Napoleons political prisoners in France moments before the guillotine blade fell.

When Kelly left to join Daphnia my mind said, "OK…now just take it easy for 'awhile' and relax". I tried. As I was going over that 'awhile' word again Daphnia pushed a button and it was like the crew on Das Boat loading a torpedo for firing. Motors whirled, gears turned and my gurney moved into the abyss. I wear glasses now but even in my 20-20 perfect vision years I could never focus on anything two inches from my nose so once inside the tube I immediately gave up looking around and closed my eyes to nap. I listened to the blood running in my veins for a few minutes before Daphnia apparently pushed a few more buttons. That is when the banging started and I was glad of the sponges in my ears. The banging was not one sound but three. Each just different enough for you to know there were three muscular guys on the outside and just over your head, with mallets. I was trying to put the differing sounds into some kind of musical theme just as a cold breeze picked up across my bare chest that changed my mind about music.

Damn being macho. My brain reminded me however it was glad I had stopped into the men's room shortly before Kelly first called my name. This isn't going to be that bad.

I still had no idea how long 'awhile' was going to be.

On July 3, 1977, an event took place that would forever alter the landscape of modern medicine. Outside the medical research community, this event made scarcely a ripple at first. This event was the first MRI exam ever performed on a human being.

It took almost five hours to produce one image. The images were, by today's standards, quite ugly. Dr. Raymond Damadian, a physician and scientist, along with colleagues Dr. Larry Minkoff and Dr. Michael Goldsmith, labored tirelessly for seven long years to reach this point. They named their original machine "Indomitable" to capture the spirit of their struggle to do what many said could not be done.

This machine is now in the Smithsonian Institution. As late as 1982, there were but a handful of MRI scanners in the entire United States. Today there are thousands. Medicine can now image in seconds what used to take hours.

MRI or Magnetic Resonance Imaging is a very complicated technology not well understood by many. The machine is still a huge, noisy contraption that actually works.

MRI provides an unparalleled view inside the human body. The level of detail that can be seen is extraordinary compared with any other imaging modality. MRI is the method of choice for the diagnosis of many types of injuries and conditions because of the incredible ability to tailor the exam to the particular medical question being asked. By changing exam parameters, the MRI system can cause tissues in the body to take on different appearances. Some circles would call that "cool".

To understand how MRI works, you must first focus on the word "magnetic" in MRI. The biggest and most important component in an MRI system is the magnet. Magnets are a lot like water. Unless you understand the power of each, they can do you bodily harm as well as good. Until you have turned on a spigot in your front yard or seen a swollen river wipe away whole towns or seen a metal object magnetically pulled across a room and deeply imbedded in a wall the word 'magnet' probable means only something kids play with and it's just part of the motor that drives your ceiling fan. If not careful an MRI magnet can suck a metal watch right off your arm and eat it before you can blink. Knowing the power of a magnet made the metal questions from Kelly - personal.

For example: People with pacemakers cannot be scanned or even go near the scanner because the magnet can cause the pacemaker to malfunction. Aneurysm clips in the brain can be very dangerous as the magnet can move them, causing them to tear the very artery they were placed on to repair. Some dental implants are magnetic. Most orthopedic implants, even though they may be ferromagnetic, are fine because they are firmly embedded in bone. Even metal staples in most parts of the body are fine -- once they have been in a patient for a few weeks (usually six weeks), enough scar tissue has formed to hold them in place.

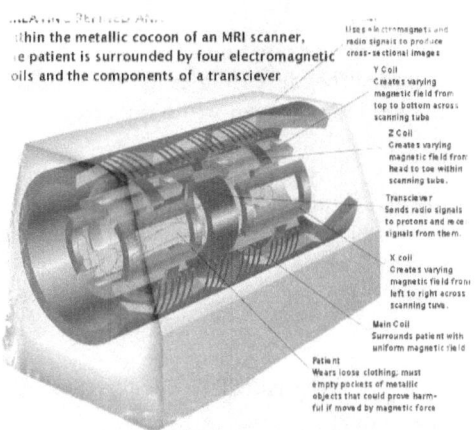

Kelly and Daphnia are not just two very pretty young ladies but intelligent, dedicated and exceptional professionals.

There are three basic magnets in the standard MRI machine but the superconducting magnets are by far the most commonly used. A superconducting magnet is somewhat similar to a resistive magnet -- coils or windings of wire through which a current of electricity is passed create the magnetic field. The important difference is that the wire is continually bathed in liquid helium at 452.4 degrees below zero. Yes, when you are inside the MRI machine, you are surrounded by a substance that is that cold! But don't worry; it is very well insulated by a vacuum in a manner identical to that used in a vacuum flask. This almost unimaginable cold causes the resistance in the wire to drop to zero, reducing the electrical requirement for the system dramatically and making it much more economical to operate. If that is not impressive enough, the next time you view your medical bills, without superconductivity try imagining total cost with three more zeros (000).

Remember when I mentioned wishing I had a blanket – *superconductivity* was the reason.

While in the torpedo tube I did learn a valuable lesson about myself. I learned that every itch did not have to be immediately scratched.

Daphnia had perfectly positioned me within the torpedo tube three different times as hammers banged, the cold winds blew, my facial itches moved from left eye to cheek to right eye to forehead to the tip of my nose then finally to an elbow until finally 'awhile' arrived. This time my gurney did not stop inside but moved to open air. I was free.

As I was re-focusing Kelly bounced next to my gurney and gave me a hand to sit. "That wasn't too bad, now was it?" She tried.

"No... not really. It wasn't bad at all." After answering her I couldn't wait and ask my question. "How long was I in there?" I had to know how long 'awhile' had been.

"An hour and ten minutes" she responded. The number surprised me a little as it had seemed a long time but not that long. "You had three procedures and each takes about twenty minutes." I grinned as I was thinking; maybe I had napped while my nose was itching.

After I had my street clothes on I cornered Kelly and Daphnia to fess-up my confusion between MRI and CAT Scan. Even though they were busy with my report they took time for me and explained in terms so I could understand the differences. They did it together and separately as they began: "Compared to most CAT Scan images, those made by MRI tend to be more detailed and often have more contrast.

Kelly covered the advantages: why would your doctor order an MRI? Because the only way to see inside your body any better is to cut you open.

MRI is ideal for:
Diagnosing multiple sclerosis (MS), Diagnosing tumors of the pituitary gland and brain, Diagnosing infections in the brain, spine or joints, Visualizing torn ligaments in the wrist, knee and ankle, Visualizing shoulder injuries, Diagnosing tendonitis, Evaluating masses in the soft tissues of the body, Evaluating bone tumors, cysts and bulging or herniated discs in the spine, Diagnosing strokes in their earliest stages.

Daphnia picked up on the few Disadvantages:
Although MRI scans are ideal for diagnosing and evaluating a number of conditions, it does have drawbacks. For example: There are many people who cannot safely be scanned with MRI (for example, because they have pacemakers), and also people who are too big to be scanned." Neither lady responded to my comment as I said, "That must have been the size pants I had to wear. If they fit, then you were too large to fit into that torpedo tube." Daphnia grinned and Kelly just shook her head.

"MRI systems are very, very expensive to purchase, and therefore the exams are also very expensive. Thinking back on that superconductivity temperature gadget made a lot of sense by putting a dollar sign to something needed to maintain a minus 400+ degrees reading. With all the disadvantages the almost limitless benefits of MRI for most patients far outweigh the few drawbacks."

Now that the ladies had me up to speed on MRIs they looked to each other, grinned and continued with: "CAT scans take the idea of conventional X-ray imaging to a new level.

Instead of finding the outline of bones and organs, a CAT scan machine forms a full three-dimensional computer model of a patient's insides. Doctors can even examine the body one narrow slice at a time to pinpoint specific areas.

The Basic Idea of the Computerized Axial Tomography (CAT) scan machines produces X-rays, a powerful form of electromagnetic energy. X-ray photons are basically the same thing as visible light photons, but they have much more energy. This higher energy level allows X-ray beams to pass straight through most of the soft material in the human body. A conventional X-ray image is basically a shadow: You shine a 'light' on one side of the body, and a piece of film on the other side registers the silhouette of the bones.

In the scanning procedure the CAT machine looks not like a torpedo tube but more like a giant donut tipped on its side. The patient lies down on a platform, which slowly moves through the hole in the machine. The X-ray tube is mounted on a movable ring around the edges of the hole. The ring also supports an array of X-ray detectors directly opposite the X-ray tube.

A motor turns the ring so that the X-ray tube and the X-ray detectors revolve around the body (in an alternative design, the tube remains stationary and the X-ray beam is bounced off a revolving reflector). Each full revolution scans a narrow, horizontal 'slice' of the body. The control system moves the platform farther into the hole so the tube and detectors can scan the next slice.

In this way, the machine records X-ray slices across the body in a spiral motion. The computer varies the intensity of the X-rays in order to scan each type of tissue with the optimum power. After the patient passes through the machine, the computer combines all the information from each scan to form a detailed image of the body. It's not usually necessary to scan the entire body, of course. More often, doctors will scan only a small section."

The ladies had been sharing dialog until Daphnia stopped, leaned back into her chair and let Kelly finish. It was dark in the monitor room where the girls were talking to me but even in the darkness I could see Kelly's eyes light up as she said, "Since they examine the body slice by slice, from all angles, CAT scans are much more comprehensive than conventional X-rays. Today, doctors use CAT scans to diagnose and treat a wide variety of ailments, including head trauma, cancer and osteoporosis. They are an invaluable tool in modern medicine."

I told you these ladies were smart.

PROLOG:
We only see 'hospital people' when we are sick and that is a shame. They come in all shapes, colors and nationalities. They wear white coats, candy-strips, flowery prints, pin adorned smocks colored from white to children designs. They wear tennis shoes made by Keds to Air-Jordan and always have that listening tube around their necks. Hospital people have their own language only understood by those in white. Hospital people are nice folks that only see us at our worse but they always have a spring in their step and happy words for us even after they have been on their feet for twelve to sixteen hours.

God Bless Um...

txe DaYinci CoDe Commentaires De Roman

The Da Vinci Code novel raised many questions for me. I am sharing some as I sort others.

What do you know about the Holy Grail?

What do you know about Leonardo Da Vinci?

What do you know about the Last Supper?

Why is the lady of the Mona Lisa smiling?

Just when I think I have life figured out something changes. As for the Holy Grail, I always though I knew 'what' the Grail was and the 'where' question was either France or England. Wars have been waged, fortunes made and lost, people have killed or died seeking the Holy Grail for two-thousand years and it is still being sought, for many reasons. All but one of these reasons comes from people much higher in the food-chain then I, so, I just figured they would tell me when they knew. I think the DaVinci Code did that, but...I wonder.

I have just finished reading and thoroughly enjoyed the novel The Da Vinci Code and now feel I may have been misguided in my cloistered thinking about life. Why? Because, now grays have overtaken the "blacks" and "whites" of truths as I know them.

Libraries, book stores and many homes have books and novels. I have only a few; but, Barns & Noble and Amazon have millions. Have you ever wondered where those books and novels come from? Do you even know what a novel is? Where they come from is easy. Folks like you and I write them. Those of us that are really bad at telling stories are called Wannabees. The rest of us authors are called Writers. Writers are better at telling a story then the Wannabees; but, never-the-less only a story teller. Writers do it on a regular basis but every once in awhile a Wannabees will get lucky and write an untold story which may have many gray areas, half-truths or fabricated facts which reads well. It is most probable the kind of story which puts a tear in your eye and a smile on the lips at the same time it is putting doubt in your mind. You writers do that with ease, grace and intelligence. Even when telling true accountings from life we Wannabees are prone to have us our license-to-fib to embellish or make the story-line more readable or as my publisher once called it, tongue-in-cheek Literary License. As a third-class Wannabees I use that license when the truth just doesn't sound right or makes my protagonist sound too lackadaisical or wimpiest or I am trying to make a point and the truth doesn't do it. Hay, it is my license to fib.

True, writers are not Wannabees like I and can get their point across in a normal gender non-specific structured action verb, adjective, noun, pronoun or adverb sentences and not need to ramble in run-on sentences looking for meaningless words which go on and on until readers decides you forgot where the period key is so you just keep writing until an idea entered your head. Dan Brown is a Writer.

I almost didn't write this short story; but after the germ of an idea took shape and the first draft was outlined in my head, the idea would not go away. So…as a Wannabees I have to say once again I really enjoyed **The Da Vinci Code**. It was a page-turner, a bit hard to follow in spots but nevertheless a damn good tale. Those parts I did not understand, I knew (hoped might be a better word) their true meaning would somehow sneak into my subconscious before the story ended. For over 450 pages and many sleepless nights the novel has made me think, and wonder. Sitting here at my keyboard watching the sun transition from a dark orange to a brilliant white and the black of the sky adjusting from its grays to a majestic unambiguous blue, the morning comes to life and bewilderment and awe deepen and…I wonder.

Is it Memorex or is it real?
Is it just an accomplished story told by a master writer?
Is it truth or just an Urban Legend or maybe just a hell of a story?
Who or what can be believed?
My dad always told me "…don't believe anything you hear or read and only half of what you see…" but, dad was never sober long enough to tell me why he felt that way.

Words written two thousand years ago… are they factual? I have a tendency to believe ancient words because it was not until the turn of the 21st century it became fashionable to lie. If an answer is hard to come by, think about the year 4008AD. Two thousand years from now. As these words are read then, will they be believed as factual?
Vitruvian Man (1485) →
As a youth, I attended a Baptist Church in the south. It was not the Southern Baptist which comes to mind with fire and brimstone sermons, even though I had an uncle that was your typical Southern Baptist minister who singed his mustache

every week. My Baptist church was just a church which happened to be in the south. I have never liked the idea of believing in Heaven because I was terrified of a fire and brimstone eternity. During my clumsy years and to this day during my stupid times, I sometimes severally burn parts of my body and can not associate that kind of pain - for an Eternity. My head tells me no God can be that cruel. Having said that, streets paved with gold, fluffy clouds, eternal happiness and winged, perfect people is also difficult to believe - sometimes. Imagine it, yes hope for it, yes but, actual belief is difficult for anyone that can use only a small percent of a mediocre brain to begin with. It is estimated that Einstein used only 10% of his brain; so, we mere mortals use a lot less.

Have you ever noticed older people always have well-worn bibles or qurans and even ouija boards close at hand? They are studying for finals.

Truth or literary license? If ancient words can't be believed and if there is no after-life or life everlasting, I feel the real waste of a human life are those that take a vow of poverty or chastity. An unadulterated belief in anything is all powerful and the cornerstone of family and respectable human beings. I envy a person who can devote a life to a Belief. Personally, I am too weak and always tend to bend with the wind. Creature comforts, the feel of smooth, hot flesh and the cooling down afterglow while you catch your breath from making love with another person is indescribable. I am weak, but I... wonder.

What are my religious beliefs? Many times they are confused. I do not attend church on a regular basis; but, I believe in and chat with God daily. As a baptized, Protestant I spent many years on my knees in Catholic schools and attended daily Mass listening to "...hail Mary full of Grace..." until I was afraid of girls. As time passed and I traveled the world I, witnessed Buddhist monks reduced to ashes for a belief, youth defying military tanks for a belief and groups drinking arsenic-laced tea while others commit suicide in their bunk beds as comets passed. They had a belief and... I wonder.

I raised a son in a Methodist environment; had a Seventh-day-Adventist brother-in-law, have lived in the Far-East where Buddha was the law of the land, enjoyed mass participation and group sing-along of black gospels and the full music and stage productions of present day Lutherans. Our world takes all kind of people...and every person is an individual and we all have our beliefs.

All religions have the word of their God.

It is the interpretation of that word is turning my hair gray. For example, I can understand the statement, "...will always be...", but, the one that gives me the most trouble understanding is, "...has always been..." Doesn't everything begin – somewhere? Or maybe, it's just that percentage of my intellect again? Kinda makes a person.... wonder.

My son with a 3.8 GPA is an EE college graduate and agnostic who believe in the big-bang theory of creation. A very close and ultra-religious friend that is true -catholic believes in God, Purgatory, hell and the sanctity of women and family told me unequivocally the DaVinci novel is "…Pure Fiction". Makes me… wonder.

Of the twenty-two Major religions of the world which include: Christianity, Islam, Secular/Nonreligious/Agnostic/Atheist, Hinduism, Chinese traditional religion, Buddhism, primal-indigenous, African Traditional & Diasporic, Sikhism, Juche, Spiritism, Judaism, Baha'I, Jainism, Shinto, Cao Dai, Zoroastrianism, Tenrikyo, Neo-Paganism, Unitarian-Universalism, Rastafarianism, Scientology and also includes the 45 churches grouped under Christianity… ALL BELIEVE. I personally don't understand the difference between the Sunni and Shi'ite but then when a billion people practice it, I don't need to know, but… I wonder.

Silas – the Ghost Monk →

Would you like a bit of food for your brain so it does not atrophy today? Think about this: Was Jesus married? Was Mary Madeleine a prostitute or wife of Jesus? Did Jesus have a family, a daughter? Is there a Holy Grail? Is the Grail a 'thing' or something else? Don't answer off the top of your head, think about it. I did and some of the answers made me…wonder.

In my early twenties, I was fortunate to live in 1950s Paris, France. Monuments were black with age and soot, untainted beauty on one side of an avenue and darkness on the other. It was the City of Love and physical loving could be witnessed most any day down by the banks of the Seine. Artists lived and created on broken sidewalks, whores became wives and mothers, and white-flag factors flourished, but sometimes…I wondered.

In my four years in Paris, I spent endless hours in a rundown building called the Louvre. I was twenty-four years old and dumb as a stick by any measure. I graduated college but that was all book-knowledge. I didn't have a clue about life and especially life of other cultures and times. Until I left home for college, I thought all people were red-necked white hillbillies who spoke with a southern accent. Fifty years later, I still have a Texas twang and am completely people color blind.

The last Supper (1498)
← Who is this lady??

It is stupid people that roast my chops. But, I do know that …stupid is that stupid does… The Louvre then and now is a treasure house of the Masters – painters and sculptors alike, it is those that create using God-given talents. Be it commissioned or individual ideas, master pieces were created and survived. Paintings are more than pictures. Sculptors do more with marble and limestone than merely sculpt. Did you know or are you cognizant that all painting and statues tells stories? The Sistine Chapel is a prime example as is **the Last Supper** and as are the undeveloped pictures in your camera. Winged Victory is…. well, I don't want to go into that.

My well read and religious friend who told me the DaVinci Code was fiction is infinitely smarter then I, so I will merely pass on his and a few other comments from people of influence that now reflect, after reading the DaVinci Code novel, some of my new thinking: But I still… wonder.

"1. Has this book changed your ideas about faith, religion, or history?

2. Would you rather live in a world without religion…or a world without science?

3. Will you look at the artwork of Da Vinci any differently now that you know more about his "secret life?"

4. A stunning new thriller that will provoke much debate. Dan Brown's extensive research on secret societies and symbology adds intellectual depth to this page-turning thriller. His surprising revelations on Da Vinci's penchant for hiding codes in his paintings will lead the reader to search out renowned artistic icons as The Mona Lisa, The Madonna of the Rocks and The Last Supper. The Last Supper holds the most astonishing coded secrets of all and, after reading The Da Vinci Code, you will never see this famous painting in quite the same way again."

EPILOGUE:
1.   Although the Grail myths and stories date to 5 BC, there is no mention of the Holy Grail in the Bible.
2.   Leonardo Da Vinci lived in the fifteenth century and was an Italian painter, draftsman, sculptor, architect, and engineer whose genius, perhaps more than that of any other figure, epitomized the Renaissance humanist ideal.
3.   The Last Supper is not a "picture" but a fifteenth century interpretation and pure conjecture of Jesus and his disciples gathering for a last time – Matthew 26
4.   Conjecture can be typified by the disembodied hand holding a dagger and the presence of Marie Magdalene depicted in the supper.
5.   Mona Lisa's face is androgynous and is smiling because her name is an anagram of the divine union of male and female – **AMON** (Egyptian god of fertility) and **L'ISA** (goddess of fertility) AMON L'ISA or *Mona Lisa*.
6.   A novel is new and unusual, can be fictional, is length and is about people.
7.   A story can be fictional but is more about "things" and is shorter than a novel.

If you don't read the novel then the movie is now a DVD.

Pietà
Michelangelo, 1499
St. Peter's Basilica

This sculptor by *Michelangelo* has nothing to do with this short story on the Da Vinci Code and *Leonardo Da Vinci (1452-1519)* but I wanted to share with you a work by a master that I had the opportunity to stand before, to touch and to marvel at the genius of such masters so many years ago. Touching the fine marble I felt so small and insignificant in comparison to them. There is so much I wonder about...

Sometxing I need to say...

Alternate Title: The Crime I got away with...

If you only do two things today, read this first.

"When beggars die there are no comets seen. The heavens themselves blaze forth the death of princes."
William Shakespeare

REASON for this short story: It is something I need to say and I hope it comes out on paper (screen) the same as it has inside my head for ooooh so many years. Why this format? Why not? If you speak with another person only that person hears your words. If you speak to a large gathering only those present will hear, the same for television and radio. BUT if you write your words they are indelible for the ages and for all mankind.

There are many truisms in today's world:
You use less then 10% of your brain's capacity.
The brain never rest.
You can not get out of life, alive.
You begin dying the moment you are born.
All mammals and living things die.
When given chooses, it is better to kill then be killed.
My mother's favorite - "I had druther see you dead and in your grave then...."

And... there are many truths:

The body you come into this world is small, naked and being developed. When born, the only organ that will not develop further are your eyes. Your body is delicate, vastly complicated, and vulnerable as most anything can cause harm to it. It is one reason Nature and God encased our brain with thick bone. Even as careful as the designer of our body was it can and does still get hurt; A fall; shaking; poison; drowning; obesity, bulimia, sugar, fats, etc... You get the idea.

Noise is bad for the ears, but that is their function.
Some food is bad for you, but we need substance to live.

Sex is bad, but only if you get caught or a rain coat is not used with strangers.
Anything you enjoy… is either bad for you or against the law.
To complicate this living process we have to factor in
The Eight Deadly Diseases: Heart Disease, Cancer,
Stroke, Diabetes, ALS, Osteoporosis, and Arthritis and
of course Alzheimer's.

Then just as things couldn't get any worse they throw
in problems called common denominators for major
medical problems; unstable molecules; the high
homocysteine level; mineral deficiency; bad toxins; parasitic infections such as worms,
fungus, bad bacteria. Anything in our body such as a bad microorganism. And then, we
have damage inadvertently caused by medications, surgical procedure, a side effect of an
outpatient surgery, basically a medical mistake. If we look at drug side effects
individually, every year there are showing thousands die of adverse drug reactions.
Actually the group of drugs used to treat arthritis is now the 15th cause of death in the
US.

Have you ever wondered why they say doctors *Practice* Medicine?

I only have this one life so I am not really concerned with 1 thru 15 or all the things that
are bad for me. There is only ONE out there for me – trouble is I don't know just what
that ONE is.

They told me in Vietnam if I could hear the bullet it would not harm me. It is the one(s)
you don't hear or the mortar or the rocket you don't hear that is of concern.

What cause of death do I fear? Burning or being buried alive. ALL forms of death are
unacceptable but those two are the ones I fear most.

I have killed the enemy but it was quick and I hope only briefly painful.

I recently saw the 2004 Clint
Eastwood movie, *Million
Dollar Baby*. One of his
last lines in the movie
struck me as most
profound. As Hillary
Swank, in her rehab bed lay
paralyzed and with absolutely NO hope of any kind of
life other then life support he said, "I'm going to unplug
your oxygen and you will go to sleep." He did and she
did. He then took a full syringe of adrenaline and as he gave it to her in her IV he

said, "...now you will stay asleep." I cried. I am crying now just remembering the scene and my feelings toward death and dying.

Do you know where feelings originate? Why you blink your eyes, move a finger, lift an arm, feel an organism, know love, hate, and how you control bodily function?

I have held many in my arms as they passed from this life and in most cases appeared peaceful. No pain, no discomfort. One minute they are here and the next all the bodily systems shut down and they no longer are a living being. *They are dead.* Do you have any idea how many systems it takes to operate your body and how they all depend on each other? There is some redundancy built into our bodies, but even extra parts wear out. All humans come with a few extra parts and some parts you really don't need, but on the whole this most complicated pile of chemicals we call a body will one day, die. If you are about to stay asleep forever how do you do it gracefully and with dignity?

Control! With all these vast and complicated systems we call a body do you have any idea how it is controlled? Your bone encased 1400 gram (just a bit over 3 pound) brain is your control room, your Captain Central, the place where ALL decisions are made and carried out. What tells a finger to move? When a germ is encountered, what tells the body how to protect itself? When you burn a finger, what tells the body it has sudden pain and what to do about it? People can and do "Will" their body to get better or to give up and know when it is time even to die. Your brain can do wondrous things as it can cure or kill you. When the time for death is near, how do you think your systems know to shut down? Yep. Your brain tells them.

How do I know all this?

Let's digress for just a moment to the living by saying, if you factor in accidents such as: auto, doctors, clumsiness, not paying attention or just being in the wrong place at the wrong time, chances of longevity is decreased.

Hunger, biblical and modern day diseases, famine and drugs affect hundreds of thousands from around our globe. Not to mention natural disasters. Tornados always seek out Mobil homes and dismember a few folks that have no basement or safe room. Then you have an earthquake that can and have taken the lives of many tens-of-thousands in less then a dozen heart beats or in the blink of an eye. Don't forget no one is really safe from these disasters. You can be on a vacation, tanning, drinking and enjoying life when an earthquake thousands of miles away can not only sweep you out to sea in Tsunamis.

Have you read the stories about Lois and Frank?
I will not go into ALL the stories but their last episode is interesting and ties to this theme.

"How do I tell friends and family what is going on inside my head?" The statement was not a conscience though but just words and feelings floating around inside Lois's head. Floating is not a good words as she heard herself say to no one in particular. "Screaming, demanding, yelling all are better adjectives." Lois smiled to herself but it was not your everyday happy smile. Lois is in-between major emotional viewpoints and some say emotional instability.

The Heavens are putting on a grand show this evening. Jagged ribbons of highly charged electricity race and dart at the speed of light across the black threading sky creating a night of wonderment. Down, across, up, across resembling a teen-ager with raging hormones or an addict between fixes. Lighting reflections and rolling thunder are dancing around Lois's bedroom but she didn't notice. She was lying on her back on top of all bed covers, eyes open as her brain was dancing around others and in other places.

The stormy night intensified to the point the room was constantly bright as day-time at high noon. It was a light show beyond all others. It was the kind of show she didn't want or need this evening. Frank was dead and in the ground. This evening not even four double Manhattans could help the total emptiness in her gut.

Lois had a few gold fish as a child but they all eventually learned to float on their backs. A Doberman puppy she had raised until it was four year old died when a tree fell on it during a summer soaking rain and wind storm. That was an act of God. Her grandparents had all passed away, but that was expected as they were old. They were well into their sixties. Old.

The world outside had not changed and that bothered her. Her world has changed, drastically and she wanted others to change – and now. It wasn't fair. Life isn't fair but life had never been this close before. Lois knew about life but she had not lived it yet. Not in her thirty-five years had she been made to see that all living things die. Maybe not all will die today, but someday they will. Nature said so and that is how Nature designed all living things. Rocks were safe from this fate but then they had to worry about being crushed, broken are made into molten lava. A few become diamonds but most just turn into coal.

"Hello." Lois answered the phone with a sullen voice not unlike normal, but not really normal either.

"Lois. Hi…. It's Maryyyyy."

It was the voice only a mother could love and now was not the time to carry on any kind of conversation with the bubbly Maryyyyyy, but she tried.

"Hi . Nice to hear from you. Are you home?" Lois's tongue was already getting thick and she knew it would only get thicker the longer she lied. This was not going well and Lois knew it but was reluctant to do otherwise so she continued pretending to be interested in the conversation.

Isn't that what everyone does?

There was no way Lois could tell Mary or anyone else how she felt, what was going on in her head and gut. How could she explain to others something she didn't have a clue about? Shopping she could handle, love, sex and family were OK also but life and death subjects give her a hard time thinking about. Everything yesterday that was normal was a blur today. Yesterday things were normal. Now normal is out the window and reality is here. Is there a Heaven? A hell? Is there a God? A Lucifer? Is there such a thing as Eternal Life? Why did Frank have to die? I needed him… her head was saying but somewhere in her head was that little voice saying, …or did I? Now Lois has to face some sort of reality that only others had to do before. Death only happens to others. Accidents only happen to others. Bad things only happen to others and the ones you read about or the evening news tells you about.

Lois turned into a local news channel and listened. She was not mentioned.

She then switched to National news and again she was not mentioned.

No need to listen to the international news because if she was mentioned then she had more problems then she first thought and that she did not want to think about. This is hard.

"Do you feel like talking about it?" Mary tried.

Lois's voice was barely audible as she whispered, "Yes… no… maybe… I don't know."

Mary took that as a blank check and began: "What have you heard from the authorities?" This looked to be a long afternoon for Lois but she sipped her Cherry flavored Manhattan, crossed her long legs her head was saying, it could be worse Lois… go along with her. About that time her mouth said, "Not much." They have no suspects, no motive, and nothing as far as I can tell. They are kinda just doing routine investigating for now. They told me not to worry and they would get in touch if they needed me."

Conversation was tight and increasingly difficult with each passing minutes until Lois finally excused herself. Mary went along with the excuse up to a point before saying, "Frank just up and died for no reason? Surely the cops know something or maybe suspect something, right?"

Lois didn't answer as she cradled her phone.

Chief Light, grand master of his Free Mason lodge and Chief of police in charge of the case and as of today still had no hard evidence if Lois or anyone else had caused Frank to die. Lots of suspicion but thinking and proving are two different bed-fellows "It's an open case." He has said many times to the press. "At this time we have no evidence to suspect anything of Mr. Steele's death other then by natural causes."

In private, Chief Light was overheard in a conversation with his deputy saying: "How do you catch a killer who can murder from a distance without leaving a trace? There were no ordinary clues at the scene, but there may be other information available. Light's underling that most referred to as simply "L" thinks he can solve this puzzle. In only one day he has come up with some ingenious ways of narrowing down the search. Adding to the story's complexity, Light believes that he is doing a good thing. He feels that he has been given this opportunity so he can make the world a better place by eliminating those who are truly evil. This vigilantism is reminiscent of the comic The Punisher. Light's father is a policeman so perhaps he wants to prove he can deal with criminals more effectively than his father.

Ryuk, the Shinigami, follows L around and talks to him, but only L can see him. Over time, Light learns from Ryuk that the Death Note is more complicated than it seems. Ryuk looks kind of like a very tall goth clown, with sharp teeth and spiky hair. The trouble his Death Note causes in the human world seems to amuse him, but he refuses to take L's side. Takeshi Obata, the artist who also created Hikaru no Go, does a great job of putting this strikingly odd character into what is otherwise a very realistic world. Because of the overall realism, unlike most manga Death Notes would probably work well as a live-action movie, but this is no movie. It's real. It's life and it's a death.

Lois killed Frank because she believed him to be wasting his life. He was doing what he wanted, when he wanted and with whom, he wanted. He was mid-thirties, had a white-collar job but no direction. When he married his child-hood sweetheart in his mid-twenties Lois did not want to start a family so he volunteered to be sterilized (vasectomy). It was non-reversible. Lois loved Frank deeply with few reservations but as each birthday passed and her bio-clock was ticking the womanly urge was stronger then the laws of the land and God's law. Frank is a writer of fiction, mostly horror. He is always killing off people so Lois uses one of his techniques to do him in..... He wrote in his first novel, January's Heat, "…Dark Yagami has a magic notebook, originally the property of a Shinigami, or death god If Dark writes someone's name in the book, that person will die. It sounded like a clever story idea…."

How did Lois kill Frank? There are over six billion humans on this Earth so that makes the number six-billion ways to kill.

The one way that doesn't readily come to mind is: She wrote his name in a secret place and wished him to pass from this life, and he did. The next time someone you know passes away and there is no apparent reason, look in secret places to verify if their name is written there.

Life expectancy has increased from 35 years of two-hundred years ago to close to eighty in the early 21st century… that is… *if no one writes your name in a secret place.*

Enjoy the day as it could very well be your last on this Earth.

With all this death and dying stuff and before I close I have one final word. We know for a fact we will all someday die. So what do friends or family do with the dead body?

Do not put the body I left behind in the ground. *Cremate my dead body.* I do not want to lie for years rotting and be food for things that live in the earth. God will take care of my eternal soul but I do not desire to be food for any of His earthly creatures.

IF you put me in the ground, surely some dark and stormy night a family of worms will make a dinner of me, I will become their energy for a few hours then turned into worm poop. No thank you.

ARLEE

How I Learned to Speak DOG

Always leave your mind open to learn.

PROLOGUE:
Henry is a grown man that grew up in the southwest. Growing up he was blessed with the required two parents, a sister, two dogs, a couple cats, caged canaries (until the cats ate them), a manual push lawnmower, raging hormones and can speak or understand several languages. Max is a dog that speaks only DOG but has a knack of teaching grown men what he wants them to know. Time is the present. Local is on Mother Earth most anywhere except in Korea where dog is considered the *'other white meat'*.

Understanding DOG is a lot like the dog whistle, not everyone can do it.

"Woooof... woooof. woof... blink... blink...yawn... Rignare".

Henry had heard this before and responded "Ok, OK, I'm coming. I know little buddy, I know. I know. You're ready to eat. I'll be there in a minute."

Tail wagging and soulful eyes said Max understood.

"Do you really understand what he wants or just guessing?" Lynsey asked from the kitchen. She seemed serious and actually wanted to know if there was anything to this man-dog bonding thing she needed to know. As an after-thought she said, "You remember Max graduated first in his Dog-Obedience class when he was only six months old so he responds to sounds he knows. Certain sounds mean different things to him. Remember 'Uuk'?"

Henry had forgotten 'Uuk' so he tried it and Max immediately lowered his eyes and assumed a prone position. To Lindsey's first question he said, "Yea.... well kinda.... I think." The anguished look on his face and his muted stuttering caused Henry to rethink his attitude as it looked as though Lynsey had hit a nerve. His wrinkled brow and speech impediments cleared when it dawned on him that he really didn't know the right answer, if there was a right answer.

If yes, he understood Max might mean his mentality had digressed to the level of a dog or his mind had exponentially expanded during the summer to levers where he could now actually communicate with another species. Or...or...or NO would mean he was guessing. His head was saying I understand what Lynsey means when she tells me things when she really is saying one thing but actually means the opposite, and I am suppose to understand. He blinks a few times while his head worked out the details before it said 'if I can handle Lynsey and other females' it stands to reason I can handle a dog. Not real sure his heart actually believed what his head was thinking but for now let it pass. 'Yes… No?' His head yelled, but his mouth did not respond.

"I don't know." Henry was saying as Lynsey left the room.

Max and Henry have had many long talks over the last few years and Henry thinks they understand each other. Max doesn't have a clue what all the fuss is about.

Henry thinks Max thinks of him as: The kind of person that enjoys life to its fullest. He use to tell Max of his world travels when he would walk the Apian Way in the ruins of Rome and let his mind see merchants and soldiers of twenty-five centuries ago. His mind saw all the wondrous and spectacular sights inspired and directed by Augustus, Caligula and Julius as he stood in the center of the great Coliseum and before the three remaining pillars of the Vestal Virgins. The smallish Sistine Chapel was as large as the Grand Canyon as his mind witnessed

Max is fully enthralled →

Michelangelo working on its ceiling and the war-torn battle grounds of Vietnam were flower gardens and perfume hills as his mind saw beauty. He still took a good M-16 sight-picture of the bad-guys but that was part of the job. Even walking the streets of Pigalle in the City of Light (love) he saw the day-time purity of the ladies-of-the-evening and street whores.

Max thinks of Henry as: Abbaiare, Latrare and sometimes Uggiolare.

Yes, Henry understood Max.

Max is a Black Lab and as gentle as God made.

Max is the only male dog anywhere that does not lift his leg.

Max has huge brown eyes and the makings of gray whiskers under a mostly happy face.

Max is basically a pussycat and has taught Henry how to communicate, for example:

How does a dog tell you he's hungry? Do you look for sounds, looks, actions any combinations? What does it mean when a dog stands cross-legged or his eyes look watery?

Dog meal times are a lot like humans, breakfast when you get up, lunch at mid-day and dinner when the work day is over. Dogs, the lucky house pets, mostly have an early and late meal. Its fun to prepare Max's food. The morning meal is the same as the evening minus the beans. Max always shows his appreciation as he yelps smiles and bounces on his front legs. He's relatively quiet right up until the time the water is added to his silver serving bowl then he really shows his appreciation.

Don't ever get between Max and his meal. A huge paw from a 100 pound dog will get you stepped on 9 out of 10 times because you didn't get out of the path to the food dish quickly enough, but that's OK.

There is only one thing Henry has ever considered cruel toward Max. Sometimes, and it is rare and normally only during the summer months, when ice-cream is being shared after a dinner meal that he feels sorry for Max. Lynsey is only playing with him as she works her way toward the bottom of her ice-cream dish when she will click the dish several times with her spoon. This clicking has been in his vocabulary

since he was a pup and means 'goodies'. Click-click-click-click translated means you can have what's left. I have known humans to salivate over dessert (especially Crème Brule) and when Lynsey tells Max he can have some of her dessert he assumes the position.

←Would you share YOUR ice cream??

Directly in front of his benefactor, long front legs straight, paws turned inward and sitting on his bottom – waiting with panting breath, open mouth and a twinkle is each brown eye. Henry has always been a push-over when it comes to animals and particularly Max so when the discipline of Lynsey says, wait… wait it hurts to see Max sit at attention, waiting and drooling. Drooling!!

So far he and Henry have survived, but just barely. They both love ice-cream.

After several happy slurping sounds, it was now the moments the wet mouthed grinning black lab head sneezed twice then rubbed the side of his face on your pants leg. It was a ritual Max had used in training Henry, and it worked.

"You understood that?" Lynsey said.

Henry didn't mouth the words but simply nodded.

"Thanks buddy." It was the friendly phrase of a human toward his four legged buddy.
"Abbaiare, Latrare, Uggiolare…"
"What?"

"Abbaiare, Latrare, Uggiolare!!" Max emphasized.

"What does he want now?" Lynsey asked.

"Not sure. Almost sounds like he is trying to bark and yawn at the same time. Those must be the new words he learned over the holidays." Henry said as he seemed to concentrate on Max's head and face seeing if there was something he missed.

With a wrinkled brow Lynsey ask the simple question, "Henry…why do you call Max Buddy?"

The question was a good one but he had never given it any thought before. With down cast eyes then looking at the ceiling then toward Lynsey then in the vicinity of where Max was sprawled in the middle of the floor Henry finally muttered, "Not really sure. I probable mean it as a term of endearment. Rather then calling him by name four hundred times a day, I mix in *Buddy, Hay you and You Dumb Shit* sometimes. He recognizes the sounds as his and, I don't know, maybe it's because everyone else always calls him by the name you gave him eleven years ago. I try to keep him on his toes, so to speak." Henry continued with "I guess it's just my way of personalizing us. He and me. Us. Me and him. Max and Henry. Man animal and dog animal." Henry shut up as soon as he recognized the shut-up stance from Lynsey. His mouth was open to say something alone the lines, '…would you prefer me calling you Lynsey all day or would you mind if I threw in… 'Honey, Sweetheart or I love you', but he shut his mouth quickly and with his right hand made the jester of zipping his lip. She grinned.

"Gagnolage" Max tried from his prone position.

Later that day Henry sat in front of his keyboard remembering Lynsey comments and questions. It made him curious.

When you have the world in your keyboard and access to over eight billion web sites and most words that have ever been published, you use it. Henry typed "Define the language DOG" into his favorite search engine.

The query results were instantaneous. Well maybe not but 0.02 seconds is faster then quick but a bit slower then instant and just short of infinity.

Many of the 1,368,992 results were basically the same, same meanings, different wording but they all answered his query, more or less:

'On this earth there are eleven major languages spoken by over 2.8 bllion people. There are more then 6 billion human here that leaves something less then 4 billion other people speaking languages that only a few rapper and young people can understand, and that is if you don't count dialects. Just in the United States we have four major dialect regions: the Inland North, the South, the West, and the Midland not to mention pure Southern, Yankee, Eastern, Hollywood, and several dialects each spoken in Philadelphia, Connecticut, Maine, Arkansas, and Rhode Island. Then you have Proper English, Broken English, the Kings English, Pigeon English and American English spoken with rolling R's to 277 accents all with misplaced vowels. The written word in this hodgepodge and patchwork languages is a bit easier to understand but then you have DOG.'

Dogs can not "human speak" but can be understood.

Speaking Dog requires a tongue that can reach all parts of the anatomy to include the complete nose and "other parts". Understanding Dog is easy because all you must do is be able to understand body language, moods and bodily noises, but you have to pay attention. Dog owners in the world are in the minority of those that have pets. Records and polls tell us there are only 43 to 68 million of us kept dogs.

Still further down the minority food chain or those that actually speak DOG. Speaking may be a misnomer as 'understanding' may be the better word.

As Henry read his screen his mind was saying, "…I just added DOG to my resume."

One whimsical web site from his query said, 'Would you be interested in knowing there are 238 vowel systems? No wonder the tongue gets tired at parties and eating tough steak. Dogs tongue never gets tired from barking or eating.

Dogs do not have vocal cords that can pronounce words, but they communicate nicely. They have no cuss words that we know of but they leave nothing to the immigration through innuendos or body language. How do you learn DOG? Why would anyone even be interested in knowing what an animal was saying or trying to communicate? Dogs are another species not as developed as some but more so then others – say for example… cats.'

Normal breathing was coming from Max curled at Henry's feet on the carpeted computer room. Henry was busy reading and Max was busy, well he was busy doing, just busy doing his thing – nothing. Henry had become absorbed in his computer and had not noticed Lynsey standing behind him. He hated when she did that.

His heart skipped a couple beats when her silky voice came from just over his head, "Hi there. What up?"

It was a short minute before he responded. "We were talking about understanding Max earlier and I was just looking up what others say about understanding dogs and how to communicate with them. What I found is interesting. You want to read over my shoulder for a while?"

Lynsey didn't bother answering as she pulled a chair from across the room and settled in. With her face almost resting on Henry's shoulder and her honeyed breath on his cheek she said, "...sure." It was most erotic.

Henry slowly scrolled the black lettering down the white monitor screen:

The screen said in part:
'It's important to understand what dogs are saying with their bodies, not only to know your own dog but to better predict what other dogs are doing.

To really read dog body language takes experience. We encourage you to watch your own dog(s) and others. Go to the dog park and watch dogs interacting. Watch different body parts (ears, tails, eyes, lips, hair, and overall posture) separately for a while. See if you can predict which body stances lead to which activities or outcomes.'

"Henry this is boring." Her tone was of pure exasperation.

He quickly changed three pages of instructional data with a couple key strokes. He did leave one more paragraph that she skipped.

'If you find that your dog is "protecting" you, consider that your dog thinks of you as a valuable resource that he must guard, like a prized bone. Yes, he possesses you.
Sounds of Dog's 'Laugh' Calms Other Pooches Researchers: Canine Laugh Is Long Loud Panting Sound. Researchers at the Spokane County Regional Animal Protection Service in Washington State say sometimes a bark is just a bark -- but a long, loud panting sound has real meaning.'

Maybe saying that Henry learned to speak and understand dogs is not entirely accurate. Understanding and just paying attention may be better words.

At times Max's sounds are different. His hip movement is sometimes different when they were out for walks. At times Max would swagger while a normal walk was just that – a walk. At times he would poop in places that were off limits he always had a gleam in his eyes and would either wink or protest his innocents. He acted differently at different times of the day; when he was taken to the Vet, when being boarded out for a humans long week-end and when he knew being thrown into the lake for a bath rather then for play…. He was always different.

Max has developed a new trick while on his walks. He limps. At the beginning of the walks Max is full of energy and wonderment of the surroundings, sniffing, barking and enjoying life. As soon as Henry lets him know it is time to head back to the barn... Max limps. Mostly on his left front but when he forgets, the limp is on the right front. Two weeks ago Max could not remember so he dragged a rear foot. His brown eyes always become soulful and ears droop. Poor guy. Henry had been well trained so the walks are normally extended until Max agrees to go home.

Henry doesn't have a clue what is going on inside Max's head when they talk. Maybe it is just the different sounds of different words mean different things to Max and Henry.

Today walking Max was approached by Blackie the neighbors black Coonhound. They did their sniff, nipping and growling routine when Henry said, "Max HEEL" The command he knew to get his butt to his master and heel. The coonhound took off with its tail between its legs.

Buddy as a Pup

Buddy second from left

Apparently 'heel' meets something bad to Blackie.

Chances are Max doesn't have a clue either what is going on inside Henry's head. Many times even Henry doesn't even know.

BUT... whatever is happening between their collective ears, they got along nicely.

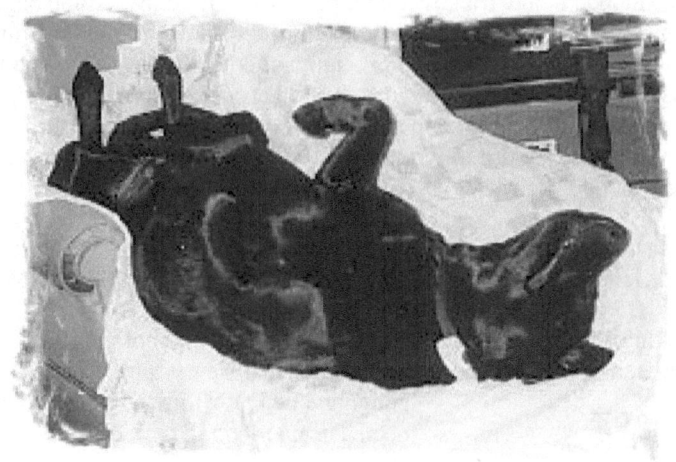

The attitude I got when my stories bored him.

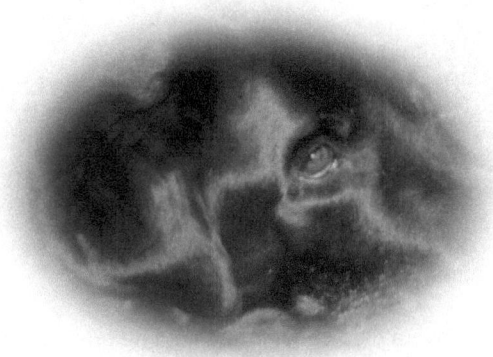

Max just moments before going to sleep at the vet's office.
My heart cried.

Steve Rogers

Honesty, complete honesty is sometimes rare but always welcomed.

*Honesty **and** Intelligence are rare…*

1. Question: If you could live forever, would you and why?

Answer: "I would not live forever, because we should not live forever, because, if we were supposed to live forever, then we would live forever, but we cannot live forever, which is why I would not live forever"
---Miss Alabama in the 1994 Miss USA contest.

2. "Whenever I watch TV and see those poor starving kids all over the world, I can't help but cry. I mean, I'd love to be skinny like that, but not with all those flies and death and stuff."
---Mariah Carey

3. Researchers have discovered that chocolate produces some of the same reactions in the brain as marijuana. The researchers also discovered other similarities between the two, but can't remember what they are."
---Mat Lauer on NBC's Today Show, August 22.

By nature I am a Cynical person.

Why? It can be argued there may be good reasons, maybe not.

I grew up in the south in the 1940s in a small town where gossip was faster then the town paper. We knew for a fact when Betty Sue got '…in a family way…' she was trash or when Frank Jay did not go to church on Sunday, he was still drunk from booze and drugs from partying all night and when Ruth Ann's five children all looked like they had different fathers, they did. Rumors, gossip, and hear-say that were never true, well maybe, but made you wonder. When you are a teen-ager talk kinda made you suspicious but you never ventured out from behind snickering hands and back yard hearsay to look at the real person where the talk was aimed. It was always easier to listen to gossip and believe the worse of a person. Some folk's call that Human Nature, while others call it being suspicious or skeptical. The word cynical has the connotation of evil but because of my nature when I see a spade..., I call it a spade.

Learned teen habits are hard to overcome in later years.

But I did... I think.

After college, I had a career in the military and can cuss like a drunken sailor when my brain goes into its stupid mode and because of my youth I have been known to do many wild and not so smart actions against my fellow man. In those twenty military years I saw all sides and traits of mankind, from the pentagon where I helped make life and death decisions normally with intelligent and hopeful honest people to the battle fields of sunny Vietnam where many of my decisions were made thought the sight-pictures of my M-16. In the jungle I never knew who was smart or honest only what uniform they were wearing. You don't have to be smart to pull a trigger nor do you care about the image that is your target. You don't know nor care what that target had for breakfast, if they had children or if they were an honest, caring, intelligent person or if they have lied in the past. Your cynical mind always justifies they are the bad guys and deserve their fate.

After the military I worked another career for our government in Washington D.C... That was scary.

I saw first hand that Cynicism is rampant in politics and right or wrong it is the bed we vote for ever four years. Who can you believe? When my President tells me folks are bad and deserve to die I figure he/she has gone beyond the gossip mill and know what he is saying. I believe because, after all, I am not a teenager any more. I listen to all the news from the Right, from the Left, the Liberals the

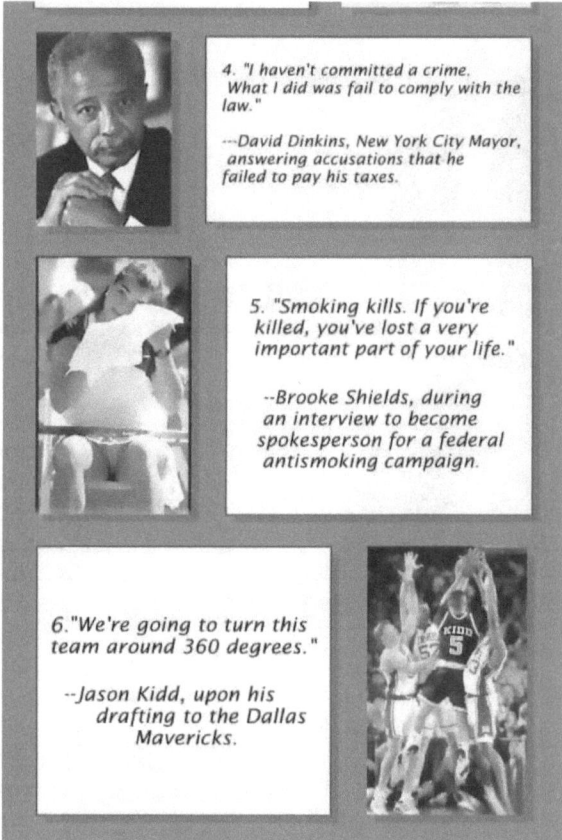

4. "I haven't committed a crime. What I did was fail to comply with the law."

---David Dinkins, New York City Mayor, answering accusations that he failed to pay his taxes.

5. "Smoking kills. If you're killed, you've lost a very important part of your life."

--Brooke Shields, during an interview to become spokesperson for a federal antismoking campaign.

6."We're going to turn this team around 360 degrees."

--Jason Kidd, upon his drafting to the Dallas Mavericks.

Conservatives, the good, the bad and the ugly and I usually make up my own mind, but still there is cynicism.

The last time I was in Lafayette Park there was a protesting group of ladies advocating carnal knowledge to protect Virginity? Go figure.

I am not a teenager any more but I sometimes feel I have not out-grown my stupid and suspicious stage. I still only believe half of what I see and nothing I am told.

Then Steve Rogers enters my picture.

I have never actually met Steve, but we have talked on the phone and I am not cynical or suspicious or distrustful of him. He is an Honorable and honest person.

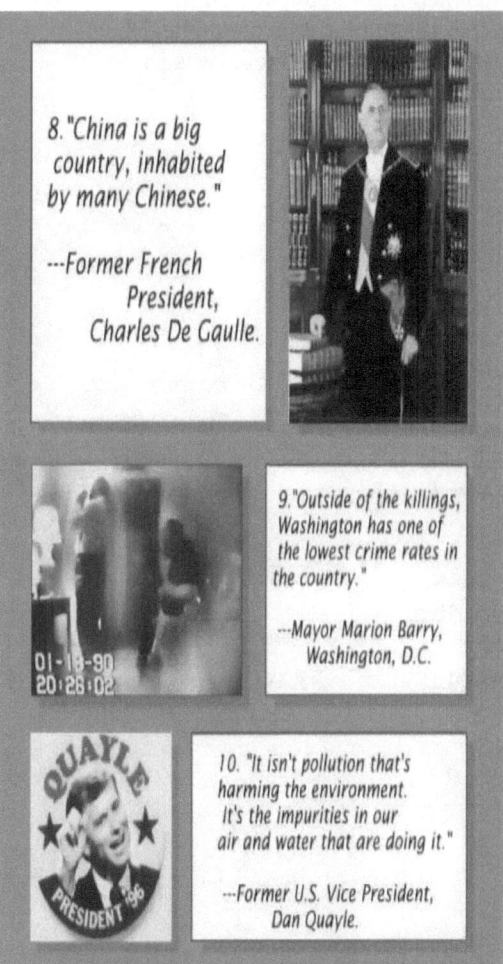

8. "China is a big country, inhabited by many Chinese."

---Former French President, Charles De Gaulle.

9. "Outside of the killings, Washington has one of the lowest crime rates in the country."

---Mayor Marion Barry, Washington, D.C.

01-18-90
20:28:02

QUAYLE
★ PRESIDENT '96 ★

10. "It isn't pollution that's harming the environment. It's the impurities in our air and water that are doing it."

---Former U.S. Vice President, Dan Quayle.

How do I know that?

Steve runs the South West Optics business in the UK and is incredibly trustworthy. What makes me so positive in this conviction?

Real time is November 2005 and the time of the year I begin making my Christmas list, checking it twice and trying to find that all important perfect gift. I listen to suggestions, to innuendos to body language and I always listen very carefully to that that is not said. It is amazing the ideas you can come up with to what is not said. For this very special person I came up with Optics as their gift. Not your everyday optics but special and the kind Wal-Mart, Best Buy and Radio Shack don't carry. I found the perfect gift online, on the Internet. The store was seven time-zones away but the gift had to be just perfect with no substitutes. IF I had been able to find the same optics in my U.S. Central time zone I would have been happy to pay a reasonable price but because all stores and internet stores where out of stock and would have to backorder I choose **South West Optics.** Because of the weak dollar again the Pound Sterling my special optics were almost twice what the item would have cost IF I could have found it in the States.

Why do I still say the nice things about Steve Rogers if he was charging twice the going U.S. price? My reasoning was his phone call and his words.

Backordering gives me the chills and is a hold-over from my early cynicism as a youth, as a military person and my face-to-face reality of the world I live in today. The last item I backordered at this time of the year arrived the following May.

Steve Rogers called me a couple days ago. It was a Sunday evening and he was seven time zones away but he called to tell me I would be wasting my money if he filled my order. He had researched my order and found where I could buy my Optics, in the States, for a fraction what he would have to charge. We chatted for several minutes about backordering and need as a Christmas gift before it dawned on me he was paying international phone rates which can be an arm and a leg sometimes.

He made a business decision that cost him a nice sale by allowing me to cancel my order, but his voice inflected what he had done was his character, his nature, his personality and temperament and the right thing to do.

My youth and much of my adult life was remembered as I re-cradled the phone. I do not attend church as regularly as I should but I am a religious person. As the years go past faster in retirement, I sometimes do some cramming for finals from King James, just in case. I just re-read Jeremiah 5:1-3 and *smiled as I remembered Steve Rogers.*

Then there is Christopher Morley and folks like Scrooge and Bush II, but they are other stories. Read some of their writings when you have time.

Good Morning Betty Sue
(As told with a wee bit of literary license)

Sex, Love, Rape, The Internet, Death … all to no avail

Sunday the first of July has the beginning of just another day for Betty Sue. Two of her three grown children have come over for breakfast and as always the discussion was what Mom needs to do about her nightmares now that Dad has moved out of the house and in with a woman half his age.

"Dad has been gone four months now" Mary said as she stared at her mother, "You have to get out of this house, do something; hobbies, part time work, volunteer at the hospital… something."

Betty Sue did not disagree with her daughter. She had been telling herself the same thing for almost two months but she just didn't know how to go about it. She didn't have a clue what her first step should be. She had married right out of High School, three kids before she was 21 and a homemaker for over 20 years. "Your right, of course and I agree with what you are saying, I really do." Her eyes welled and she made no effort to stop the tears from flowing. They had seen her cry almost daily the year before dear ole dad left and more so these last months. Cheeks had ringlets of water as she finally said, "Now that I have the house all to myself, what do you suggest?"

Eileen Rasmussen pictured on the right is Betty Sue for this story.

This may have been the question Billy had been waiting to hear from his mother. Instead of words, he fished into a pocket of his jeans and placed a bright blue box on the table in front of his mother. The box was smallish, less then a couple inches square and about a half-inch thick. Gold flake raised lettering in a slight curved arc near the top of the box had one word, "TROJAN". Betty Sue had not seen a box of these since before her first child when she practiced birth control.

Mary looked at her brother and through him. He returned the gaze but with shrugged shoulders and a why not grin as he answered her unasked question. "Why not, Mom is free now and over 21". As Mary dropped her gaze he had the offensive so he looked at his mother and continued, "Mon… you need to get out. You need to meet people. You need…." He was busy telling her what she needed and she knew all along what she needed, just didn't know How to go about GETTING it.

Maybe it was time to have that family chat about the birds and bees but kinda in reverse. As motherly as she could muster with a new box of Trojans sitting on the table between the butter and the grits she told them that their dad was the only man she had even been with, and the only thing she knew about life outside raising a family was what she had read in dozens of Harlequin sex books and watching Doris Day movies.

Mary interrupted with, "Mom, Doris Day movies are…" Betty Sue cut her short with a huge grin saying she was just rattling her cage and yes, she knew Ms. Day was Little-Miss-Goody-Two-Shoes and that she had seen a few hard core movies and even some staring John Holmes. That shut Mary up.

"Kids… my problem is I don't have a clue how to meet men. I kinda know what to do with your Trojans Billy but THE problem is getting a man here for me to try on him." The kitchen was so quiet even the Grits were still as Billy ate his last spoonful.

Billy swallowed hard as he looked toward Mary as she looked at him, her mother and back, then toward her mother again and finally said, "Mom… we need to go... for now. Love you very much." And with that said, Mary motioned for her brother to follow her outside as she had a plan.

Mary was in command as she said to Billy just before getting into her van and leaving. "Meet me at Best Buy in twenty minutes" and she was gone in a cloud of dust and flying pebbles.

In less then two hours Mary and Billy were back in Betty Sue's driveway. Mary held open the front door as Billy muscled in one large cardboard box after the other. Betty watched as the kids opened each box, assemble parts, plug in things and hand their mother a brightly colored yellow and black soft cover book titled "The Internet for Dummies".

Mary took charge saying, "Here you go Mom. Here is the world at your fingertips."

Betty Sue was quiet as Mary talked then Billy would interrupt with spurts of knowledge as he would be interrupted by Mary doing the same. During the next hour they had the computer up and running with the Internet. They explained Google, Dog Pile, Mr. Jeeves, A9, Chat Rooms, Email, IMs, Passwords, Log-in IDs and even opened an Internet account.

The kids were very proud of themselves.

Betty Sue was as confused as a human could be and if you looked into her eyes you would not see any Xs and Os, let alone 0s and 1s connected, but over the course of the evening with some hands-on keyboard action, Betty Sue Soloed.

Monday was overcast and rained all day. Tuesday was a steady downpour as was Wednesday. The days were warm but dreary but Betty Sue never saw them.

She had pulled all the blinds and shades in her den, turned on the computer, propped up her legs and pulled the key board into her lap. One bottle of Zinfandel disappeared as did another then another as day time turned to night to day to night back to day before Betty Sue signed off her window to the world.

Betty Sue was hooked.

When you are chatting with another person on-line you never know if they are on the other side of the world or next door. Most times if you asked they tell you they are in

some exotic world famous location and they are the perfect, or near perfect specimen of human. They mostly lie. As luck would have it she met and chatted with a very nice sounding man that lived only a few miles away. They agreed to meet for lunch.

"Good afternoon Ms. Betty Sue, my name is Albert. It is so nice you agreed to meet for lunch. I have made room reservations for a couple hours at the Motel just down the street so if you don't mind we can go down there first then come back here for coffee." He was serious.

Her hand was still stinging from a wicked hard open right hand slap as she drove home.

Throughout the history of mankind a turn to the right causes one thing to happen whereas if that turn is to the left another set of events happen. Sometimes even the sting in a hand will cause events to happen.

Today Betty Sue took her first major step away from the Doris Day mold into the world of reality as she discovered the Internet was bottomless.

"There are tens of millions of people on the internet. Logic tells me half of those have to be men, so there has to one out there for me." Betty Sue argued with herself. "If I have to, I'll type my fingers to the bone and will not rest until I give them all a try or until I find the one that can be the other half of this couple." Her brain paused before it said, "I really want to be a couple". She paused again, looked sideway into the hall mirror. "So what I'm a little short. I'm in shape... pear is a shape. My hair is blond, I am witty and I am cute so there has to be someone out there – for me." The tears that eased from the corners of her eyes and escaped down her cheeks went unnoticed.

A car trip into New York City for a Broadway play produced another stinging hand.

A plane trip with a best friend to Texas and a night out bar hopping produced still two more stinging hands.

More car trips to Philadelphia, Washington DC, Boston, Hartford, Trenton and another United flight to San Francisco produced still more stinging hard right hands.

Then there was Geoff. The box her son had given her many months ago was used as was several others. Geoff was educated, intelligent, good company, fair sex, good conservationist, witty, good looking, handled himself well at parties and in crowds but as soon as the glow of the physical began to wear thin and the reality of being a couple sank in he stopped calling, stopped all E-Mail and dropped off the face of the earth as far as Betty Sue was concerned. Bastard. There was never any closure with Geoff, never any satisfactory stinging hand – nothing but more emptiness and more tears.

Frank knew of Betty Sue and several of his on-line friends talked of her in chat room and at the many rooms Bashes. He always listened but being a man that has had foot-in-mouth disease many times knew when to be quiet especially at the many week-end parties where no door is locked and few wear underwear. The Internet did itself a favor when it created the venue for grown people to get together where there were few rules and call them bashes.

Betty Sue will give the shirt off her back to anyone in need and will drive 300 miles if invited to a friend's house for pizza. Betty Sue is a good person that believes in God, family, country and all people are basically decent but Geoff was almost that straw that broke the camel's back... almost.

After Geoff, Betty Sue turned thoughts into more positive action as she screened potential lovers/partners as carefully as she knew how and was lucky in one respect. She never ran across the axe-murders, rapist, sadists, con artists (well a couple), and habitual liars that could cause further hurt, but she did have several more false starts with different men until she accepted the advice of a friend to spend some time with a man she had casually met at a birthday party given for her by an internet friend in another state. His name was Frank and he came with references. Her friend told Betty Sue, "...I have known Frank for several years and we are good friends."

"How good is good?" Betty Sue asked.

Bess was ginning from ear to ear as she said, "Good. Good like in I took him to bed a few times and he is good." That was a scary answer to a still coming of age 40 something year old.

"I haven't been with that many men...." She was interrupted by Bess saying "Not to worry sweetie, he will teach you all you need to know."

Now that was scary but if you looked real close into Betty Sue eyes there were little devils at play.

The internet is finally becoming fun. A few taps on the keyboard and he was there with you in your house, your studio, your room, your bedroom. Where ever you have the computer. Click, click, tap, tap, tap, tap and you have the world in your keyboard. "Hi Frank. My name is Missy." Frank's screen suddenly had an IM note.

"I don't get many Instant Messages lady, do I know you?" He IMed back.

"No."

Franks instinct was to turn off his IMs or just block her but he didn't. He sat staring at the terse IM as him mind went through many gyration. After several minutes he sipped his watered drink, squirmed a bit in repositioning his bottom then keyed, "No... what?" If she wanted to play games, so could he.

The IM response was slow in coming but finally the screen said, "No. Well not really. We were introduced once at Bess's house. It was my birthday party."

Frank is a man with a man's mentality and hormones. He didn't have a clue who or what Missy looked like or who she was. That birthday party was a bit like a hangover haze.

His IM response was a lie but until his brain drew him a better image that this haze he is looking through he keyed, "Well yes. How are you Missy?"

The IMs went back and forth for a few minutes before Missy said her doorbell was ringing and she had to go. That was a lie also but that is what people mostly do on the internet.

Frank was quick to the telephone. "Hello Bess.... Who is Missy?"

She filled him in on female attributes until he had a good idea now that Missy was Betty Sue and Bess had given him a glowing reference.

"You gave me a reference? What am I suppose to do with that?"

Bess had to be having a fun time toying with Frank. "Well if I were you fella, I'd make reservation somewhere for the weekend and give her a call."

As a small light appeared over Franks head he said, "Now I remember. That was the girl that was there with her boyfriend, a Geoff something and I think I remember hearing they were planning on spending that night and the whole next day in bed. It was her birthday right?"

"Yes she was and yes they did." Bess said. She wanted to say more but held her tongue.

"You're crazy, you know that?" Franks voice was smiling at the prospect after a few hormones got his attention and as he held the phone slightly away from his ear, suddenly prospects of a weekend of sex, fun and games didn't sound that bad. Bess was quiet on her end of the phone waiting for Frank to continue his thoughts. There was nothing now but dead air then he said, "...but she has a man-friend. What does she need with another?" Stupid question from a no-nothing man about women and all Bess did was silently shake her head. She wanted to tell him that a woman can not have too many men friends and seldom can a woman have enough sex, but again held her tongue after saying, "Just do it dummy... trust me on this one. Have I ever lied to you or pointed you in the wrong direction?" But quickly added, "Don't answer that, just go and have a good time."

It was nice chatting over the internet and telephone but real life is better. Betty Sue described her first week-end with him in a brief note to Bess simply as "WOW".

In the following months they found many facets of their lives that gave them pleasure. Sex? Sure lots of sex, and it was always good as they learned to share, but there was one hard headed Betty Sue idealism that caused Frank concern. He was ex-military and knew weapons were good to know and understand, but he couldn't get that point across to Betty Sue. The argument was the same he had heard time and time again, "...I don't like guns..... They are dangerous.... and I don't need nor want one... They scare me...." There had been no way to get the point across that guns don't have to be bad, but sometimes you really need one.

Frank tried the old truisms, "They are what their owner makes them. Guns don't kill people... People kill people", etc...etc.. even the argument, "Would you druther be dead or use a gun in your defense?" Good arguments for someone interested or listened but not so to Betty Sue. This is an opinionated woman that knew her mind and right or wrong, she had dug her heels in. Frank knew he was losing the battle, but in the back of his mind, he didn't mind losing a battle or two, if he could just win the war. And that was all important to him. She had become a part of his life he wanted her around for a while so was trying to do what he knew could very possible, someday save an innocent life.

It's hard to understand how someone else feels toward any particular subject or thing, that's why we have to rely on speech to communicate feelings. The hard part comes when you know in your heart that knowing about things, in this case, guns, would benefit you. Some people don't like dogs, and they are man's best friend. The same can be said about cat lovers or anyone that has an animal for a pet. I know, I know... don't push your beliefs onto someone else; let them learn the hard way. A lesson leaned the hard way, though experience and hard knocks is a lesson that will stay with you a lot longer then just being told something. If you live though it that is.

Betty Sue lives in New Jersey. The rolling hills of Northern NJ are lust green during the summer months and brilliant reds, oranges, and yellows of fall. Winters are cold and for the most part with a white covering of snow or ice. For Betty Sue, it isn't a fun place for

the cold parts of the year. Betty Sue's spacious and comfortable home sits geographically in the center and highest point of five acres. There was a barn that held live stock at one time in years past, a wooden fence that could use a handyman's touch and a bottom flat couple acres that you could always see deer, bear and other smaller creatures roaming at will. The property was perfectly safe from predators. Unfortunately it was during the drab morning hours of one of these nasty cold monotonous dreary days a weak knock on her front door Betty Sue welcomed a two-legged killer into

her home. He didn't look like a predator, he had no scales, his tongue was not forked, his feet were no cloven and his eyes were round and not cat-like. His clothing and manners suggested he was affluent and innocent. He said his name was Louis. He said he had lost control of his car on the dangerous curve at the bottom of her knoll near her driveway and destroyed her mailboxes. He was sorry for that, and he would be more then willing to pay for their replacement, but his main problem was the front end of his cheap air-bag less Japanese car. He was pretty sure he had damaged the left front of the car and couldn't move it. Could he use her phone to call a garage or toll service to come get him? Please.

Sure. With a smile on her honey lips and the graciousness of a sophisticated lady, she said if her mailboxes caused him harm, the least she could do is invite him in and the warmth of her home for the use of phone and facilities. "Sure. Please come in."

Betty Sue is a pretty woman. Blond hi-lighted close trimmed hair is shiny, healthy, doesn't quite brush the top of her shoulders when she laughs and uses her arms to gesture or to welcome Louis with a friendly hand-shake. Her Brown eyes sparkled as she sympathized at his story of her mail boxes. In the 22 years in her home, more then just Louis had run down her mail boxes. She smiled to herself as she remembered one time one of her lovers from Maryland had been visiting and she scrapped the side of her own car on one of the three mail boxes. Louis's hand was cold as she welcomed him inside. Out of concern for his well being Betty Sue used both her hands over his for warmth and a gesture of friendliness. She was a bit careless. Her silk morning robe had been properly belted and pulled closed under her chin, but with the extension of both her arms and influenced by her amble breasts the robe parted slightly and reveled the deep valley between two creamy perfumed mounds of white flesh. Louis recognized the scent of Opium and smiled to himself. The last women he raped and murdered just last week was also wearing Opium. He liked it. Louis was thinking today was going to be interesting. Betty Sue didn't have a clue. Lately she has been meeting more and more people, especially men so she took Louis at face value. She didn't know at the time, but unless she stopped him, stopped events he would put into motion, an innocent person was going to die today.

Louis was shown a wall telephone in the kitchen area and was left along for his call. Betty Sue returned to her computer in her warm and cozy den area just opposite her spacious kitchen. She was comfortable. The fire in her wood burning stove in the far corner had recently been fed; its door closed and was happily radiating heat. The sun is probable shining somewhere but here on Sid Taylor place in Lafayette Township the sky is low and drab and shuddery and trees boarding Betty Sue's property were still glistening from frozen dew. Funny, for no reason as Betty Sue was standing behind her computer chair facing glass doors leading to a patio area looking outside toward her friend Mary's house, thoughts not of her visitor but of her lover and how he liked the idea she sometimes didn't wear underwear. I will have to slip out of these before Frank gets here she thought to herself as a tingle of pleasure ran from the tips of her hard nipples to her breastbone then straight down to a damping . Her OB-GYN doctors told her she was perfectly normal and that she was actually jealous of a woman her age could still have those very human reactions through thought and action. Betty Sue grinned and subconsciously looked at her watch. 10:26 AM. Frank should be here before 2 PM. He called yesterday and said he should be on the road before 9 AM and with the way he drives, he never makes it less than 5 hours coming up from the South. One of these days, I'm going to have to take him out on the open highway and teach him how to keep up with traffic. Here it is already 2 years into the 21st century and he still drives like the roads were gravel and there were police out there trying to control speed. They stopped that practice at the end of 2001 and changed their priorities to helping those that asked for it. Few asked for speeding tickets now days.

Louis passed some pleasantries by saying "Thank you very much Miss for the use of your phone. The garage said they are a bit backed up right now, but should be here in an hour or so. Is it all right if I warm myself by your fire and wait inside?" Sure. Coffee was offered and accepted. Louis's was black, Betty Sue's with just a trace of low calorie half and half. Louis is a big man. Maybe 6'-3" probable in the 220 weight range but could have been 170. It was hard for Betty Sue to judge until he took his tailored suit jacket off and draped it over her washing machine next to the phone he had used.

There is light conversation as coffee is sipped, then without any warning Louis gets up from the couch and started opening cabinets in the kitchen area. "Say, Mr. uh, Louis I'm not real sure what you are doing, but whatever it is, please stop. This is my home and I don't remember asking you do go through my cabinets." He didn't bother answering. Just as she was about to say her piece again he apparently found what he was looking for. A well stocked liquor cabinet. He was not careful looking thought the bottles, rattling them and knocking two over reaching for a full liter bottle of I.W. Harper. He took a deep swallow.

Well damn him to hell, he has no right to go against my wishes. There was rancor in her mind and body but the thought of danger never crossed her pretty head. Betty Sue's second mistake was trying to reach the wall phone. The bottle was switched to his left hand as he brought his right hand back as if getting ready to throw a baseball and slapped her hard against her left cheek. The open hand was huge and rough against her delicate skin, as the blow knocked her glasses off and hurt like a son-of-a-bitch. She had never been slapped in anger before, and certainly never this hard. From her view point the blow sounded like a clap of thunder inside her head, didn't knock her down but did stagger her back into the den area and turned her all the way around. It crossed her eyes and by the time she could focus again she was still bend slightly at the waist looking for her glasses and trying to think. We're in trouble!! Her brain yelled at her. Why in the hell did he do that? Shit... I didn't do anything to him. Where is Frank? What time is it? Damn.

The clock on her microwave read - 11:03 AM

The atmosphere in the den was becoming highly charged with more then just emotions. Over the years this room has seen its share of human drama; kids growing, parties, school events, dogs barking, laughter, typical family problems, crying over a failed marriage, loving, procreation and your every day sex; sex by the kids, the husband, his lady friends Betty Sue's friends, the lovers, but never bodily injury. These walls didn't have a clue what hard, permanent, premeditated type violence was. The theater sized Television opposite the couch didn't help matters. It was never turned off and Queen for a Day was just starting with the typical topic for today's audiences, "Sex - To Orgasm or Not". The fireplace in the corner was not a lot different then roaring fire in her head form the slap and the confusion of what was happening to her, she could barely heard words and parts of sentences over the real live shouting and rambling demands from Louis being made in the den. "... Clit... rubbers ... erection... the last time was... sensitivity.... The theme of the show was for this group of six ladies on the show to come up with the sadist sexual episode they had ever had to endure, and the audience would decide who would win the likes of, washing machines, microwaves, portable hair dryer, or six months vacation to a place of their choosing. A real grab bag prize list so sometimes the topics were really juicy. From the

 couch she thought she heard the words – "When was the last time you was fucked little lady?" Pardon me? Betty Sue heard herself saying. "Are you deaf, cunt? I said when the last time you got a good fucking." His voice was calm and even, maybe a bit horse from being in the cold but very understandable. Betty Sue straightened and looked him straight in his gray eyes and said, "...none of your fucking business - now I want you out of my home. Now!!... Understand? GET OUT!" She was angry, her face hurt and she was scared. The first dish she threw at him, missed. He slowly turned his head from side to side. He was serious. It

must have been at that moment the reality of the moment hit home and she became more frightened. He repeated his question through clenched teeth and glaring stare. His size made him menacing and him drawing his arm back again in the same manner when he first slapped her, made her re-think her original thinking of physically matching up him. Betty Sue thought about her answer for a full second before straightening to her full 5'- 1" and now calmly saying. "When Frank gets here you're in trouble!"

Good, that was a good answer. This woman has some spunk. He liked that and laughed while taking another long pull from his bottle. "Well little lady, consider this your lucky day, because I am going to f*ck you - and you need not have to worry about winning any trips either. When I fuck a woman she is never satisfied with anyone else, and the thoughts of a trip are soon forgotten. Well actually, when you come to think about it, for many I am the last screwing they get." Then he laughed at his private joke. "Little lady, do you have any idea who I am?" He paused then said, "...no, you probable don't, but IF you did, you would know I am no man to mess with. In my time, I have killed 16 women and you want to know what I did to them just before I killed them? Well pretty little lady, I don't think I'll need to tell you, cause I'm going to show you."

Betty Sue's mind was a whirlwind of thoughts, idea and fears. Her brain yelled this is a god-damn psycho. You are in for a bit of trouble if you can't get him out of the house. Get your gun? Where did I put that damn gun Frank gave me last year? Not sure why she was so calm and didn't seem to bother Betty Sue, her guts may have been on fire but outwardly, she was as calm as if the pool man had just told her pool maintenance wouldn't cost any more then last year. Frank always told her that the only way to survive in combat was to keep your head and operate within your emotions.

She didn't notice, but this maniac was talking and moving forward one small slide step at a time until he was within arms length of her. She was standing as tall as she could in her bare feet and defiant as her Yankee heritage would allow.

RAPE! There's hard sex, there's demeaning sex then there's brutal mean sex where the sex act is nothing more then a mask for brutality. He smiled again as he grabbed the front of her robe and torn its top open. The pink teddy lost its top three buttons as he ripped downward leaving her right breast exposed. Betty Sue is petite in most areas, but not her breast. She was almost fully developed in the 8th grade, and by the time she was dating in high-school she was know as Larry's girl friend with the big tits.

← **The Rape of Polyxena**

Now 30 years later she was still very well endowed. The breast sagged just a bit and was rose tipped by bullet hard nipples and oracles that looked as hard as pink skating rinks. She was embarrassed at being exhibited and angry enough to bite a ten-penny nail as she struck out. She threw her right hand at his head... and connected. That was a mistake, but at the time it made her feel good. He laughed once again as he dropped his Harper and grabbed the bodice of her shirt pulling her close to him as he hit her first with an open right hand then a backhand.

The pain in his hand was nothing compared to the stinging in Betty Sue's cheeks and pounding in her head as he grinned through clenched dirty yellow teeth. His eyes were wide and there was drool on his chin. His breath smelled like a sewer in Paris. He was standing with legs spread so he could get a better swing. Holding her with his left hand as he raised his right hand again. It seemed the perfect time to knee him hard in the crouch. She would show him. She has seen this exact scenario many times in the movies and they always got away from their attacker. All she had to do was knee him real good and send his balls high into his chest and walk away. She tried. Damn. She tried to get to her feet and throw her good right hand. For her efforts she got slapped again, really hard this time. Betty Sue's eyes crossed again and her mind became a jumble with what was happening. Why her, why was this happening, where did this animal come from?

Deep within the collage of her mind she saw scenes from her block in New York, the Brownstone, the yard, she saw herself sitting on the front steps, then in the front seat of a car. Betty Sue blinked then blinked again. It was her all right and her boyfriend at the time, her bodice open, both breasts free of her bra, her panties hanging over the steering wheel, her legs in the air and a huge man moving in rhythm to her giggles. She saw herself playing poker with a Mafia gunman friend - wish he was here now. Another stinging right hand snapped her back to the present and a very real danger from this animal now clawing at her panties. Louis was not being careful as he was tearing at the skin of her stomach searching for the elastic top. He finally gave up the search and grabbed a hand full of silk and flesh and torn.

The pain in her stomach was nothing compared to the back of her head when he slapped her once more and punched her hard into a book case. Betty Sue had lost her glasses with the first slap an eternity ago, but she could make out what was happening. The back of her head felt damp and her back hurt from the force of being pushed across the room into a sudden and violent stop against the wall and book case. Louis had opened the fly to his jeans and was holding what looked to be not that large, but a very hard and crooked cucumber. It had warts and scabs around the shaft and two on the little head. His shirt was open and she could also see sores, nasty looking reddish and purple sores. She had seen this same picture in her doctor's office during a class last month on advanced AIDS. She felt sick to her stomach. She had to stop him... somehow.

"Now my cute little cunt you are going to get the fucking of your life." She heard the words but didn't see his lips moving. He seemed to turn loose of the cucumber as he grabbed both her ankles and pulled her to the center of the brown deep piled carpeted room. Surprisingly the rug burn didn't hurt and the new pain of her ankles was somewhat muted as it finally registered that if she didn't get her gun and stop this son-of-a-bitch if he didn't kill her on the spot, the disease would in a few years. What was it that Frank use to tell me, a gun can be your friend, it never sleeps, is always ready, willing and very able. Her mind calmed momentarily with thoughts of family then her brain reminded her, "I hate guns, am afraid of them, have always been afraid if I had one, I might hurt someone. Hurt someone? Yea right. That is exactly what I need my gun for right now... to hurt this SOB." The human mind is a strange and wondrous organ. It can cause pain as well as mask it. It can compute at the speed of light or decipher a shopping list at the grocery store, and it can recall pleasant and unpleasant events almost simultaneously.

When her eyes finally uncrossed she realized she was looking at the ceiling fan and a now drunken Louis was between her legs clawing at her panties and mauling her exposed breasts at the same time. He was intent on rape and unlike one other time she had been in this kind of situation in NY following a pleasant dinner and a couple bottles of wine, her potential lover (sex partner) for the evening had her in the same position. Rape wasn't the intent then, but sex sure was. Legs in the air crouch open and dick in hand. At that time, she yelled "STOP" and Angel did. She tried it for Louis. "STOP"!!! Don't think it was working this time. This wasn't a date-rape; this wasn't just rough sex, as this was shaping up to be a violent violation of her body. This was the true meaning of rape. Her brain took over and shut out the pain of his entrance into her body. He wasn't being careful, loving, and considerate. He had not bothered to open her lips, but had forcible pushed his smallish hard diseased crooked cucumber into her pulling hair and barren skin inside as he ripped and torn her dry vagina. Her mind helped by feeling no pain, discomfort, or anything between her legs, but he had not stopped. The smell of him was sickening from his exposed genitals to the fowl methane gas he was letting. She knew, but her mind was not accepting what was happening to her as she felt nothing in her body. Her hips were hurting and both legs were numb and heavy but her arms still worked as she hit him over and over on the head and shoulders. He liked her struggling. The more she struggled the harder that damned cucumber seemed to get.

"Hi sweetheart, anyone home?" It was Frank. He was early and coming in the front door.

"Who's that… you expecting company?" Louis demanded. Betty Sue didn't answer but struggled with flailing arms and legs to get out from under this pile of useless humanity. Her cheeks were still stinging and her stomach and insides of both thighs were already heavily bruised and becoming painful. "FRANK!!! RUN!!! Don't come in! Run!! FRANK... RUN!!!!" She screamed.

"What the hell is going on here?" The screen door slammed behind him as he dropped a garment bag and squinted toward the floor of the den area trying to make out the two figures. "Betty Sue?" It was a question he didn't need to ask. He knew her voice and he was familiar with violence, he knew the answer and worst of all, he saw exactly what was happening. The yelling and screaming with female legs in the air, a male bare ass facing him was picture enough. He knew... and reacted. An ear ear-piercing rebel yell exploded from his lips as his happy-go-lucky steps of only a moment ago took him the twenty feet into the pile in the den. Betty Sue's home is large and very comfortable. Ranch style with recreation room in the basement, in ground heated pool, hot tub, sun porch. The last time he had this kind of adrenaline level, he had to kill.

Ex-military aren't the brightest candles on any tree, but they do have a tendency to get the job done. Betty Sue was still on her back on the floor; Louis was between her open legs still holding onto his crooked cucumber like member while turning to see just what was going on just as Frank hit him with a flying tackle and an elbow upside his head. The force of the blow sent both men hard against the wooden wall breaking a VCR storage cabinet in the process. A lot of things were happening at the same time and there were arms, legs and torso's all in a pyramid with Louis pinned against the wall with Frank pounding on him with bare knuckles and a plastic VCR movie housing that somehow had found itself into his hands.

As Frank pounded the container shattered and the jagged plastic was taking chunks of skin from Louis and also leaving long slices of deep red wounds on his face shoulders and upper torso. Anything that Frank could hit was being cut and gouged. Betty Sue somehow managed to scoot out from under the fray and crawled toward the now open bedroom door only a few feet away. My gun... I have to get my gun!! Air coming from the bedroom was cool. The window shades were pulled and the room was a deep gray, but you could easily make out the huge master king sized bed, a dresser and night stand. The sound of the fan running in the air-conditioner filled the room, but was unnoticed in the commotion of the men fighting. Betty Sue crawled to the side of the bed and put her back against it, feet almost touching the dresser. The .38 revolver was in the night stand. Get the gun Betty Sue. Get the gun. Get the gun. Now!!!!

Her head hurt, her dressing gown was torn, her stomach and inner thighs hurt and her breast were tender from the mauling Louis had given them. Damn. Get the gun Betty Sue!!!

Seconds passed that seemed like long minutes.... Get the gun Betty Sue. NOW!!! *God, please make this go away...* Someone or something was slammed into the wall again and again as the two men fought and violent angry words were being said and shouted by both. Another minute passed with noise and fighting when suddenly, the den area was silent. The hum of the AC's fan became the only sound in the house other then Betty Sue's heavy breathing. She noticed the noise of the silence and began crawling toward the closed door to the den. She slipped her hand between the door and the jamb and pulled it open only to see Frank lying on his back only a few inches away. His face was bloody and there was a knife handle sticking out of his chest. Somewhere during the two men struggling, they had fought their way through the kitchen area and Louis had apparently grabbed a large bladed, black handled 11 inch butcher's knife and buried it in Frank's chest.

Frank was dying and no one could do anything about it now. It was too late. Louis was sitting on the floor with his back braced against the glass outside door next to her computer. His face was more blooded then Frank's but he was smiling and even worse, he was still alive. Betty Sue crawled over to Frank and took his head in her hands and kissed him. His lips were motionless and sticky with blood. She put her hand on the handle and thought about pulling it out, but Frank winced in heavy pain, so she stopped. He looked first toward Betty Sue then to the tip of the handle and back before weakly saying, I may need a band ad. He coughed a couple time as fluid and blood built in his lungs and he looked tired. "I am so sorry" Betty Sue said. "I love you so; I tried to warn you, to run, to not come in... God Frank... I am so sorry... Please forgive me.... I love you so very much, please don't leave me... Please." It was too late. At best he had only a few more seconds left on earth and he used them to express him love to this very special woman in his life. "Betty Sue sweetheart... not your fault... I love you too, so very much...." Then with his last breath he said, "...the gun.... night stand... protect yourself..." then he winked and grinned as blood ran from the corner of his mouth across her hands and pooled on the dark brown rug.

An eternity passed in the next three seconds. As Frank's body was shutting down it twitched a couple last times as Betty Sue held his dead body close to her breast and her whole being was racked with soul searching sobs for the lose of her love and the complete emptiness she now faces. Louis took it away from her. Louis has caused her great and unrelenting pain. God Damn him to Hell. How dare he come into my home and do this to me... How dare he...! Her mind was saying all the evil things she could think of as he said aloud through that same sick smile. "OK now my sweet little cunt, as soon as I get up it's your turn. I'm going to finishing fucking you then I'm going to cut your heart out and eat it after I slice it up using that knife in your boyfriend's chest." He said the words and made a few jesters with bloody hands but didn't move any of his body parts. Frank had put up a pretty good fight and during the scuffle had opened several gashes that were leaking lots of Louis's blood. He looked to be in a bit of pain. Frank and Betty Sue use to sit and talk for hours. They would talk about any subject that came to mind and never held anything back. If a topic was thought to be disturbing or not appropriate at the time, they would try it and see where it took them. Once he was telling her about his combat tour and how the enemy would get high on opium and heroin type drugs before a battle. He said it gave them courage and kept them going if they should get wounded. Louis was definitely high on something other then whiskey was the only explanation to why he could still be taunting her with sex and violence? Frank had made him pay, but not enough.

It wasn't a conscience thought or effort as Betty Sue gently lay Frank's head down on the carpet and crawled back into her bedroom. She wasn't thinking but only reacting. It was only a few seconds till she was back, standing erect, both red stained breasts now covered but still damp from Frank's blood. Heat from the wood stove could be felt on her backside. Sunlight was coming in through the open curtains. It was high noon. Outside in her yard there were birds singing and playing in the gentle air currents. The world was good. Why has God forsaken me at this time? Nipples were bullet hard and breasts swayed slightly as she took five steps toward where Louis was propped against the glass door. He didn't see the Colt .38 in her right hand.

Betty Sue had never fired a gun in anger. She had never fired a weapon of any sorts, in any condition but she held the .38 firm in her hand and walked with purpose. With each step she was remembering the instructions Frank had given her. "This is a double action .38 - 5 shot revolver. Always make sure of your first round and chances are you will never need the other 4. Never jerk the trigger. Use your thumb to cock the hammer for your first shot, take a deep breath, sight along the top of the barrel at your target and squeeze the trigger. The gun is nothing more then an extension of your hand. Point it and squeeze." She was hearing the words as if Frank was walking with her whispering in her ear. She stopped two yards from Louis. He was still smiling but Betty Sue's face was expressionless. Her right arm was hanging by her side. Thumb on the hammer, index finger gently touching the trigger housing, third and fourth fingers holding the cool plastic ladies handle. Her thumb seemingly acting as if on its own double cocked the hammer. She said nothing; her emotions were in check as she slowly raised the little gun to eye level sighted over the short one-inch barrel to where she was looking right between his eyes. He was either to stupid or didn't believe she would pull the trigger and did nothing but lay there and grin. She took a deep breath and lowered the barrel to just below his belt and squeezed. The little gun jumped just a bit. It felt good. The round hit exactly where she wanted. His screams of pain told her she had hit him right in the middle of that damnable cucumber. She was beginning to see what Frank had told her about guns. They can make you feel good as well as hurt. She squeezed the trigger once again while looking down the barrel at the middle of his forehead. Yes. Three more times she felt the .38 jump, she squeezed again, then again, then again. The little gun stopped jumping and only clicked, clicked, clicked. Her arm felt heavy. She was very tired.

To kill isn't that difficult when there is a reason.

There was suddenly a slight taste of acid in the room, Louis had his cucumber splattered, now had a third eye, three more button holes and there was blood and brains surrounding the shattered glass door where he had been leaning. He wasn't smiling.

The evening had been long and very dark but the sun was due on the Eastern horizon any moment.

Betty Sue was on her back with the bed comfort pulled up sweetly under her chin. There was a pixie little girl smile on a relaxed face and her right hand was sticking out of the covers as if waiting for Frank to hold her hand once more like so many times in the past. It had been his habit to hold her hand while gently kissing her morning lips and gently very gently running his finger tips over her naked body. He had done that one day long ago trying to find ways to wake her and still let her think it was her idea to open her eyes. He knew she liked her sleep. He knew that waking her before it was time was... well... it wasn't good. One morning long ago he rose to an elbow and gently pulled the covers down enough to expose both breast and a warm stomach that disappeared between two beautiful thighs. He had always liked touching her. There was never anything mechanical about the touching... Never five time around this breast then five times around the other. Touch one nipple, then the other. They became lovers by listening to the others body. They remained lovers by listening to the other and always putting the other before themselves. The fan of the AC humming in the background had always been only for the noise but it gave a refreshing atmosphere to this room. This was Betty Sue's bedroom. This was the room she had been with Frank so many times, making love with him till her body tingled and in her inimitable words, left her boneless. This is the room where she could be herself, explore, and experiment, be the woman she had always known was hiding in her body. This is the room where she and Frank laughed, joked, played cards and games of ever sort. God how she loved this room... It held so many memories...so many beautiful memories. Geoff never made it to her bedroom. The guestroom was used for Geoff and others... this bedroom is reserved for only the special and the loved.

There was a slight tingling around her stomach and a sensation of pleasure running from her right breast down through her stomach and trying to escape her ...a very wet. It was Frank's fingers.

Frank was leaning on his left elbow as he said, "Good morning sweetheart. Hope you didn't have any more of those horrible nightmares of you being raped and me getting killed. I slept like a log... Are you ready for your coffee??"

EPILOGUE:

Betty Sue's account of this day has been reenacted thousands of times in real life not only here in the land of milk and honey, but world-wide to humans of all walks of life, and to every color and age group. Crime and violence has no color and state boundaries and never sleeps. They are sisters in savagery where there is no age limit for violence and death. You must be 18 years old to drink and legally drive an automobile, but rules do not govern when you needlessly suffer, die nor who can kill. Knowledge of how to properly use weapons, will and very frequently extend life. This story began, unfolds, is lived out in a matter of only a few short hours, but affected many lives the duration of their lives.

During the initial years of the 21st century Betty Sue's life changed dramatically from a comfortable community oriented home life, loving wife and mother to a woman looking for her own identity. She was alone and she didn't need a man in her life, but she wanted one. Family life is good and everyone should have a family, but a human's basis instinct is to share love, physical love with a partner. She wanted to be part of a couple. Betty Sue's sexual partners in the past have been something less then satisfying and according to the many books she read, the movies she saw, and from other female conversations, there was something missing. There was a fire burning inside her and she somehow had to find a way to satisfy what to do about it... in Frank she found that satisfaction.

***

AUTHORS NOTE: Eileen is dead now...Her death was not from a rapist, an evil person, natural disaster, a war or a nice clean bullet or even those seven seconds of life you have left when your car impacts a concrete bridge abutment. Her death came from a cancer where there is little to no defense. She was 53 years old.

Josx2 txe copy

The clone of the clone had to be tested. The 12th century seemed to be a perfect time and place.

Time frame = 2117
Place = Washington DC area in Northern Virginia
Human cloning is becoming a staple
The President of the United States is female, as is most of her cabinet

Ann was on a classified conference call with the president of the United States, Ann and Harry. The conversation was not subtle but blunt, to the point so as no one would misunderstand.

"I'm telling you Madam President that for my programs to continue here at the Agency for Cybernetic/Clone Research and Development I have to do this."

"We're talking expenses that I don't see justified Ann. This is not a household budget I'm running; it's the whole United States." She paused, took a deep breath and countered, "ACCRED will just have to slow down a bit and let things happen – naturally."

It was Ann's turn to take a deep breath. She did but the determination in her voice was maybe a pitch higher now as she kept pushing with; "I have one perfect clone... I need another. With Josh, I was fortunate. All the eyes were dotted and all the T's crossed and we came out with a great product." She quickly continued with, "I need to do this."

There was complete silence on the air ways.

Ann waited.

Harry waited.

The President was silent but wasn't waiting for any more input; she was thinking and weighing consequences.

Finally after a lifetime the President said, "I don't want this expense to show up on any spreadsheets."

There it was – *Approval.* Ann quickly said, "You got it."

Harry knew when to be quiet.

The President paused then added, "Just so that I fully understand what I think I just agreed to let me say this out loud. ACCRED is a bastard organization to begin with and now you want go further against nature and make a clone of a clone. You are wanting to clone Josh because he seems to be perfect for your purposes and you feel your chances of success are better if you start from a *know* going toward an *unknown,* does that sound about right, so far?"

"Yes madam president." Ann whispered toward to conference VIACOM (Video screen).

"Harry any comments?" The President said.

Harry had been quiet for so long he had to clear his throat before saying, "No madam president. Ann pretty well explained the situation and you have a perfect understanding of the way I think it will go."

"A copy of a copy!" The President exploded. "Second generation… I don't like it." She paused briefly then as air was escaping from lungs long overdue for a relaxed breath said, "If this Josh clone… this Josh2 or whatever you call it, comes out fuzzy, I don't want to hear about it. You guys are the experts; just don't step on your foreskins on this one."

There it was, Approval.

Now all they had to do was test Josh2. Beta testing is always better done outside curious eyes and outside nosy folks and of course, the budget folks. So how do you test a clone of a clone?

The future is too uncertain and you always had to be most careful when operating in the past… but the past was certain.

I realize this picture may LOOK a bit like the author but I assure you this is Josh the Clone. Trust me.

Lois and Frank had been notified they were needed for a trip and as always they showed up, on time. They visited with Ann Folk for less than an hour than with Josh2 in tow were off to the airstrip where the Lakehurst had been made ready. The Lakehurst is nothing but aluminum, titanium, a few rivets, a lot of glue, 128 kilometers of wiring, two standard jet power plants for the atmosphere and another apocalyptic superconductivity engine needed to obtain orbital flight than speeds in excess of light are required for time travel. Sitting in the shadows it looked quick and was as beautiful as a mistress on a Saturday evening.

The ride into orbit had been smooth and flawless, but you have to remember the word smooth is relative. Flawless is a good straightforward word but when used in connection to moving a 47,000-pound aircraft from point A to point B, which happens to be in another time frame, can be a bit bumpy. Flawless is; the always present hint of kerosene in the cabin cooling system, the low steady pitch of Pratt & Whitney engines gulping air and pushing your silver beauty toward the taxiway, the groaning of brake pads turning onto runway 27W, an intercom message saying you are ready for takeoff, a brief but bone rattling ride as you accelerate from zero to 130 knots rotation speed, the lump in your gut as the mains are seated in the wing roots, flaps and slats repositioning and mother earth dropping away and disappearing as you pass through low layers of mist and clouds on your way to orbital speed and altitude. Flawless.

Frank and Lois had departed ACCRED Headquarters in the suburbs of Washington DC on time, and following the approved flight plan for going backward in time, achieved orbital speed and altitude away from the earth's normal rational direction. Once satisfied of all instrument reading, Lois rolled the craft over on its back, pulled her seat belt a little tighter and flipped the toggle switch by her right hand marked, "LIGHT SPEED". Inside the craft nothing appeared different. Lois was in the left seat with Frank holding down co-pilot chores on this trip; Josh2 was busy looking out a right side portal toward a distance blue planet 186 Kilometers below. Fred had been content on the ground to just walk the companionway but in orbit, he was now having a really difficult time trying to act nonchalant about his flaying wings and incessant shrieking. Fred was a klutz on the ground and even more so in weightlessness. But he tried.

At a normal 23,412 KPH orbital speed the Lakehurst completed one orbit of 87 minutes. As the superconductivity engines kicked in and came to full potential, the distinct cloud covering far below became blurred as continents existed without boundaries and oceans became continuous. Within three seconds the Lakehurst was circling the earth at more than nine and one-half times a second and Frank was counting down critical elapsed time. "... 13... 12... 11... 10... 9... 8...get ready to break... 5... 4... break on my mark... 2... 1... **Break**." He said emphatically.

As Lois flipped the toggle to OFF the high pitch of the superconductor subsided, the blue earth once again became distinct in shape and colors and Frank said in a mechanical voice, "...OK boys and girls, we are here. Touch down in approximately twenty minutes."

With that Lois rolled the craft back, positioned the wings with the horizon and pointed its nose toward the East and began looking for a flat level area to set down.

Fred had not paid attention when Frank warned of breaking and had bumped his beak on the lavatory door and gotten a little disoriented, but other than being his normal klutz, was quiet and still for the time being.

Directly below the Lakehurst was what appeared to be waste land, or what could graciously be called a vast frozen white wilderness... virgin... cruel and unforgiving. It was Russia of 1100 years ago and was that vast section of Europe and Asia whose area comprised one- sixth of the globe and inhabited by Slavic stock at least from the 1st millennium BC. But now there is a young woman named Katrina who lived and died and has left her mark on the world for generations well into the 22nd century.

Katrina family history began early in the 9th century AD about the time adventurous Swedish Vikings, inspired by the hope of developing trade relations with the Orient via the Russian watercourses, with the establishment of trading posts on Lake Ladoga and along the rivers to the south and east. It was shortly after the death of Yaroslav, who had been the principle architect of Russian Christianity, a period of disorder existed which terminated only when the throne of Keiv fell in 1113 to the lot of Yaroslav's energetic grandson Vladimir Monomakh.

In his short but spirited rule he established hamlets throughout his territory known for their breeding farms. One such farm, located on the Western shore of the Black Sea, whose serf village was named Tuapsee, was to be Joshua's assignment, and the rest of Katrina's fruitful life.

Her 11th century existence began her adult life in dirt poor surroundings and flat of her back, as did many Russian girls of this time in history. Existence was on the barest of diets and survival depended on how well you tolerated brutal winters lard and potato diets and birthing babies.

Tuapsee's streets were poor excuses for widened paths of nothing more than hardened earth and rocks that turned into a sea of mud when the snows melted or it rained for any lengthy period. Dwellings were crude even by poor Slavic standards and seldom more than one story. Windows all appeared as afterthoughts and many constantly open to the elements.

One known lesson, however, is that life is not a contradiction. On the contrary, these poor but resourceful people were conscience of the world around them to the extent not only the selection of materials but the weather itself played a considerable part in the design and construction of the enclosures called home. No openings faced north. Normally no more than two, sometimes three opening were left in the walls facing South or leeward depending on surrounding terrain. All windows were diminutive to keep out the cold and sometimes covered with animal skins but usually rags that could not be used for anything else. The walls to these huts were mud for the most part, sometimes wood, and never finished. The only ones with proper fireplaces and chimneys were the breeding huts, the nursery and the kitchens.

Women cooked on open fires or in clay bake ovens and they ate with fingers because they were not allowed knives. Their privies were holes in the ground that were covered as a cat naturally does when it thinks no one is watching, but only when the ground was soft enough to push and dig in.

In 1016 AD an imperial edict was passed making breeding farms legal. Part of a state run charter was to not only bringing currency in the coffers but also to build a strong country. It worked... sort of. Mature men and women products of the breeding farms alike became pure of blood and oneness of mind and steadily spread to the points of the compass throughout the massive country. Fortuitously, this spread could not be controlled outside the preview of the farms so the more Westward the migration the more intermarriages losing genetic purity, or cloning.

Strong, young, healthy farm girls were recruited and promised good lives for themselves and their families. The head of household, so to speak, was paid in cash and the young girls were taken away never to see her family again. Males were also recruited in the same manner, but never bought or bartered for as the females. Their lot in a breeding farm was considered a privilege, however because of the lack of rapid or wide spread communications the vast country side had to be searched. Criterion used was participates must be sexual alert, capably, strong bones and passable appearance. Age was never a consideration.

Mating was always detailed.

Those in the breeding farms lived life on a grander scale than their counterparts, but not much. Their food was somewhat better and they were warmer but only when they were producing what the owner wanted. They had bathing huts but were still subject to the whims of the owner and the overseer.

The year Josh2 came back to abound with royalty, and it was they who controlled most of the more lucrative farms. There were a few horse breeding farms and many agriculture types to produce food, but the main staple for the Tuapsee estate was the breeding of people, to be sold.

As the sun tried to burn off morning haze and mist, the day promised to be just any other day. Today was not unlike yesterday or the days before that and days and

weeks ahead. Josh's first impression of the weather was as if it or someone, or something was terribly wrong in the universe. The wind and temperature were more than bone chilling cold. The air was extremely heavy and hard to breathe. Men's mustaches and beards were frozen the moments a face was exposed and the normally warm and invitingly soft flesh of a woman's inner thigh was elapsed till spring. The bare trees were storing their sap so they would not turn into living petrified wood, the snow was cold, the day was cold, and Josh was cold.

Even the pigeons of the day were walking.

Josh's mind was a collage of thoughts, ideas and questions, many questions. The time of day…? Not sure, probably early afternoon by now. Hard to tell as there were no lunch crowd. The smattering of pedestrians was bundled so tightly if one did have the time, it is doubtful it would be shared. The year… the year is even a bigger question? Russia had never been famous for changing style of transportation of horse drawn sleighs on a yearly basis, and the basic grays and blacks of the men and women also gave no clues. Best guess… sometime after the turn of the 11th century. That fact was in itself, not comforting, but the fact that it was not permanent was. Soon he would return to 2117 and Keri.

Josh2 deplaned with last minute instructions as to pick up date and times and carrying little more then a shaving kit.

Within moments of touchdown the Lakehurst was again airborne in a thundering, molecular destroying blast of 20th century Pratt & Whitney J4000 jet engines. He was cold and there was little to no prospect of getting warm anytime soon.

From 1000 meters up, Tuapsee looked to be no more than one maybe two kilometers East by Southeast, should be an easy walk even in bone chilling cold, but he never made it on his own. Within a hundred-meter walk he was quickly beset by red cheeked and heavy bearded men. From the look in their eyes, they were eager to have a stranger in their mist. Josh smiled to himself as he looked into each face knowing what they were thinking was no where close to what he was thinking and the reason he was here.

"What do we have here Igor?"
"Not sure sir... looks to be a stranger. I have never seen him before and some of the boys here have never seen him either. It might be a good idea to take in back to the farm and have him checked to see if he can be used..."

"Good idea". So they did.

They never questioned how he came to be by himself on the frozen lake, maybe they didn't care, but before the sun was to set on the first day it was made clear he was now a captive on a breeding farm. And that was fine with him. His habit of storing everything he saw compelled Josh2 to retain these thoughts and concentrate on the mission. So he did.

Josh2 was introduced immediately to the ways of the farm and where most of the activities took place. It was ugly and baron. Smoke from a defective chimney filled the inside of the conception room. Bare walls, one opening in each wall that served as a window, two shelves just at eye level and a line of six cots. Four were occupied at this moment by couples.

Josh's first thoughts as he watched the gyrations out of the corner of his eye were embarrassment. The cot people were doing private things that made him feel bad having to stand this close and watch. The couple on the right side was the most active. Josh turned his head to watch and his thought were more on Keri and himself only a few short weeks ago long, long time from here. They had made love to and with each other, and it was good. As he watched this animated couple his programming clicked through love and sex categories where he found words and phases such as loving, screwing, masturbation, and f***ing. At first he thought, loving... naturally, because of their position and they were in fact, coupled. But, watching further and listening to the sounds from just one cot spoke volumes about men and how they function with their one-eyed friend. "...Oh honey, you are so good. I have never had a woman as tight and hot as you. We are going to make a beautiful baby this day. Relax and let me do it. You just lay there... lay still. I said."

The second cot was different. The man on top told him another word. He was hearing basic words for basic people. He would have put fucking before loving, but for the simple fact the woman's eyes were shut so tightly the sockets were but single slivers of flesh, she was quiet and the toes on both feet were curled into tight little balls. This woman was being used and she knew it. It was her hell on earth, as this person inside her was doing nothing more than masturbating, and using her as a receptacle. If expressions could be translated to words her thought might have been; "...this son-of-a bitch is killing me. I want no part of this breeding farm any more. I'm sick. I hate this. My legs hurt. I think I'm about to throw up on him."

A bundled pile of torn clothing piled slightly to one side and behind Josh, with a man's voice inside said in a dialect only a handful of serfs in Tuapsee understood that it was his turn next and something about he hoped his woman was as nice as the one in the right hand cot. Or, it sounded something like that. He was slobbering so badly words were coming out covered in O's and was wet and slimy. Josh turned his attention back to the cots. The couple on the right had finished by this time. The middle cot had stopped its violent movements and from the looks of the man's bottom he may have been trying to punch a hole in the cot's slight padding and bend a tiny metal coin with his hairy cheeks at the same time. The pounding of the left cot had caused it to physically move itself a full meter away from where it had been only three minutes ago. Suddenly it stopped, the man arose, pulled leather trousers to his waist and left. Just like that.

A voice from the corner of the tent sounded like it was saying, "Are you due back soon, Yorg? You looked to be especially good today. Today, you may have made a beautiful baby."

I'll be back later today. They have me scheduled for four women today."

"Four?" Josh was thinking how cold the weather was but also how cold and unfeeling these men are. They finish and just leave. No thank you, see you tomorrow, kiss my foot, or that was nice. They just up and leave. Yorg's partner's legs were still raised and involuntary muscle reaction was causing the calves to twitch and move. Her breathing appeared labored.

In a brief seven minutes Josh had learned there was no pretense of love making, affection, or emotion. The movements by both parties were mechanical and measured. The man was always on top until climax where he quickly arose and the woman held her legs together and high in the air until released. Josh learned it was a crime and punishable by whipping if any semen escaped her body. Rarely did she have the time or luxury to perspire or enjoy what her body longed for. Her position in life was to produce babies, and in this day and age, enjoying conception was never permitted.

Time passed, but all too slowly.

For the past two days he had been watching Katrina and knew without a shadow of a doubt this was one of Ms. Folk's previous lives. He had convinced himself of the fact, but every time he rationalized the thinking, there was missing pieces. If a person had a pervious life, how were they the same or different? Stands to reason that looks would be a bit different as would mannerisms, habits and likes and dislikes. When two people are blood kin they have something special that distinguishes them from outside the family. But, when a person is the same person even if separated by a few centuries, there should be similarities. The puzzle just did not fit. Close but not a perfect match, but he was still convinced... sort of. This was the second time he had been sent back into the past and encountered an earlier Ann Folk and once he had encountered a very nasty Kari. He was beginning to wonder if Ann had been truthful with him when briefing him as to the purpose to this trip. Right now it didn't matter, he was expecting a female that had been chosen for him and he had to turn his mind away from speculation to reality.

Anticipation was not one of his strong points. Josh was not looking forward to the next few minutes. Yri had given him a drink of some kind of a swill watery-like concoction as he left his hut and was told it would keep him warm and relaxed. Josh accepted it as maybe a tradition of the village and did not question it ever as he was turning green. The thin snot-like drink did go down easily and was warming his gut as he saw Katrina. The gagging reflection went suddenly to a soft smile and a warm feeling in his cloned loins.

Katrina and the old slave soon stood in the doorway of the breeding hut where Josh had been assigned the middle cot. She was wrapped in rags, head bowed with both hands clutching her chest. The old slave walked her to the edge of the cot where he carefully and with deliberation slowly unwrapped the young woman's shoulders.

She was naked.

No words were exchanged and no sly, sideways, or awkward glances look between the chosen couple. In years, Katrina had been on earth for 18 years. Josh knew that, but looking at her naked body standing in front of him like this his mind would not admit he was about to deflower this 11th century Ann Folk and start, he thought a new generation.

Her stomach looked smooth and soft with a hairy black patch and breasts high, proud and firm. The nipples probable tasted of lilacs and lime.

The thought that maybe this woman was also a clone passed between Josh's ears before he quickly discounted the idea as abused. But, her skin texture was too smooth, the muscle tone was too sharp and defined, the breasts were too young and proud with nipples that looked to have never been touched by man or baby. There was a small mole under the left breast and another 10 maybe 11 centimeters below her bellybutton. She smelled of lye soap and lilacs.

Josh's perception of his surroundings and of these people was suddenly elevated. Anyone who could come up with the scent of the delicate lilac in this frozen hellhole could not be all-bad. Maybe he was preoccupied, maybe it was anticipation, maybe it was that water swill concoction he had earlier. Whatever the cause, his body did not readily respond to her now prone attitude or mild encouragement. He knew her job. He had been told many times her job was to lay still and receive the man. Nothing more, nothing less. By Imperial decree she was not to help, and she didn't, so anyone but Josh2 could notice. Keri had done the same to him the first time they had made love but it didn't last the evening. She had told him afterward for him not to worry about it, because, '...it was a woman thing...' few men knew about, and none understood.

Katrina's breast separated only slightly as her head touched the hard padding of the cot and the fingers of both hands gripped its wooden railings. The sides of his waist felt cold to the top portions of her inner thighs. There were a number of things happening now. She felt slight inward pressure at the same place in her body where she had born two babies already, and she waited. The pressure increased slightly as it moved slowly inside her body. She had felt this same pressure many times in her young life, but this time she did not want it to end. No one had ever been this gentle before. No one had ever treated her as a human before...not even Yri.

On hands and knees on the rickety cot scent of lilacs pushed Josh to near intoxication, the feeling was very effective on limp middle appendage. He wanted to be gentle and not hurt her, but he also did not want to bring the wrath of the village or Yri on her, or himself. Touching her pubic area with

hands or fingers was not allowed and to enter her dry and without direction could be painful, for the both of them. Her legs were separated and elevated with pelvic slightly raised as he touched her scented pubic patch it opened just enough for him to feel her moisture and heat from within. The question flashed across his mind, as to wondering how she did that, but he said nothing.

Meet YRI on your left.

The moment he became completed buried in her body his mind told him who this beautiful and warm person really was and he had to grin to himself, thinking about the irony of being inside an ancestor or the same person responsible for his creation.

Minutes turned into 20 then 30 then 42 before Josh slowed and they both stopped all outward movement. Inwardly, Katrina smiled to herself as she quietly used strong vaginal muscles to massage that part of him still very much inside her.

Both partners were completely drenched with perspiration and lying in each other's arms as they finished at the same time.

Couples in the four other cots had long stopped their activities, as had Yri and six village people that had stopped by to warm themselves. Most of them also had visible beads of sweat on their lips and foreheads but their attention did not vary from the center cot.

"Who is that couple over there? Pay attention to what she is doing... I want you to do the same things." The young lady in cot number one was saying to no one in particular but was hoping her partner for the day was listening.

Katrina felt good inside, her belly was warm and alive, her breast tingled and her heart was glad. She had enjoyed this man being inside her.

Quickly, as she realized her own pleasure, she moved her head from side to side to see if anyone in the now crowded room had noticed. Two old men nearest her cot were smiling and poking each other in the ribs were committing on what they had just seen but looking at their faces she was sure they had no idea as to how she felt, nor why. She was safe... for now.

God this feels good. Who is this young man? Katrina was thinking to herself.

Try not to enjoy it again, she admonished herself.

Josh2 was up early the next morning, more from necessity than desire. His head was three sizes too large and every beat of his heart was amplified up through his neck and exploding between his ears. His stomach was queasy and he needed a privy, badly.

Josh was freezing as he stood knee deep in the mountain stream running passed his hut, but right now, there was no alternative. He tried splashing the water on his forehead, and it helped, but was all too temporary. Finally he used his soaked shirt to wrap his throbbing head... it helped. The skin on his shoulders and back had turned a light shade of blue by the time Yri came by and inquired as to Josh's well being.

There were several nasty eye gestures from Josh2 and wide eyed innocence from Yri before it registered that the reason he was standing in the stream was because of something Yri had given him to drink before coupling last evening. Just something light to relax him. Yri went on to explain the little water was a concoction the village developed over the last several years. It helped keep them warm during the winter months. A by-product he did admit was a pounding head if you were not used to it, or drank too much to stay warm. Yri seemed quiet proud of himself as he went on to explain the rather simple procedure in making it. They use left over corn, grain, and potatoes mashed into a gummy pulp, boiled it and capture the vapors in goatskins.

"Vodka." Josh2 said under his breath. He did ask how many times this concoction was boiled and captured and when given the answer as only once, he understood why his head was pounding this morning.

Yri did not understand the word, vodka and asked what it meant. Josh did not try to explain, but merely shrugged his shoulders and simply said, "Nothing. It was just a word that will not be known for another 300 years."

Central nervous system seems fine. The productive systems also seem intact and functional and now the taste buds have been checked and register correct data. What else has to be tested and where?

The *what* part of the question was easy...

As was the *where*... *anywhere* as long as it is away from here.

two

Have you ever wondered...about "things"?

Have you ever wondered, for example, why the sun always rises in the East? Why the summers are hot and the winter's cold? Why the sky is blue here on Earth and solid black to our astronauts? Why electricity tingle your fingers and why your heart keeps beating even when you aren't thinking about it or why two is better then one?

I have.

I have often heard, "...if your not the lead dog, the scenery never changes". That could be a true ism as what I have seen, most days are predictable and pretty much the same...until today. Today has been different somehow. It is not yet 6 O'clock in the morning but the day is different. The sky is blue, as usual; the lake is mirror smooth, as usual for this time of the morning. Give it a couple hours. Add a few dozen jet-skis, a few guys/gals fishing, three or four 40' cabin cruisers power boats, kids water skiing and boats pulling guys and girls on water skis and boogie boards and there you have a normal day on the lake. This morning is somehow – different.

This morning has not been normal as everything seems to have twos.

Two chipmunks running as fast as short legs   will allow. One with what looks to be a chopped off tail and the other in close pursuit. Both are your everyday cute, destructive rodent. Rodents? Sure. Those cute little guys are nothing more then small stripped squirrels that prefer the ground. Meanwhile the aerial version of the little chipmunk is alive and well jumping from tree to tree and playing between meals. The trees seem to be bursting with young fuzzy tailed squirrels chasing each other. Not sure how they do it but they defy gravity in their games and I have yet to see one fall. Complete panic sometimes when small branches are missed, but fall... never. Vertical sides of anything scare me to tears but vertical means nothing to these rodents with razors picks for toenails and ice water in their veins. If I were to climb a normal sized tree trunk it would take me the better part of a day. Not so with these young rodents. There may be a few older squirrels thrown into the fray but they all look the same to me. These rodents climb, chase and play at the speed of a blink. They aren't quiet doing it either. Not sure what squirrel talk sounds like because I am usually laughing so hard at their antics I can't hear anything over my own voice. Whatever it sounds like, they do it quickly and with twitching tail semaphore make sure their message is received.

Turtles eat our baby ducks so I have no love for those creatures that live in my lake and look like rocks with legs and ugly heads. I have a pump pellet pistol that I will plink the little brown baby duck eaters every chance I get. I have yet to hit one, but Dixie or I should call her by her professional name – Annie Oakley has been know to plink the back of their heads on a regular basis. They normally surface and hang onto the boat docks guide wires that hang in the water while they breathe and sun themselves. That is when Miss Oakley has her best shots. This morning there were two rocks with legs and those really ugly heads swimming and sunning themselves between docks away from all wires. Unusual but there they were. All the baby ducks had either been eaten or grown old enough to fend for their selves as Ms. Oakley was no where in sight. Lucky turtles.

Ducks live on my lake also and why not? The lake is pleasant, full of food and because this is a boating and pleasure Lake No Hunting is allowed. We have ducks strolling in the yard on a daily basis but if you get within a few feet they will make a major verbal complaint and are airborne over your head in a matter of a second. Don't be surprised if they deposit a bit of poop on your head either. Our ducks like life here but they mostly travel alone or in flocks. Today was different. All our Mallards were in pairs.

Now pairing is not unusual in October and November when the Drakes are horny and the Hens coy but today is the last week in July. Why today are they paired off?

Not all ducks quack; many whistle, squeal, or grunt. I heard a lot of grunting this morning, but those were mostly from those arguing. Have you even seen ducks argue? Have you even seen ducks fornicate? Takes two I know but I don't believe that is my answer this morning.

Everyone has seen mother duck and her brood stop traffic as they meander across the quiet cove but have you ever seen them in any kind of major argument? They will yell and grunt at each other on land and in the water until usually the hen will have enough and fly away, or try too. The angry Drank will always chase her as best he can but the

Hen has special flying capabilities she will throw at the Drake until he gives up and leaves her alone. Ever watch a jet airliner making a final approach into an airport. Ever notice how the aircraft will lower landing flaps to reduce speed and then lower its landing gear that will further reduce speed? Mother hen does the same in the air to anger the male. She will be flying as hard  as her wings will allow and Mr. Drank will be right on her tail screaming and grunting when mother Hen will stick her legs down and lower her tail feathers. A surprised Drake will always go flying past and has to do a wide circle to come back into his arguing position. Mother hen will do her foot dragging, tail feather routine until drake finally grunts and leaves her alone. It's all part of nature but always takes two to argue.

Duck fornication is different and sometimes difficult and embarrassing to watch. Animals hump till the male waddles off with silly smirks and the indifferent female are inseminated. If ducks hump they are quick about it and for sure they are not fish, but they seem to prefer water. The air is their kingdom but their love-making is under water and looks dangerous. Danger is the bad part. Quick is the good part for the hen. The Drake usually swims up to a chosen hen, jumps on her back while banging on the back of her head with his beak till he pushes her head under water. Drakes are a lot like teen age boys however and normally the Hens head is only underwater one or two seconds. The Human mating season has neither boundaries nor time constraints and maybe because of this are much better at loving then other animals and things that fly, especially ducks. Nature tells me two is better then one and less strenuous then three.

Being human is good.

Maybe today is different because it is a Monday, the temperature is already 93 degrees here in Mid-America and nature tells me, "…it takes two".

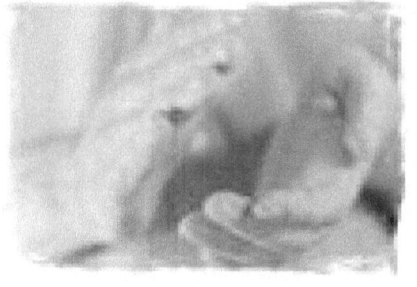

Enjoy each moment of each day and remember the next time you applaud someone or something…. It takes two hands.

Remember… This is where TWO started.

ARLEE

txe Mornina of txe Contest

A bit of frustration about the subjectivity of contests from a contestant's viewpoint

The sun was late this morning, or so it seemed. As the days go further into fall and closer to Halloween, Thanksgiving and the all important family Christmas holidays, daylight is scarce and if you get out of bed before 06:00 AM you should expect the sky to still be black, the lake and birds quiet and the fish hungry. Frank made his last trip to the bathroom a bit after 6 and his aim was as true as always. He grinned to himself as he thought about having the same target for 70 years. It should be, and is automatic now to raise, point, relax, lower and flush while wondering about the coming day. Today was normal, so far.

Lois was still hard into REM as her coffee and slightly cold buttered toast was placed on the night stand. The last few months, Frank had gotten into the habit of 'clinking' the coffee cup onto the night stand and sitting heavily on the side of the bed as he sang his good morning wake-up jingle. "Good morning Breakfast clubbers...." He was in fine voice as Lois moved first a toe, then a leg then finally an eyelid. It looked to be a real effort.

"What day is it?" or words to that affect as she muttered them without moving her lips. Retirement does that to you. One day is just like all others except the week-ends and holidays. "Saturday

sweetheart, rise and shine. The sun is up, boats are already making wakes and Max has been feed and done his thing ...In the grass". The coffee and knowing Max had 'done his thing' must have been key as she snaked her right hand from under the sheet and crooked her first finger. It was the ole coffee-finger sign. After a few unintelligent sleep-comments she, with great difficulty said, "Have you open your mail yet to see what the subject is today?"

"For the 24 hour writing contest?" Frank said with wrinkled brow.

"Yes dummy." It was a term of endearment shared by two people that truly loved each other.

"Yea. Turned the computer on a few minutes ago and I had mail from what's-her-name, you know, the contest director." Frank said then added, "Not sure how I want to handle this subject."

"Meaning?" Lois said as she blew on and sipped her coffee.

"How many times have I entered this writing contest?" Frank asked.

"Geese...not sure. Eight or nine times. Why?" Lois was still a bit out in sleep la-la land but the question made sense.

Frank was trying to make sure her eyes were open and she was not just making conversation because he turned serious. "You've read all the short stories I've written, right?"

"Yes."

"What did you think of them?" He was staring straight into her deep brown eyes as he threw the query at her.

"I liked all of them." She said with a mouth full of toast.

"Could any of them have won, or at least finished in the top three?" He hadn't said it right but she knew what he meant.

"One or two of them maybe, yes, but you did have a couple off-the-wall stories." She tried to soften the words with, "I liked them but the folks that grade your work may not have been thinking the same as you and was looking for something else."

"I know. I know. But I'm not writing for them. It's me that counts. What is inside me and what I am trying to say that matters – not their feelings or what-ever. I'm not writing to

 please them, but I have to say, writing would be a lot easier if I could at least get a door prize or acknowledgment that I had busted a few brain cells coming up with some damn good short stories and... And especially with the endings the contest director looks for - surprise. So far I have yet to get even an honorable mention." Frank seemed surprised he said that all in one breath as he took a deep breath and finished with, "Of the 500 entries you would think that it's about time

for my name to percolate to the top."

"Subject?" Lois questioned with raised eyebrows and crooked head position. He knew what she meant.

"Actually, it's not a bad subject this time. Kinda in line with the season. They gave us; the red, orange and yellow leaves traveling the river contrasted sharply against the black water. Distant thunder and a bitter wind promised an early winter storm. She shivered and walked faster, ignoring the muffled diatribe coming from the burlap sack in her arms."

Lois giggled to herself before saying, "Sounds like they want you to write about a winters thunder storm with a sweet young girl without a raincoat trudging through snow flurries on her way a river bank where she has to drown a toe sack of kittens." She seemed to ponder what she had just said, than added, "Maybe you could get dramatic and add her dad or boyfriend had forced her to do this dastardly deal because, oh maybe  because they were diseased, or the moon was full, or their yellow house cat had been tomcatting the back alleys or they didn't like the colors or numbers they were presented with on the back porch this last weekend." Lois was sure feeling her oats this morning. Normally she is too pristine to even think such thoughts.

"So…. What are you going to write about?" She said taking the last bit of toast.

"Well… I thought about it and if you look at our conversation so far, we have exchanged about 953 words, so I might just leave it at that."

"At what?" Lois was serious.

"One of the rules this time was a short story not to exceed 1100 words."

Lois was quiet.

"Before you send this story in, do you want me to proof it?"

It took Lois only a few minutes to read and rereads the "story". She grins in spots, groans in others and is most critical in more then a few spots.

"Well one thing is for sure." Lois says.

"Yes?"

Fighting back the urge to grin, Lois was calm and straight faced as she muttered, "Chances are pretty good you will be left *High and Dry again* and will finish in 500th place this time."

From the Sands came Christopher

In the year 2167 DNA was used to find artifact from WWII under the sands of Normandy.

"Monsieur Irby, would you like roulements et café?" The chief serveuse of the Chateau des Milandes in Aquitaine said with just a bit of starch in her voice.

"Veuillez oui. Monsieur Jerry Irby will be down shortly and I am sure he will also want to start with rolls and coffee." Tom said in his best high school French. He had graduated with honors six year earlier in 2161 and gone on to a higher education in DNA Polymerases with specialty in Engineering Thermostable Polymerase Trends in Biotechnology (DNA) at the Heidelberg University.

Just as he was reminiscing about his great-great grand father Louis Irby, Jerry came bouncing into the dining room.

"Tom, good morning." Jerry was happy and looked to be rested after their flight from Houston, to Paris to Normandy yesterday.

"I ordered breakfast. OK?"

"You bet cousin. I hope you ordered a side of beef and a gallon of coffee." He was serious.

"Close." Tom replied with a crooked grin. He was excited as today was to be the day he had studied and prepared for. Today he would put all his education, knowledge and experience to his one driving goal. The goal he had promised his mother on her death bed.

Looking at Jerry's attire, Tom said, "You may be a bit chilly in shorts and polo today. Don't you think you will need a sweater or jacket?"

"Hay buddy, its June, I'll be fine." Jerry said over his shoulder as he waved toward the waitress.

"OK, but just remember June in Normandy France is different then June in Houston Texas."

"6 June in France or 6 June in Texas is all the same ole buddy. I'll be fine." Jerry said. Tom had done all his graduate and post graduate studied in Germany and he knew June in Europe could be chilly, especially at the waters edge of the English Channel, but he let Tom bask in his Texan ignorance.

A tray of meats and breads was placed on the table with Tom and Jerry along with small pots of the thickest black coffee know to mankind. Jerry's cup was small and he could just fit his first finger into the handle. Small volcanic-like vapors rose from the miniature molten lava cup as he stirred the black concoction. He stopped stirring for a moment as the waitress passed and the spoon stood erect in the cup.

"Tom look!" Jerry was pointing to the spoon as if were the ninth wonder of the world.

Tom was not interested in Jerry's antics and continued munching a roll and a few slices of salami as he read and reread his journal.

"What yaw reading cuz?" Jerry said with a mouth full of bread.
Without looking up and with a single hand motion Tom slid a single piece of paper across the table coming to rest under falling crumbs.

The paper was yellowed and stiff. The words were original and more then faded from a 1944 ribbon fed typewriter.

A great invasion force stood off the Normandy coast of France as dawn broke on 6 June 1944: 9 battleships, 23 cruisers, 104 destroyers, and 71 large landing craft of various descriptions as well as troop transports, mine sweepers, and merchantmen—in all, nearly 5,000 ships of every type, the largest armada ever assembled. The naval bombardment that began at 0550 that morning detonated large minefields along the shoreline and destroyed a number of the enemy's defensive positions. To one correspondent, reporting from the deck of the cruiser HMS Hillary, it sounded like 'the rhythmic beating of a gigantic drum' all along the coast. In the hours following the bombardment, more than 100,000 fighting men swept ashore to begin one of the epic assaults of history, a '*mighty endeavor*,' as President Franklin D. Roosevelt described it to the American people, '*to preserve ... our civilization and to set free a suffering humanity.*'

Churchill warned, the beaches of France might well be '*... choked with the bodies of the flower of American and British manhood.*'

"Wow. That's heavy cuz." Jerry said with a somewhat downcast feeling.

"I know. I know, but remember, it's the main reason we're here. I made a promise to mom and I intend to find what she asked of me." Tom said.

"You know we will probable have more luck in finding the Holy Grail." Jerry still had a mouth full of bread and cheeses, but he got his point across.

"I know." Was all Tom could muster before adding, "Don't forget my expertise?"

It had taken the cousins almost an hour to climb over the rocks to the all but hidden Normandy beach. His DNA detector was strapped to his back and there wasn't any thought of others on the beach at this time of morning. It was low tide as Tom and Jerry started at the water line and began sweeping the detector back and forth. On his fifth pass, the detector gave a strong beep...beep then said in its mechanical voice.

"STOP! Here. One meter down."

Tom looked at Jerry and Jerry looked at Tom just as an uncoordinated sea gull came to a chin sliding shirking stop at the end of a three foot sand ferrule just three inches from Tom's sandals.

The digging took no more then a few minutes even in hard packed sand. There it was. A Saint Christopher medal still in its 222 year resting place and still belonging to a PVT Louis Canute Irby, 101st Airborne Infantry Division that had been blown apart as he took his first step onto French soil and his last step on earth.

A long three minutes passed before Jerry said to Tom, "What now?"

"Back to Mom. It's what she wanted."

An awkward bird pulled itself from under its self-inflected sand tunnel, yelled something in gull language and disappeared into the blinding sunrise.

It was going to be a perfect day.

ARLEE

Predestination

"If I had not flown it in myself, I would not have believed that a helicopter would fly in that condition." Crash Coe, 1969

"Destiny is what you are supposed to do in life. Fate is what kicks you in the ass to make you do it."
...Henry Miller, 1891 - 1980

The slight Texas morning breeze played in Iye and Siyeke's hair as they sat cross-legged on the leading edge of the left stabilizer pretty much minding their own business and watching the proceedings. Both Guardian Angels were dressed in silky cloud-like smoke colored jeans and boots. Both had silky shoulder-length bobbed hair and both showed slight womanly features under their long-sleeved shirts. Their luxuriantly feathered wings were tucked gently behind them, almost invisible, and they appeared as comfortable and relaxed as they could be in their line of work...for a Guardian Angel's job was never easy.

"Seems only yesterday you were taking care of David and Morris and I had my hands full watching Roger in that shooting war in Vietnam back in 1970". Iye sighed as her head swiveled between loadmaster, trucks, Roger and Siyeke.

"Silly, it's been only a heart beat in our time, you know. Remember that introductory lesson we had to have with The Creator before he allowed us to take on assignments." Siyeke replied. "Elohiym told us there were only three creative acts that were recorded for him in Genesis: Heaven, the Earth, and Life."

"Yeah, I remember, but it's still hard for me to understand a day, when a day doesn't always equal a day." Iye was struggling with it, but down deep, she knew what God had meant.
Both angels sighed and continued watching their 'charges'.

The Angels went unnoticed as they were nothing more than an imagination, a thought, a wisp of energy, a soul without form, as we know it. They were there to protect their 'charges'...humans assigned to them at the moment of their conception. From that moment their destiny was written it becomes predestination. If it's written, someone had to write it and that someone must have something to do with the outcome. The Angels couldn't change that outcome. They can help by bending it, but change, no. They are here to guide us through pre-determined life. Angels aren't there for every little thing, like bumps in a daily routine or to help win a game, get over a bad cold or a hangover.

In 1969, Iye took Roger, and Siyeke took Chief Coe and Dave on as their primary charges and passed the rest to other angels. But they were known to butterfly as needed. Since their wards were going to be in harm's way they were going to need all the help they could get, and South East Asia was a boiling pot where Iye didn't want Roger's hide boiled. It was so written.

By 1963 the United States watched Communism succeed in Vietnam and began bombing the North from aircraft based carriers. By 1965, North Vietnam was being chewed up pretty good by American soldiers and marines in a conventional fight so the North changed tactics to a more guerrilla style.

We'll come back to all that in just a bit; right now it's time to go to another war... again.

Time: 0512 hrs
Date: 01 December 1990 (Gulf War)
Place: Kelly Air Force Base, San Antonio, Texas
Temperature: 8 C

"We need to get these choppers loaded", Sergeant Rasmussen the loadmaster was complaining to a slick sleeve FNG as he motioned toward several men standing at the top of the ramp. His C-5 was majestic in the early morning hours sitting in line on the tarmac with dozens of its sister ships. Ramps down, fatigue dressed men and women scurrying around and loading crates of aircraft spare parts on 5-Ton OD trucks. Everyone had a job and as inefficiently as the military sometimes seems to move, helicopters with folder blades, support rolling stock, and crates were disappearing from the trucks and being lashed down inside the skeletal insides of the aircraft. Roger Whitley, Mike Deady, and Terry, their crew chief, had reputations as to slight of hand and an air of 'if your daughter isn't locked up, she's fair game', but they always get the job done. They were all fun loving with a serious side that came out at the oddest times.

In this cool Texas morning they were dressed only in their gray flight suits, but weather wasn't on their minds. "Do you know those guys up there? Let's get them moving and out of the way." Rasmussen said more to himself then to Irby.

"As a matter of fact I do know them. Look at the name on the chopper... the guy standing next to it." Rasmussen was saying to Irby as he squinted toward the top of the ramp saying, "Irby, look real close. Didn't you ever watch Emergency 911 on TV? That's the helicopter they used in the opening scene and that's its pilot, Chief Whitley."

Celebrities or not, there was a job to be done and Rasmussen was having the normal problems loading people and equipment on board his C-5 so he didn't need any extra headaches. This wasn't the greatest job in the world right now, sending men and women off to war, but when trouble started brewing in the Gulf; President Bush had made the decision to send troops to help and other then a few active combat type units. Roger's Medical Reserve unit was the first alerted. The unit being loaded was the 273rd Air Ambulance detachment; out of Conroe, Texas "That's Chief Whitley and his crew all right" was Irby's answer. Then just as the light went on over his head he exclaimed, "If they hadn't been on television they would just normal 40 year old guys getting ready to take their 30 year old Huey's to another war."

"Yea Right" was the response. "So? You want their autographs – or what? Get on the stick. Get these crates loaded." The words were sneered so the meaning was not just conversational. They loaded.

All wars are political and conducted to gain power or territory, for genocide or just plain stupidity.

The Gulf War: Desert Shield and Desert Storm
Scenario:

In 100 hours, was it possible to reduce the 3rd largest army in the World to the 2nd largest army in Iraq? It was over so quickly the guys and gals there never really had a chance to enjoy the war. The answer is yes.

Back to sunny Vietnam - 1969
"Remember what our flight instructors always told us. 'Helicopters don't lift as much in hot or thin air as they do in cooler temperatures'. Remember?" Roger was listening and also remembering when a guest speaker at the flight school had talked about the Huey. He had been a much-decorated Vietnam combat veteran who had been in full dress blues and stood as straight as a ruler. Roger remembered him being a bit salty, but he got his point across by telling real stories of actual events about flying the Huey and the brave kids that flew them. He was remembering as if it was yesterday and he could see and hear the pride in CW2 Wayne *Crash* Coe's voice...

..."I managed to get shot down in Viet Nam seven times, I also had two engine failures, not combat related, for a total of nine auto-rotations for real. You don't think I would make a nickname like *'Crash'* up, do you? Fucking Flight Surgeon called me *Crash*. I was a standards pilot for Sixth Army in California and no one knew my real name was Wayne." There were a few smiles from the class, but no one snickered or made a sound.

He noticed the initial indifference then continued with, "I was flying for the 187th AHC in Tay Ninh where I few with a bunch of kick ass, take no quarter from anyone pilots. Not sure if some of it rubbed off on me or I affected some of them but we got along real good."

The whole class sat easy in their chairs as Chief Coe began talking. It was if he was in his own little world and was carrying on a conversation with past combat buddies. His demeanor was professional, his tie was tied perfectly and his white shirt had just come from the cleaners. His shoes had a spit shine you could look up a girls skirt with and they made slight leathery sound as he paced the front of the classroom and down aisles to search out individual cadets and to look them in the eye to get key points across. No one took notes, but no one forgot a word of his message.

It was when Crash switched to first person Roger enjoyed most. "So Crash, do you remember doing a medi-vac near Katum where you chopped down a couple of trees getting in?" Frenchie asked me.
"The night medi-vac deep in a hover hole where I destroyed a D model getting out the wounded?" I answered.
"Yep, that's the one." The Frenchman replied.

"I didn't think we were going to make it home, in fact, I didn't think we would ever get off the ground. Class… this is a war story from my vantage-point in the left seat and meant to show you just how much punishment your helicopters can take and still get you home. They have their limits but if you're good to them, they will return the favor. Actually, I'm not real sure but from this story you may also see where the nickname *choppers* came from.

The 187th Assault Helicopter Company had been given the mission to re-supply the 25th Infantry this day, and as a member of the First Platoon, known as the Maggots, my instructions had been simple. "Blackhawk 54, Contact Manchu 6 on his ground push, don't let them keep you past 1900 hours." Growled Major Bauman. After our evening briefing my platoon leader Captain Billie Presson was next to get my attention, he assigned me an aircraft and gave me a list of frequencies to contact the ground troops. I was happy to get Billy for my Crew Chief and Frenchie for a gunner both from Boston, both with thick Boston accents.

It would be fun to hear them talk on the intercom; some of guys from the Deep South needed translators just to work with these two.

We started early in the morning hauling water and ammo.
I could see the red smoke coming up through the hole in the Jungle. We were out near Katum. It was a long flight from Tay Ninh to that hole in the jungle.

I made a high pass over the Hover Hole and looked down into the dark green eerie pool, I could see nothing in the darkness and the smoke coming up made things worse.

I approached into the wind and when I got right over the top of the hole my crew started clearing me down. About half way down my eyes had a chance to adjust to the dim light in the Jungle and I could see between my feet the Grunt with the rifle over his head guiding me in to touchdown. The red smoke flair at his feet puking out clouds of the acrid red smoke that burned my eyes and lungs at the same time. The rotor-wash turning the air pink all around us.

Once I had the guide on in sight, the rest was easy and they had a pad marked and markers for us to land on.

I went to flat pitch and had a look around. The Grunts were dug in, but the only light was from straight over head, it was dark under triple canopy jungle early in the morning. The crew helped the Grunts take the ammo off while the Sergeant I would be working with came up to the helicopter to shoot the shit. I told him this helicopter was a good one and we could take seven men. With simple hand signals the Sergeant pointed who was getting on and with thumbs up and a big smile it was time to go.

I pushed the mike button the cyclic to the first détente, the intercom, "Coming up" I was telling my crew to clear me on the vertical departure. "Clear right" from Frenchie, "Clear left" from Roger. The UH-1D started to climb straight up. With help from my eyes in the back we threaded our way out into the bright sunlight. At the top of the hover hole I eased the nose over and gently started to get enough airspeed to fly home.

Time after time we went in and out of the hover hole until very late in the afternoon just before sundown when Manchu 6 let us go.

That last trip out of the hover hole empty was like being born again. With an empty chopper and the radio playing "Please release me let me go...." we were all singing along with the radio grabbing some altitude on the way home.

"Mr. Coe, you said I could get some stick time if..." I cut him off. Usually after a long day of flying, I would let the crew fly home. Some of them like Frenchie became proficient flyers. I always thought teaching the crew to fly was insurance. The 187th

Assault Helicopter Company already had a time where both pilots were hit and the helicopter was flown to the hospital by the crew chief saving all their lives.

With the Flying Frenchman at the controls and clearance from the Tay Ninh tower, we terminated at a hover twenty feet over the top of POL. "I've got it" I said, and I hovered down to a refueling nozzle. I was about to take my helmet off when the call from operations came in over the company frequency.

"Blackhawk 54 we have a medi-vac for you, shut down on the operations pad."

I climbed out and made the short walk to the inner sanctum, Blackhawk 6 territory. Major Bauman always talked very formally to the Warrant Officer pilots in his command, "Mr. Coe, the troops you have been supporting today was hit hard just a few minutes ago. They are requesting medi-vac. They have at least two very seriously wounded men that need medical attention immediately. You have been operating out of that Landing Zone all day and know the area, so I am sending you back to get the wounded. Grab something to eat while the gun ships work over the area, this could be a long night."

I felt sort of numb on my short walk back to the helicopter; the thought of flying down in that hover hole in the dark was not what I had in mind for this evening.

I told the crew of the mission we had been given; they were ready to go, not one second of hesitation. I felt better; they obviously had faith in my ability to get in and out of the hover hole one more time in the dark.

Major Bauman's runner found us all at the mess hall. "There is a break in the action, you need to depart now." And he turned on his heel and was out of the tent in a flash, we looked at each other and dropped what we were doing and ran back to the helicopter.

We were in the air in minutes, the darkness closing in around us as we left civilization and headed out over the jungle. I checked in with *Paris* Radar and they started vectoring me to my target. I could hear the Guns on *Victor* coordinating their attack; I broke in with "Blackhawk 54 in bound for a medi-vac, over." The Rat Pack fire team leader came back with "Roger 54, they seem to be pulling back, I would not call it quiet, but we are not taking fire at this time." Rat Pack 18 Art "Killer" Cline had my life in his capable hands.

I switched to FM ground frequency and called the ground commander. "We have two hit very badly and five that will make daylight." Was his comeback, I knew I could get all seven; we had been hauling that many all day.

Rat Pack 18 called for flares, and the Grunts responded by shooting one out the top of the landing zone. The wildly swing flair clearly showed the hole in the trees and I was over the spot in seconds. Searchlight and spotlight on and at first look down I could see tree limbs that had fallen across the opening to the landing zone during the battle. My crew was clearing my tail boom, and about half way down our rotor wash dislodged a large branch sending it through the main rotor. To up the pucker factor, the Viet Cong started shooting at the light in the trees with everything they had. I could clearly see the landing pad had a large branch leaning out over it; I had not chopped my way in this far to pull pitch and leave without my wounded Grunts. I chopped and chopped until I got on the ground. When I shut off the light we were plunged into an inky darkness with the only light coming from tracers crisscrossing the landing zone and the dim red light of the instruments.

My D model blades were thrashed. I had lateral vibrations, I had vertical vibrations, and it seemed as if she was going to shake herself to death. We were taking a huge volume of fire on the ground, and everyone with a weapon was using it. The Sergeant I had been working with all day ran up to the door and told him to just put on the critically wounded patients; my beat up blades would not lift very much.

The Grunts loaded two very badly wounded men and a medic to help keep them alive. I called out "Coming up" and as I started pulling pitch I knew we had big problems with the main rotor.

As soon as I broke ground I turned on the lights, which seemed to focus the tracers on us. We still had some chopping to do to get out. By the time I got to the top of the hover hole I was pulling all the pitch we had. The Rat Pack was working out on the steady stream of tracers coming up from the jungle.

I was trying to get some altitude, but the old girl had given her all chopping in and out to get the wounded Grunts. I was able to get some forward airspeed and with the pitch pulled under my armpit we limped back at 40 knots low level the aircraft shaking so hard I was afraid we were going to come apart in the air. I did not lower the collective until we were over the hospital pad.

"Blackhawk 54 turn on your position lights." The call from Rat 18 boomed in my ears. I turned everything I had on. "Tally ho" was the response and soon a light fire team accompanied me on my slow trip home. It took an

eternity to get back to Tay Ninh. I made a straight in controlled crash at the hospital pad, my Rat Pack escorts streaking over the top of us low level, in 90 degree banks, thumbs up, a salute from the Bad Dogs. I started to breathe again.

The 45th MUST hospital triage team swarmed our chopper and I shut her down after cooling the engine for the required two minutes. As the blades turned down I could see the end piece was gone off of both blades. When I climbed out to have a look myself, my knees got a little wobbly from what I saw. *The blade leading edge had been beaten flat, and about the last three feet of both blades was gone, they just had the flat lumpy leading edge, and the rest was gone. We had a couple of bullet holes and the dents in the leading edge went all the way back to the rotor head. The tail boom had dents all over it and the tail rotor leading edges were all flattened and dented.* We had also broken out one of the greenhouse windows, and my chin bubble. If I had not flown it in myself, I would not have believed that a helicopter would fly in that condition."
The class hadn't moved a muscle throughout the entire presentation and it was if they were spell bound now that the Chief had stopped talking.

There was slight clapping in the center of the class and as the cadets got their senses back and realized they were not in Vietnam but still sitting in a classroom in Texas, the applause escalated to a steady thunder with everyone standing and smiling. There were tears on many cheeks and Roger's wasn't the driest eye there.

Without Chief "Crash" Coe at the controls this would have been pictures *that were never taken.*

Max

The 1 to 5 ratio for large dogs is unfair to humans.

Max is a Labrador Retriever that is a loving, affectionate, lovable, patient dog. He is highly intelligent, loyal, willing, and high-spirited and very lively and good-natured; he loves to play, especially in water. In addition he has an excellent, reliable, temperament and is friendly, superb with children and equable with other dogs.

Having said all that we need to get to the truth about Max.

Actually the entire first paragraph is true and most of it's true about Max… mostly. This story is about a Max that's going on nine year old (or more then 57 human years) and is a house dog. This Max is a Full bloodied Black Lab and probable the laziest dog known to man but has the biggest brown soulful eyes and he talks. Well talking may be the wrong term, but he does communicate very well.

Max is also a bit pigeon-toed but he loves to go on walks. Walks up steep hills are his favorite as he normally stops several times to mark his territory and usually once to poop. Max has great bladder and bowel control and a storage capacity most humans would kill to have. Max lives on a lake and its level has been known to rise by two inches after his morning pee. Max can pee on command and go to the grass (poop) anytime he comes across an area that has not been marked yet. Max on a leach is a contradiction in terms. You don't control him rather he controls you and always the first half of a trek he pulls on the leach until your arm muscle and shoulder socket aches but on the way home your shoulder doesn't get any rest either as you're pulling him.

Max is no dummy. He was second in obedience class; beat out only by a tie for first between the New Guinea Singing Dog and a Miniature Australian Shepherd. He can Heal, Sit, Backup, Stay, Come, Free, poop and pee with the best of them. Ooh yes, he will also *uook* on command.

In Max's youth he would run like the wind and could jump with the best as he controlled his 100 pound mass with the grace of a mountain lion. In the years Max has been on earth his jump has gone from a 24 inch vertical leap to a struggling two inches and then just at feeding times. Max has terrible table manners but he always acknowledges the bowl of chow with several yelps of glee and get out of my way there buddy, I'm hungry nudges. It has been the mystery of the ages how a dog with relatively small paws can always manage to step on or stand on your feet especially when you are bare foot. Dogs, as all four legged creatures are marvels at how they can control which legs goes where and at what speed and in what rhythm. It's a guarantee of nature that it doesn't make much difference if those legs are going up or down stairs, flat terrain or grassy knolls when your feet are in their proximity at least one paw will find the top of one of your feet.

In the *How do you handle it* category, during Prime Time TV viewing, the show you are interested in and trying hard to follow the good guys winning and the bad guys losing themes that Max will always start talking to you. Doesn't make any differences if there are other people around are not he will always get your attention by focusing those huge brown eyes on you and speak. To you it probable sounds a lot like gargling or a swallowed bark but to Max it's Come on… I'm hungry… I need to go potty… or I need my ears cleaned out please. The forehead may look Neanderthal but under all that fur are love, contentment, and friendship. The really sad part of all this dog chat is that you understand it, especially when he lays that large chin down in your lap or on top of your leg the same time rolling those brown eyes. That's all well and good but Max will always blink a couple times just to make sure he gets your attention.

All animals have a personality but many can not reason. If his favorite ball gets loose and rolls all the way to the lake from his back yard he hasn't figured out yet that every time he drops it, the ball goes to the lake only to be retrieved by wading by his master. In canine language Max is probable thinking between those Neanderthal ears; I don't know what happen Ms. Dixie. I dropped it and it just ran away… will you please wade out those 5 meters and bring that ball back? I will try to hang on to it in the future… honest. Isn't that what kids do to parents? A baby cries and a parent jumps. A baby looks cute and the proud parent beams as he metamorphosis into a horse to ride the kids around the room while on his hands and knees making horsy noises or simply says isn't that cute the way he throws the food all the way across the room.

When Max is alone for more then a few minutes be prepared for some hard nose punches and a few well aimed sneezes and having your feet stepped on a few times when you come back. He deserves the attention. If I was in the same predicament I would want more out of life then having my ears rubbed ever once in a while as a passing jester of love and affection.

Max sometimes seems part human, but I got to tell you he isn't. Humans know when other humans don't feel good and when there are certain things one can and can not do, for example: Let's say you come home from the hospital following a hernia operation and your doctor instructions are to take it easy. You need to take it easy because you've been cut on, have a mesh now inside you that is tender but Max doesn't know that. He is just glad to see you and he is dying to give you his patented poke in the stomach then run up behind you and stick his big head between your legs all the while being friendly. Ouch.

Remember TV time? Have you ever enjoyed a bowl of ice cream during a romantic movie? Try eating the whole bowl with a fuzzy chin and large brown eyes resting on your

ARLEE

legs? Max will clean your bowl in a heart beat along with any jelly beans or puppy biscuits that aren't tied down. Max could be the cat fish of dry land or a canine vacuum cleaner if he had his way with food.

Max hasn't been around many male dogs. Max is probable the only male dog anywhere that squats to pee. The only time he raises a leg is to scratch behind an ear.

Max is dragging his left hip now but you would never know he is hurting. He is always in good spirits and still walks like a lion but is actually just a real cat.

I will miss Max when his time is up and I will always remember his idiosyncrasies because he loved me as much as I love him.

Authors Note:
February 2007 Max was outside wandering with no apparent destination or purpose. When it was time to come back inside I had to go get him. The look in his eyes made me cry. He was sorry he didn't know where to go. He was sorry he was limping. He was sorry I had to come after him. He was sorry...

The Vet took many x-rays and examined Max as he would his own child.

Cancer.

There wasn't an organ or bone without cancer. He was in dire pain.

Max's veterinarian, Dr. Tom told me this one story of the many Lab puppies and dogs he had treaded over the years and they all had a similar thread running through the dog's character. *They never show pain.* "There was this one lab I will never forget..." Dr. Tom was saying... "...a yellow lab that his master carried into my office not long ago. He had been run over by a car and broken both front legs. They were compound fractures and even the right leg was pointed in the wrong direction. I cried as I examined him as he was licking my hand and wagging his tail just being happy to be here."

As Dr. Tom was telling me the story as he gave Max a shot "This will let his sleep" He said with tears in his eyes. I was saying my good-byes as he gave him one other shot that would keep him asleep and comfortable.

I miss him.

ARLEE

A Beautiful Sunday on the Lake

If you live near the water you need to know where to store "stuff"

Have you even wanted to live on a lake, a river, the ocean or any kind of body of water? I never though about it much… until one day I found myself on the tranquil *Lake of the Ozarks* in a quiet cove writing my third novel. I was soon to find out water is either meant to drink or you best learn about it if your living on or near it.

Keep in mind there is a difference between living on the water and in it. We will talk to that later. Water people are different then normal folks. Water people get away for the weekend to a quiet condo where they spend two days relaxing as they are going as fast as they can on water. They normally don't have any particular direction and seldom have a destination in mind. They are tanner than most and they and rust are first cousins. Water people all have boats and have no compunction to constantly throwing money into that hole in the water. Water people are good at docking in all kinds of weather and they are good people. They are good at knowing all the places you can get to by land or by water. The first time I was on the water a new water person friend pulled into our boat slip in a magnificent 32 foot something or other that would go like the wind and hardly get you wet. It was pushed by two throaty in board V-8s that sounded like constant rolling thunder. Nice. There are rules for everything. Rules for driving on the right side of the road, who has the right-of-way stuff and rules for the land and rules for the water. When you have a four thousand pound twin driven Fiberglas beauty on the open water doing over 60MPH it's kinda like driving an ocean liner. You can't turn it on a dime nor can you stop it quickly so you go by the rules. When I was flying I use to have a plaque at home that said, Flying is like the ocean, Safe if you play by the rules, extremely unforgiving if you don't.

With the wind blowing over my bald head, lake water forming a magnificent bow wave, our Fiberglas ride was bouncing and spraying and everyone was smiling or grinning from ear to ear. That's what you do in a boat when you're skimming the water. Speaking as loudly as I could over the wind, the V-8s and my insecurity about water, I said to the driver in an honest voice, "Say Gary… I see several boats coming this way, right at us. What's the rule for meeting or passing them?"

If I hadn't been busy wiping the spray off my glasses I would have kissed him when he gave the golden rule of waterdom. "…just try to miss um…"

I won't mention the price of gasoline that it takes to drive those throaty monsters but I did notice that a hundred bucks got us just passed the 10 mile markers and back home. Where do boats live? **FYI** = Water gas normally runs 0.50 to 0.75 cents higher then land gas.

Boats live in two places. On trailers and in slips on docks. Water people normally either own a dock or rent a slip.

All docks have stuff. They have stuff to sit on, stuff to swing from, dive off and places to store things. Things you need to live on the water like life jackets, floatation devices, anchors for that hole in the water and fishing stuff. Where do you store this stuff? Usually in Boat Boxes. Now boat boxes aren't cheap. Many times you can go to a marine store with a thousand buck in your pocket and after buying a boat box you will have just enough left to stop at McDonalds for a dollar meal.

For the landlubber a dock can be either anchored or floating. The dock can be constructed from steel, concrete, wood or any combination but keep in mind that floating docks usually have lots of water under them.

Our dock is steel and concrete and floating on 30 feet of blue-green water where fish and snakes live and swim. I swim with them many times and most leave me alone when the water temperature is above 60 degrees.

Water people never make mistakes about their water stuff. They always take very good care of their boats, their water gear and their boat boxes.

Did I mention that there is usually wind on a lake? Wind on a body of water can and will come at you from all directions and it will come at you as a gentle breeze, gusty zephyrs or drafts. Wind on lakes loves boat boxes just as tornados love trailer parks and wind celebrates ever
occasion when it happens upon a new white beautiful Fiberglas expensive boat box filled with expensive stuff that is not anchored to that steel and concrete dock decking.

My illustration pictured above was taken during the winter months but shows exactly what we are talking about.

Saturday had been beautiful. The sun had been out, the weather perfect, the company had left early but not before everyone had several drinks and all had a wonderful time. Once you have a few drinks and you have a nice fire going in your gut, the world is a beautiful place so you have a few more knowing if a few drinks are good, more will be better. Ever hear of a hangover?

The sun was just burning of the morning mist Sunday morning as the words that would occupy the whole day were uttered.

"Honey the boat box is gone."

"What do you mean the boat box is gone?" The landlubber said.

The experienced water person just repeated the statement thinking the landlubber would understand *gone.*

"Gone! It can't be gone." From the second floor bedroom window not more then 50 feet away from the dock even a person that didn't need glasses could see the dock clearly and there was no box to be seen.

All the ducks in and around the dock were busy with their morning bath and breakfast. The squirrels were busy running up and down the trees playing and carrying stuff. The family black lab had just finished doing his morning thing and four yellow finches and three humming birds could care less at what the landlubber refused to believe.

The boat box was gone.

"Maybe someone stole it during the evening." The landlubber tried. All he got from that effort was a dirty and questionable look on what to do next. "Should I call 911?" he tried.

He got that same look as before.

"I knew that box needed to be anchored" the water person said.

"Anchored? Why? The damn thing weights a ton and has been sitting on the dock for nine months." The landlubber innocently said.

The water person wailed, "It had all the life vests, ropes, anchors, towels…. There was lots of stuff in that box and now it's gone."

"Should I call 911?" The landlubber didn't have any solutions for this water problem.

"Over there. Look over under the neighbors dock and shoreline." The water person said excitedly.

It was as if the stuff on the Titanic had all washed to shore. There were life jackets, and some towels but no ropes or water shoes. It was definitely our stuff from the boat box.

"Well doesn't look like anyone stole it last night. What's that stuff doing over there? How did it get out of the box?" This landlubber was not the brightest bulb on the tree so the water person told him. "The box fell off the dock and apparently the lid popped open."

"The box… how?"

The water person in all her experience said, "The wind must have blown it into the water last night."

"I don't see it in the water."

By this time the experienced water person's neighbor came over to the landlubber standing on the sea wall scratching his bald head and said something along the lines *of "… if your looking for your boat box it's **between** our docks…"*

Sure enough if you stand on their bouncing wave runner float and look down 20 feet between the two docks there was something white and you kinda hoped it was the boat

box because if it wasn't it meant you were looking at a eight foot mean white shark.

There was lots of discussion the next few minutes on how to retrieve this great white boat box. Scuba divers, kids with snorkels, wait till the lake goes down, or forget it and buy another were some of the options.

"That's $900 down there and it still has *stuff* in it." The water person said and it didn't sound like she was going alone with *the forget* it option.

Some people are cut out to be hunters. Some outdoorsmen, foresters and fishermen and then there are landlubber. If you fish and successful you piss off a lot of fish plus you have to clean them. Cleaning to a water person mean more then a shower and deodorant. It means skinning, gutting and filleting. The eating is the good part but that's only in nice restaurants.

"I'll fish it out." Talk about an innocent statement from the landlubber that didn't have a clue what he was saying. "I can do it... trust me." He was serious but ooh so dumb. The boat box is Fiberglas with nothing to grapple or hook onto. "How are you going to get hold of it?" That was a really good question from the water person and the landlubber didn't have a clue.

The landlubber did do one thing right as he started fishing as he did tie one end of the rope to his wrist so when he threw out the 30 feet of rope with the four prong grapping hook he could reel it in. "Sure hope that's the box down there and not a shark."

For twenty minutes with no bites from the landlubber's dock he decided that the neighbors dock was a mite closer to the white shadow but he would have to stand on a floating wave runner ramp that bounced with every boat that went by, and they all make huge wakes.

For the next 45 minutes the landlubber had several bites before he finally hooked the white shadow. He was almost seasick from the bobbing float but he managed to call for help. "Bring a longer rope... I got it but now I don't know what to do with it.... It weights a ton... literally."

The water person brought the longer rope and between a few well chosen military terms of endearment the landlubber and water person was able to snake the longer rope under two steel guide cables while keeping the tension on the white shadow and pull it to shallow water, lid open and full of water. There was still one towel in the corner alone with three 7 inch crappie and three inexpensive water shoes.

SUCCESS!!

The boat box was on dry land, emptied of water and all but a couple towels. The landlubber had had enough dumb luck to snag the one place on the box that was snag able and strong enough to drag it to shore. The rest of the story should have been that all he did then was drag the box back to the original dock, retrieve all the stuff that had floated out, anchor it to the steel and concrete dock and have a good lunch after he scared off a 4 foot water moccasin 200 meters down the shoreline that had found a new home in the missing water shoe.

Success?? Not yet. It was still windy and the landlubber was still just as dumb about water stuff as he was when the sun came up.

Don't laugh and I'll tell you the rest of the story?

One remaining problem to take care of before lunch. The landlubber had a new concrete bit, plenty of self tapping concrete bolts, a new expensive De Walt cordless power drill and enough engineering and architecture knowledge to anchor that white box. No problem.

Squatting inside the box drilling the first anchor hole the bit came loose but stuck in the hole. No problem just pull the bit out, put it back in the drill chuck and continue the project. As the landlubber stepped out of the box to get a pair of pliers from a tool box the wind saw what was happening and did the same as it did the night before. Blew the box into the water – again. The landlubber was standing no more then a foot away as it went over board and he was thinking, "No problem as I had the forethought to tie both end of the box down before I started drilling." All true. The box was floating just out of arms reach – full of water again and all our dumb landlubber had to do was drag it back to shore. All he had to do was untie the ropes that was holding this now water filled 1000 pounds white monster, don't let it sink again, tie a long rope to it as it bobbed like a cork in cold 20 foot water just out of reach, get it to shore and back on the dock before the water person saw what had happened. Damn.

An hour later, many well chose military words and the box was sitting back on dry land, wet and covered with moss but as the water person snickered she never asked why it had been moved.

There was a tornado two day later with high winds and as golf ball sized hail went through the area destroying trees, plants, roofs, windshields and denting cars, trucks and metal roofing of docks, the newly anchored boat box didn't budge.

Have you even wanted to live on a lake, a river, the ocean or any kind of body of water? I

didn't… until I did and I learned living on the water is a real experience. Sometime in everyone's life they should own a convertible, a pickup truck, a sports car, travel to many foreign lands, live with two or more partners and live on the water.

BTW: Did I mention…. The expensive De Walt power drill is still in 20 feet of cold lake water?

But never mind. I took the boat 21 miles over to *Party Cove* and looked for it there where there were more bikinis and mono-kini clad young ladies to help me look.

Life is good.

ARLEE